ALTERED EUROPA
An Exploration of Passed Possibilities

Edited by
Martin T. Ingham

Published by:

www.martinus.us

Cover art by Denise Roos
Check out her work at http://dementedpirate.deviantart.com

Special thanks to William Rade for invaluable proofreading and editing assistance.

First Edition, Released April 2017

Table of Contents:

The Public Execution of Winston Churchill
by William Rade

"One should forgive one's enemies, but not before they are hanged."
                                                    -Heinrich Heine, 1848.

Ruined parts of the city had been left deliberately as ruins since February of the previous year. A peculiar scent was subtly present in this damaged quarter of Dresden. It was long-ago burned wood, since waterlogged by rain and growing fungi, mingled with vehicle exhaust, tobacco smoke and boot polish. *The new smell of the new Third* Reich. *And this*, Winston thought, *is the glorious phoenix risen from the ashes! Or an eagle, perhaps.*

Those buildings that had been rebuilt boasted the familiar and disgusting swastika banners, in sizes so large that they may have been comical under different circumstances. *We fly the Union Jack from our buildings, but at least we maintain an appropriate flag-to-building ratio.* Winston stifled a sigh. *Well, we did.* Unwelcome images of even more decimated sections of Britain, now flying their own massive swastikas on backgrounds of red, served to diminish his already guttering mood. *Must be strong for her, for Mother England and the Empire. It's just a pity they're flying the wrong flags back at home, that's all.* Winston moved his tongue around in his parched mouth. Desperate for moisture, he made do with a swallow of his own saliva. *Bloody thirsty!*

Every possible space and vantage point was filled with jeering Germans, waving flags of their own, as Winston was led toward the city center. While none of them were close enough to touch him, save for his gaunt-faced military escort, Winston still inwardly recoiled at their numbers and vehemence. *It looks like all of Dresden has come out to see this. Well if there's this many of them left, I didn't do nearly as good a job here as everyone has been saying.* Then Winston took in more of the panorama and began to understand the scale of today's event.

He saw regimental standards from all across the *Reich* and her allies. Civilians, not just from Dresden, but from every part of the war-ravaged continent. A glint of sunlight on brass. *Good Lord, that's the Vienna Philharmonic!* Winston felt a rush of guilt at owning a copy of their phonograph long before 1939, only because Beethoven and Mozart couldn't be blamed for Hitler. At least, not at first. *Well,* Winston resolved to himself, *after today I do solemnly swear to never listen to the Vienna Philharmonic again!*

At that moment the Philharmonic struck-up. They played nothing from the great composers but instead some nationalistic filth the crowd immediately recognized and commenced to sing. Flags waved enthusiastically and streamers flew. *Trust the Krauts to bring streamers to a ruddy hanging!* He was so very thirsty. He knew that this way he was unlikely to disgrace himself when he died, and that some sense of dignity and decorum needed to be preserved. But, at that point, a wet trouser leg would no longer be of concern to Winston. He wished his friend had visited his cell one last time this morning. Well, not exactly his friend. The closest thing he'd had since his tearful farewell to Clementine and his boarding of the *Lützow*, in chains, at Harwich harbor.

* * *

The German had visited his cell unexpectedly one night last week. His sentence was long public by then, not that there had ever been much doubt.

"*Herr* Churchill?" the man had whispered into the darkness, from the other side of the bars. Winston had earned the nick-name Secretary for Insomnia during his time in the House of Commons. He was, naturally, awake. Winston had studied the concrete ceiling above his bunk for a time and considered the childish impudence of pretending to be asleep so as to avoid conversation.

"*Herr* Winston Churchill?" the voice continued, a little louder. *Damn,* Winston had thought with a wince, at hearing his full name spoken by the stranger. *With the Jerries now in charge back home, that's another thing that's going to go to the dogs: the pronunciation of the W.* Winston heard the speaker outside his cell shifting his feet anxiously. Winston sighed under his breath and decided to humor whomever it was who was calling at this hour. He spoke in a voice heavy with exhaustion and exasperation:

"I prefer Mister *Herr* Churchill, if you don't mind." After a brief pause, the speaker composed himself.

"My apologizing, Mister *Herr* Winston Churchill. I am *Deutsch* and not so good, always, with English and English speech conventions, myself."

Despite himself, and the hour, Winston found himself indulging in a brief chuckle.

"Nonsense! You sound as though you've read the Classics at Cambridge! If there's one thing I won't abide, it's false modesty!" A long silence. The man on the other side of the bars shifted uncomfortably again. Winston let out a dramatic sigh that wouldn't have been out of place in one of George Bernard Shaw's ridiculous socialistic theater farces. Summoning his extraordinary and legendary willpower to stubbornly face adversity, Winston hauled his 65 year old body into a seated position to face the speaker. There was almost no light.

"You joke, Mister *Herr* Churchill?" the man asked, after a great deal of thought.

"Well, I tried to, but I'm usually better when I have time to prepare. What time is it, anyway?"

"It is 2:30 tomorrow morning," the German answered. Winston decided to let that one go through to the keeper.

"You will be dead in one week, your country lost the War, you will be hung for all the world to see, and you are joking with the prison guard?"

"I would have said that I will be *hanged* for all the world to see, personally, but I agree with you, in principle. I try to find whatever is humorous in any situation, condemned prisoner or no. For I myself am an optimist—it does not seem to be much use being anything else." Winston's voice trailed off and he looked around his cell once again. The guard, most annoyingly, shuffled again in his place during the ensuing silence. Winston, ever the military strategist, decided to go on the offensive.

"With whom do I have the pleasure of speaking?" he asked, in what was the most convivial tone Winston could muster.

"I..." the man began, "I would prefer not to give my real name. I am not here as official prison guard, just now, today." Winston found himself nodding. Whether the speaker could see his head at all from the other side of the cell bars was unknown.

"Understandable," Winston allowed. "Then I shall pick a name for you. How about Fritz? May I call you Fritz?" There was the beginning of another awkward pause, but Winston spoke again before the man could jolly-well shift about on his legs for the sixth or seventh time in less than two minutes.

"It's decided! I'll call you Fritz." Winston clapped his hands together once. "What glad tidings do you bring me this morning, Fritz?" Only a small part of the man's face was visible in the darkness. Winston was confident the anonymity of the shadows was also deliberate, and didn't blame the man for being cautious. His was a regime that killed people simply for being born of an inconvenient race, let alone for fraternizing with a convicted foreign war criminal. But why was Fritz fraternizing at all?

"No news, Mister *Herr* Churchill. There is no change to your sentence, or the date of your execution. All of your Kingdom continues to be under the rule of the *Reich*, though there is still some fighting on most of the other big island they call the Irish Free State." Winston almost smiled. Almost.

"I don't suppose you have a newspaper?" Winston asked. What he could see of Fritz's head shook in an emphatic no.

"If you were found with a newspaper, in English, in your cell..." Fritz began, but Winston waved him to silence. The man shifted from one foot to the other yet again.

"Out with it, man!" Winston suddenly demanded. Some of the strong leader remained in him, however imprisoned and condemned.

"I was at London!" he suddenly blurted. The longest silence between them yet ensued.

"London." Winston finally echoed.

"*Ja*, London, and all around your countries in the United Kingdom. I saw it all. They had us learn English for years, to be ready. I too went to Manchester and Bristol and... the place of the Scots where your king had his summer palace?"

"Edinburgh," Winston supplied in a quiet voice, "it was called

Holyroodhouse." Fritz was warming up to the conversation and became a little more animated.

"*Ja, ja*, Holyrood! I have a brick at home from Holyrood," he began, before remembering to whom he spoke, and cut-off what he was saying with a sudden sound—almost like a choke. Winston just shrugged, his face stayed impassive. Fritz cleared his throat and continued.

"But nothing I saw anywhere else was like my visits to London," Fritz shook his head sadly, "it was like nothing else in the whole world." Both men were quiet for a time.

"Have you been to Auschwitz?" Winston asked.

"Where?"

"Auschwitz, Poland. Thirty-two miles southwest of Krakow. From what I hear, you can't miss it."

"No. I have not been. Have you, *Herr* Churchill?"

"No, Fritz, I haven't been there, either. Not in person."

"What happened there? Was it like what happened to London?" Winston shook his head.

"No, it wasn't. There wasn't a whole skyline of buildings to be leveled in Auschwitz. Nothing like London. Of course, I only saw pictures smuggled by the intelligence service, heard reports. London was what we did here, why they're hanging me. Just on a much bigger scale. And against a people already much closer to defeat. It was war, Fritz. But places like Auschwitz... and there are many others like it. What happened there was not war, it was something we couldn't even name. Something that has never happened before, since civilization began. Something dreadful, which we couldn't stop. Haven't stopped." Aghast, Winston trailed-off. During the ensuing silence, Fritz stood perfectly still.

"Maybe I will visit Auschwitz, Poland, southwest of Krakow, Mister *Herr* Churchill," Fritz mused.

"Fritz?"

"*Ja?*"

"Don't visit Auschwitz." A pause.

"*Jawohl*." Fritz replied. Winston was grateful Fritz didn't click the heels of his boots together and snap a *Sieg Heil* salute, along with giving that customary military response to an order. Winston winced, then let out a low sigh that was more like a grumble.

"If you've seen London, that's more than enough for one man's soul." Another brief pause, then Winston began to pace slowly the length of his cell, as if he were back in the War Office, dictating a speech to a secretary.

"The only reason I mention Auschwitz at all is for parity. You suggested that London is now the worst place in the world. It's gone downhill since your lot have been there, I'll grant you. But those who remain are Britons. We are a proud people, indomitable. Even from under the jackboot, we shall rebuild and continue to prosper. We in the government made some posters for the people which you might've seen around the place. The Crown, with the words 'Keep calm and carry on' below. On a background of red, like your blasted swastika, except ours is on a more British red. Like that which the Redcoats wore proudly one hundred years ago. Carry on, Fritz. That is exactly what we all intend on doing!" *Besides, I can't bear the thought of the worst place in the world being in Britain, no matter what they've done to it.*

Winston stopped his pacing. Suddenly frustrated with himself for his inexplicable need to babble to the closest thing to a confidant he'd had since his capture, he turned and walked right up to the cell bars. He noticed that Fritz reflexively took a step backward, seeking more shadow and distance from Winston's reach.

"Why are you here?" Winston demanded.

"Like I told you, I was at London," Fritz answered, a little defensively.

"And you dropped bombs on the Tower and the Old Bailey, and the tenements, and now you want my absolution. Is that it?"

"*Nein*, not me. I am only a corporal, I am not a pilot in the *Luftwaffe*. I was infantry. I was sent in after the *Luftwaffe, und* the big guns of the *Kriegsmarine* ships. *Und* the V2 rockets. *Und* the paratroopers. *Der Blitzkrieg* strategy."

"Oh. Infantry." Winston had gone a little more quiet at the word. "An infantryman."

"*Ja*, infantry. So I saw London *sehr* closely. That is, I mean, very, very closely." Winston looked away and found his throat had gone dry. Eventually he managed to mutter,

"Indeed. You would have done. You would have done, at that."

"*Ja*," Fritz agreed, solemnly, as he busied himself with something in the darkness.

Winston heard the rustle of clothing followed by the clink of metal on glass and a bottle being unstoppered. Then came the unmistakable sound of a liquid being poured. A kind of peace welled up in Winston. *Merciful Heaven! Potassium cyanide?* When the odor reached Winston, however, he was not sure whether he felt more of relief or disappointment. It was clearly a strong liquor. *It might still be poisoned,* Winston realized. *But even if it isn't, I'll be sure to drink it all, anyway.* Finished with his task, Fritz came closer to the bars again holding two dented metal cups. The kind he had seen British soldiers use as far back as when they were fighting the Boers, while his rank and title made sure he always drank from porcelain or crystal. *Or at least bloody glass!*

"Scotch?" inquired Winston, not yet reaching for one of the cups. Fritz shrugged by way of apology.

"Schnapps," he replied. Winston shrugged too.

"Local stuff," he said to himself. Then, a bit more loudly, "very well, Fritz. Thank you. That is, *danke schön.*" He decided not to ask whether or not his portion had been poisoned.

"*Bitte schön,*" Fritz mumbled reflexively in reply. *You're very welcome.* Winston put an arm through the gap between two of the cell bars and Fritz took a step forward. Winston took one of the cups by its handle. Slowly he brought it to his nose and gave the liquid a swirl. Its bouquet was fruity and definitely alcoholic. Other than being certain he would have preferred scotch, or gin at a pinch, Winston could determine nothing else about the drink. He opted for a sigh and one last question.

"You said you were involved in the sack of London, Fritz. I am the deposed British Prime Minister. Your people put my countrymen and I on a show-trial in Nuremberg. Hanged most of them right there, God rest their souls, but thought I deserved to die in Dresden, because I had ordered its destruction last February. So here I am, Fritz, awaiting poetic justice. While they're building the scaffold and foreign dignitaries are still *en route*, you come to my cell at 2:30 AM and risk the Lord-only-knows-what punishment to sneak me schnapps, ostensibly to drink a pre-dawn toast of some kind. To *what*, man? Whatever are you and I going to toast together?" After it was clear Winston had finished his diatribe, Fritz took another step closer to him, so their two metal cups were in range of one another.

"To London," Fritz supplied simply, in his heavily accented English. He held up his own cup a little higher. It shook slightly in the man's tight grip. Winston visibly composed himself and took a deep breath.

"To London," Winston agreed. The metal cups clinked together and both men drained them with a single swallow.

* * *

In the long days and nights that remained before the hangman, Winston had a great deal of time to pinpoint exactly what had gone wrong with the War. With some paper and a few pencils his jailors had finally agreed to give him, Winston wrote a list in a rough chronology. *I should have written a list of what had gone* right *with the War. It would have been much shorter.* For brevity's sake, he started only with events following Great Britain's declaration of war with Germany after the invasion of Poland on 1 September, 1939. Though Winston was convinced a great deal went very badly even before that date. Nevertheless, part of the way through his list, Winston went back to the start and added just one event prior to 1939, and then gave it an underline.

20 April 1889: The birth of Adolf Bloody Hitler

8 December 1941: "The day that will live in infamy." (Understatement of the War, by Roosevelt). Simultaneous attacks on all three US Pacific Fleet Aircraft Carrier vessels by the Empire of Japan, before any new declaration of war was made by her. (N.B. City of Dresden: An *actual* war crime.) *USS Saratoga*, irreparably damaged by Japanese fifth columnists in an attack while she was being refitted at Puget Sound, off the US mainland. *USS Lexington* attacked *en route* to the Philippines by torpedo aircraft and submarines, and lost with all hands. Finally, and most inconceivably, *USS Enterprise* sunk the very day after her return to Pearl Harbor in a devastating attack by aircraft from Japanese carriers. We only understand the importance of aircraft carriers after Japan uses them successfully to destroy two of the Americans'. Also destroyed or crippled in the Pearl Harbor disaster: a stunning eight battleships, other vessels and vital naval infrastructure, and thousands of lives. Not a great start for our erstwhile allies.

11 December 1941: The so-called "silver lining" of the Pearl Harbor attack was that US troops would be sent to Europe, where we were definitely struggling to stem the flow of fascists.
"We've won the War!" I exclaimed, a little prematurely, on hearing

about Japan's reckless attack on the sleeping American giant. Only, in a rare show of fascist caution, Hitler and Mussolini *didn't* immediately declare war on the US. A tactical masterstroke. The US was only at war with the Japs, while it was just the rest of the civilised world at war everywhere else. Roosevelt had been wanting to come to our aid for some time, but the isolationist cowards in Congress had blocked him at every turn. They obviously had to engage in hostilities with the Empire of Japan, following her attack. But since Germany and Italy didn't declare war on her, neither did the US declare war on them. They were not friends. They were the allies of the enemy, and enemies of their allies. But not, immediately, at war. American tanks and aircraft were still available for our purchase and use in Europe, but no American servicemen were coming with them. That, I think, made all the difference on the Continent. We would not be able to retake France and the Low Countries without thousands of Yankees. Yet the Yankees were only going to the Pacific.

15 February 1942: What I accurately described as the worst disaster and largest capitulation in British military history. A force of Japanese we outnumbered almost two-to-one, some of them using bloody *bicycles*, captured our strongest fort outside of Britain herself. When Singapore surrendered, Great Britain was brought so very low. They captured 80000 British and Empire men. What happened to those poor devils at the hands of their inhuman captors, I shall not dwell upon for longer than I must. May the Lord rest the souls of those who did not survive the rest of the War, and comfort the scarred waifs who did. The fall of Singapore started whispers around Westminster that we might, in all honesty, lose this War. It was a blow to our morale from which we did not, could not, recover. Not for all of my rhetoric and rousing speeches.

Suddenly overcome with the enormity of their defeat, *his* defeat, Winston snapped the stub of pencil in two. He slammed the bits on the simple wooden table with an open hand. With the list abandoned unfinished, Winston wept.

* * *

Winston doubted he had slept more than an hour in total during his last evening. More Krauts than usual assembled outside his cell in the morning. Some of them were clearly in the kinds of clothes military people wore when others deemed them to be terribly important. One of them, as an underling jangled a key in the lock, uttered one word to Winston:

"*Heute.*" *Today.* Winston gave the smug man a grimace in reply. *Thank you so very much for reminding me today is my last day on earth. I may have forgotten, otherwise, and that would have been so terribly embarrassing.*

"*Raus!*" another of the important-looking men barked, equally unnecessarily.

"Yes, alright then, I'm coming," Winston huffed as he rose to his feet. "Don't get your *lederhosen* in a knot." *Bloody Nazis. Always so impatient and ill-tempered.*

There were armed guards, too. Winston had the delirious thought of rushing one of the guards, scrabbling for his holstered pistol and making the bastards shoot him in the back rather than dangle him on a stage. He shook his head, as if to clear the foolish desire. Winston knew that this public hanging was from the sick mind of Joseph Goebbels himself, then rubber-stamped by the unquestionable *Führer*. There would be no quick and comparatively private death for such a seminal enemy of the *Reich*. They would subdue him with their boots and rifle butts, but take him alive to the scaffold nevertheless. Instead, Winston chose to go to his end in a manner as dignified as possible.

He walked, unrestrained and with his head held high, all the while mentally rehearsing his last act of defiance. He permitted the corners of his mouth to curve upward slightly as he thought fondly of how his final few moments on the scaffold would be remembered by history. Winston began to whistle a few bars of "Rule Britannia" before one of the brutes behind him gave him an angry shove. Down the corridors, military men stood to attention, flanking them as the solemn procession marched. Winston met the gaze of one young corporal. *Fritz?* The man's eyes widened minutely before he snapped them forward and stared past Winston. *Yes, Fritz, dear fellow!* Danke schön *again, and cheers. I hope you, at least, survive these maniacs who are now running Europe.*

* * *

Though he had lived through it only days prior, Winston could still scarce believe he had been at the rehearsal. *I knew the Jerries were a cruel lot, but to make a man rehearse his own execution, well in advance?* There would, however, be an unexpected variation from the script at the real event. Winston's stomach acid was in full revolt up through his esophagus at the thought of it. He did his best to swallow it down. *For England. I am calm, strong... unshakeable. And thirsty.*

From his place on the stage, Winston could see all of the elements for the day's piece of theater. The gallows, with noose strung and waiting, swinging only very slightly in the breeze. The trapdoor, whose mouth opened up to the drop Winston had been promised would lead to a snap and a quick death. *But that could change when I don't keep my end of the bargain.* The confession and apology he would sign on the stage, as if it were the Magna Carta. A list of all of the titles and awards the King had stripped from Winston. King George VI and what was left of the House of Lords had been required to do it, just as they had been required to hand over Winston and his cabinet for trial, in the United Kingdom's conditions of surrender to the Nazi occupiers.

Most unnecessarily, there were several of Winston's own paintings—oils on canvas—and copies of books he had authored. These were to be burned while he hanged. Hitler was fond of burning any books or paintings that were by Jews, or were better than his own for any other reason. Winston took pride in the knowledge that his paintings and books were among those better than Hitler's. *Art-school dropout! Philistine, cretin, hack!* Long before the War, when the Nazis began burning books in public, the British newspapers quoted a German playwright from the previous century. Heinrich Heine had written in 1823: "Where they have burned books, they will end in burning human beings." Had Heine been writing in Germany in this century, Winston supposed they would have burned his books first, and him not long thereafter. Heine was born Jewish. Winston thought of the photographs of the smoke rising from crematoria and the accounts of black snow falling in winter, and wondered whether it was for the best he would be shortly leaving Europe forever.

There was the minister to pray for Winston's soul as it was sent either upward or downward. The Nazis were God-fearing men. Prior to the rehearsal, Winston had been given the mercy to choose whether he wanted a Catholic priest or a Protestant minister to officiate. Winston's query as to whether a rabbi would be available was not well received. *I suppose that was what they call "gallows humor."*

Though he hated them, Winston could not resist looking at the VIPs assembled with a clear view of the stage. They were surrounded by walls of thick glass, probably some new bulletproof technology from Nazi scientists. Heavily armed guards in SS uniforms maintained cordons around their enclosure and scanned the crowd with eyes looking for signs of trouble. Theirs were the only guns Winston could see in the immediate area. After the events of the 20 July plot and assassination attempt on Hitler by some of his highest ranking military officials, no doubt the men permitted to hold the guns near the *Führer* were unswervingly loyal Nazis, likely hand-picked from the extermination camps by Himmler for this very mission. Winston felt a twinge of pity at having to die in such company.

The German elite were easy enough to identify, in their drab uniforms. They were too far away for Winston to make out particular faces, but he knew which of the Party would be surrounding Hitler for this occasion. Back at home a few years ago Winston had files on every single one of them. Closer to the stage were the foreign dignitaries. There was Franco of Spain, Benito Mussolini, and the Vichy French puppet that was a fraction of the man of the late Charles de Gaulle. The pro-Nazi leaders of all of the other occupied nations of Europe were there. Looking out of place were a few faces from Latin American fascism, but most striking of all were the Asian dignitaries. Winston doubted it was Tojo or Hirohito themselves in attendance, but he could not be sure. Prince Asaka, perhaps? There was certainly enough brocade on one of the men's military uniform to indicate he was someone of importance. It would have been relatively easy for the dignitaries to travel from the Japanese-controlled side of the former Soviet Union through to the German occupation of all of Eastern Europe, and onward to Dresden. *All that fuss, just for me! Really, chaps, you shouldn't have gone to the trouble.*

Finally, there was Winston's confessor. He had forgotten the man's name. *Did it matter?* The man insisted on being addressed only by his rank of *Gruppenführer,* anyway. *The sanctimonious git.* The Vienna Philharmonic finished the song with an extended orchestral flourish. Germans cheered and waved flags while confetti and streamers flew. *This really is getting ridiculous.* Still, the most ridiculous part was about to happen. Winston had an agreement with *der Gruppenführer.* Winston would speak an apology to the German people into the microphone, in both English and *Deutsch.* Translators were on hand in case Winston muddled his final words. In exchange for this undignified concession, the hangman's drop would break Winston's neck. He would not suffer. Nor, according to *der Gruppenführer*, would more than one thousand British resistance partisans who had been captured and were being held back home.

If Winston had refused to recant for his crimes against the *Reich*, he would die slowly by strangulation on the gallows. The brave British men and women caught plotting to plant bombs or trying to assassinate occupying Krauts would suffer much worse. Winston had no doubt as to the reality of his own final suffering. After a great deal of thought, Winston was convinced the claimed thousand hostages to his apology were likely a fabrication on the part of *der Gruppenführer*. If such poor devils did exist, they were either already dead, or marked for death no matter what Winston did or did not say.

The *Reich* had made many promises of peace and mercy. The *Nazi-Soviet Non-Aggression Pact* of 1939 lasted less than two years before Hitler broke it. Then there were the untold millions of Jews and others who were told they were merely being deported. If they boarded the trains peacefully, they would be given new lives in Eastern Europe. Winston examined his conscience about deceiving *der Gruppenführer* on the gallows. Much like his conscience about the bombing of Dresden, Winston found he had no case to answer.

Der Gruppenführer ranted into the microphone, his voice echoing his clipped and furious *Deutsch* across the square. The audience hissed and grumbled as Winston's crimes were read out, and cheered at the appropriate bits about his conviction and sentence. Another German in uniform translated and spoke in surprisingly clear English, for the films that would be shown back home for propaganda purposes.

"*Herr* Churchill, you have had time to consider your actions during your nation's war of aggression against our *Reich*. For those actions, you have already been sentenced by our highest court to death by hanging. There can be no commuting of that sentence. However, you have a chance to make amends to the people of *Deutschland* and her allies. If you confess your sins in true repentance, God. who is merciful and just, may take pity on your soul today. Have you anything to say to the people of Dresden?"

It was time. Winston took a deep breath and a small step towards his microphone.

"*Ja, und danke schön, Herr Gruppenführer*. I am grateful for the chance to make my soul clean and fit to meet the Lord." The translator rendered Winston's English into what he hoped was accurate *Deutsch* for the crowd, by means of his own microphone. Winston, as he had been instructed, gave the translator time to keep pace.

"I, as Prime Minister of Great Britain, personally oversaw the plans for the aerial attack on the city of Dresden in February of 1945. I am ultimately responsible for the conduct of my nation's Royal Air Force. I instructed them to do as much damage as possible to the city, including the bombing of targets known to be civilian or non-combatant, in order to cripple your nation's ability and willingness to fight." The crowd was shockingly silent when Winston began speaking, but the angry murmurs rose steadily in volume the more he said. By the time the German translator had rendered this part of Winston's speech completely in *Deutsch*, the crowd was shouting. Many waved pictures of loved ones who had been killed in the attacks, no doubt another of Goebbel's clever propaganda designs.

Der Gruppenführer officiating at the proceedings allowed the noise to go for a while, but eventually held up his arms in a placatory gesture. The translator spoke something further into the microphone. Silence descended. Winston leaned in closer to the microphone.

"You ask if I have anything to say to the people of Dresden. I do. I say this:" Winston paused to let the translator finish.

"I say: London." There was at first a confused silence, then more murmuring. The translator, remembering his task, repeated the phrase in *Deutsch*, though it seemed most of the audience had gotten the gist. Winston stood up straight as he continued. He thought he saw some disturbances break out within the crowd but could not spare the attention to look more closely.

"I could say the names of many places. Paris, Amsterdam, Athens, Warsaw, Moscow." *Der Gruppenführer* had turned to stare at Winston, his face a mixture of fury and terror. Winston would not be surprised if the *Führer* himself later personally ordered the officer to kiss his long-barreled Luger for allowing this embarrassment to occur. The look in the man's stricken eyes said, "But you gave me your word!" Once more, Winston examined his conscience, and found it to be clear.

Winston's eyes saw more clearly some of the scuffles in the assembled crowd. There were a few pockets where men and women were trying to unfurl Union Jack and St George's Cross banners. Winston was stunned. *British resistance? Here, at my execution?* He was certain the crowd had been searched for any weapons that could be used against the assembled fascist elite, but smiled as he realized these flags had been successfully smuggled into the square. The guards had been searching for guns and bombs. Cloth banners could have been sewn into clothing and gone undetected. Some of the late de Gaulle's Free French men were trying to do the same with banners of their symbol, the *Croix de Lorraine*. Like England's St George's Cross, it too was red on a background of white.

Simultaneously, Winston saw flurries of cloth of other anti-fascist groups and subjugated states. It was a coordinated disruption. Not all of the flags were recognizable to Winston, and not all of them were fully unfurled before the agitators disappeared under a flurry of fists, stomping boots and shouts from the surrounding loyalist Germans. Any survivors would no doubt be dragged away to somewhere not at all pleasant.

Over the sound of the fracas, Winston all but yelled into the microphone, "But I am an Englishman, so I say: London! London!" The translator was no longer translating. Winston heard the whine and hum of his microphone as the cable to the speakers was torn out. He thought he saw the German who did it stamp on the cable underfoot. The foreign disruptors and their illicit flags were quickly subdued. The audience bellowed. Glancing to the German VIP section behind the thick glass, Winston could make out most of the men on their feet in rage, but one of them looked particularly apoplectic. He appeared to be banging on the table in front of him. *Ah! So that one will be Adolf, then. Splendid.*

Some barked commands from *der Gruppenführer* had the hangmen adjusting parts of the scaffold. *Oh yes, I shall be made to squirm for that one.* Winston almost smiled. There were tears in his eyes, but they were not tears of self-pity. Rather, they were the result of fierce pride in his countrymen being beaten in the square, clutching the Union Jack. *Britain remains!* His view went dark as a black fabric bag was pulled over Winston's head from behind. It was not total blackness, however, as rays of light filtered through the weave of the fabric. Still, Winston could no longer make anything out clearly.

As he was being manhandled towards the waiting noose and trapdoor, Winston tensed as he heard gunfire. He wondered for a moment whether he had been shot instead, but felt no pain, and the hangmen were still working to get him into position. When the noose tightened around Winston's neck, he realized it must have been his countrymen and their allies in the square, being summarily executed by the armed SS guards. *Brave fellows. Poor devils.*

Winston had no regrets as such, but finally reflected that, had he been executed in France he would have been given brandy and a cigarette first. A cigarette and vodka instead in Russia, and even that would have done, at a pinch. But these Germans were dangling him bone dry.

A dastardly, barbaric and monstrously efficient people, these Nazis. How terribly uncivilized and ungentlemanly, to hang a man stone-cold sober.

The crowd roared.

Foundation and Evil Empire
-by Sam Kepfield

"First Solzhenitsyn, now this!"

Mikhail Ivanovich Gromov winced as his host tossed the thick paperback book down on the desk. The thousand-plus pages made a satisfying but ominous *thud*. Gromov picked it up, and studied the gaudy cover. The lettering was in English. The art showed stylized rocket ships soaring over a futuristic metropolitan skyline, with several characters in heroic poses reminiscent of the thirties Socialist Realist posters in the foreground. The men wore tunics and trousers. The women wore short dresses that left little to the imagination.

"*Foundation*," his guest translated. "A trilogy."

"Ah," Gromov said. "We turned it down five years ago. I heard it was kicking around in *samizdat* for a while." *Samizdat* was a tradition for Soviet authors whose works were censored by the State. Unlike in the West, where it tended to be an admission of failure, in the Soviet Union self-publishing only enhanced a work's reputation and worth.

"Apparently it was kicked to the right people," his host noted acidly. "It was smuggled out of the country two years ago, sent to Great Britain. No one would touch it there, so it went to America. Apparently Ace Publishers thought it worthwhile. I'm told it is selling rather well, though why anyone would pay two dollars and ninety-five cents for it is beyond me."

"You've read it?" Gromov asked.

"Of course. Every word."

"It's not exactly Pushkin. Or Tolstoy. The style is quite unadorned, almost simplistic."

"The quality of the writing is irrelevant," his host spat out. "It's the theme of the book. That's why you're here."

Gromov felt his heart flutter. As the head of Goskomizdat, the State Committee for Publishing, Gromov had final say on every printed word that was published in the Soviet Union. Hundreds of books and articles were suppressed every year by both Goskomizdat and Glavlit, which controlled the release of information that could be considered state secrets.

What happened to the writers who penned potentially subversive literature was the responsibility of the man in whose office Gromov now sat.

"We turned it down," Gromov said defensively. "I can't help if he passed it around to his friends. Others do it –"

"I'm not worried about *this* book," the Chairman of the *Komitet Gosudartsvennoy Bezopasnosty*, or KGB, said. "What concerns me is not so much the ones he's managed to publish so far. It's the ones he has in his desk drawer."

"He's quite prolific," Gromov said dismally.

"I know," the Chairman said, flipping open a thick manila folder on his desk. "Ozimov, Issak Yudovich. Born 1920, Petrovichi. Nationality – Jewish," the Chairman raised an eyebrow. "Degree in mathematics, Moscow State University 1941. Served with distinction in the Red Army during the Great Patriotic War. Faculty of Moscow State University, denounced in 1948, sent to the camps for ten years, released and rehabilitated in 1956. Member, Academy of Sciences since 1957. Worked on rocketry program while in camp. Noted lecturer. Recipient of Lenin Prize, 1966. Ah, here," the Chairman put a thin finger down. "Authored of works of fiction. *Rabotniki*, 1957. *Contend in Vain*, 1961. *The Fall of Night*, 1963, and a dozen others."

"All published under The Thaw," Gromov said. "Chairman – er, the late pensioner Khrushchev cleared them."

"I'm aware of that," the Chairman growled. "A big mistake, if you ask me." Following the Twentieth Party Congress in 1956, and Khrushchev's denunciation of Stalin's Cult of Personality, the Party relaxed censorship. Solzhenitsyn's scribblings had seen the first light of day in '62, with *One Day in the Life of Ivan Denisovich*, the first work on the camps.

Ozimov's works of fiction were not as blatantly political, and had slipped through earlier, almost unnoticed, which was why Solzehnitsyn had won the Nobel Prize and then been deported, while Ozimov had gone nearly unnoticed.

Gromov cleared his throat. "I should point out that he has authored a number of non-fiction works, published by Novosti Press."

"Indeed," the Chairman said. "A number of works on mathematics and physics. Also *Ozimov's Guide to Pushkin. Ozimov's Guide to Tolstoy. Ozimov's Guide to Marxism-Leninism*—"

"One of our best sellers," Gromov beamed.

"—*Ozimov's Guide to the Works of Lenin*—"

"Another best-seller. Along with *Ozimov's Annotated Das Kapital*. Most of the Politburo have copies handy." He glanced at the shelf behind the Chairman, to a gap where the well-worn red-bound volumes of Ozimov's works normally sat.

"—*Ozimov's Guide to Soviet Science and Technology.* Which," the Chairman looked up, "was quite controversial since it criticized Lysenko and his theories."

"But Ozimov was ultimately correct," Gromov said.

"*Ozimov's Annotated Yevgeny Onegin.* And so on." The Chairman closed the folder and sat back in his chair. "Not exactly someone we can take to the basement, eh? Ozimov presents a problem."

"What is to be done with him?"

"I have an idea in mind," the Chairman said. "And the good doctor should be here any moment to learn his fate."

He was able to intellectualize the whole situation and detach himself from it, having endured it once before. Oddly, though, the fact that he was traveling to Dzerzhinsky Square in the brightness of a Moscow spring day in the back seat of a Volga sedan was disconcerting. Usually the *chekists* came for you in the middle of the night, when the disorientation factor was the highest.

Dr. Isaak Ozimov, like anyone who was a potential threat to state security, kept a suitcase packed and beside the door at all times, just in case. The suitcase sat on the rear seat next to him. It bulged with a dozen pair of warm socks, woolen underwear, shirts, sturdy shoes, which might or might not be stolen by the guards or the *zeks* who were in for real crimes, not political falling under Article 58. He could deal with them, though; he'd learned plenty while at Perm, and then the *sharashka* in Moscow. A few hundred ruble notes were tucked in the lining. Those, too, would have to be guarded, as they could buy special privileges.

What awaited could take a few days or several weeks, depending upon his attitude. First they would announce the charges, in the vaguest terms possible, and use persuasion to get a confession. That having failed, the chekists would resort to cursing, intimidation, maybe a mock execution, physical humiliation (like laying facedown on the filthy concrete floors for hours). They would lie about how bad it would be for a friend if he didn't confess, play on his emotions for Lena, his wife, and his beautiful blond daughter Zoya, now at Moscow State University. Physical tortures like sleep deprivation, water deprivation, standing at attention for hours would be next. Confession signed, he and his suitcase would be loaded into a railway car, sent to a bleak transit prisons somewhere in the Urals, and from there to a camp beyond in Siberia. If he was lucky it would be below the Arctic Circle. Vorkuta (again) at his age would be a death sentence.

Then again, things were different now. Stalin and his brutish methods were dead. They didn't shoot people for telling jokes about Lenin or Stalin anymore. *Trotsky calls Lenin, and asks that two tankers of grain alcohol be dispatched to Liski Station. Why? Lenin asks. The peasants have sobered up, Trotsky replies, and they are curious why the Tsar was deposed.* He'd gotten ten years for that one, but it still made him smile.

Nonetheless, it still didn't pay to pry too deeply into the history that everyone knew, whispered stories of those who vanished in '37 and never came back, taken in the dead of night for a slip of the tongue and denounced by a spiteful neighbor or toadying co-worker. And if they found the manuscript with all the jokes in it, he was well and truly done for.

The Volga stopped in front of No. 2 Dherzinksky Square. The huge white stone baroque building dominated the area. The Bolsheviks had confiscated it from the Russian-American Insurance Company after the Revolution and turned it into the headquarters for the *Cheka*, the successor to the tsar's secret police. Knowing that this might be the last glimpse he ever had of the world outside as a free man, Ozimov gathered his briefcase and got out of the car.

There were two grim-faced men in dark ill-fitting suits waiting in front of the huge door.   One was large, dark-haired with bushy eyebrows, resembling a bear.   His partner was scrawny, with mousy brown hair and a rat-face. "This way. You're expected," Bear said. The other opened the heavy door and they entered the headquarters of the KGB.

The inside was anything but grim; parquet floors, elegant light fixtures, heavy mahogany woodwork, hardly the image that Orwell had conjured up for the West.   Rat-face directed him to a metal cage elevator.   The door opened, they entered, and it slammed shut.   Rat-face pushed the third floor button, and the cage ascended rapidly.   A bell chimed when it reached its destination.

They walked out into the hallway, wordlessly, and paused before a door.   There was no nameplate on it.   Agent Bear of the agents knocked, and the door swung open.   Bear pushed Ozimov through the door into the office.   He halted inside, seeing the man behind the desk.

"Have a seat, Doctor," the Chairman said.   Ozimov swiftly recovered his composure, and did as he was told, setting the suitcase beside the chair.   "You've brought me more of your works?" the Chairman said softly.

"Not exactly.   Woolen underwear.   Archangelsk is chilly this time of year," Ozimov replied casually, sitting down.   "Mikhail Ivanovich," he said airily.   "Suppressed any good books lately?" Gromov scowled in acknowledgement.

The Chairman sat back.   "You do know why I have summoned you?"

Ozimov pointed to the copy of *Foundation* on the Chairman's desk.   "Indeed. If you wanted an autographed copy, you could have simply written me a letter. I'm fairly prompt about such requests."

The Chairman brought his fist down on the desk, making the thick book bounce.   "Subversion! Article 58, anti-Soviet propaganda. That is why you are here, Doctor."

Ozimov blinked, then laughed.   "Subversion? You give me far too much credit. *Foundation* is hardly on par with *Doctor Zhivago.*"

"True, the subject matter is somewhat juvenile, and the writing style is inferior –"

"I refuse to indulge in style for its own sake," Ozimov said.   "A good story stands or falls on its own merits, not any useless ornamentation by the author."

"Don't interrupt me," the Chairman warned.   "For all its faults,

Foundation is a subversive book."

"How so?" Ozimov asked.

"To begin with, this 'psychohistory.' A means of predicting the future. Specifically, a means of predicting the fall of the Galactic Empire, and the shortening the ensuing Dark Ages."

"So far, correct."

"Clearly, this goes against the dialectics of Marxist theory on history."

"All empires fall. They must."

"Historical materialism holds that human society evolves in stages. You would have it regress and advance, in endless cycles, from a slave society to feudalism, capitalism, socialism and then communism and back again. Apparently this Galactic Empire is a capitalist society, meaning that communism was never achieved on Earth – you *do* mention Earth, Doctor. The hidden message is that the Soviet Union failed in its historic mission to liberate mankind."

"Oh, nothing of the sort," Ozimov waved his hand. "It's fiction. The Galactic Empire is a mere construct of my very active imagination. Although," he said with a twinkle in his eye, "I'm flattered that you believe I can bring down the Union with this one book. My modest self-image would never have allowed such a thought to occur." Beside him, Gromov snorted. "Honestly," Ozimov spread his hands, "I wasn't thinking in those terms when I wrote it."

"Eh? Really?" the Chairman furrowed his brow. "What of these?" He picked up a phone on his desk, muttered into it, and a minute later a side door opened. Three men wheeled in cardboard boxes stacked on handcarts. Ozimov's heart sank.

"Ah. You recognize the boxes. We got them from your friends Andreyev and Kuzmov."

"Don't do anything to them," Ozimov pleaded. "They merely agreed to store the boxes. I didn't tell them what was inside."

"Knowing you, they might have guessed. As it is, your published works are troubling enough. This *Fall of Night*, about a civilization that breaks down every two thousand years, when night falls. It fails to take into account the progress of socialism. Surely the New Soviet Man would never panic over such a thing – we abolished such peasant superstitions years ago."

Not as much as you would believe, Ozimov thought, recalling his own upbringing in Petrovichi. The Old Russia lived yet there, surviving both the Bolsheviks and the fascists. "But, comrade Chairman, if you look carefully, you can see that the structure of the society is clearly capitalist, and therefore lawless and decadent, which causes the superstition and panic that erupt in an orgy of self-destruction. Isn't that what we've been predicting will happen to the West for decades?"

"Hmmph," the Chairman said, momentarily mollified. He stood, as the men set the boxes on the ornate Persian rug. He got up, and walked over to the stack. He took the lid off the first box, lifted a dog-eared manuscript out and began flipping through the pages. *"Eternity's End,"* he said.

"Time travel," Ozimov explained. "A traveler from the far future is stranded in Moscow in 1945, and provides the knowledge necessary to construct an atomic pile, and atomic bomb –"

"Ignoring the role that our own scientists played in developing the first bombs, to challenge the threat from the Americans," the Chairman snapped.

"And ignoring the role that our spies played in stealing the secrets from the same Americans," Ozimov fired back. "Really, Comrade Chairman, Gorky's Socialist Realism died in the Thaw. There's no sense in trying to revive it."

The Chairman's eyes narrowed. "You were in the camps once before, Doctor."

Ozimov stood, drawing himself up to his full height, his eyes glinting beneath the heavy black-framed spectacles. "I was. I was denounced in 1948 for telling a joke, and spent the next eight years of my life in the Gulag."

"A pretty easy time of it," the Chairman said. "A *sharashka* in Moscow, working with rockets captured from the fascists." *Sharashkas* were camps designed for prisoners with special scientific or engineering skills. Conditions there were generally better than in hard labor camps.

"I spent a year in Vorkuta." A hundred kilometers above the Arctic Circle, Vorkuta housed German POWs, and dissidents from Poland, Hungary and other European nations. "I caught pneumonia and nearly died. If you're going to send me back there, you'd best do it now. I'm prepared." He locked eyes with the Chairman, until the latter blinked and looked away, began digging into the second stack of boxes.

"Ozimov's Guide to the Bible?" the Chairman said incredulously. "In

an officially atheistic nation? By a *Jew*, no less?"

"It's an informative work," Ozimov said calmly. "Debunking myths of the Bible, explaining historical context."

"It'll never see the light of day," the Chairman growled, tossing it on the floor. He dug further, bringing up another sheaf of papers bound with thick rubber bands. "Limericks?" He began thumbing through the pages. "A certain old harpy from Omsk / Who was wholly unable to 'comsk' / Would ecstatically shout / When a *samovar* spout / Was shoved up her Muscovite 'rumpsk'." Gromov, who had been invisible up to this point, stifled a laugh; the Chairman glared at him, then continued to flip pages. "Filth," he muttered. "Pure filth." Ozimov stood his ground, a faint smile on his face.

It went on for another hour, the Chairman removing manuscripts and speed-reading through them. Each one, in the Chairman's view, was a heresy against Marxism-Leninism at best, at worst a threat to state security. Ozimov steadfastly maintained that all the works were merely entertainment, nothing more, no political motives involved and no publication of secret information.

"What about this?" the Chairman pointed at one short article. "Thiotomoline, which dissolves 1.12 seconds *before* water is added! The defense applications are boundless – surely our best academicians are working on this substance right now, and you're about to divulge a state secret –"

"It's not real," Ozimov said.

"Not real?" the Chairman sputtered. "But you claim that a relay of batteries using this solution relayed information back in time to our rocket scientists, who would then alter the designs accordingly –"

"No such thing occurred, I assure you," Ozimov said patiently. "It's purely a mental exercise in scientific absurdity. I have no intention of submitting it to the Academy of Sciences for publication. The success of *Sputnik* and *Lunik* and *Vostok* was solely due to the genius of our scientists and engineers. I'm not divulging state secrets."

The Chairman scowled, and continued with another bundle. "Your laws of Robotics exalt the individual over the State, and its property. It would thwart the robots' duty to improve class conditions. You cannot bend the interests of a class to one person – that is individualism, the curse of the West."

"But," Ozimov countered, "robots prevent the alienation of the worker from his labor, as Marx warned. That prevents the alienation of man from man, which paves the way to true communism. It's in there, if you read carefully enough." The Chairman pondered that for a moment, then moved to the next.

At the end, he dumped the last one on the floor and crossed his arms. "You present me with a rather perplexing problem, Doctor."

"Really?"

"This material, when viewed in a certain light, challenges the basic tenets of Soviet socialism. It could be considered subversive."

"Nonsense," Ozimov said. "I find writing to be a joy. I can't stop when I start. If I have this affliction, I reasoned I might as well do something creative with it. Even if it may never see the light of day, and the world knows me only as a scientist, or explainer of the theories of Marx and Lenin."

"And Stalin," Gromov said, pointing to one of the piles on the floor. *"Ozimov's Annotated Bibliography of the Works of Iosef Vissarionovich Stalin* is extremely –"

"Oh, stop it!" the Chairman ordered. "Even though the *Vozhd* has been rehabilitated, it wouldn't do to publish it. Not yet." He ran a hand through his thinning hair, removed the thick glasses and rubbed his eyes. "We are somewhat limited in what we can do to you. This is the era of *détente*. We have to take world public opinion into account. We can't simply shoot you. And you won't need your suitcase. You're not going to the camps."

"Thank you," Ozimov said, with a sigh of relief.

"We could revoke your citizenship and put you on a plane to America, like Solzhenitsyn. But that simply made the crazy bastard a martyr, and even more popular. Exile would mean you'd have even more time to write your damnable books. No, I'm not making *that* mistake again."

"I don't suppose a small fine and a warning would suffice?"

"Don't push your good fortune, Doctor. Very well," the Chairman said, peering down his nose at Ozimov. "There is an expression, 'be careful what you wish for, you may get it.'"

"I've heard of it." Ozimov's heart fluttered in anticipation.

"You insist your writings are nothing more than the whimsical scribblings of a compulsive bibliophile. Very well then, I grant that. I would go so far as to say they are unworthy to bear the name of someone as distinguished as yourself, a member of the Academy of Sciences, a pioneer of rocketry. As such, the last thing such an esteemed figure would want is to be identified with this drivel."

"You are a wise man, Comrade Chairman. It would cause me great embarrassment." Ozimov fought back a grin.

"You shall get your wish. I will arrange for your works to be sent to America, where they can be published. Assuming anyone would waste money and newsprint on such trash."

Ozimov's eyes gleamed. "You are most merciful, Comrade Chairman. I will somehow bear this humiliation and punishment, and redouble my scientific efforts in service of the State." He strode to the chair and picked up his suitcase. "I presume you are finished with me?"

"I am. I wouldn't look for any more Lenin Prizes anytime soon."

"I won't," Ozimov said sorrowfully, and left. The door closed behind him. The Chairman heard a noise, which sounded like laughter, fading down the hallway.

The Chairman picked up one of the bundles. "'A Galactic Patrolman from Venus / Had a hyper-extendible... Rubbish!'" He moved to throw it to the floor, but hesitated. He waited until Gromov's back was turned, then picked it up and slid it into his desk drawer.

Fenians
by Dan Gainor

The Union troops were moving across the large, muddy field. It was a majestic sight watching two whole corps, nearly 50 000 strong, advance toward the Confederate line. The men marched crisply in formation, drummers beating a strong cadence.

Gen. George McClellan could see it all despite the smoke from the artillery. He watched the state flags move forward with their regiments – New York, Ohio, New Jersey and Maine. His heart leapt just a bit as he watched his native Pennsylvania flag held high.

There was sudden firing from off of the right flank. Even over the noise of battle, he could hear that damned rebel yell. He turned his binoculars and saw a large force of Confederates hitting the flank like they had come from out of nowhere. The Massachusetts troops that held that part of line quickly gave way.

What started as a retreat in good order soon turned into a rout. The men weren't backing up and firing, they were running. Several tossed their guns away in absolute panic. They collided with others and made it impossible for any to make a stand.

McClellan turned to the front and the scene looked even worse. The rebs had massed artillery. Those weren't 12-pounder Napoleons. They had heavy guns up on the ridge and they were smashing the Union center.

He could hear the screams of the men as the massive cannonballs carved canyons through the Federal lines.

McClellan called for his staff, but they just stared at the carnage and watched as the army dissolved. From behind he could hear Confederate cavalry attacking the reserves.

The Army of the Potomac was finished.

He, Gen. George McClellan, had lost the war.

* * *

Gen. McClellan could hear someone call his name. He felt a gentle hand on his shoulder.

"George. George!" The hand shook him harder.

"Wake up!"

He opened his eyes and the battlefield disappeared.

It had been a nightmare, a subconscious twisting of Gettysburg or some other battle he had only read about.

"It was just a dream, a soldier's dream is all." He tried to smile and knew he failed.

McClellan looked out at the city beyond the balcony — Rome. It was a truly glorious place, filled with beauty and history, even if it was too papist for a good Presbyterian.

Still, the food was excellent and the people were kind. Even young Mary had picked up a few words of Italian. The young learned so fast. The thought of his first child had him thinking of his second.

He smiled at Nelly – more genuinely this time.

"That's better George. Maybe you need a change of scenery." She pointed at the London Times on his lap. "And maybe you should stop reading of the war. Especially now that it's over and done."

The U.S. Ambassador had told McClellan, but he had to see it in print. Here it was, right in his hand; the April 24, 1865, edition of *The London Times*: "America. Surrender of Lee." The paper was a few days late arriving in Italy, but the news was solid. It was all over. Restoring a nation would take decades more.

"Do you want to go home?" He shook his head no.

"In a manner of speaking, only." Now she smiled back at him. If Helen had a face that could launch a thousand ships, Nelly had a face that had inspired two generals. George still patted himself on the back that he had outdueled that damned rebel A.P. Hill for her affections.

George waited patiently. He knew he'd agree no matter what. It had taken him nine times to get her to say yes to his proposal. He'd been saying yes ever since, trying hard to make her happy.

"You've talked about going to Ireland sometime. Let's go there and see where your family came from in Ulster."

It would probably be raining, but why not? Without realizing it he was smiling broadly now. He scooped up little Mary and told her:

"We're going to the land of the leprechauns!"
* * *

Dublin was beautiful and remarkably dry for an early May day. George found a carriage with an unusually large driver. The man helped the family settle in and then grabbed a heavy trunk in one hand like it was filled with air.

The city all around them was bustling. It was barely nine in the morning and the streets were crowded with shoppers, merchants and delivery men.

"Where to, me lord?"

"The Shelbourne," answered George with confidence. The hotel was the finest in Ireland and its reputation had spread.

"Ye ain't English, are ye, me lord?"

"English? Heavens, no! We're American." McClellan reflected a commonly held bad opinion of Britain for her casual support of the South. War might have gone faster without that trade.

Big Mike, as he called himself, took off his hat and sat it down next to him. George noticed the crowd react as their eyes moved away. Within seconds, they descended on a nearby carriage. They pelted the two men it carried with small stones and bits of garbage. McClellan noticed the driver still had his hat on.

He leaned forward and whispered to Big Mike. "Are things that bad that you have to signal the crowd not to attack visitors?"

Mike nodded somberly, surprised the signal had been recognized. "If you have any problems with anyone here, just tell them Big Mike says he owes you a whiskey. They'll know what means."

McClellan changed topics and moved back to his spot in the carriage. "Do you have any children, Mike?"

"The good Lord's only blessed me with five. But I'm holding out fer a few more," he said with a bawdy laugh.

The carriage pulled up in front of the Shelbourne. McClellan paid the man with a nice tip, "for the young ones," and was soon surrounded by bellboys taking their luggage to their room. The man at the desk had a winning smile that matched the class of the hotel.

"How many in your party, sir?"

"Just my wife and daughter and I."

McClellan signed the register and dug in his purse for English money.

The desk clerk saw the purse held mostly American bills and

glanced at the signature on the register. "Sir, would you be Gen. George McClellan?"

McClellan smiled and nodded his head. Few in Europe recognized him. It was nice to feel the tug of celebrity once more. With so many relatives in America, the Irish followed the fight closely. The desk clerk whispered quickly to the bellboy and turned back to the family.

"We will put you in the royal suite, general. It does us proud to welcome a former presidential candidate to our fine hotel."

The general thanked him and reached for another tip, but the clerk shook him off. "Please, sir, you do us a great honor. We will do all we can to live up to it."

He reached into a locked box under the counter. "We can exchange some of your money if you wish. Most establishments in Dublin only take English currency."

By the time they were done, McClellan was whistling to himself. The reception was grand indeed and the room more so.

* * *

It hadn't taken too long to unpack. Nelly was a whiz at organization, thought her husband. Mary was eager to see "leper-cons" before lunch.

"Nelly, why not take her across the street to see what's happening on St. Stephen's Green? I'll sit and have cigar and catch up on the news."

She frowned ever so slightly at the word "news," but took her daughter's hand. "We won't be long. Just enough to get our land legs again," she said smiling again.

George sat down and buried his face in *The Irish Times*. Even a casual reader could tell Ireland was in trouble. The paper was filled with little bits of rebellion – street protests, vandalism, even the occasional attack on one of the English visitors.

It was a sentiment he knew well. Fenians filled the ranks of both North and South during the war. An officer in the Irish Brigade had once told him they had joined up to fight so they could train to fight the English. Irish pipe dreams. The Irish had found freedom – as immigrants in America.

He scanned through the paper and finally found what he sought – two full articles on the end of the war. One was devoted solely to politics now that Johnson had succeeded Lincoln. McClellan felt a twinge of guilt. He had never liked the president, but to die that way was dishonorable.

He dove into the stories with both feet.

* * *

Nelly held her daughter close as they approached the crowd on the green, the Irish term for park. The gathering was a few hundred strong and they were listening to some man talk about freedom. She and Mary had barely crossed the street when screams pierced the din.

She turned toward them and saw cavalry riding toward the crowd pushing their way through those who refused to move. She watched in horror as the horses squashed a man against a carriage.

The crowd grew angry. Rocks and bottles began to fly toward the hated English cavalry. Too late Nelly tried to head to the hotel. The growing mob blocked her path.

* * *

George heard sounds of fighting, but that was so common to a soldier's life that he had ignored them. He suddenly remembered his wife and jumped out of his seat – only to see Big Mike carrying Nelly's battered body.

He barely heard as they told him Mary had been trampled. Time later to grieve. Time now to heal the wounded ... his Nelly.

George McClellan had seen enough combat to be used to bloody bodies. He'd seen comrades, even friends, butchered by war, but never someone so close. Big Mike carried her all the way to their room, tears streaming down his cheeks.

He placed her bleeding body gently on the featherbed and shook his head at McClellan. "Sorry, I can't stay, me lord, there's more to be helped."

It wasn't long before a doctor arrived. The hotel staff were doing all they could. Something like this had never happened to one of their guests.

After a little while, the doctor told him to take a walk. George checked his watch and realized it was barely two hours later. It seemed like years.

He stepped into the hallway and saw two men, both with pistols in their belts. One was standing just outside the door. The other was watching the window.

George examined the one closest to the door. He seemed no threat. In fact, he seemed to be on guard. He was a good-looking, well-dressed man with a close-cropped beard. Before George could speak, the man held out his hand.

"Begging your pardon, sir, the name's James Stephens."

"Why are you and your friend standing at my door? There's been an accident and we don't have any time for visitors."

"'Twas no accident," the man said, muttering "bloody English," under his breath.

"What do you mean 'no accident?'" George felt his temper rising.

"It's how they treat us all the time. Once they realize they've done it to an American, they might well come along to get rid of the witnesses."

George could barely speak. The English had murdered his daughter and his unborn son. Nelly herself might be lucky to live through it. And now they might come back? It sounded preposterous. But Stephens looked grim-faced.

It was impossible not to believe.

"Wait here."

George went back into the room and came out bearing a .44-caliber Colt Dragoon revolver.

* * *

The pair talked all day and night. Stephens told McClellan about the IRB – the Irish Republican Brotherhood. He explained how there were plans to rebel both in Ireland and even invade Canada to create a second front.

George tried hard not to laugh. He knew you didn't build an army out of wishes and good intentions. It took men, weapons, supplies and a commodity in short supply. It took time.

Stephens nodded at each point, listening intently, taking it all in.

Gen. George B. McClellan was mulling the task. Thinking of what he would need. Mentally calculating guns, provisions, men and whether it could be done.

It all made him think back to the Crimean War, where he'd been sent as an observer. Then Capt. McClellan had set Washington on its ear with 360 pages of what he'd learned. It had put him on the fast track to command. Even his detractors knew he was a skilled organizer.

Stephens waited. He had baited the hook. But the fish had to decide to bite.

George sat on the top step, his head leaning in his right hand. A million details and no nation to provide them. Yes, Stephens said there were friends in the U.S. with money who would help. But could it be done?

Each time he made lists in his head, the images changed. A box of cartridges morphed into a soldier in green gunning down a red-coated cavalryman. A crate of bayonets was soon deployed across a whole company eagerly charging a collapsing English line.

George didn't just want victory. He wanted justice. For Nelly. For Mary and for thousands more like them.

There was silence in the hall. Worlds turned when great men thought such thoughts.

"You'd have to let me do it my way, with my people and put off these other little bits of foolishness you have planned."

Stephens wanted to shout. But he hesitated as well. Was Ireland making a bargain with the devil giving over power to the man they had called, "the Young Napoleon?"

It didn't matter. Street riots and a poorly organized invasion of Canada would never make Ireland free.

Maybe this way would work.

* * *

Prime Minister Henry John Temple sat with his former rival, Lord John Russell, who was now also the foreign secretary. They relaxed in the study, enjoying a nice after-meal port, and finally worked their way around to what the papers called "the American problem."

"I sent one of my best men over to the hotel to explain the situation and express the government's disappointment," Russell explained, taking a sip. "That damned American actually pulled a gun on my man Hastings and said he didn't care if the queen herself came begging."

"He insulted Her Majesty? The gall."

"What's more, the Americans have filed a formal complaint. They demanded an apology. Demanded!"

"It's a bit like the Trent Affair," said Temple. "It will blow over and cooler heads will prevail. The Yanks don't want a war with the mightiest nation in the world."

* * *

Stephens didn't like having so many important IRB leaders in one place, but what was being decided demanded it.

Big Mike took his third drink of whiskey. It didn't make him feel any better as he muttered, "my fault." "Let's show off fer da Yank, sez I. I got dem kids killt."

Stephens patted the big man on the shoulder. "No, you set it in motion. But, 'twas the English that did the deed. It's on them. Not you." Mike silently shook his head in agreement.

"I don't like it. Sure, he's part Irish but he's not devoted to the cause," said one who went only by the name of Taffy.

Stephens gave the man a look. "I'll grant, he's no Irish patriot. But he hates the bloody English as much as we do. And he's got a name and a story that can win us friends at the highest levels of the American government." He paused. "And he knows how to build an army."

There were nods all around the table at that, even Taffy. "Then we need to send the word to our friends in the States to make sure he receives the proper welcome."

Stephens laughed quietly. "That much I've done already. The ship left this morning."

* * *

McClellan stood on deck as the ship steamed into New York harbor. He thought on the oath they had made him take. It didn't seem to overrule the one he had taken as a union officer. Still, he quietly recited the new one once more:

"I, George McClellan, do solemnly swear, in the presence of Almighty God, that I will do my utmost, at every risk, while life lasts, to make Ireland an independent Democratic Republic; that I will yield implicit obedience, in all things not contrary to the law of God to the commands of my superior officers; and that I shall preserve inviolable secrecy regarding all the transactions of this secret society that may be confided in me. So help me God! Amen."

No. It wasn't an oath. It was stepping stone. To avenging himself. He'd take the devil's oath if that's what it took.

* * *

The Inman Line's City of Manchester churned the water slowly as it came close to shore. Finally healthy enough to move about, Nelly joined her husband on deck to watch home come into view.

Cheers rippled across the water. Nelly turned to George. "That crowd, they're for you, you know."

He put his arm around her. "They're for us."

"No. George. They expect you to do what no one else has and give them freedom." She turned to face her husband and stared at him. "I know you can do this. You know you can as well. I've been a soldier's wife and I know the risks." She hesitated for a moment and looked up at him. "They took our children away. I want you to give birth to a nation instead."

He hugged his wife. She had been his strength during the war. She was telling him she was strong enough to do so again.

"George, one more thing. The English will believe all the press about you. They'll think you are afraid to fight. Use it against them."

Despite the emotion he felt, George began to grin. Nelly was also a damn good tactician.

* * *

George helped Nelly into the carriage and the crowd grew quiet, respectful. Grown men were crying as the carriage passed by.

McClellan ascended the hastily prepared stage and looked out at the crowd. It was huge – far bigger than anything he had seen during the presidential campaign. Many of those still wore union blue.

But there were those in gray in the crowd as well. The tale of the attack on a woman had inflamed Southern chivalry. And McClellan was more pitied than hated in the South for his war record.

North or South, red hair was there in abundance.

The crowd waited. George thought of Mary and Nelly and smiled, summoning his best orator's voice.

"My friends. And I do mean that. Nelly and I thank you. Your love and friendship will help us through this trying time."

The crowd applauded, respectfully.

"There is no time now for grief. That will come later. There is only time for the work ahead. England has killed too damn many innocent women and children. It's time for them to learn that men – Irish men – know how to fight back." As he said it, he pounded his fist into his hand.

The crowd went wild. Cheers and anger overflowed. Somewhere a band started playing but even it could barely be heard. McClellan climbed down and began to shake hands with people in the crowd. It might have been the shortest speech in history.

It was more than enough.

* * *

Gen. George B. McClellan sat in the staff meeting and looked at the men he had gathered around him. Gen. Francis Meagher, former leader of the Fighting 69th, was to his left as second in command. Brig. Gen. Charles Tevis sat across from the table, in between Col. John O'Neill and Brig. Gen. Samuel M. Spear. Those last three had been in charge of the original planned Fenian invasion of Canada. "Planned" was hardly the right word. The operation had no organization, few supplies and little order of battle. McClellan had changed all that in the past few months.

Gen. Hermann Haupt was seated on McClellan's right side. Haupt was far from the only non-Irishman in the army. McClellan had recruited him personally. His railroad expertise was key to any attack. A youngish Maj. Sean Barry was the only unknown at the table. He had been with Gen. Butler at Petersburg and had a unique skill set.

"Gentleman, the planning and training go well. You are all to be congratulated."

That summed up herculean efforts. There were now three separate training camps scattered across New York. Men were easy to find. Many brought their own weapons. The rest of the supplies were war surplus, purchased on the cheap from a very accommodating U.S. government.

The table was filled with maps of the planned three-pronged invasion into Canada. Some of the invasion might even take place. McClellan knew it would be hard to keep a rein on the eager men much longer.

As if on command, Gen. Meagher chimed in. "Begging your pardon sir, but when do we go. It's already August."

"Don't worry, Thomas. I too am eager for a taste of revenge. I have a meeting with some of our, er, backers in New York. When I return, we will talk about specifics."

He turned to face the others. "Meanwhile, keep drilling them. The English are good at what they do. We need to be better."

McClellan felt bad lying to them. But he knew the English had spies in their midst. Only Stephens and he knew the truth. Orders were about to be issued and then it would be too late.

No aide had written the orders. McClellan had penned every last one in his own hand, till the hand ached from it. Even now, those orders traveled with him. He left nothing to chance. The train car was full of guards. Though if the English tried anything in the United States, they'd face an all-out war.

That fact had been made most clear to Britain by Charles Francis Adams, Sr., the ambassador to the Court of St. James. Britain was worried about fighting a re-united America and didn't want that conflict. The U.S. had taken an officially neutral stance. Unofficially, the army still loved McClellan and he got whatever he needed.

The train pulled into New York siding in the early afternoon. McClellan made an ostentatious display of meeting with several old veterans he knew from the war, along with a group of New York and Massachusetts politicians. He told them all that the invasion would have to wait another few weeks. One last bit of misinformation, he hoped.

When the dinner was over, he got back on the train, rather than stay in a hotel.

Stephens was waiting for him in his car, dressed as a conductor. The pair shook hands like old friends. "You've done an amazing job with the army and everything else."

McClellan nodded in appreciation but was all business. "Is everything in readiness in Ireland?"

"Yes. We've put the English to sleep. We've told all of our people that the invasion of Canada is our first step. After that succeeds, we'll worry about Ireland." He took a sip of whiskey. "I even sent a few high-level IRB members to Canada. I didn't tell them that I thought they'd be in the way," he laughed.

Turning serious, he looked at McClellan. "When?"

The general checked his watch: 6:57. Three minutes earlier than planned. "Tonight."

Stephens nearly choked on his whiskey as McClellan reached into the case he carried. "Orderly!"

A young captain rushed through the door. "Yes sir!"

"Take several men and get on the 7:05 to Albany. You are going back tonight with these. Stop first at the camp in Newburgh and then on to see Gen. Spear." He handed the captain an envelope filled with orders.

The rest would be in the hands of Herman Haupt.

* * *

Gen. Haupt was sitting in his tent when the captain arrived. "General, message for you from Gen. McClellan."

Haupt read the note and smiled. He wasn't in this fight for glory or Irish freedom. He was in it for the challenge and McClellan just gave him one: Move the entire camp to New York harbor to ship out as fast as possible.

Haupt smiled. The men didn't have to move anything but their own equipment. He had pre-positioned supplies in a New York warehouse. He was prepared to move either the men to the harbor or the supplies on north. "You'd better get on that train, captain. I'm taking every train I can find and heading to New York!"

The captain saluted and ran out of the tent.

Haupt and McClellan were both railroad men. They had many friends and those friends kept a few trains always "on maintenance" nearby. The first one began to load in 15 minutes.

* * *

The initial ship left the dock at 3:05 a.m. and headed away from shore and away from the others. It had another mission.

The men moved fast, eager to for action, even if they doubted the strategy. The men on the ships were veterans, many from the Fighting 69th. They didn't know where they would land, but assumed it would be Nova Scotia. If the English fleet let them land.

McClellan tried to relax in his cabin, mentally going over the moving parts. Every military action had too many of those. His had a few key elements.

First, supply. That much was assured. Benevolent Irish in America had been shipping food and clothes to Ireland for months to stave off any chances of starvation in winter. Instead of trying to avoid blockades, they welcomed English inspection of the ships and even asked for soldiers to guard the warehouses to prevent theft. English officials agreed, to try and smooth over the anger in the states.

The Englishmen found large stores of flour, salt, salted beef and pork, as well as hardtack. The last was purchased as war surplus and gave the inspectors something to laugh about.

The clothes were sturdy wool – all designed for winter months. None of the inspectors noticed that they were all in adult sizes. Enough for 50,000 men. And enough food for six months without forage. It was the first time in history an enemy army stood guard over the very supplies its attackers planned to use.

The guns and ammunition had left the port of Charleston, allegedly destined for sale in South America. Only they and the ships that carried them had turned north, not south. They'd been escorted by two war surplus Confederate ironclads. They weren't as ocean-worthy as some of the English ironclads, but they were a match in a fight.

McClellan knew he needed luck. He needed to rendezvous with them before being spotted by the British navy. And good weather was essential.

The Canadian campaign was left in the hands of Gen. Spear. His orders were clear. He was to muster all of his forces and push across the border into Canada and move against Montreal. From there he was to go forward toward either Quebec or Ottawa.

Spear didn't have many specific commands except to keep his force together and do what he could to protect both Canada's Irish immigrants and the French-Canadians who had no love for their English overlords. The original three-pronged attack had been scrapped. McClellan wanted to field a large, powerful army in Canada.

* * *

He woke to a pounding on his cabin door. "General, lookout has spotted several warships, off the starboard bow."

McClellan struggled to throw on his coat, fighting to remember which side was port and which starboard.

He walked calmly to the bridge, his stomach doing somersaults. McClellan asked for binoculars and just told the man to point. "There, sir," he said, his hand directing the general to the right.

The general mouthed a little prayer of thanks. "Signal them and all other ships to open Order A2."

McClellan watched as the first officer did just that. The man fought hard to contain himself. "Pardon me, general, might I share this with the men?"

"Please do. They have a right to know."

"We're going to Ireland," the man screamed over and over, again.

Ships bells and whistles sounded throughout the fleet until officers calmed their men. There were still perhaps eight days of travel to go. Either Poseidon or the English navy could stop them.

* * *

The English hunted for the Americans at sea. It was just a matter of time till they were found. Much of the British Atlantic fleet had been directed to protect the east coast, especially Nova Scotia. Sooner or later they would be found and 10,000 men that could be used to attack Canada would instead learn to swim.

Rear Admiral William Loney waited for the message. He could

hear the midshipman's tiny feet. It would be Murray. He had the honor of bringing the news.

The midshipman knocked and saluted impeccably. "Admiral, one of our picket ships spotted smoke, but the ship ran away before we could make chase." The midshipman handed the details to the admiral.

Loney checked his watch. It was more than three days since the expedition had left New York. They were right on time. "Make sure this message is relayed to shore at once. Now we'll see action."

* * *

Admiral Loney had been wrong. The only action they'd seen had been smoke or occasionally one ship, just at the edge of the patrol area. He'd finally designated a few faster vessels to give chase to see what was going on. It had been more than a week since the ships had left harbor. Already Irish troops had crossed into Canada and defeated a small force near Montreal.

England had sent reinforcements but more troops had to be pulled from the colonies and would take time to gather.

Still no invasion by sea.

* * *

The City of Dublin was the first steamer into Cork. It came in just as the sun peaked over the horizon. It was flying English colors. McClellan figured that technically true since Ireland was part of the empire.

For now.

Gen. Meagher's Fighting 69th had been drilling for weeks on how to get off the ship quickly and quietly. They did so to perfection. Half secured the city and warehouses and the other half seized the coastal defenses without firing a shot. They just marched up and were waved through with some hastily forged papers claiming they were a colonial unit from South Africa.

The other ships docked, spewing out men and equipment. McClellan had the ships and coastal batteries stripped of their guns. He even took the armor plating off the ironclads and ordered them sunk in the mouth of the harbor after the task force had retired.

Big Mike greeted the general with a bear hug. "'Tis good to see you, sir. I'm to be your contact with the IRB."

Mike's energy was infectious. The long voyage wore off and McClellan smiled. "We need all the wagons, horses and trains. We're pushing north, away from the ocean where they can get at us easily."

Mike raced off to organize the eager Irish and get the transportation McClellan needed.

* * *

Prime Minister Temple and Lord Russell were studying the map of Canada. The situation looked grim. It would take months to muster force to counter the invasion and Canadian Irish and more American recruits were flocking to the cause. Montreal had surrendered and the army had pushed onto Quebec which declared itself independent of England.

An aide brought in a message. "Well, read it young man. Don't just stand there," said Russell.

"The Yanks have finally landed, my lords, in Cork."

The aide beat a hasty retreat as the leaders called a war council.

* * *

The Army of Ireland had made its base at Portartlington, which many Irish still called Cooletoodera. It wasn't a port. It was an intersection of several railway lines part of Ireland's premier line, the Great Southern and Western Railway.

The base was 45 miles west of Dublin, just far enough to make it tough for the English to reach quickly. McClellan and the IRB had commandeered (the Irish loved having that word work to their benefit for a change) every train and car from Dublin south. IRB agents had managed to capture several others from the northern lines and sent them west before the English could react.

Train travel anywhere but between Belfast and Dublin had ground to a halt. Herman Haupt had the men build two large roundhouses to store the trains. And he set to work fixing the cars the way he wanted. American railroad men wouldn't let him rip the backs out of the cars so men could get in and out easily. Here, no one stopped him.

* * *

September was a busy month of training. McClellan had no trouble finding Irish who wanted to fight. The problem he had was limiting it to 50000. Every Catholic in the south wanted to join the army.

But the army lacked the resources to train, equip and, most importantly, feed that many. Recruiters required high standards and still had to draw lots to decide.

New recruits were set to work digging, building fortifications and securing the army's artillery. By the time fall hit, the Army of Ireland was dug in deep enough that even Bobby Lee would be impressed.

McClellan almost laughed aloud at that thought. He was sure he was right. He had several of Lee's officers on staff. They knew how to fortify.

And fortify they had done. The big guns were dug in on two small hills that overlooked the area. Three sets of lines surrounded the training area. It would take a major British invasion to dislodge them. There were only a few permanent structures below. Haupt's roundhouses, three small supply warehouses, and Maj. Barry's training building.

That last was the strangest of the buildings. It was two stories high – high enough no one could see in. Only part of the large building even had a roof and there were no windows to see in. The rest was empty. Barry's hand-picked men were in there every day drilling.

With what, no one knew.

The English didn't have the manpower for a full-scale attack. The navy had blockaded Ireland so no American ships got through. Still word of the slow-moving Canadian campaign leaked. England had used its fleet to reinforce Canada, but its troops were still outnumbered.

The navy had been gradually landing troops in Dublin as well and they were camped just west of the city.

McClellan dispatched Gen. Meagher with the 69th and four other regiments – 5,000 men – to serve as a blocking force. "General, I want you to make their lives difficult. I want you to make sure they don't forget we're here. But under no circumstances are you to engage a large or superior force," he said, as he reined in the angry general.

He let the veteran have his say. Then he reminded him. "Gen. Meagher, you are there because I trust you. You are ready. Your men are ready. The rest of this army is not. When it is, I promise you as God is my witness, you will not be forgotten."

Meagher had reluctantly agreed.

As weeks ran on, he almost regretted it. Keeping the 69th and the other hotheads in check was a 24-hour-a-day job.

* * *

October came and went. Then November. By mid-December, morale was bleak throughout the Army of Ireland.

The English army outside Dublin numbered 25,000 strong. It

wasn't even dug in. The English were daring the Irish to attack. The officers had already moved into the city for winter quarters. Fall was cold and wet and camp life was miserable for both sides.

The Irish papers were filled with stories about McClellan's American campaigns. The papers had dubbed him "The Littlest Napoleon" and depicted him as a child unwilling to play with his toys for fear of breaking them.

McClellan knew the risk he took. Every staff meeting was a battle. Every trip to the latrine had to be escorted by guards. The Irish was itching for a fight – against the English, McClellan and anyone else.

Worse still, he had given them the tools, the training, the ammunition. And they knew it.

On Dec. 17, just after many of the men had attended mass, McClellan called in Big Mike. Stephens had long since stopped speaking to the general. Only Mike was willing to talk to both men.

"Mike, I want you to do me a favor."

"Yes, me, lor…, I mean, general. Anything."

"I want you to take a detail down to Cork and round up every barrel of whiskey you can find. I want enough alcohol that we can float a ship. The men have worked hard. They deserve a Christmas present."

Mike was silent. "Go ahead, Mike, what is it?"

"Sir, I know you mean well, but what the men want for Christmas is lobsterback, not whiskey."

McClellan nodded. "I know. Just trust me on this. Take as many men as you need, but only Irish ones. I want to keep the American regiments here. Why not take a few Cork boys and at least they can see their families."

* * *

Mike obeyed the general's order like he had done each time. He gathered more than 100 men, nearly all from Cork and headed south. Haupt allotted a few wagons to the expedition. The rest they had to acquire in Dublin.

At least Big Mike knew he could pay for the whiskey. That would make it easier.

Everywhere they went, the men told of their planned expedition. McClellan's Christmas bribe to the troops. Mike had yelled at the first man he heard telling the story.

Then he realized how stupid he was being and stopped saying

anything at all.

The whole trip took exactly a week and more than a dozen huge whiskey wagons rolled into camp Christmas Eve afternoon. The camp was in a good mood for the first time in months. Christmas and the promise of an ample share of whiskey boosted morale.

McClellan waited for the men to finish dinner and grabbed Mike and went to the nearest wagon.

Eager men gathered round, hoping to be first in line. Big Mike quieted them down with a few yells and one terrifying glare.

McClellan climbed onto the wagon and then atop the barrels, standing precariously on hundreds of gallons of Ireland's finest.

"Men, I've worked you hard and you've earned every drop in these wagons!"

The men cheered and cheered some more.

The general waited for them to grow quiet. "And I would like to lift a glass and have a drink with each and every one of you…"

He hesitated. The soldiers grew restless. For the first time, some sensed that something else was going on. Something more important than whiskey.

"I'd love to drink a drink to Irish independence, but we're not yet bloody independent!" he said with a roar that surprised his men. Then he pulled out his saber and pointed it in the air. "But we're about to be. This is Christmas Eve and the English think we aren't going anywhere. That we're just a bunch of drunken Paddies. And they're wrong."

The stunned looks on the men showed excitement, eagerness, even fear.

"Now we've convinced them we're not going to attack. And that's what we're going to. We hit them tomorrow on Christmas morning!"

The camp started to cheer again but he waved them to quiet.

"Now, to your tents, boys, first train leaves in 15 minutes." Then he looked into the crowd. "Gen. Haupt, get this army moving!"

Haupt simply nodded and raced to the roundhouses.

* * *

The first train left 13 minutes later. The GS&WR was rolling again with a vengeance, loaded with troops and guns.

McClellan and his staff joined Barry in the second train. His surprise lay waiting beneath canvas on several flat cars.

* * *

It was a short trip to reach Meagher, about an hour and a half. The general himself greeted McClellan's train. "Then it's true, sir?"

"Yes, Thomas. And I don't forget my promises."

Even as McClellan's men unloaded, he could see the next train in the distance. Meagher was a good two miles from the English. He hoped they wouldn't think a few extra trains were unusual.

He headed right to Meagher's camp and the staff meeting began.

Men checked and rechecked weapons throughout the Irish line. Bayonets were sharpened. Metal buttons dulled. Anything that made noise was tied off or cut off. This was an army with one purpose, now, to defeat the English in open battle.

* * *

Haupt walked into the tent and interrupted McClellan. "Sir, one of the engines broke down. It will take us a good hour to clear it to a siding."

McClellan looked at his watch. It was 3:46. Moving men quietly in the dark was dangerous and took time. Precious time. Even now they might be lucky to get all the men into place.

He looked at his muster – 13 000 men, a few cannon and Barry's unit. And the element of surprise.

Opposite them sat 25 000 or more English soldiers, but with few officers to organize them. Those we all asleep in warm city beds.

Gen. George B. McClellan, head of the Army of the Potomac, would never take that risk.

That general had died in Dublin with his children.

He turned to face the staff. "We go." He stared at Meagher, "General, your veterans will lead the attack with two of the newer regiments and push the English south to north. We will leave one blocking regiment on our left flank with Barry. The rest will advance forward. We will hit them on the flank and on their front simultaneously."

Meagher looked at his watch and silently asked when. McClellan said simply, "Sun up."

* * *

When sun came to the Emerald Isle, Dec. 25, 1865, all hell broke loose.

McClellan didn't even use his artillery. He didn't want to alert the enemy. He sent out troops to silence the few enemy pickets and then watched as the tide of green swept over the English troops, hung over from the night before.

The attack was swift. Meagher's men didn't yell, or scream or even curse. They moved quickly through the tents, killing or capturing the men who had haunted their native land for hundreds of years.

The English were no pushovers, even this day. Small units began to form and fight. The first sound of musket fire echoed over the battlefield.

Defeating them took time. Each pocket of resistance slowed up Meagher's advance just a bit. Gradually, the English formed a line facing south. They threw everything they could find into makeshift barricades and the Fighting 69th paused.

A cheer went up from the English line. They had stopped the advance.

Then more green troops crashed through the western part of the line and that defensive position folded. Once more, men were on the run trying to find a way out of the pocket. The defenders drove north with Irishmen close on their heels.

* * *

Col. Damian Cullum had been rebuffed by one Irish lass. So he decided to check on his men instead. Cullum was the only officer above lieutenant anywhere on the line that night when the fighting began.

He had seen his share of action abroad and knew how to rally the troops. Only about half the English force had been engaged. Junior offices readied the remaining units but lacked any coordination. Cullum figured with proper leadership – his leadership – they should still be able to turn the tide. This was one of those times when colonels became generals, if they acted decisively.

Cullum sent messengers to nearby regiments and soon had five foot and one light cavalry regiment under his direct command. He urged the remaining forces to dig in against the Irish advance coming from the south.

The colonel had better things in mind. Cullum noticed the Irish had left their own flank exposed. It was guarded by just one regiment and two batteries of light artillery that must be low on ammunition. The guns hadn't fired a shot. He dispatched the cavalry to circle from the north and flank the defenders. He ordered his remaining men to advance.

The light horsemen were led by a young lieutenant eager for glory and a chance at promotion. They didn't wait to coordinate the attack. His units charged the Irish, the hooves of the horses pounding out a deadly tune.

They never reached the Irish line. The men manning the first battery turned their guns and fired, cutting down men in horses with hundreds of rounds fired within seconds. It sounded like a horizontal hailstorm or perhaps thousands of bees. It was a never-ending horror roaring guns and death.

Horses and men screamed and the first rank of the charge was cut to pieces. The second rank crashed forward and the attack turned into a mass of dead and dying. There was so much blood that troopers couldn't tell their comrades from the horses they rode.

Cullum felt sick. Too late he realized that the light cannon weren't cannon at all. They were an American invention he had read about – Gatling guns.

The infantry attack was committed, as well. The front ranks couldn't turn and run because of the men behind them.

As soon as the cavalry attack collapsed, both batteries turned on the slow-moving infantry. The eight guns spewed close to 4,000 rounds in a minute. The supporting regiment added their fire and rank after rank of redcoats fell, turning the ground as red as their uniforms.

It was a disaster. The only thing Cullum could do was save whatever men he could. Instead of being the hero, he would be remembered as the man who lost the Battle of Dublin and maybe the war.

He ordered the bugler to call retreat.

* * *

American ambassador Adams, the descendant of two U.S. presidents, had helped mediate the surrender. He had "accidentally" been in Dublin on business when the battle occurred. In all, the English lost 3,491 men dead or wounded and another 2,410 missing, some so chewed up they were unrecognizable. The remainder had been captured.

Stephens was once more talking to McClellan and they both admitted 25,000 men made a big bargaining chip. Irish successes in Canada did even more.

But what tipped the scales was America's sudden interest in a free Ireland. Adams had a letter from President Johnson written just for this occasion, in the slim case the Irish were able to win a major victory. It was written in flowery ambassadorial language, but it emphasized that the United States would encourage the Irish to release *most* of the Canadian territory they had gained and cease hostilities in return for Irish freedom. Quebec would become independent – backed up by U.S. ground forces.

The ambassador handed McClellan copies of some of the American newspapers. They were screaming for war with England if the Irish weren't set free. Now that Ireland had won a key victory, those cries would only grow louder.

The general figured the rest was in the hands of the diplomats.

Little Mary would soon be resting in a free Ireland.

Afterthought:
Both McClellan's trip to Europe and the Fenian invasion of Canada actually happened. However, McClellan apparently never made a trip to Ireland. Had he done so, would the Little Napoleon have changed both his history and Ireland's?

The Twenty Year Reich
by Dave D'Alessio

Reinhard Heydrich had been told that the *Führer's* bedroom door was soundproof, but he could hear muffled voices inside. He made no attempt to eavesdrop, and with a cold look made sure his aide kept his curiosity in check.

The fat doctor, Morel, came out first, followed by Himmler. "If you would be so good," Himmler asked Morel, the *Führer's* personal physician, "would you explain the situation to my deputy?"

Morel wheezed to Heydrich, "The *Führer* is resting comfortably from the sedative I gave him. I would say he has reached the advanced stages of Parkinson's disease."

"And that means?" Heydrich asked. He knew that Himmler thought Morel was a fool and a quack with obnoxious personal hygiene. He shared those opinions.

"At this stage the patient is generally confined to bed. I, however, shall be using the most powerful treatments available and will soon have him back on his feet," Morel wheezed, cheerful as usual.

Morel seemed unaware that the SS had doctors of its own. Heydrich had spoken to a number of them, and he knew that Himmler had consulted astrologers as well. The predictions were unanimous: the *Führer* would be confined to his bed for the rest of his life. The dementia he was suffering would continue to increase. No one, let alone a fool like Morel, could reverse it. Adolph Hitler, who ruled the world from the Urals to the Emerald Isles, from Murmansk to Cairo, was dying.

He was weak.

Himmler caught Heydrich's eye, and nodded once, slowly. They had planned for this day. They had known it was coming since the '40's, when the *Führer* could no longer hide the trembling in his left arm. "Contact your staff," Himmler told Heydrich. "Tell them I would like them to execute Operation Bumblebee."

"Do it," Heydrich ordered. The aide at his side snapped out the Hitler salute and ran off, leather boots slapping against the marble floors of the *Reich* Chancellery's halls.

"That sounds ominous," Morel wheezed. "I thought operations were more my department." He chuckled weakly, his stomach jiggling like an aspic.

Himmler ignored Morel. He turned to Heydrich and said, "I shall be in my offices." They exchanged salutes, arms stiff, hands open. Himmler left.

Heydrich waited until Himmler was out of sight and then drew his automatic. He shot Morel twice in the chest, the flat gunshots ringing off the corridor's walls. As the fat man slid to the floor, incomprehension his final expression, Heydrich shot him again behind the ear.

He went into the bedroom, pistol in hand. *Fraulein* Braun looked up to stare at him, eyes wide like those of the deer in the spotlight at the sight of the gun. Her eyes came up to meet his. "Reinhard, no," she said. She was sitting straight, clutching Hitler's hand to her breast.

Heydrich shot her once, between the eyes. She slid to the floor, Hitler's hand slipping from her dead grasp.

The *Führer* was sleeping poorly, Morel's drugs be damned. He twitched in his sleep, cried out incoherently as he dreamed. Perhaps, Heydrich thought, he was fighting against Morel's sedative. Perhaps he knew what was coming.

Heydrich took one of the overstuffed pillows from the head of the bed, and pushed it down over the *Führer's* face.

Hitler thrashed more frantically. He was weak, though, too weak to resist. And if he was too weak to resist, he was too weak to lead. National Socialist theory demanded the survival of the fittest. This empty shell of a man no longer had any right to rule the *Reich*.

Heydrich held the pillow down until Hitler's body stopped twitching. Then, in the name of efficiency, he fired through the pillow, the gunshots muffled by the pillow's down. He left the stained pillow in place over the crimson ruin of the *Führer's* head.

* * *

Orders raced through the halls of the *Reich* Chancellery as fast as black-clad SS men could carry them. "Hitler is dead," they told everyone. "It is a coup by *Reichsmarshall* Göring. We must restore order!" Hitler had named Göring his heir. If Himmler could put the blame on Göring, he'd be finished. What was one lie more, with the entire *Reich* at stake?

SS men secured the entrances and seized switchboards. Any civilian, any man of the *Wehrmacht* or *Luftwaffe* or *Kriegsmarine*, who failed to do exactly as told was shot. *Luftwaffe* men were shot even if they obeyed. Hadn't their leader killed the *Führer*? The SS men wept for their lost *Führer*, and killed anyone they pleased.

Hess refused to take orders. He was shot. Von Ribbentrop, shot. Goebbels would have been useful, but he refused to believe the story about Göring. Shot. Bormann obeyed. He was shot anyway. No one had ever liked that slimy prick.

Blood pooled around bodies on the immaculate floors, and spattered the walls that Speer had designed to demonstrate the power of the Nazi party. Armed men ran up and down the wide staircases, ready to enforce their orders with bullets. In one hallway a group of Hitler Youth, inconsolable in their grief, had gathered around a hand grenade. The SS men avoided that hall.

But in the screaming and the gunfire and the death, there were those who kept their heads.

* * *

Himmler wasn't the only one who could talk to doctors, and the *Wehrmacht's* physicians were better than the sycophants kissing up to the SS. The army knew this day was coming, too. The SS controlled the *Reich* Chancellery switchboard. They had no idea that there were a dozen telephone lines out of the building they didn't know about.

"The blackshirts have gone crazy," a *Wehrmacht* major hissed into his phone. His sidearm was in his hand and he planned to murder the first SS man who walked into his office. "They're killing everyone in sight."

A machine pistol stuttered in his outer office. A voice shrieked and cut off sharply.

"Long live Germany," the major said. He crouched behind his desk, pointed his pistol at the door, and waited.

* * *

The aide glided into Chief of Staff Jodl's office, saluted, and handed over the flimsy he was carrying. Jodl glanced at it, then out the window. Half-tracks full of *Waffen* SS men were surrounding the Oberkommando *Wehrmacht*, the regular army's headquarters. Black-clad troops leaped out of the tracks to set up machine guns.

"Notify the reserve battalions," Jodl said. Three-quarters of leadership is looking calm. "They are to resist any attempts to disarm them. They are to accept no orders from the SS until told otherwise."

"*Jawohl*," the aide saluted.

"Contact von Manstein," Jodl said. "Order him to hold the Ural front." If the commanding general in the east wanted to send his reserves back to fight in Germany, neither Jodl nor Himmler nor orders would stop him, but whatever von Manstein decided, the Soviets needed to be held at bay.

"*Jawohl*."

Jodl checked his automatic. The SS scum weren't going to take him alive. Those sadists knew too many interesting ways to inflict pain on people they didn't like. "Tell the *Reichsmarshall* what's going on," he added. "Tell him the *Führer's* dead and now Himmler's bastards are acting like they own the place." Göring, if he didn't have a head full of morphine, could figure out what that meant for himself.

Downstairs the machine guns were starting to fire.

* * *

Erich Hertel had been grounded in '51 after shooting down over 300 Russian aircraft. The *Reich*, though, still had need of experienced officers. Now Hertel was a group leader, commanding three fighter squadrons by flying a Big Metal Desk for the last two years.

His boss, Field Marshal Hermann Göring, always liked to have some of his "young eagles" around him as he hunted. With Hertel's group refitting in Frankfurt, he was close enough to Göring's stomping grounds north of Brandenberg for the *Reichsmarshall* to invite over.

Hertel was always nervous about these trips. Depending on how deeply Göring was into his morphine haze, friendly fire might be a bigger threat in the hills of Germany than it was on the eastern front. Plus Göring always wanted to talk politics. Hertel hated politics. He was a flyer, nothing less, nothing more. And if Himmler's SS snoops overheard something, Hertel could be yanked out of his office and left to rot behind barbed wire fences with the other enemies of the *Reich*.

The beaters flushed a pheasant. Göring pulled his shotgun to his cheek and fired both barrels. Hertel watched the dying pheasant flutter to the ground.

Göring broke the weapon open to eject the spent cartridges, and loaded two fresh rounds. Hertel envied him the shotgun, one seized as loot from an English castle the *Luftwaffe's* Stukas had spared during the winter of 1940. The panzers overrunning Great Britain from Brighton to Aberdeen had savaged the countryside, but at the end England, Scotland, and Wales, and all they contained, had fallen under the swastika, and there was still plenty of plunder to be had.

One of the gamekeepers came running up. Not a military man, he tugged at the bill of his cap in an awkward salute and handed Göring a scrap of paper.

Göring read it. His face remained passive. The note read, he snapped the shotgun closed. "*Danke*," he told the gamekeeper, and then smoothly turned and pointed the shotgun at the SS man in the party. Hertel froze in shock.

"The *Führer* is dead," Göring announced. He pulled both triggers, nearly cutting the SS man in half.

* * *

"Alarm! Alarm!" Electric bells screamed around the camp. The 14th Panzer's replacement battalion was working up outside of Berlin, new recruits joining veterans on R&R or just back from the hospital, learning or relearning the business of war before heading to the front.

Heinz groaned, "Another damned drill." Drill or not, he moved quickly, pulling on his grey jacket and steel helmet.

Max was right with him. "We're refitting, not resting," he snapped. He led his team out of the barracks and onto the parade grounds.

"This isn't any drill I've seen," Fritz said. It didn't look like one, no, not the way the sergeants were screaming at everyone. Max's team ran to their positions and fell in with the rest of their platoon, buttoning the last button and pulling boots on with the rest.

Major Ausberger didn't wait for the military niceties, or even for the alarms to cut off. "Now hear this," he yelled, used to making himself heard on the battlefields of the Urals. "This is the real thing. Those SS bastards have killed Hitler…"

The roar that rose from the men was feral. Many of them had known no other leader; all had been singing about their love for Hitler since their short pants days in the Hitler Youth. And all of them had sworn their personal oaths of loyalty to the *Führer*. "I said those SS bastards have killed Hitler and now they're coming for us!" Ausberger screamed. "Full alert! Draw your arms from the armory! We resist until relieved, got it?"

"*Jahwohl*!"

Lieutenant Jahns caught up with Max as he was running out of the armory with his machine gun on his shoulder. "I want you to dig in over there," Jahns pointed out the spot. "I'll have the squad bring sandbags. Dig deep!"

Max eyed the position. He'd have a clear field of fire down the road. But if the SS had air support, they were cooked. "*Jawohl*," he said, and added, "Is it true about the *Führer*, Lieutenant?"

"Not a damned idea," Jahns snapped as he looked around for his other machine gun crews. "But Hitler picked Göring as heir. I follow my *Führer*."

* * *

Gunfire rattled through the streets of Berlin. Heydrich could hear it from his office. Damn those people! Double damn the *Wehrmacht* men! Why couldn't they have simply obeyed Himmler's orders?

Their resistance had set off the fanatics in the *Waffen* SS. Teams of black clad men roamed the streets. *Wehrmacht* soldiers who refused to surrender were killed. Civilians who interfered were murdered. Kreigsmariners, *Luftwaffe* men; if they would not swear loyalty to Himmler, they were butchered.

Through the door he heard, "Come here, Reinhard. I need you."

Heydrich went into Himmler's office. Himmler started to say something, but when he caught sight of Heydrich he blanched and gulped. Looking down, Heydrich saw that he had blood on his trousers. It was probably Morel's. Not looking at Heydrich, Himmler said, "We've intercepted Jodl's commands. The *Wehrmacht* is to resist until it receives further orders."

Jodl had killed himself when the SS had overrun the OKW. He wouldn't be issuing further orders.

Himmler turned away from Heydrich, away from the blood, and looked out his window. Heydrich looked outside past him. Two *Wehrmacht* men hung from lampposts, strung up by their own belts. A truck full of stormtroopers sped by, the men firing their assault rifles toward windows across the Vossstrasse. Smoke rose from a dozen spots across the city that Heydrich could see, fires started by grenades or artillery or just sheer blind rage. A platoon of Hitler Youth trotted past in step, coal scuttle helmets bouncing on their heads, rocket launchers on their shoulders, tears streaming down their baby faces.

Himmler said, "The Werhmacht will yield to my orders or they will be disarmed by force." He turned away from the window. It was worse than the Night of the Long Knives, much worse. In '34, when the SS men had eliminated the Sturmabteilung as a force in the nation, the SA men had barely fought back. Their deaths had been clean, clinical executions. "Have we any word of the traitor Göring?" he asked.

"No, my *Führer*," Heydrich said.

* * *

Göring's estate in the hills of Brandenberg was only 35 kilometers north Berlin itself. "Too close to that poison dwarf, Himmler," Göring had told Hertel. They were riding in the back of Göring's Mercedes. Both fighter pilots, they constantly scanned the way ahead and behind for signs of trouble.

Göring had his motorcade on the road to the *Luftwaffe* base at Stendal. There were bases closer to Brandenberg, but Göring had his reasons. "Von Ohlen's commanding up ahead," he told Hertel, eyes still on the move. Fighter pilots learned that. Spot the other guy first and you win.

Hertel knew Adolph Von Ohlen, of course. They had been decorated personally by Hitler once Moscow had fallen, and gotten drunk together afterward. "Good old Adi," he said.

"*Ja*," Göring answered. He lapsed into silence, planning, perhaps, Hertel guessed, or wondering where his next fix was coming from.

Hertel kept his eyes open. Outside the car he could see no threats, only the quiet German countryside.

The rolling hills and lush forests of Brandenberg were nothing like the Russian steppes he'd spent a decade driving across or flying over. Out in the steppe roads were flat and straight, and usually unpaved. In Russia you could see the camps for miles and smell them even further away. Himmler and his SS men were ridding Russia of her Slavs, to create *liebensraum*, living space, for the German aryans. Here in the heart of the *Reich* there was no sign of the butchery, no, not here, not where the sight might offend the German people.

Hertel saw a mile marker and guessed that it was still twenty minutes or more to Stendal, and there could be an SS roadblock around any of the many curves between here and there. But once they were there, they could count on Von Ohlen. "I'll be heading to Peenemunde as soon as he can lay on transport," Göring added, breaking his silence.

A Volkswagen had skidded into a ditch, run off the road by Göring's motorcade. The driver stopped screaming curses and gave the Hitler salute when he saw who was in the final car.

"Peenemunde, *Reichsmarshall?*" Hertel asked. The experimental base was 300 kilometers northwest, almost directly away from Berlin. He tipped his cap toward the Volkswagen's driver, the only apology the man would get.

"Westau is there," Göring said.

Hertel ran over *Luftwaffe* dispositions in his mind. "Bombing Group 200," he said. The elite unit had always experimented with novel tactics and aircraft. "But how will that help?"

UNITED PRESS INTERNATIONAL HEADLINES

MUNICH: Dozens of Nazi party members storm the Burgerbraukeller beer hall on word that Hitler is dead, chanting, "Kill Göring."

DRESDEN: Bishop van Zandt calls for peace in cathedral service. "Keep your heads," he urges.

REICH PROTECTORATE ENGLAND: Rioting in London streets met by machine gun fire. Truck bomb explodes outside SS barracks Portsmouth.

ROME: Mussolini sends condolences from Italian Empire. "The world has lost its greatest hero," he says.

MOSCOW: All quiet on Eastern front.

JERUSALEM: Grand Mufti mourns loss of "the man who made the world safe from international Zionist gangsters."

WASHINGTON: Spokesman for President Dewey: "No comment at this time."

REICH PROTECTORATE FRANCE: Premier Laval shot. Condition unknown. Large sectors of Paris on fire.

"Keep it coming, Heinz!" Max shouted over the tearing rip of the MG-42. He was firing as he had been taught, in short bursts, but the SS men kept coming.

The SS troopers fought stupidly. They had no sense of cover, didn't use terrain, had no coordination between units. But there were thousands of them and they kept charging even as they were mown down.

Heinz was feeding belts of ammo into the weapon. "Plenty left," he grunted. At this rate they'd be overrun before they ran out.

Looking out of the gun pit Fritz swore. "*Scheisse*! Damned Maus!"

Max looked up and swore as well. The SS men knew nothing of war. None of them had fought in the streets of London or Leningrad or Moscow. Around him the rest of his squad banged away with their Mausers rifles, picking off the SS men by the score. But the SS had all the latest and best equipment, the Sturmgewehr assault rifles with their 30-round magazines, and the giant, 100-ton Maus tank. Wars are won by men, not machines, but the machines can kill so very many brave men.

He traversed the MG to cover the tank. His bullets would have no effect on it, but if he could drive back the infantry with it, trotting as it ground along in first gear, maybe something good would happen. That was a hard-learned lesson, too, one the Russians had taught the men of the 14th Panzer the hard way: the tank protects the infantry, but the infantry protects the tank.

Max held up for a few seconds, keeping his head down as Fritz swapped the hot gun barrel for a cool one. Fritz patted him on the shoulder and Max held down the trigger, able to give the advancing troops a good, long burst with the cold barrel in place.

The SS infantry melted away from the tank, dead, dying, or fleeing. Max grinned even as the Maus's turret started to swing in his direction, the mouth of its huge 128 mm gun gaping wide. He'd done his job. Now it was up to someone else. He held the trigger down until the belt of ammo ran out, and then the three of them ducked and waited for the belch of the tank's gun.

It never came. Max grinned again as he heard the familiar chunk of a panzerfaust being fired, and then another. He looked up in time to see the Maus run off its treads, the rocket propelled grenade having struck the tank's only weak point. Max used the MG to drive the SS men further away.

A squad dashed forward, three of them clutching bags of grenades, as the huge tank ground around and around in circles on its remaining track, doing nothing but digging a deep gouge in the square.

Two of the men were shot as they tried to scale the three and a half meter wall that was the side of the tank. Another slipped, and was ground to mush under the Maus's treads. Max had to gulp and look away.

There were grips and maintenance handholds on the Maus's sides, and the rest of the squad made it up top. One man pulled the hatch open. A second fired his machine pistol inside. The third threw his sack of grenades down the hatch. They went off with a hollow ringing inside the giant metal tank. It burned for twenty minutes, until its ammunition exploded with a roar.

Those SS bastards. They were brave enough for bullies and thugs, but they didn't know a damned thing about war. The only question was whether the SS would run out of men before the soldiers were all dead. No one would be surrendering here today.

* * *

"Theo," Göring said, extending his hand and ignoring Colonel Westau's salute. "Good to see you again. Wish the circumstances were otherwise." He showed no sign of the flight up, made in one of the new jet transports.

For himself Hertel was tense and exhausted. No one knew whether any *Luftwaffe* units had thrown in with Himmler, and so the flight had been made at tree-top level the whole way, piloted by Von Ohlen himself. "Just like the old days, eh, *Reichsmarshall*?" Von Ohlen had asked, and Göring had agreed, "*Ja. Ja*! But faster, Adi, much faster!" They had all laughed at that, old pilots three.

Westau took Göring's hand and said, "Agreed, *Reichsmarshall*. Is it true about the *Führer*?"

"That he's dead?" Göring asked. "Your guess is as good as mine. That I did it? That sounds like something the poison dwarf thought up." Himmler was as despised among the *Luftwaffe* men as he was by the *Wehrmacht*.

"If the *Führer* is dead, *Reichsmarshall*, isn't your place in Berlin?" Westau asked.

Göring grimaced. "Not with that limp dick Himmler running things there." He motioned to the operations hut at the side of the field. "What kind of communications do you have?"

Westau led the way. The hut was a simple wooden shack, much too flimsy for the winds off the North Sea, in Hertel's opinion. "Only local. I'm afraid, *Reichsmarshall*," Westau answered. "Our radios have been jammed for half an hour now, and we've got no telephone contact off the island."

"But local service, *ja*?" Göring asked. Westau held the door, and Hertel and Von Ohlen followed Göring into the hut as he absently returning the salutes of the office personnel with his field marshal's baton. "That's all I need. I want to talk to Professor Bohr over at the Research Center," he said. He held out his hand and waited for someone to put a loaded telephone receiver into it. "Theo, I want you to listen to this. If Bohr tells me what I think he will, I'll have a job for volunteers from your group. Men with real guts and total loyalty to the *Reich*."

Westau clicked his heels together. "It will be done, *Reichsmarshall*. This is Bombing Group 200!"

Göring took the phone. "Professor," he said. "Do you know my voice? You do? Do you recognize my authority as *Reichsmarshall*? Say that you do aloud, *Herr* Professor." Göring held the receiver out so the others could hear Bohr's voice, tinny over the telephone, saying, "I recognize your authority, *Herr* Göring."

Putting the receiver back to his ear, Göring said, "What follows is a direct order that I intend to enforce with the personnel under my command, *Herr* Professor. Say that you understand." He held the phone out again.

"I can't see what this is all about," Bohr's voice squawked, "but yes, I understand."

"Good," said Göring into the phone. "*Herr* Professor, I am ordering the immediate release of the *Ragnarok* weapon to my control, to be used at my discretion."

As Hertel watched, Westau turned white. Von Ohlen asked, "What? What?"

"The atomic bomb," Westau whispered.

* * *

"Where is Göring?" Himmler demanded. He was facing his window again, staring through his spectacles. Smoke hung dark across the capitol.

Heydrich's people were all over the roads between Brandenberg and Berlin. All he'd learned was that the *Luftwaffe's* SS liaison was dead. He said, "Gone from his usual haunts, *Führer*. He must have fled the *Reich*."

"Fled? Fled?" Himmler repeated. Heydrich had changed his

trousers, and now it seemed that Himmler could bear to face him. Turning from the window, Himmler's voice increased in volume until he was shrieking. "Fled to where? To black Africa, perhaps? To Switzerland? Across the ocean to America, even? In one of Donitz's U-boats, perhaps?"

It was impossible. Heydrich stayed mute, having nothing to say.

Himmler turned back to his window, now speaking conversationally. "It should have been easy, Reinhard. Hitler was leader of us all, but he was sick, going mad. I am the one who purified the nation. I purged the *Reich* of the Jews, the homosexuals, the gypsies, the Slavs, the Negroes, the insane and the retarded, the Communists and the intellectuals. I understand National Socialism. I live my life by its tenets, without drugs or liquor. Why do people follow Göring?"

"He was Hitler's designated heir," Heydrich suggested.

Outside Himmler's window another body had joined the two hanging. Faint wisps of smoke curled upward from a burnt out staff car. There was still gunfire: the rattle of assault rifles, the crump of artillery, the flat crack of Mauser rifles. Heydrich imagined that the latter was growing closer. SS men didn't carry the obsolescent weapon.

"What has gone wrong, Reinhard?" Himmler asked, turning away from the window.

Heydrich stood silent.

Himmler pounded his fist on the window sill. "Göring! No one can find him, no one hears from him, but there," he waved his hand to the window, and the sounds of combat in the city. "People fight for him, Reinhard. People fight for a ghost! A fat, useless, drug-addled ghost!…What is that?" he finished. In the distance horns were sounding, wailing dissonantly.

"Air raid sirens, *Führer*," Heydrich said, diplomatically.

Air raid sirens. Civil defense was in the hands of the *Luftwaffe*. "Göring," Himmler spat out. "He's showing his hand, Reinhard! Now we can finish him!" He looked up, avoiding the sights of destruction in the street below.

Heydrich joined him. High in the sky he could make out a six-engined aircraft, one of Messerschmidt's heavy Amerika bombers, escorted by the smaller shapes of fighters. They were turning lazy circles above the capitol.

An armored half-track clattered by. Equipped with a loudspeaker, its driver announced, "Emergency! Emergency! By order of *Führer* Göring, evacuate the capitol immediately! Tune radios to 1200 megacycles to hear *Führer* Göring's speech!"

Himmler turned back from the window, trembling with rage. "Have that stopped!" he screamed.

Heydrich left immediately. Outside the office he found Hitler's secretary, now Himmler's. "*Frau* Eisen," he asked the mousy woman, "have you got a radio?"

She blanched. "Sir! It is an execution offense!" she protested.

Did he dare listen to Göring? Did he dare not? Was there even a radio here? Would Himmler murder him, too? "Arrange for one," he said.

One of the *Luftwaffe* hymns, "Wir Fehren Gegen Englland," was playing. Heydrich listened impatiently. Göring was reminding people that his *Luftwaffe* had won the Battle of Britain. That had been more than a decade ago, though.

Göring's voice came out of the radio clearly, more clearly than Heydrich could recall it sounding for years. "Loyal citizens of the *Reich*," he said. "I have heard the lies spread about me following the death of our beloved *Führer*. I did not kill the *Führer*, whom I loved as I loved my own father. I did not order him killed, or ask for his death. I believe that the man who has usurped the *Führer's* position did so. Ask the liar Himmler why there is no investigation.

"People of Berlin! Those of you who obey the traitor Himmler deny the inevitable course of history! The *Wehrmacht* stands with me. The *Luftwaffe* stands with me. The *Kriegsmarine* stands with me. The *Reich* outside of Berlin stands with me. Abandon this lost cause now! Leave the city now!

"Look upwards," Göring's voice went on. "There is a bomber in your skies. It carries a bomb so powerful that its effect is measured in hundreds of thousands of kilos of ordinary explosive. Abandon Berlin now! Abandon Himmler, the pretender, now! I have warned you." The music repeated, and then Göring's announcement. It seemed to have been recorded.

Himmler's voice came through the door. "Heydrich!" he shouted. "Have that signal jammed!"

It seemed pointless. "*Frau* Eisen, I suggest you visit your cousin in Mainz," Heydrich said.

Above, a tiny black dot separated from the bomber, and started its long fall toward the city below. "Or try to find a shelter," he said.

* * *

It was as though the sun had touched Berlin. A pillar of smoke curled into the air, the head flattening into a mushroom shape as it reached into another layer of the atmosphere.

Hertel stood and watched, his sense of revulsion slowly growing. It was all so awful, so like the dread feeling of the walls closing in around him each time he sent men out to fly against the enemy. Each time he gave those orders he wished he was in the seat of his own Messerschmidt, free in the open sky, still responsible for his men's asses, but there to fight for them if they got into trouble. Now he was powerless. All he could do was wait and watch.

Göring had excused himself and slipped into Westau's private office. When he returned, he seemed more relaxed, with better color in his face. Hertel guessed he'd taken more morphine.

The phone rang and Westau snatched it up. "*Ja*," he said, and listened. His face turned white, whiter than Göring's had been before his moment with the needle. He replaced the receiver gently into its cradle. "Success, *Herr Reichsmarshall*," he said. His voice was flat as he continued, "The bomb detonated within a hundred yards of the chancellery. *Herr* Himmler was inside at the time. They estimate..." Westau's voice cracked, and he swallowed and went on, "...estimate one million casualties, dead and wounded."

"A million!" Hertel breathed. All at once. One bomb. Von Ohlen excused himself hurriedly and stepped from the room. Hertel could hear him retching through the thin walls of the shack.

Westau said, "*Herr* Himmler could not have survived. You are now undisputed *Führer* of the Third *Reich*, *Herr* Göring. What are your orders?"

"Eh?" said Göring. "Orders?"

"Yes, orders," Westau said. He was starting to tremble. "The government is yours, my *Führer*! The nation is yours! We serve your will! Heil Göring!" he shouted, throwing up his arm in the Hitler salute. "Heil Göring! You, too, Hertel! Salute! We are in the first moments of a new age of the Third *Reich*! Heil Göring!"

Hertel remained silent. The world was tumbling down around his ears. Hitler, Himmler, the thousands upon thousands of others, all dead to make this obese drug addict *Führer* of the murderous *Reich*.

Göring stirred himself, smiling faintly. "Thank you, Westau. My orders? Carry on."

"Carry on? Is that all?" Westau asked.

"Yes, carry on," Göring said, his voice firmer. "The future of the world, of all humanity is in our hands." There was a glitter in his eyes. The morphine was hitting his system now, Hertel guessed. "We are the ubermensch, the superior man! It is our destiny to rule the world!" Göring spat out.

Westau barked, "First Russia!"

Göring was in full roar now. Hertel could only imagine what people in the other rooms of the flimsy shack were thinking. "*Ja*, first Russia! And then America, with her Jews and her negroes! The yellows of China, the browns of India, the blacks of Africa, degenerate breeds all! We will purge humanity, Westau! We will put the nozzle into the world and give it a great enema! And when we are done, the human race will be pure!"

"And the dead? The dead of Berlin, *Herr Führer*?" Westau asked.

"Martyrs! Condemned by that maniac Himmler! Just like Horst Wessel, we will sing their praises forever!" Göring said. It was as though he were on the rostrum at Nuremberg, speaking to a half million true believers, but here it was only Hertel and Westau, and they were pilots, not true believers.

"A million Berliners, a billion Chinese. What is more dead, after all the dead already?" Westau asked.

Göring bellowed, "A purging! It is needed!"

Deliberately, Westau drew his sidearm and shot Göring, The light slug punched him in his obese gut. Göring grunted, his eyes wide. His fat fingers scrabbled at the holster on his hip. Westau shot twice more, the smell of burnt powder filling the shack. Göring leaned over, fell to his knees, and then pitched forward onto his face without a word. A trickle of blood ran from his mouth.

"A purging," Westau repeated. "I don't know what happens next, but the world can't be worse off than it is now." He reversed the pistol and held it out butt first to Hertel. "Place me under arrest, Group Leader," he said.

Hitler was dead. Göring was dead. Himmler was dead. Hertel could hear gunfire in the distance. War. Civil war. Someone would rule the *Reich*, but if God could find a way to love Germany, it wouldn't be a Nazi.

Hertel looked down at Westau's pistol and shook his head. "It was needed," he said.

N'oublions Jamais
by Tom Anderson & Bruno Lombardi

April 28, 1916 – Halifax, Nova Scotia, Dominion of Canada
"Now *that's* an impressive boat!"

Sergeant Booth—the duly designated guide of the soldiers that were following him by lieu of the fact that he was the oldest (at a ripe old age of 29 years), the highest in rank, and had actually been to Halifax just before the War—came to a stop and made this announcement. The dozen or so members of the 3rd Reinforcing Draft of the 10th Canadian Mounted Rifles that were following him came to a halt and took a good long look at their home for the next nine days.

They had seen a great many things in the last seven days. The vast majority of the 10th had been born and raised in Saskatchewan and Manitoba and the four day train ride from Saskatoon was, for most of them, the first time they'd seen any part of Canada outside the prairies. The stopover in Montreal was… eye-opening… for those who had never seen a city bulging with half a million souls—the entire population of Saskatchewan in one city, in essence. Sadly, the city was wracked by protests from Prime Minister Borden's recent announcement about conscription in general and French Canadians in specific. Needless to say, the announcement had not gone over well, necessitating having the stopover cut short. A relatively short but very picturesque ride up the St. Lawrence River and then across New Brunswick later, they then found themselves in Halifax.

And staring at the biggest ship any of them had ever seen.

"Bloody Hell!" shouted Private George Lane. "She's a cruise ship!"

"She looks vaguely familiar," said someone in the back. "I'm sure I've seen her before."

Booth nodded his head and, with just the hint of a knowing smirk on his face, spoke. "Aye. She's called 'Old Reliable' now but her name is *Olympic*." Booth took a quick glance at the men and smiled when he saw several of their faces contort in varying degrees of vague recognition or confusion.

"Hey, hang on," said Trooper Michael Smith, "Wasn't that the sister ship to … to…"

"The *Titanic*," finished Booth, barking in laughter at the looks of the men. He was enjoying this all too much. A small ember of compassion flickered within his heart and he felt compelled to add, "But unlike her sister ships, she's shrugged off all manner of disasters. She's not called 'Old Reliable' for nothing, after all!"

The dozen men seemed to relax ever so slightly.

"So," said Booth, "Isn't she a beaut?" A chorus of vaguely affirmative grunts and moans indicated a general consensus on this question. "Hey, Beauty," continued Booth, turning his gaze to a quiet man standing near the back of the group, "What do you think?"

'Beauty' was a tall, lanky, black-haired man of about twenty years of age, and with altogether too many elbows and knees. He had that fresh-scrubbed look of a man who had just discovered the art of shaving and was upholding to it enthusiastically. His great-grandfather had been born in France, his grandfather had been born in Quebec, his father had been born in Manitoba and he himself had been born in Saskatchewan, so, in a very roundabout manner, he was going home again.

His name, of course, was not 'Beauty', much as the members of the 10th seemed to insist otherwise. His name was Joseph Bell. However, he (rather insistently) preferred to pronounce his surname as 'Belle'. Almost all of his fellow countrymen – even those who had no truck with French (a rather larger than usual number these days, alas) – knew a smattering of the French language and knew what the word meant. Trooper Claude Felton – who, ironically, was the most vocal supporter of the War despite the fact that he was an American and his country had steadfastly remained neutral – knew not a single word of French and had inquired of the meaning of 'Belle'. When informed that it meant 'beautiful', he immediately announced that 'Beauty' shall be Joseph's new nickname, this being what passed for high humour in the 10th.

Trooper Joseph 'Beauty' Bell simply smiled at Booth's question and took a long look at the *Olympic*, as his practiced artist's eye examined every nook and cranny and curve on it. He smiled again and turned to face Booth.

"Indeed she is. Shall we get on board?"

* * *

Joseph pulled his coat tighter against the bitter damp North Atlantic air and, pausing briefly to take a long drag on his cigarette, took up his pencil once more and resumed drawing. His current work-in-progress was a tableau of a section of soldiers lounging near a lifeboat. He had completed five such drawings in the seventy-two hours since leaving Halifax and was eager to have a sixth completed when the *Olympic* reached the mid-point of the Atlantic.

He had just finished adding a mustache on one soldier's face when a meaty hand clamped down on the paper and tore it out of his hands.

Joseph looked up to see that the hand belonged to what on first glance he thought to be some preternatural offspring of bulldog and human, but soon resolved into the face of a scowling soldier.

The paper – with its half-completed drawing – vanished as a breeze caught it and carried it off the side of the ship.

"Weel, swatch at whit we've got haur. A goddamn Frenchie," said the man. His Scottish accent was almost incomprehensible. "We dinnae loch yer kin' haur, Frenchie. Whit wi' yer popery an' treason." The man's face darkened. "They got mah grandpa killed at Balaclava an' now mah brither!" The man drew his fist back and was about to swing it when –

"Stand down, Trooper!"

The large man hesitated as another man – a Captain – came into view. The Captain had a look that could only be described as 'livid'. Two other officers – lieutenants as best as Joseph could make out – appeared behind the Captain. They were significantly younger but no less livid than their companion.

"Trooper," said the Captain. "I will repeat myself once more. I will not repeat myself a third time. Stand. Down."

The Trooper – incredibly – for a brief moment looked as if he will disobey the Captain. And then he put his fist down and stood at attention.

"Trooper, if I see you so much as *stare* at another man until we reach Liverpool, I will personally put you in the brig. Do I make myself clear, Trooper?"

"Aye sair!"

"Dismissed!"

And with that, the Trooper turned smartly around and marched away.

"Trooper...Bell," said the Captain, reading Bell's dog tags. There was just the tiniest hint of an Irish accent in his voice.

"Yes sir!"

The Captain raised an eyebrow in something akin to vague bemusement. "French-Canadian, I assume, Trooper Bell?"

"Yes sir! Born and raised in Saskatchewan, sir!"

The Captain smirked. "Well, contrary to what *some* of my country folk may think, even you people – and indeed all of Canada - are part of the Empire-wide war effort."

"Yes sir!"

"Looking forward to showing the enemy that Canadian troops are made of steel, Trooper?"

"Yes sir!"

"Excellent! Carry on!"

"Yes sir!"

And with that, the three officers walked slowly away. After a long while, Joseph sat down again and, pulling out a new sheet from his notebook, began making a new drawing.

* * *

September 1, 1916 – Ruins of the Village of Frise, Somme, France

Lieutenant Pierre Ranier grabbed a stone from the nearest makeshift rubble bulwark and struck a match against it, lighting a cigarette. Two years ago, in that vanished world of peace, he might have made a face at the stink of the impure phosporus, and he'd certainly have turned his nose up at the quality of the tobacco itself. Now, the chemical smell was a welcome respite from the stench of the trenches he and his men called their home, and he counted his blessings that he had cigarettes at all. Not all of the tobacco-producing countries were willing or able to trade to France, and soldiers like himself had top priority for the rations.

Pierre ducked his head under the *abri*, the little shelter built into the trench, to hide the smoke as he took a pull. Yesterday he had seen one soldier, a new recruit barely out of short trousers, take off his

Adrian helmet to catch the smoke in it instead. Pierre had smacked the thing out of the hands of the stammering *bluet*—'blueberry' in trench slang—and had almost yelled him out himself before remembering to let the sergeant do it in his place. He was still getting used to the officer's stripes he had been breveted with. He thought the kid had got the message: the only reason Pierre had those stripes was because too many good men had been slaughtered in the early days of the war, when everyone had been wearing kepi hats and they would have killed for an armoured helmet like the Adrian.

The decisions of those *limogers*, those incompetent officers who had sent them into the bloodbath of the Marne in '14 and so many others with unprotected heads and brightly visible uniforms—"The red trousers, they ARE France!" the conservative fools had cried—still made Pierre almost as furious as any of the *Boches'* depredations.

Almost. Pierre stubbed out his cigarette and put it in a metal case; at the start of the war he might have put it behind his ear, but he had learned what even the smallest telltale wisp of smoke could do if there happened to be a keen-eyed enemy sniper on duty. He went to the front of the trench, giving a nod to Sergeant Pierre Marceau as he knelt beside him. Marceau, a *midi*—a soldier from the South of France—was manning a *banquette*, a protected station at the front of the trench where he could rest his Lebel rifle and scan the horizon.

What there was to see of it. Pierre had heard one officer say the valley of the Somme looked like the surface of the Moon. Pierre didn't follow astronomy and his only point of comparison was the film *La Voyage Dans La Lune* he'd seen as a child, which seemed altogether too jolly in retrospect: the Earth of peace to which he had stepped out of the cinema with his parents and his dead brother now seemed just as remote and alien as Georges Méliès' vision of what the Moon was like. Pierre would prefer to compare the landscape he now observed to Hell, one level of Dante's *Inferno* maybe. Where proud trees had once stood in pleasant fields there were now only stark, blackened skeletons in miserable piles of mud, hammered too frequently by artillery fire for anything to grow. Maybe nothing would ever grow here again. And wouldn't that be God's final joke on the French nation: to expend an ocean of blood to regain these lost lands under the German jackboot, only to find they were now worthless?

Somehow, even that thought didn't sway Pierre's resolve. He might be bitter and cynical, but this was still his *patrie*, his fatherland,

and if it came down to it, he'd give his life to defend it. But not throw it away for no reason.

He brushed the uncomfortable thought aside, pulled out a telescope and sighted in on the enemy trenches across no-man's-land— or the *bled*, as some troopers called it, copying the Arabic name used by the Algerian conscripts. There was an almost darkly comic symmetry to the whole affair, the enemy trenches looking identical to the French ones. Trenches, barbed wire, seventy or eighty metres' worth of hell, and then the enemy's barbed wire and trenches. Pierre wondered how many skeletons were buried in that muddy ruin by now, cut down by machine gun fire as they tried futilely to break through after hoping that *this* time the artillery barrage would do it. With no-one to dig their graves, the next set of shells would cover them in mud as it showered from their explosions. And then the whole cycle started again. Maybe it would last until one side or the other ran out of men, and Europe was emptied.

"Look, sir," Marceau murmured, pointing without exposing his arm to sight: the little tics of a veteran. The mists and smokes over the Somme cleared sufficiently for Pierre to see what the sergeant was looking at—an *aéro*, a plane, flying over the battlefield. He recognised it as one of the new Nieuport 11s, a plane that was finally a match for the Fokkers that had previously shot down anything the French and their allies could throw at them. A cold smile stretched beneath his moustache as he saw the Nieuport dive and rake the enemy trenches with machine-gun fire, dodging the hail of bullets as the Germans tried to respond. The Nieuport swerved low over no-man's-land and waggled its wings in salute as it flew over the French trenches. Pierre gave the pilot a salute. At the start of the war they had viewed the pilots as aristocratic fools and half sympathised with the enemy when they were attacked in such a way, but two years of blood had changed things. There was only one France now.

But one France could not stand alone against the German war machine. "Everything fine here?" Pierre asked. After a comically timed pause, he added "Relatively speaking, I mean."

It was a weak joke but Marceau smiled anyway. "As well as can be expected. Henri thinks he may have got a Fritzie officer yesterday: silly fool forgot to blacken his tabs and we had enough sunlight for once for them to reflect."

"There's one born every minute," Pierre said. "And rather more than one of 'em dies every minute, these days." He shook his head. "Anyway, I'm going to go and check on the new shipment of allies."

Marceau rolled his eyes. "Good luck. Let me know if we'd be better off sending them to the other side."

Pierre grinned, slapping the sergeant on the back. Comradeship was precious these days. Still, France needed allies if she was to emerge victorious from this war—or emerge at all. He used the *boyau*, the communication trench behind the front line, to connect to the neighbouring trench system which the French's allies had inherited from a decimated regiment. He incautiously stepped through into the main trench to be confronted by the sentry in his exotic uniform—

* * *

Joseph took a long drag on his cigarette and then slowly exhaled, letting out a low and almost orgasmic moan. As far as Joseph was concerned, there were very few things more enjoyable than the first cigarette of the day. Alas, ever since he had stepped off the boat in France a week earlier, more often than not the first cigarette was also the *only* cigarette.

How hard can it be to get more tobacco for us? thought Joseph, with more than a twinge of bitterness. He took another long drag on the cigarette and slowly exhaled, as he turned to examine his surroundings once more.

He wasn't entirely certain what to expect when he first arrived. He had heard all the stories about the trenches, of course, and had imagined that the trenches on the front lines were simply a hodge-podge of trenches dug every which way with no rhyme or reason. Instead, he had discovered to his dismay that there was an actual *system*. The firing line – of which he was in, naturally – was the first line of defence. Dug in clever 'zigzag' sections to minimise damage, only a small area would be affected if it was attacked by enemy forces or hit by a shell. Dug several hundred yards behind those trenches were the support trenches, ostensibly to be used as a second line of defence. And several hundred yards behind *those* lines the reserve trenches stored supplies and offered a meagre dose of comfort to troops en route to the front. Connecting the entire network, a massive lattice of communication trenches enabled soldiers to travel quickly; keeping the army, its supplies, its reinforcements – and its casualties, of course – on the move at all times. Joseph had heard stories that soldiers could spend literally *weeks* at a time without once poking their heads out the

trenches and, given what he had seen so far in the last few days, he had
no reason to doubt them.

*We're becoming experts at building an underground city. I
wonder if this is how the Morlocks in Welles' novel get their start?*

Joseph took one last drag on the cigarette, hissing slightly as
the burning end of the cigarette scorched his fingernails, and threw the
remnant onto the ground. It fizzled for a brief instant as it hit the wet
mud and then vanished from view as the earth slowly swallowed it up.
In the space of a few seconds, there was no trace of the cigarette.

Heh – how so very appropriate of this war…

Joseph let out a sigh and stepped out from the small shelter—
little more than a dugout cut into the side of a trench with a tattered
blanket to keep out the rain and wind—that he had curled up in and
stood up suddenly, ignoring the pops in his knees that sounded like
distant artillery explosions. The military had instigated a rotating
system for all its troops and, true to form; its intricate system was both
fascinating and horrifying. Troops would spend a few days at the firing
line, then be moved to the support trenches for another few days and
then to the reserve trenches. And then—for a precious few days—the
troops would be sent further back to hunker down in billets and
bivouacs in camps far behind the battle line for training and rest and—
yes—even a bit of recreation. And then the process would start all over
again. *Ad infinitum.*

Joseph smiled fondly at the thought of his first five days in
France. They had actually held a medal ceremony and parade! And
then the smile faded as he realized that this trench was going to be his
home for a week.

Shaking his head in a futile attempt to remove the unpleasant
thought, Joseph walked to the sentry on duty and relieved him.

He had only been here for barely two days now and, like
everything else in the military, a mindless routine had already started to
come into effect: 'Stand to' order before dawn while everyone gathered
their weapons. All soldiers taking a place on the 'fire step', and as the
sun rose, firing a volley of shots towards enemy lines in a daily ritual
called the 'morning hate'. A breakfast meal of meat, cheese, bacon,
bread and vegetables. Then a wide assortment of chores, from sentry
duty to trench maintenance. Spare time spent on catching up on sleep
or writing letters. Then the 'stand to' was repeated at nightfall. Groups
sent into the treacherous and deadly No Man's Land while others

fetched rations, went on sentry duty, or left the firing line altogether.

And then the process would start all over again the next day. *Ad infinitum.*

And always, at the back of the mind, the fear, the terror, the gut-wrenching horror of that one order that everyone knew could come at any moment... *"Over the top!"*

Joseph shook his head once again to shake the thought.

No! Focus on the here and now! You have a job to do now! Sentry duty! Be vigilant!

It was, perhaps, a sign of either divine humour or human hubris that at precisely the instant Joseph was admonishing himself for his lack of focus and duty, a soldier appeared in his field of vision.

A soldier in a uniform completely different than any of Joseph's regiment.

Enemy! was the first thought that ran through Joseph's mind and he went to lift up his rifle – and hesitated.

Wait! Spiked helmet. Field-grey uniform. He's not *the enemy!*

"Oberleutnant Bluhm," said the German officer, introducing himself. "Welcome to the front, soldier," he continued, smiling. His English was quite good. "May I speak to your Captain?"

Joseph nodded his head. He wasn't entirely certain what the protocol was for allied officers. *When in doubt, salute, unless you're in the field* was an order driven into his head from his first day of enlistment, so Joseph did the next best thing he could think of.

"Yes, sir! Right this way!"

* * *

"So how were our...erstwhile allies?" asked Sergeant Marceau. After Pierre had given the password, of course: just because you had known a man for years was no reason to get sloppy.

Pierre held his hand out flat and waggled it in a dismissive gesture. "Could be worse. Not like those Portuguese fools who got themselves killed at the Marne. At least these Italians have some experience. They previously served on the Sudeten Front with the Austro-Hungarians."

Marceau nodded. "Quiet compared to here, but that mountain stuff is still real fighting from what I've heard." He snorted. "Don't tell them I said that."

"I won't," Pierre said with a skull-like grin. "Their commander's a bit of a new boy but with time I think he'll do."

"If he *has* time," Marceau reminded him. "If any of us do."

Pierre winced, then nodded. "If. Anything to report?"

Marceau ran a hand through his filthy hair. "Maybe. Boucher reckons he saw something while he was on his *banquette*. Corporal?"

The young man nodded, his youth showing in every part of his face but his eyes. Boucher wasn't his real name: he was called 'Butcher' for two reasons, firstly because he had the stereotypical butcher's first name of Roger and secondly because he had been responsible for taking out an entire squad of advancing Germans with one well-placed improvised mine. "I definitely saw it, sir. Glint off a spiked helmet..."

Pierre blinked. "Not many *Boches* still toting those things nowadays. Staff officer who doesn't know what life is like at the front..." He frowned at Marceau. "Which suggests what to you?"

The sergeant bared his teeth. "That our friends across the *bled* have got some reinforcements as well, and instructions are being sent to them."

"And there's only one kind of instructions you send a staff officer for, barring a court-martial," Pierre muttered to himself. "I'll go to the *boyau* and get the Village Idiots of Faucoucourt on the line." By which he meant the brass safely behind the lines. "We'd better brace for an attack."

As usual, Pierre spent twenty minutes getting the field telephone apparatus to connect and then another twenty minutes arguing with the stuffy lieutenant on the other end that A, he wasn't a nefarious German infiltrator born in Alsace-Lorraine and conditioned from birth into service to the Kaiser, and B, that he knew what he was talking about when it came to predicting attacks. As a result, he only bought the French forces perhaps half an hour before the first shells began to fall. He prayed it would save some lives regardless as he huddled in an *arbi* with Marceau and Boucher.

Being in an artillery bombardment was utterly indescribable to those who hadn't lived through one. Pierre remembered seeing a newsreel about the earthquake and fire in San Francisco ten years ago, and at the time he had thought that horrifying, but nature couldn't hold a candle to the terrors unleashed by the ingenuity of man. These were not the crude howitzers of Marshal Turenne's day, or even Napoleon the First's. The enemy guns blasted brass shells filled with deadly new explosives, both horizontally across the *bled* to pound away at the French fortifications—Pierre felt a trickle of dust down the back of his neck, but that was not so much of an itch to a man used to the lice of the trenches—and, even more terrifying, some were mortars that shot their shells in ballistic trajectories to land among the trenches. One could come down on Pierre's head at any time, and he would hear it coming: that deadly whistle, rising and rising in pitch as it grew nearer and nearer...

That whistle sounded odd. Marceau clearly realised at the same time. "Those aren't German guns!" he yelled: veterans became used to picking out words even over the demonic chorus of the exploding shells as they hurled mud and shook the earth. "Heard them once before. British!"

British. So the Germans were having to turn to their allies as well. It was small comfort. "At least we don't have to worry about gas!" he yelled, patting the gas mask at his hip.

"I thought the—" Boucher paused as a shell detonated in the *bled* and hurled an orphaned string of barbed-wire overhead. That could be as deadly as any bomb-casing shrapnel if it hit someone, as Pierre knew all too well. That decapitated comrade from Ypres still haunted his nightmares. "I thought the Englishmen were supposed to be making mustard gas in their factories as well now!"

"Propaganda!" Pierre cried dismissively. "The *Rosbifs* can't even make decent mustard, so how are they going to make the gas?!"

Despite, or because of, the situation, the two other men laughed. It was that or turn your pistol on yourself and save the Germans—or the British—a job.

The shells had been drawing closer and closer for a while now—it seemed like years, it always did—and, as a titanic explosion in a trench behind the French suggested a lucky British shot had hit an artillery dump, the guns finally fell silent. Pierre knew what that meant. The British had been tutored well by the Germans. Their troops would be advancing across the *bled* with the artillery fire rolling before them like a deadly rainfall, detonating mines and clearing obstacles.

At least, in theory. "They haven't cleared *this* obstacle," he muttered to himself, showing his teeth. He gave a nod to Marceau, received one in return. He filled his lungs. After shouting over the world-filling noise of the bombardment, his voice sounded unnaturally thin in his still-ringing ears. Nonetheless he yelled the battle cry he had learned from a politically inclined comrade, a man now as dead as Marat in his bath. *"Aux Barricades!"*

Pierre rose to his feet, Lebel rifle already in hand, and turned the face of the nearest khaki-clad Englishman into a red ruin.

* * *

"Over the top!"

The words were still ringing in Joseph's ears.

It was, to be sure, rather odd that they were still ringing in his ears. There were, after all, a great many sounds that should be ringing in his ears.

There *should* have been the sound of the artillery shells exploding, the shockwaves travelling up your legs and rattling your teeth.

There *should* have been the sound of his companions shouting 'Tally-ho!' and 'Give them Hell!' and a wide assortment of utterly pointless epithets to convince oneself to charge into the clouds of smoke and dust and darkness itself.

There *should* have been the sound of rifles and machine-guns and pistols firing and then, the gasps of shock with the realization that the sound of gunfire was not only coming from behind you but from ahead as well.

There *should* have been the sound of men that he had come to know as friends screaming and falling into the morass of mud and debris and feces and bones that made up No Man's Land.

There *should* have been the sound of men shouting out for their mothers or the sound of men gurgling and choking to death on their own blood.

There *should* have been the sound of the few – so very few - enemy soldiers rising up from their shelters and screaming curses in their language – no, *his* language – before being cut down.

There should have been any of these sounds ringing in Joseph's ears. Instead, there were only two.

"Over the top!"

And Joseph's quiet muttered reply to himself just as he did so –
"Maudit."

He had no idea how long it had taken for him to run to the enemy's trenches but he was only yards away from one particularly large section when he saw Henderson scream in shock as a French soldier rose up out of the smoke and flames like a demon arising from hell. And then, as if the demon called upon the legions of hell itself, more French soldiers rose up out of the flames.

Henderson's face vanished in an explosion of blood and gore and skull fragments as the first French soldier fired with a rifle. For the first time in his entire life, Joseph knew fear. As if some supernatural force had cast a hex on him, Joseph found himself unable to move or even make a sound. Dimly, he was vaguely aware of the sound of his companions behind him screaming and yelling and, yes, even running away. And then, as suddenly as it had overtaken him, the fear and shock vanished.

Joseph had just enough time to swing his rifle towards a man to his right as the soldier turned his rifle towards him in turn. There was the thunderous sound of a gunshot –

* * *

For a moment, Pierre feared that the British would overwhelm them. That artillery dump had been a bad blow and its explosion had broken a hole in the *boyau* and the other secondary trenches that allowed reinforcements to be sent along the line. There were a lot of khaki-clad forms rising out of the smog and ruin of the *bled*. Too many, maybe. He saw one Englishman snap out of the daze that afflicted many first-time soldiers, dodge the shot from a Frenchman and take him out in turn with a bullet from his Lee-Enfield. Pierre took a shot at the enemy, not pausing to see if he hit him or not, then turned on another target, ducking behind his *banquette* to dodge the return fire. He knew he was living on borrowed time and it could all come to an end at any moment—

Then the regular whistles of the rifle bullets were overshadowed by a furious staccato roar, nothing compared to the lower-pitched thunder of artillery but nonetheless like a guillotine blade of sound cutting through the chaos of the battlefield. It was obvious why Pierre's mind had chosen that metaphor when a British soldier was virtually sliced in half by what had made the sound. Pierre looked quickly to his right and saw that reinforcements had got through the blocked trench after all, and Sergeant Marceau had helped them set up a Saint-Étienne *mitrailleuse*, what the British called a machine-gun. France had invented those weapons way back for the War of 1870, and if the French army had had a few more of them at the time, maybe Alsace-Lorraine would still be free today. Marceau grinned savagely as he swept the battlefield with the weapon's deadly fire as though watering his garden with a hosepipe. Khaki turned to red, like the uniforms the British had worn in his father's day. There was a pregnant moment as the enemy hesitated—

And they broke. Pierre let out a yell of triumph as the khaki forms fled back into the mist. Marceau kept up his fire and shot several men in the back. At the start of the war, many had refrained from such cowardly and dishonourable actions. Two years of misery had weeded most such idealists out of the army, and shepherded many of them into the grave. He heard some traditionalist cry *"Montjoie! Saint-Denis!"* and he grinned tightly: the battle cry of the French armies of the Hundred Years' War. *We threw the English out of our country then and we'll do it again. Just let them thin their ranks by throwing themselves uselessly against our defences, and…*

Pierre belatedly heard a second cry. French, but accented and clearly not the speaker's first language. "They break! After them! Their trenches will fall to us!" He spun around to see the Italian captain standing atop his neighbouring trench, his medals glittering in the light of a distant melinite explosion, his sword in his hand. The man charged after the retreating British and, after a moment, his troops rose out of his trench to follow.

"Voilà le branleur!" Pierre bit out, giving his opinion of that fool. The man was clearly brave, at least, but he was going to get himself and his men killed.

And, Pierre realised to his horror, if he did then his trench would be undefended. The British might be decimated but he was sure their German allies had forces nearby. The Germans could be very good at storming depleted trenches and clearing them out with their potato-masher grenades. Which meant the only way to stop the Germans snatching victory from the jaws of defeat was to ensure the Italians succeeded… *"Sacré merde,"* he swore again, and filled his lungs. "All right, you *connards*, do you want to live forever? OVER THE TOP!"

* * *

Joseph had no idea how the French soldier missed hitting him but he – blindly – squeezed the trigger on his rifle. He almost shouted out in joy as he saw the man go down when he saw, out of the corner of his eye, the soldier who had shot Henderson swing his rifle towards him.

He actually *felt* the bullet hit his helmet. There was a flash of light, a sound of a gunshot, the pain of his rifle being flung violently out of his hands, and then a feeling of dizziness…

There was the sound of thunder.

Joseph opened his eyes and mouth – and immediately began choking on mud. For a terrifying brief instant he thought he had died and was now suffering some kind of damnation of eternal choking. But a quick twist of his head revealed that he was, in fact, very much alive.

For the moment, at least.

And then Joseph realized that the sound of what he had thought was thunder was nothing of the sort.

It was something far, far, far worse.

Machine gun!

There was, thankfully, only the one that he could see. It was situated far to his left and focused – for the moment at least – on a group of twenty or so soldiers. He saw the number reduce to a dozen in a space of a few heartbeats. More shouting and yelling – this time from his right and directly ahead of him – drew his attention away from the horrifying tableau.

There were at least a dozen members of the 10th running towards him as if the Devil himself was on their heels.

A moment's glance indicated that it wasn't the *one* Devil.

There were well over a *hundred* devils leaping over the tops of trenches instead.

"*Tabarnak!*" Joseph swore as he leapt up and ran.

Joseph could hardly hear any sounds around him, what with the sound of his blood pounding in his ears and his breath sounding like a steam engine.

He was immensely glad of that; it blocked out the sounds of his friends being shot in the back and the sounds of the devils behind him howling like wolves.

Please God. Please God. Let me make it to my side. Please. Please. Please. Pleasepleaseplease...

A flash of light ahead of him distracted him for one horrifying instant, as he involuntarily came to a brief stop. Thankfully the – one? – enemy soldier directly behind him came to a stop as well. Joseph found himself recovering a split second faster than the Frenchman behind him.

It was all he needed.

Truthfully, Joseph didn't care very much for his nickname 'Beauty'. It didn't really bother him either, to be honest. A soldier must learn to live with some ribbing and joking, after all. But he never told anyone what his *real* nickname was. The one that all the children in school used to tease him with.

His nickname was 'lapin' – Rabbit.

And, with the Frenchman screaming curses behind him, Joseph reached far down into his reserves of strength and showed the enemy behind him precisely *why* they called him 'rabbit'.

He had just leaped over a crater when he realized with a shock just what the light ahead of him had signified.

Some fool had fired an artillery shell! And right at him!

He had just enough time to hear the whistle of shell rise up in volume when –

* * *

For the second time, Joseph woke up with the taste of mud in his mouth. He couldn't hear. Or see for that matter. Where the hell was he? Was he finally…dead?

As his vision slowly cleared, he saw that – once again – he was *not* dead.

The same, however, could not be said of the six fresh bodies – all enemy soldiers, clad in blue where it was visible under the mud - around him.

Twice in one day! God must really be watching out for me! was Joseph's first thought. And then, because he had already seen far too much than one man must see on their first day of combat, a more cynical thought bubbled to the front. *The Devil must really want to torment me!*

No Man's Land was empty of any other living soul, a thought that made Joseph's blood run cold.

Who won? Did the enemy advance? Or did our side advance? How long was he out this time?

So engrossed in what his next task should be, that Joseph almost didn't see one of the 'dead' soldiers twitch and then, slowly start standing up, until it was almost too late.

"Non!" screamed Joseph in French, as he reached for his pistol…

…that wasn't there!

The Frenchman, incredibly, seemed to blink in shock for a moment. And then he shook his head and reached for his own pistol and pointed it at Joseph.

"You're my prisoner!" shouted the Frenchman.

* * *

Pierre's muddy hand was slippery on his pistol and he wasn't sure if there were any bullets left in the chamber. But the Englishman didn't have to know that. "You're my prisoner!" he shouted, and then belatedly remembered his opponent might not speak French.

He haltingly tried to repeat the phrase in what English he knew, but was cut off by the man, who reluctantly raised his hands over his head. "*Je vous comprends*," he said in strangely accented but fluent French: I understand you. "I surrender," he added bitterly. "Trooper Joseph Bell, 10th Canadian Mounted Rifles, service number 5201."

"A *beautiful* cavalryman, eh? Where's your horse?" Pierre said mockingly. It was a bit of black humour that had also cropped up among his own side: traditional cavalry hadn't lasted long in the misery of trench warfare, and most titular cavalry regiments were on foot these days. Then he belatedly registered the rest of what the enemy had said. "*Canadien?*"

"Yes," Bell said, and nothing more, keeping to the rules of war.

Pierre waggled the pistol at him, almost dropping it in the process. "With me! This way!" He could just glimpse the trenches in the distance and hoped like hell they were the French ones. As always, the artillery bombardment had changed the landscape beyond recognition and any landmarks from a few hours ago had been obliterated.

"Your men will shoot at me when they see my uniform," Bell pointed out. He kept glancing around himself and shivering: clearly the horrors of the battle were catching up with him.

"Of course they will if they just see you, you're a goddamn Englishman," Pierre snarled. "Put your hands above your head and stay close to me if you want to live."

Bell obeyed and they began to slowly pick their way across the mutilated *bled*, avoiding fragments of barbed wire and suspicious half-buried metallic objects that might be helmets from fallen soldiers—or might be unexploded shells. "I'm not a goddamn Englishman," he said mildly as he extricated his trouser leg from a coil of barbed wire, ripping the khaki cloth and leaving behind some threads.

Pierre wasn't surprised that the man had given up on strictly following the rules of war when it came to name, rank and serial number: most inexperienced men did so in a situation like this, thinking they were fine so long as they didn't give away military information. But then they often did so without realising it. So he kept Bell talking. "You're an Englishman," he repeated. "I don't care if you were born in Montréal or wherever—"

"Saskatoon," Bell said. Pierre had never even heard of that before. "My grandfather was from Montréal though, and *his* father came from here. France."

Pierre jabbed the finger of his other hand at Bell. "You wear that uniform, you're an Englishman. What would your ancestors think of you now?"

Bell shrugged. "What would any of our ancestors think of us?" He kept his hands above his head but still managed to wave them in such a way to take in the battlefield. "What'd they think of all this? Do you think they'd be proud of us?"

Despite himself, Pierre took his eye off the Englishman—the *Canadian*—long enough to look around. He saw the hellish landscape, the mud and corpses and barbed wire and ruin, as though for the first time. "Perhaps not," he allowed. "But what can we do?"

"We could just…stop," Bell said. "Did you ever hear about that football match at Christmas a couple of years ago? I heard stories that the French came out of the trenches and played football with our boys—the British soldiers, I mean."

Pierre winced at that last. "I heard. It was a lovely story, but it couldn't last. We can't just stop, or all the blood and sacrifice will have been for nothing."

"What was it for in the first place?" Bell asked sardonically, stumbling as he climbed over a half-buried remnant of a blockhouse destroyed in an earlier bombardment. "Some German communist takes a shot at Franz Ferdinand on his visit to Munich, kills his wife instead and so we have to send the world to hell?"

Pierre hesitated. "Our alliances…"

"Are a historical accident," Bell snapped. "They told us you Frenchies are monsters just because one of *your* lunatics shot King Edward when he came here thirteen years ago. We didn't have to go to war then, so why now?"

"I don't have answers," Pierre said. "Ours is not to reason why, ours is but to do and die—that's one of your poets, isn't it?"

"About the Charge of the Light Brigade, yes," Bell said. "But I prefer what one of *your* people said about that – it's glorious, but it's not war, it's stupidity!" He waved his hands around again. "And what is this?"

"Halt! Who goes there!" came the cry from the trenches before them, saving Pierre from thinking of a response. In French, gratifyingly. Pierre had guessed right. "Lieutenant Ranier," he called back. "The password is 'Marianne'!" He winced at that – they really had to come up with some less obvious ones.

The shadowed sentry, barely visible through the mist, raised his rifle. "Pass," he said. Pierre saw Bell close his eyes in mute acceptance.

* * *

There was a few confusing moments for Joseph as the soldier holding him prisoner – Lt. Ranier? – seemed to get lost, forcing Joseph to stop and double back a few times before getting his bearings and, with increasingly more confidence, marching him onwards. Joseph didn't blame the man for his confusing lack of direction; it was fairly obvious that the maze of trenches had taken a terrific pounding during the artillery barrage from earlier. Entire sections of the trench system were blocked by debris in some places; in other sections, the bombardment had – almost – created a whole new system of trenches.

Blue-clad French soldiers – many of them obviously injured – ran to and fro within the maze of trenches. Like confused rats, in Joseph's mind.

"I have to ask," said Joseph, as the two men walked.

"About what?"

"Why didn't you just shoot me back there?"

"Because I needed a prisoner."

"C'mon, lieutenant," admonished Joseph. "If you're going to lie, at least make it believable."

"You're upset I didn't shoot you?" asked Rainer incredulously.

"Upset? No. Just…curious. There was no reason to spare my life. No reason at all to take me, a lowly private, prisoner. And yet you did. Not that I'm complaining, of course, but something like that makes a man curious."

There was a snort – whether of derision or amusement, Joseph had no idea – and Rainer came to a stop. Joseph came to a stop a moment later.

"Well, if you *must* know," said Rainer, smiling. He waggled his pistol for a few seconds. "Out of bullets when we were on the field. I couldn't have shot you even if I wanted to. I assure you, that is not the case now, though."

Joseph stared in open-jawed silent shock at Rainer for a full ten seconds before a wave of the pistol indicated that he should start marching again. As he began walking once more through the mud and debris, Joseph let out a loud *"Câlice de Crisse!"*

That got a guffaw from Rainer. "You Canadians have very strange curse words. Who uses 'the chalice of Christ' as a curse when there's perfectly good other words that can be used?"

"Learned it from my grandfather," explained Joseph. "Heh, grandma used to slap him if she caught him saying it in front of the grandchildren," said Joseph, laughing as an old memory drifted up from his mind. It took him a moment for him to realize that Rainer was laughing too.

"My grandmother did the same to *my* grandfather, Canadian."

With the two of them still laughing, they marched onwards.

* * *

There were a lot of injured Frenchmen.

There were also quite a few dead Frenchmen as well, their battered and bloodied corpses (and in some cases, fragments of bodies) laid out in several rows. There seemed to be an animated discussion going on with several of the still living soldiers.

Probably running out of places to bury them was Joseph's silent thought.

Right next to the spot where the dead bodies lay, the ones that were too injured to walk and in need of immediate medical attention were lined up in row after row as well.

Joseph knew that if the French trenches were anything like the Canadian and German trenches, there were dressing stations near the front lines which provided immediate medical treatment to the seriously injured before they were shipped out to more 'proper' hospitals far behind the lines. It was obvious that the dressing stations – if they had even survived the barrage – were completely overwhelmed and now it was a race to bring as many of the seriously wounded to the hospitals. Wagons and carts of all shapes and sizes were being prepared, while stretcher after stretcher was loaded onto them.

It was clear that there were far too many stretchers than stretcher bearers.

Joseph turned his head and faced Ranier.

The two men stared at one another in silence for a long

moment – and then Ranier nodded his head. Putting his pistol into his holster, Rainer walked towards the wounded, Joseph at his side.

* * *

Joseph had no idea how long he and Ranier had worked nor did he have any idea how many wounded soldiers they had carried, but he saw it as a relief when Ranier had finally marched him to a quiet shelter in one of the trenches and motioned him to sit.

"What now?" asked Joseph.

Ranier put a cigarette into his mouth, paused as if to reconsider this, and then put another cigarette into his mouth. Lighting the two cigarettes with a foul smelling match, he handed one of the cigarettes to Joseph.

"We wait for the military police. They will take you to a prison camp, I would imagine." Ranier exhaled a puff of smoke. "I'll tell them that you helped with the wounded."

"Thank you."

"No, thank you."

The two men sat in silence, smoking their cigarettes. And then—

"Canadian. A question to ask you."

"Yes?"

"Was today your first day of combat?"

"Yes."

Ranier snorted and took another drag on his cigarette. "Something to write home about?"

Hesitantly at first, but with ever increasing volume, Joseph began to chuckle, Ranier joining him a moment later.

* * *

Joseph was abruptly awakened from his doze by shouts and screams. He had collapsed in the corner, exhausted after his frantic work. Ranier was gone, yet Joseph felt he could barely stand, never mind make an escape attempt. He finally managed to drag himself upright, wishing he had another cigarette. Belatedly his mind made sense of the shouted French words he was distantly hearing—yet when he did, they seemed like nonsense. "*Un cuirassé! Un cuirassé sur terre!*" "A battleship on land?" Joseph repeated, shaking his head in bewilderment. He staggered out of the trench and cautiously glanced over the side.

Now he could understand what the French had meant. That

didn't mean he had to *believe* it. Slowly, steadily, a monstrous iron juggernaut was rumbling towards him, smashing barbed wire and concrete and corpses beneath it. Everything about it seemed alien: the bizarre rhomboid shape, the moving belt travelling around it in lieu of good honest wheels, the two heavy guns sticking out of sponsons on the sides which indeed looked like weapons from a warship. Hellish black smoke spewed from what were presumably engines near the back. Only one thing revealed that it was not a terror sent from God to punish Man for his brutality: the front was painted with two flags, the Union Jack and the black-white-red stripes of Germany, and below them was printed the name PRINCE ALBERT in white.

Joseph's mouth dropped open, but he retained enough presence of mind to stand up and wave his arms about, making sure the iron monster could see his khaki uniform. For one heart-stopping moment one of the guns tracked towards him, but then halted. He saw soldiers in khaki and field-grey emerge from behind the...thing, clearly following in its path along the track of devastation it had cleared. *A trench-breaker!* Joseph suddenly realised that those belts meant the vehicle could drag itself up the side of any trench. Suddenly all those defences had become irrelevant. "Trooper, state your name, rank and serial number!" yelled one of the British soldiers over the roar of the land-ship's engines.

He did so, and allowed the soldiers to interrogate him before they were satisfied, but he spoke without much thought: his attention was still consumed by the steel bulk before him. The soldiers called it a 'tank' for some reason, which seemed a rather mundane name for a weapon that would change the war—and the world. For the tank was not unique; there were dozens more crossing the battlefield, breaking through the French trenches as though they weren't there. They were not invincible—Joseph saw some French artillerymen blast one with a heavy shell and he shuddered at the thought of the crew trapped in there—but their offensive seemed unstoppable. Machine gun fire spattered uselessly off their heavy armour. What could stand in their way...? He swore out loud at the thought.

Somehow, Pierre Ranier held onto a sense of satisfaction that he had smoked all his cigarettes *before* being taken prisoner and thus the *Boches* and *Rosbifs* had nothing to take. Sergeant Marceau, who hadn't been so lucky, kept giving him dirty looks. They both held onto that petty matter to avoid thinking about their situation. Prisoner! There had been stories about what the enemy did to prisoners, maybe not all of them exaggerated...

"Lieutenant Ranier?" Pierre turned in surprise to see a khaki form dumped in the same holding trench as himself and the other French POWs. It was Bell, the Canadian.

"What are you doing here?" he asked.

"They weren't sure to believe my story so I have to stay here until they find someone from my regiment to attest for me," Bell said sourly. "Swearing in French when I saw those new tank things was probably a mistake".

Despite himself, Pierre burst out laughing at that. "As though what you do even counts as swearing. Well, we're together again."

"We should do him in," muttered one of the other French soldiers. "If the island monkeys are stupid enough to give us one of their own, and a damn race traitor to boot, we should take the opportunity—"

Pierre smacked him in the face. "*Fermez la bouche!* This man helped save our wounded." He turned back to Bell. "When you see your superiors, tell them I would do the same for you."

Bell nodded. "When I see them." He hesitated. "I just heard some news about the wider war. I probably shouldn't tell you, but..." He shrugged. "I owe it to you, I think. Anyway, this little German corporal with a moustache told me that the Russians have just been beaten at Warsaw and Salzburg is besieged again. And there's a rumour that a French *sous-marine* has sank an American cruise ship by mistake..."

"*Sacré merde!*" Pierre swore. His fellow soldiers had shocked expressions as well, even the usually unflappable Marceau. "If the Americans join the war on your side, it's over." His tone turned bitter. "All that blood and misery, all for nothing..."

"Not for nothing," Bell said, though his own tone seemed equally bitter. Even the victors in this war would have lost so much. "Not for nothing, if we learn at least one lesson from it: let this be the war to end all wars. *Never again.*"

Pierre nodded. "Let us drink to that, at least. And never forget it."

"*N'oublions jamais,*" Bell agreed.

A Damn Foolish Thing
by Cyrus P. Underwood

As John Manning looked out over the field outside Paris, he still could not believe it. One hundred years. One hundred years since Germany became a true superpower. Though the field he was standing in had long since been overgrown with grass, there were still unexploded shells around. Not that he was worried about them. And anyway, he just wanted the tour. Didn't he?

Because standing here on a battlefield of that long ago war made him uneasy, John started when he heard footsteps through the grass coming up behind him. He turned as his girlfriend Suzette Clemenceau joined him.

"What are you thinking?" she asked.

"I was wondering what would have happened if the British had intervened in the war."

Suzette smiled sadly. "You and I both know that would not have happened after France invaded Belgium. Britain decided to stay out after that."

John nodded. " I know. I know. Still, it might have been better if France had let Germany invade first. Given the British the perfect opportunity to come in."

"What's past is past, John. You and I both know that."

"It still affects us though. We shall never get away from it."

Suzette smiled. "The past is not what *was.* The past is what *is.*"

"Exactly."

"Why are we marking this occasion anyway? I mean, Germany becoming a superpower on par with Britain is historically significant, sure, but why mark it with a centenary?"

John smiled. "I'm not sure, sweetheart. Want to skip the tour of this battlefield? It's just going to be the same thing as all the other ones."

Suzette glared at him, then softened. "I suppose your right. Come on. There is an exposition on some of Adolf Hitler's street scenes at the Louvre."

They climbed into their French made Limon and drove toward the city. Suzette turned on the radio:

"American President Henry Steward today welcomed Kaiser Otto I in Washington. They are discussing a new trade deal with the German led European Economic League," the announcer said. "In other news, Britain has had to relinquish control of another colony as South Africa was finally granted its independence. King Richard IV said that it was about time that Britain started to pull back her empire."

Suzette looked at John and said, "Why didn't America join the fight? Maybe they could have tipped the scales in France's favor."

"Many Americans didn't see it as their fight. Sure, some joined, but they were few and far between. And by the time President Albert Cummins was elected in 1916, the war was already over. Still, both Cummins and Theodore Roosevelt did manage to convince the Germans to go lightly on France. Even joined in on the economic alliance between Germany and Britain."

Suzette smiled. "*Oui*, there is that."

As they made their way back into the city, Suzette and John listened to the radio, without talking for a while:

"In other news, Czarina Catherine III created the Kingdom of Ukraine, a new autonomous region within the Russian Empire. Foreign policy experts are already calling this a step forward in Russian/Western Relations. Turning to Sports, the Olympics in Rome this year are going to start soon and-"

John turned off the radio. "I don't want to be talking over that. I would rather talk to you, sweetheart."

Suzette smiled broadly. "Is there anything in particular you wanted to talk about?"

"Well, this Hitler guy, whose pictures we are going to see."
"Yes?"

"Wasn't he a raging Anti-Semite?

"Well, yes he was. Though he was tremendously popular in

spite of that."

"Or maybe because of that."

Suzette's face fell. She was silent for a moment. "Well according to my old Art History professor, Hitler was only accepted into the Viennese Art Academy because of his time in the army. They were more willing to accept soldiers back then. Before the war he slept on the streets and he may have picked up his Anti-Semitic leanings then."

"There you go. What do his paintings look like by the why?"

"You know what they look like. That painting of the Berlin skyline that I was appraising on *Antiques Showcase*."

"Oh yeah. He's no Cezanne or Monet," (Suzette blushed and giggled at this), "but he was ok. For an Anti-Semite."

There was silence again while they drove into the city. Paris had rebuilt after the war. It was a vibrant, thriving city again by the mid-1920s. Eventually the hatred of the Germans faded. Suzette's great-grandfather Georges Clemenceau tried to build nationalist outrage against the Germans for what they had done. Eventually, everyone stopped listening to him. The French had gone up against the Germans twice within 50 years and were defeated both times. No one was willing to do it a third.

"Are you still bitter about the loss, Suzette?" John asked.

"A little. My great grandfather apparently talked about it a great deal. But I did not know him nor, anyone of that generation. So I do not have that sense of loss that they felt."

John smiled. "Well, at least there wasn't another war. That would have been disastrous."

Suzette nodded. "And we haven't felt the need to use nuclear weapons."

"Every country has been tempted to use them since the Germans invented them in 1957. Just because no one's used them does not mean that someone won't find some excuse to."

Suzette sighed. "That is true. Here we are."

After parking the car, John and Suzette got their cameras and notebooks (the better to remember things by). Though the Louvre was damaged during the Great War it was repaired and looked better than ever. Of course some pieces of art, like the Mona Lisa, were lost or damaged in the shelling, but there was nothing that could be done about that now. Going towards the Louvre they passed a newspaper stand.

The headlines read: *President of France Alexandre de la Coeur dead of heart attack; Prime Minister Helene Beauchamp to take over.*

As they entered, John and Suzette shared a quick kiss. Suzette, as she looked at the paintings, thought about how lucky they in fact were. She and John had just graduated from university. They were seeing the world. Sure they would have to start looking for jobs but that was an experience that they would share together. When they got home to the United States—it was weird for her to think of the United States as her home now—but John had made it like that.

"The past may still affect us," she said. "And the future is still unknown. But right now we are happy. That is all that matters."

They held hands and went to the show.

The Great Bear
by Alex Shalenko

As he lies dying, he dreams of thunder. It is a sound of spring, forerunner of a warm May rain that washes the streets clean and turns cracked asphalt into the vinyl soundtrack of a million lives. In his dream, thunder is his wake, man-made harbinger of a metal bird out to challenge heaven itself - but it is also a softer sound, a bombastic cannonade enfeebled by the walls of a run-down cafeteria and youthful laughter. It is the sound of defiance, the roar of the Bear in his ears. The thought brings a crooked smile to his face until he remembers.

There is no thunder on Mars.

* * *

The general's steps are hard iron upon the marble floor, and red stars mark his passage. The guards salute with mechanical precision, machine guns only one quick movement away from tracking him. There is a slight twitch in the corner of the general's mouth; a less casual observer might even consider it a beginning of a smile.

He hears the faint chatter of a dozen fearful voices, all talking at once. Arguments, mutual accusations of incompetence, even declarations of misbegotten innocence. One by one the voices go quiet as he walks nearer, the drumbeat of his iron-shod boots echoing through the corridor. His feet are thunder, and where there is thunder, there is lightning.

He glances to his sides, where portraits of great men stare down. Judging, measuring. *Are you worthy*, they ask. He allows himself a moment to look at the folders in his hands. Will he be worthy?

He pushes the door open to nearly absolute silence. The room smells of stale sweat and cigarettes, and the men within look at him with trepidation approaching terror. He fights down the temptation to keep them guessing and reaches for a cigarette of his own. The general lights it, inhaling the harsh fumes of *Belomorkanal*. He winces, an old habit he picked up during the war. *The war is over*, he tries to remind himself. *No*, he corrects the thought. *The real war has never stopped.*

"Take your seats... *Comrades*," the general squeezes the word through his teeth as if it was an insult. He takes a piece of newspaper from the folder before setting the heavy binders down. A foreign language headline is followed by a photograph - a man in a bulky white suit upon the cratered alien surface. A flag waves in the background. The wrong flag.

"But... Comrade..." one of the men wheezes, a fat, bald, sweaty functionary surrounded by small crowd of younger sycophants.

"The Party does not want excuses," the general curtly interrupts him. "I heard enough excuses from you *and* your colleagues." The others - all premier physicists, engineers, and chemists - look visibly more pale. In a different time, a different place, the general might have enjoyed their discomfort. Now, he thinks, they represent the nation's best hope.

"You know why you are here," says the general before one of the scientists has a chance to blurt out something stupid. He motions them to take the folders. "Take it, read it, pray on it, but know that we cannot accept any more failures." He lets the words ring out a second longer than he had to. "Your job," the general smiles with little mirth as he points to the folders, "is this."

"What is it?" This time it is another scientist, a younger fellow with the cocksure appearance of a former fighter pilot. The scientist reads the inscription. "Project... Great Bear? Like the constellation?"
The general breathes the fumes, heavy and bitter without a filter. He grimaces as he exhales a thick cloud of smoke.
"This, comrade, is the Soviet answer."

* * *

He lays on his back on a field of green, a blade of grass idly turning between his teeth. The only sound is a distant roar of industry assimilated into the chirping of crickets, and rustle of small animals in the nearby wood. He looks at the night sky, and the Bear stares at him.

His finger traces the lines between the stars, connecting the torso to the legs, head to mighty jaws. He imagines the glint in its eyes, the hungry snarl of its bestial mouth, and he smiles.

You are no match for me.

His muscles hurt from the day's exertions. Exercises that tested his body and mind should have left him exhausted, but nevertheless he smiles.

Five years of the nation's work led to this moment. Five years of labor and sacrifice unmatched anywhere in the world. He still has a hard time believing it as the day's memories cycle through his thoughts.

The others' faces are vivid in his mind, their expressions a range from jealousy to pity. They are the nation's brightest, the Union's best, the epitome of what it means to be a New Soviet Man. Fighter pilots all, they will challenge the Bear. They will ride its coattails above the horizon to go where no man has gone before.

No, he smiles, they will not. *I will.*

The thought had sustained him in the centrifuge as it subjected him to stresses the human body was not meant to endure. It made him strong where they faltered, gave him solace in many lonely nights in Star City. He feels a tug of pride, almost comparable to the sensation of soaring at the very edge of space with only the plane's thin metal separating him from the unknown. He reminisces about the curvature of the Earth beneath him, almost close enough to low orbit yet so tantalizingly far.

Thunder roars in his veins, tic-tock, tic-tock, like beating of an atomic timepiece. It raps a staccato rhythm that promises greater glories, greater honors than his collection of medals could possibly match. It is a testament to his strength where others have none, a proof of his courage beyond even that demanded by the stringent criteria. In his blood, he hears the roar of the Bear.

* * *

"You can say no, son," the general tells him with as much gentleness as the old man could muster. It is odd to see the grizzled veteran in this state, he thinks as he vigorously shakes his head in denial.

"Very well, Colonel," says the general with the air of resignation - or is it a tired sigh at the task successfully completed? He has a hard time telling. "Here are your orders." The general hands over a thin folder. His hand shakes, and the colonel notices age spots and grey hairs sneaking out from beneath immaculate sleeves. "They'll give you a Hero's Star for this, mark my words."

The general reaches for a bottle kept inside a redwood cabinet. The colonel takes quick stock of the label and almost winces in surprise. "The good stuff?" he half-asks, half-exclaims, as the general pours two shots to the rim.

"You'll need it, son," the old man says. He almost spills the precious liquor onto the table, where thick glass keeps aged photographs and design sketches safe from the passage of time. There are dark spots on the glass, some suspiciously round, and just about the right size for a glass. For a second, the general's eyes wander towards a picture on the wall. There he is, looking much younger, in full parade uniform, shaking hands with a heroic-looking officer, golden star on his chest. Same golden star as the one on the general's chest.

"Sometimes I wish I was thirty years younger," the general says after a weighty pause. He downs his drink in one gulp, shaking his head at the potent taste. The shot glass is a singular boom of thunder as it is smashed against the table. Broken pieces fly in all directions. "Just between me and you, son, take a look. I will not hold it against you. There is still time."

"I will ride the Bear, comrade," says the colonel. His eyes are blue steel and diamond, icebergs refusing to melt in the sun's raging corona. "The motherland demands no less."

"This is why we picked you," the general whispers, shaking his head either in amusement or in bitter denial. Forbidden words from another age, anathema to the nation that believes in secular truth and scientific progress come unbidden to his lips. "Go with God."

* * *

He opens the door with heavy heart. Water drips down from his raincoat to the linoleum floor, gathering in small pools upon the dark green and burgundy checkered squares. He hears the sound of thunder outside, like the roar of something out to prove his relative insignificance.

A seed of doubt festers in his mind, a potent poison that even years of Party teachings cannot completely erase. *Do I have a right to do this?* he wonders.

"You home, honey?" His wife's voice is tired, but she hides it well in anticipation of the big news. He never dared to tell her the whole truth. Now, he wonders if it would have been better to risk the displeasure of his superiors, or even worse. It would have made this moment so much easier.

"Hello," he answers, but there is no joy in his words. He looks at the folder in his hands, wishing that he could somehow magically wave its contents away, and yet chastising himself for the wanton thought. *I must be strong*, he thinks, mostly to reassure himself. *The Bear will only yield to the strong.*

She practically runs towards him, as much as her swollen belly will allow, lines of concern on her face. "Is... something wrong?" she asks hastily, holding on to the wall after a brief burst of energy. "Did they... reject you?" There is disbelief in her voice, a strange notion in his mind. He competed against the very best to get here, and there would have been no shame in accepting it.

"No..." he shakes his head. Thunder gives him strength, and he looks at her with newfound purpose. "I have been chosen."

His wife smiles with unbridled happiness, and he feels guilty. No, guilty does not even begin to describe it.

"Are you worried about being away from home?" she winks at him, patting her belly. "Just think of the stories you will have when you get home."

"I am not coming home." The words cut like industrial lasers into a section of hull plating, each syllable like a thunderbolt underlining the message. He took a deep breath, unsure of what made him blurt it out.

He saw shock on his wife's face, a concoction of hurt, disbelief, and anger. No matter how many times he played out this encounter in his mind, he could not prepare himself for this. She held on to one side of the narrow passage, as if in pain.

"How can you do this to me?" Her voice suddenly became shrill. "How can you do this to our child?" It was almost a scream now. "What will he say when his friends ask him where is his father?"

"He will tell them his father made his country proud," he said, cold iron in his words. "And his country will remember that. His country will take care of you and him."

His voice is the Bear's roar, indomitable and indefatigable. It is the voice of a nation that suffered and sacrificed everything for this moment, bringing its best, brightest sons to its victory altar. This noble sacrifice, for all mankind.

"I am the hammer of the Union, and I will not break," he says,

as he holds her in his arms, her fists beating uselessly against his chest.
* * *

The g-forces press down on his chest, and every breath is a struggle. He hears a countdown at the periphery of his perception, announcements of used-up rocket stages separating from the heavy lifter and disintegrating in the atmosphere. Inside his mind, the Bear roars, triumphant, its voice drowning out all doubts.

He looks out as the curvature of the Earth announces his departure from gravity's clutches. The sky is velvet black against the hulking mass of Eurasia, above the national borders and human aspirations. He sees the stars, not diamonds but eyes of the hungry unknown accepting his challenge. He is this world's thunder and lightning, writing his name upon the fabric of heaven with exhaust fumes and vapor trails, a lost comet returning to the abode of false angels.

He has never seen anything this beautiful. This must be what Gagarin and others felt, he thinks, taking in every second as if it was his last.

It was worth it, he smiles as he rides the Bear on the contrails of crimson flame.
* * *

The first rays of the rising sun bathe the alien world in rust. He goes through his final checks, making sure the systems are functioning as intended. His fingers dance over the switches, left, right, up, and down, muscles nearly atrophied after prolonged weightlessness despite a strict regimen of exercise. To his side is the mission's most valuable possession - a banner of blood-red, with hammer and sickle proudly embedded in top left corner. The *right* kind of a flag to fly over the Red Planet.

Glory to the explorers of Mars. Glory to the courageous Soviet conquerors of space.

He repeats the mantra as if it is the sole reason for his existence. In his mind's eye he imagines a poster, a heroic, benevolent figure larger than life itself reaching out for a young boy, whose stature suggests awe at being in the presence of the hero. He knows whose face will be staring down from the poster to inspire the future generations, and feels a moment of pride - or is it vanity? - at the thought.

His memories harken back to another little boy, all those decades ago, obsessed with the drawings of rockets and strange planets that no man set foot on, drawing sustenance from fantastic stories written when the world was still young and naive. He wonders if his unborn son will some day look at the stars and see more than just distant points of light. Will he see adventure, purpose, the call of something primal and irresistible that forces the human nature onward?

Will he feel pride at the thought of the father he will never know, or will he boil with resentment? Will he seek to give his life and dreams to the Bear, just like his father?

The world beneath him is dust-red and orange, brown and dead and cratered. It has little in common with the ancient domain of Wells' Martians, or the scene of John Carter's adventures. He feels a longing that no amount of pride can overcome, knowing that no one has ever been this far away from home. He is the first, he thinks, and then wonders if he will be the last? The first of many? How many noble sacrifices must be made for the sake of humanity, for the sake of the way of life he swore to uphold?

He feels the capsule starting its descent, and swiftly straps himself into the chair. This is it, he thinks, the culmination of his entire life, the sum of efforts of millions upon millions of people. It all came to this.

He thinks he can hear the roar of thin Martian atmosphere as the capsule penetrates its upper layers - the roar of triumph, the inevitable victory of those determined to pay any price for this accomplishment.

As he descends, there is thunder on Mars for the first time in a billion years.

* * *

After the cameras stopped rolling, after the final transmission to Mission Control was sent, after the flag was planted into the red, oxidized dust, he sits alone. Even the weak Martian gravity makes every movement a painful reach and he winces in discomfort, reaching for the bottle.

It is the good stuff - the best that could be procured. The motherland knows its heroes, he thinks with a bitter smile.

His eyes shift to a box of pills, white and innocent like the first snow of winter, teeth of the Bear. He knows there is not much time left. The capsule was never designed to last long after the landing, and the life support systems that sustained him over months-long journey are beginning to go out, one by one. Even the rugged Soviet engineering can only take so much abuse, and strangely, he takes comfort in the thought.

It is almost over.

He looks at his life, a series of pictures in kaleidoscopic slow motion. One by one they go away, fading into faint remembrance until they are vague and indistinct. His mouth swallows the bitter taste of alcohol and he feels light-headed as the pill dissolves in his stomach. He already feels the heaviness in his limbs, a pleasant embrace of death-like sleep. As he falls down, no longer able to control his fading muscles, he hears thunder in his veins, the sound of victory, the roar of the Bear.

And as the gasses vent into the thin atmosphere through the cracks in the capsule, he remembers.

Verum Fidei
by Charles Wilcox

The alarm bells rang out from Fort Saint Angelo across the harbor inlet. Philippe jumped up from his bed and rushed to don his armor. He struggled with the chain mail and quickly pulled the white cloak over his head. The cloak with its dyed red cross shone proudly as he stepped out into the harsh mid-morning. He rushed along the north coast of the Senglea peninsula and around the inlet to the fort at the end of the narrow spit of land.

Philippe ran through the landward gate to Fort Saint Angelo. On the parade ground of the fort, over one hundred soldiers of the Knights Hospitaller had gathered. The alarm bells meant the dreaded day had come. The Knights assembled in neat ranks as Grandmaster De Vallette surveyed them atop his horse. Philippe and the men sweated profusely as the sun baked them inside their metal armor.

"My Knights, you have been called upon by the grace of God to give your life to defend him!" The Grandmaster shouted. "And now, your day of judgment is finally upon you. You, who have devoted your lives to protecting Christendom from the heathen advance, are now its last line of defense against the Turkish horde." The Grandmaster paraded back and forth in front of the assembled soldiers as he spoke. Similar speeches were surely being given a few miles north at Fort Saint Elmo.

Philippe stood proudly as he listened to the Grandmaster, but secretly he was worrying. The Knights, with their formidable fortress of Malta, were indeed the last defense of Christendom against the Turks. He had known this day would come. After the fall of Djerba and Rhodes, Malta was the only stronghold left between the Ottoman navy and the Italian coast.

"Our spies in Constantinople relayed word of a large fleet setting sail from Athens intent on taking this island nearly a week ago," De Vallette continued. "Scouts spotted ships bearing the Ottoman ensign off Saint George's Bay this morning. We must be prepared to endure a long blockade, so I want you all to take shifts up in the ramparts. Now go, and Godspeed my brothers."

Grandmaster de Vallette rode to the gatehouse and the crowd of soldiers quickly dispersed. Philippe made the sign of the cross as he ascended the stairs to the ramparts. It, plus the fleeting shade of the stairwell, provided a brief calm before the wait and constant worry of when the Turks would launch their attack. With the Lord on their side, surely they would be victorious.

Philippe took his position with the team manning one of the cannons on the northeast battery of the fort. The battery faced toward Fort Saint Elmo and the entrance to the Grenade Harbor. The sun beat down overhead as Philippe stared out at the water. Waves crashed against the rocky coast as the three Knights peered out at the harbor waiting for the Turkish ships to arrive. He soon collapsed into a seated position against the wall.

Thirty minutes passed without incident. Philippe was nearly dozing off when one of his companions shook him awake.

"Philippe, look!" Philippe slowly rose.

"Unh, what is it, Felix?" He blinked at the afternoon sun and peered out over the harbor. As the harbor came into full focus, Philippe took a quick breath in shock, the dusty air of the fortress rampart sending him into a coughing fit.

Fifteen ships had appeared from beyond the spit of land opposite Fort Saint Elmo. They were moving at half sail, and Philippe could barely make out the flags flapping from the masts. A yellow crescent on a green field: the Ottoman naval ensign.

The three men stood and watched calmly as the ships glided further into view. "A little light for a full assault," the third Knight said, leaning on his musket. "I would have thought they'd send at least three times the fleet."

Philippe turned to him and nodded thoughtfully. "You think so?"

"Most definitely." The man said in Spanish accented Latin. "I was part of the Spanish regiment at Djerba five years ago. The Turks had brought upward of a hundred ships to attack the island. Why would they send only fifteen ships here?"

They continued watching the ships slowly move across the harbor entrance. "So, if the Turks are here, then why aren't the Spanish? Shouldn't your king be sending reinforcements from Sicily?" Felix huffed.

The Spanish scoffed, putting his hand to his chest as if clutching at a mock sword wound. "I am deeply hurt, my friend. Do you seek to bleed my honor so, after I bravely fought to defend your Knights not five years ago?"

Philippe chuckled and shook his head. Even Felix smiled as the Spaniard continued his theatrics, staggering a pace before dropping to his knees. Philippe took the flask from his hip and swallowed a brief sip of wine.

Their brief respite from the tense standoff a mile away was broken by the low boom of cannon fire. The Spaniard shot up from his praying position and crossed himself. "Dios mío!" He shouted, breaking his conversational Latin.

The three soldiers looked across the harbor as the Turkish ships began firing at Fort Saint Elmo. The fort returned fire. Blasts of orange flame shot from both sea and land. Loud cracks emanated from Fort Saint Elmo's walls as the Turkish cannons smashed against the heavy stonework.

The three soldiers watched on edge as the first line of the Maltese defense traded blows with the Turkish ships for several hours. Other Knights brought them a small ration of hard bread as the sun fell low in the western sky. The three men only briefly conversed, preferring to remain silent as they remained fixed on the beginnings of the battle for Malta unfolding in front of them.

Fort Saint Elmo, situated on the northernmost end of Mount Sciberras and one of the most solid fortresses of its day, appeared to be holding out well against the naval bombardment. "Looks like we're going to be here for a while," Felix said wearily after they had finished their meager supper.

"Yes, but with God's will and the estimate of the size of the Turkish force, we should survive," Philippe replied, taking a swig from his wine flask.

The Spaniard remained standing as Felix and Philippe slumped down against the cannon. The sun was finally setting and a cool breeze swept a collective sigh of relief over all Fort Saint Angelo.

The sun finally began to dip below the horizon. The rhythm of the cannon fire had become regular, like a rolling thunder of a distant storm. Philippe stood peering at the orange bursts of flame when the thunder was broken. A nearly blinding flash of light and a great crack jolted through the three Knights and rattled the entire area. The three looked across the harbor toward Mount Sciberras just in time to see a lingering glow from the top of the hill. Another loud crash emanated from Fort Saint Elmo. Their eyes moved over to the landward walls of the fortress and saw a gaping hole in one of the walls.

"My God," the Spaniard gasped, "that must have been a Great Bombard!"

Philippe and Felix jerked around to face him. "A what?" said Felix.

"The huge cannons the Turks used during the Fall of Constantinople," the Spaniard replied. "I thought they had been retired by now. I have only heard stories, but they supposedly fired shot nearly half as big as a man and blew holes in two of the sets of Constantinople's walls in one shot."

Felix's eyes went wide as he turned back to look at Mount Sciberras. While the cannon remained invisible, they spotted a thin grey trail of smoke rising up over the hill. The smoke was nearly black and thick enough to be plainly visible against the dim orange of the sunset.

"If they have brought the Great Bombards here," the Spaniard began making the sign of the cross, "then we truly are in need of God's help. Sultan Suleiman is sparing no expense in his desire to make the Mediterranean a Turkish lake."

Philippe and Felix silently crossed themselves and looked solemnly out at Fort Saint Elmo as a fire flared up inside its walls.

The night guards came a half hour later to relive them, and the three walked back down the hill. The Spaniard and Felix parted ways with Philippe in Birgu. Philippe continued on around the inlet to Senglea. Gratefully, he shed his armor and sword and knelt wearily by his bed. The thunder of cannons rumbled in the distance still as Philippe brought his palms together, closed his eyes and said his nightly prayer.

The next few days consisted of more waiting as the Ottoman

force continued its siege of Fort Saint Elmo. Philippe, Felix, and the Spaniard remained together as they manned their cannon on Fort Saint Angelo's ramparts. From their vantage point, Fort Saint Elmo held out valiantly against the ships' fire. Although large vertical craters had been blasted in the coastal stonework, none of the fort's outlying walls had collapsed into the sea.

The land war, on the other hand, was going worse for the Knights. The bombards continued to pound at the smaller series of walls and earthen barriers through most of the day. De Vallette had considered sending a force to rout the Turks camped on Mount Sciberras, but the Knights Hospitaller were facing a shortage of manpower around the island already. The only thing they could do was hold out until Don Garcia's expeditionary force arrived from Sicily.

On the fifth day of the Siege of Fort Saint Elmo, Philippe mustered along with the rest of the Knights in Fort Saint Angelo's parade ground. Even in the early rising the cannons could already be heard across the harbor.

"Soldiers, once again we gather to defend Christendom from the fear of Turkish invaders." Grandmaster de Vallette stood in front of the men, making his daily speech. His voice boomed out over the parade ground, but something seemed off. De Vallette's resolve seemed to be wavering with the length of the siege. His motions with the reins were more abrupt as he led his horse in front of the men.

"But today, we shall face our greatest test yet." The Grandmaster's voice dropped low and solemn. "For I have received reports that the attack here is not the only assault the heathens have made on our shores." Murmurs erupted through the crowd. "Along with the ships attacking the harbor, a large Ottoman force led by Mustafa Pasha has come ashore on our island bastion. They have already captured Il-Bahrija and are now closing in on Mdina."

A wave of shocked gasps rippled through the soldiers almost as fast the Grandmaster's words themselves. Philippe shuddered as the thought of a Turkish victory now became a much greater possibility. "When is your esteemed Don Garcia going to get here with his relief force?" Philippe hissed at the Spaniard, standing next to him.

The Spaniard frowned under his thin black mustache. "I do not know, but he had better come soon. For the sake of all, God better truly be on our side." The look in the Spaniard's eyes was enough. It was the first time Philippe had seen genuine fear in the man's face since the beginning of the siege.

Grandmaster De Vallette continued his speech. "We must meet Pasha's army and destroy them before they can incur further into the island. Therefore, I am sending several regiments including many of you here to go and meet the Turkish army on the battlefield."

Philippe and Felix exchanged concerned glances.

The small army was assembled within two hours. Philippe, Felix, and the Spaniard lined up in double file ranks, halberds at their side. De Vallette rode by and Philippe glanced up at the grandmaster. If Jean Parisot de Vallette himself was leading them, then surely the Lord would protect the Knights and save Malta, right? Philippe turned his gaze back to the column of soldiers in front of him and bit his lip.

"Have you heard the rumors too?" The Spaniard said as they began to march forward.

"Which ones? About how many men the Turks have, or about Piyale Pasha sending his fleet to attack Tunis?"

"The strength of the Turks," the Spaniard replied. "An attack on Tunis would be foolish at this juncture." The Spaniard waved Philippe's concern away from a potential distraction. "The reports I heard say that Mustafa has over twenty thousand men unloaded on the island."

"Twenty thousand?" Philippe nearly stumbled as he tried to comprehend the force they might face. "But De Vallette is only sending a thousand soldiers to relieve the garrison at Mdina, and that's already leaving the forts back at the Grand Harbor poorly defended."

"We had better put our faith in the Lord to provide us with a victory," the Spaniard sighed. "At this point, that would be a miracle."

"And Don Garcia?" Philippe said, exasperated. "Are we unable to count on your government to defend the Christian faith in its hour of need? Or has the king become too stricken by his treasures in the New World to worry about religious concerns?"

It is amazing how a dire situation can quickly sour one's opinion of another country, and how quickly others will come to defend it. "Oh, and what of your home country, Frenchman?" The Spaniard returned Philippe's glare and mimicked his exasperation and vitriol. "Your king Charles, rather than defending the one true faith, has chosen to continue France's traitorous alliance with the Turk."

Philippe seethed at the Spaniard's accusation, but could come up with no rejoinder. It was true. For decades now France had forged an informal alliance with Istanbul.

After nearly three hours of marching, de Vallette informed the men they were nearing Mdina. The thousand Knights fanned out and set up camp on a hill north of Mdina. The old capital was set atop a ridge with cliffs falling away from it to the east, and a slope to the north that led down to a ravine across from the camp. Philippe looked out at the city perched atop the hill. Once the capital of Malta during Roman times, it had fallen in importance and become just one of the small villages dotting the island.

The army set up camp in the heat of noon. During one of his rests, Philippe found comfort in the shade of a tree atop the ridge and knelt to utter a small prayer.

"Praying for our survival again, Philippe?" It was Felix, standing quietly next to him.

"No, to Saint Paul the Apostle." Philippe looked out at Mdina's city walls. "Paul sought refuge and resided in Mdina after he was shipwrecked here on his way to trial in Rome. If the Lord is not favoring us, perhaps one of his Apostles will help save this place from the heathens."

Felix's jaw dropped at his friend's worries. "Why would the Lord not favor our cause, Philippe?" He put a hand on Philippe's shoulder. "The Lord has his plan for us, and that is surely to defeat the Turks here."

Philippe shook his head and let out a slow sigh. "I don't know. I wish I had the faith you had, but against this force of Turks, I just don't know."

"Come friend; let us rest before we meet the Turks on the field." Felix turned and walked back to the Knights' camp. Philippe gazed out at Mdina one last time before he got up.

The approach to the old city was a steep hill contoured with terraced farms and vineyards. The city itself stood proudly at its crest, dominating the skyline. Mdina's white walls, bathed in the white glow of the sun, seemed to shimmer. Philippe took a deep breath, which seemed to cleanse the doubt from his mind and refill it with hope for victory. He stood and joined Felix.

The two armies had set up camp on opposite sides of Mdina. That afternoon, Philippe was walking through the camp when he saw a man rush past toward the Grandmaster's tent. He stopped just short of the tent as the messenger entered. Philippe started to continue his walk, but stopped. He looked to see if he was alone. Slowly, Philippe pressed up against the edge of the tent.

The messenger nearly collapsed as he stood heaving in front of de Vallette. "Sir, I have a report from the harbor!" he gulped.

"What is it," de Vallette said tersely. He waited patiently for the messenger to regain his composure, a constant scowl on his face.

"The Turks have captured Fort Saint Elmo and butchered the defenders!"

For the next few seconds all Philippe heard from the tent was silence. He peered around the flap and saw de Vallette's pallor had become as pale as his linen tunic.

The messenger looked pained as he spoke again. "And a larger fleet appeared in the harbor. They are now attacking Fort Saint Angelo itself. They don't know how long the harbor will hold out before it becomes a safe port for the Ottoman fleet."

De Vallette's color changed from the white of the tunic to the red of its cross. He banged his fist on the table. "Goddamn this infernal invasion!" Philippe immediately looked away from the tent and crossed himself on hearing the grandmaster's blasphemy. "Any word from Sicily on Don Garcia's force?"

"No, grandmaster," the messenger shook his head and braced for de Vallette's fury. De Vallette punched the air, sparing the messenger, and whirled around. "Those Spanish devils, at this rate Don Garcia will be facing Suleiman's army while still on Sicily!"
De Vallette leaned over the table and stared at the map below him. Another lingering silence passed.

"Fine then," the grandmaster said, clutching his forehead. "I see what we must do. Our only chance, and let us pray that God will grant it to us, to defeat the Turks is to face them here, now." He traced a finger around the crude map of Mdina and its surroundings on the table. "We shall muster at once, and take our forces around the north of the city through this valley. Mustafa Pasha will be expecting a relief of the city, so we should be able to attack his camp from the flank. With Mdina's garrison we should be able to force Pasha to retreat from here and we can return to the harbor."

The messenger nodded as de Vallette scrawled his decision to be taken back to the garrison in the Grand Harbor. Philippe ducked behind the tent out of sight as the messenger took the parchment from de Vallette and returned to his tent.

Jean de Vallette assembled the small Maltese army outside the camp. Philippe had gathered his halberd and stood in close rank with his brothers as they advanced north through the valley around Mdina. As they rounded the city, the Turkish camp came into view. Tents sprawled out across the fields in front of them. The camp was enormous compared not just to the size of the Knights' small encampment, but to the entire city of Mdina. Janissaries prominently patrolled the Turkish camp, and soldiers were busy wheeling cannons out to face Mdina's western wall.

De Vallette ordered the Maltese army to stop short of a small ridge and relayed the plan to his men. Philippe heard the plan spreading down the line and he felt a knot in his stomach. "We're going to attack now?" He hissed at Felix in front of him. "Why are we not waiting until dark?"

Thinking, however, Philippe knew the reason and grimaced. With the way the siege was going in the Grand Harbor, they might not be able to get back before the Turks took the entire area if they waited to attack the camp. If the situation was that desperate, they had to attack the Turkish army here as soon as they could.

Philippe spread out with the rest of the army along the top of the ridge. He crouched next to Felix, both of them clutching their halberds in a ready position. A tense air grew around the army as they waited for the fateful command. "I pray to you, Saint Paul of Tarsus, give me the strength to fight," Philippe paused before continuing under his breath, "and let me live."

"Attack!" De Vallette's voice called. Philippe and Felix rushed down the slope toward the Turkish camp. Philippe saw de Vallette and the few cavalry the contingent had rush ahead of them. The grandmaster slashed at a Turkish soldier with his saber as he rode deeper into the camp. Philippe saw the soldier fall screaming, and it urged him forward.

"Saint James, and at them!" Philippe could hear the Spaniard yelling the battle call of the Spanish amid the ensuing chaos. Out of the corner of his eye, Philippe caught the Spaniard thrusting a sword into a janissary as the Turk tried to fend him off with a musket.

Suddenly, Philippe's attention was jerked straight in front of him. His legs still carrying him and the rest of the army, he realized they were running toward a group of janissaries between them and the Ottoman tents. The janissaries were aiming their muskets. The halberdiers were still in tight rank. Any shots fired by the janissaries would surely hit one of them. Instinctively, Philippe yelled out as they continued running, throwing up dirt. "Loosen formation!"

The halberdiers widened just as the janissaries were set to fire. It all happened in a split second, but the formation split open enough that only a few men fell to the first volley of bullets that whizzed their way. Philippe felt the rush of adrenaline as the man to his left yelped and fell. The fallen Knight was quickly replaced by the man behind him, and the formation kept running.

The halberdiers closed ranks with the janissaries only losing seven men after another round of musket fire. Philippe swung his halberd at the nearest Turk as the two armies met. The heavy polearm tore through the unfortunate janissary's leather armor and he fell to one swing. As the two lines met, the camp erupted in chaos. The janissaries, not used to close combat, began a hasty retreat back into the camp, and Philippe followed blindly.

Soon he found himself separated from much of the formation amid the maze-like layout of the tents in the camp. He swung at any Turks he came across, killing two more enemy soldiers.

The adrenaline pumping through him, Philippe's vision began to blur. He looked around and started to hear a loud thumping sound. A glint of steel flashed from beyond an open space in the camp and he swarmed ahead, pulling the halberd back for a swing. The thumping quickly got louder. Philippe's vision of the camp was suddenly obscured by a shimmering white, as if he were adrift in a snowstorm. Philippe shut his eyes and blindly swung the polearm, hoping to hit something, anything.

The halberd connected with a squelch. A loud neigh and a scream followed and Philippe felt a crushing weight for a few seconds as he fell to the ground. He lay breathing heavily as the weight was lifted and opened his eyes. HIs vision returned and he saw a horse bolting away from him, red streaming from its side. The light sky became shrouded as a dark skinned man stood over him. Philippe thrashed at the Turk with his dagger and the man kicked him. Pain shot through his ribs and around the rest of his body. Philippe, already weak, dropped his dagger and succumbed to the tranquil darkness of unconsciousness.

When Philippe awoke, the cacophony of the battle had died down. He was groggy and pain shot through him every time he tried to roll onto his side. Philippe flailed his arms a while, groaning out cries for help and that he was still alive. He lapsed back into unconsciousness for a second time.

Philippe next awoke on a bed in a large tent. Judging by the coolness of the air around him, Philippe guessed it was evening. He looked around him. He did not recognize the tent. Unlike the stark white burlap tents of the Knights Hospitaller, this one was lined with vivid strips of pink and blue silk.

"Felix, are you there? Spaniard? Grandmaster? What happened? Have we won the battle?" Philippe mumbled. Instead of Latin, his words gurgled out in his native French.

"Do not worry," came a soft reply also in French. "You are alright."

Another face loomed over him suddenly. Unlike the Ottoman soldier, this one had a more Mediterranean complexion.

"Who are you?" Philippe wondered before realizing he was speaking aloud.

The face laughed and gave Philippe a thin smile. "I am Mustafa Pasha, general of Sultan Suleiman's army here in Malta."

Philippe gasped and tried to scramble back on his bed. He fell when he tried to prop himself up.

"Don't worry, you are not in any danger. My men were clearing the camp after the battle and came across you. I told them to spare anyone who looked or sounded French."

"So does that mean Felix is still alive?" A glimmer of hope for his erstwhile friend came to his eye.

Mustafa shook his head and frowned. "I do not know. You were the only French speaker my men recovered. Your Grandmaster foolishly retreated two hours ago back to the harbor with several men, so it is possible."

Philippe tried to get up but the pain in his side still overwhelmed him and he sank back down in the bed. "What are you going to do with me?"

Mustafa smiled. "Well, since you were speaking French, I assume you came from France before you joined the Knights Hospitaller?"

Philippe nodded.

"Then we shall return you to France. The Sultan has an envoy on the way to France right now, and he will be briefly stopping in the harbor should we secure it. I can load you on that ship."

Philippe's face hardened. The heathens were going to spare his life? This had to be a trick. "And what if I refuse? What is it you want from me to spare my life so?"

Mustafa gently laid his hand on Philippe's shoulder. "The only thing I ask is that you renounce your allegiance to the Knights. We have an agreement with your French government, and I can guarantee you safe passage back to France should you accept. If you don't, you will die here just like your fellow Knights, fighting a futile battle." Mustafa left the tent.

Philippe lay back on the bed and looked up at the roof of the tent. His eyes followed the silken strands across the ceiling as he mulled over the offer. Giving up his responsibility to the Knights Hospitaller was highly ignoble of him, but what choice did he have. If the Ottomans took Malta, then the Order would collapse. It was already a miracle that God had spared him during the battle. He could not hope for another miracle to save the island and the Order from the Turks.

That night, Philippe called for the general and gave him his word, provided he make it back to France. Mustafa and the Turkish field doctors tended to Philippe for the next three days as they finished off the remaining holdouts in Fort Saint Angelo and the rest of the island.

* * *

Philippe sat on the rampart of Fort Saint Angelo looking out at the harbor. The cannons that had accompanied his view were now silenced. The flags of a red cross on white that had flown over the forts overlooking the Grand Harbor had been taken down and replaced by the white crescent and star on red. Activity in the villages surrounding the harbor was slowly returning to normal. The bulk of the Ottoman fleet still moored in the harbor, but they were slowly thinning out.

As Philippe gazed out sullenly over the harbor, Mustafa Pasha joined Philippe on the fort's wall. "Hajji Murad's fleet should be arriving here soon to take you to France." Philippe glanced up at Mustafa and continued staring blankly out over the harbor. Mustafa stood at Philippe's side and followed his gaze. "I know you are shaken by this turn of events," the Turkish general said. "The great loss of your fellow Knights must be hard to comprehend fully."

"It's," Philippe hesitated, wondering whether he should be

talking so cordially to a Turkish general. But Philippe had nobody else to talk to. "It's not the loss of them, as much as the loss of the battle. We all put our faith in God, me especially. Before we stormed your camp at Mdina, I prayed both to the Lord and to Paul the Apostle for victory, and yet we still lost. I don't know why the Lord would let the Knights down so badly like that."

Mustafa stifled a laugh. He betrayed his disdain only with a slight smirk. "Paul the Apostle? You mean Paul of Tarsus? Do not worry, Philippe. You are just the latest in a number of Christians to fall for his deceptive teachings."

Philippe shifted nervously. "What are you talking about? Paul was a good man. He spread Christianity and was one of the first to martyr himself for the Christian faith!"

Mustafa raised an eyebrow and replied calmly. "Nonsense. Paul was an arrogant fool who led early Christians to believe he himself was a Prophet of God. Just as he led early followers of God astray, he deceived you and led your Knights to their demise. It is fitting that we shall bury the Knights in Mdina's catacombs, I suppose." Mustafa chuckled. "You must not lose faith in Allah, but you must also recognize when the Lord has steered you on the proper path. Your belief in Saint Paul led you and your fellow Knights astray, and you were punished with a crippling defeat. That is what you must learn from this."

Philippe let Mustafa's words sink in as the two stood on Fort Saint Angelo's walls. The waves softly crashed against the rocky coast of the Grand Harbor. Philippe remained contemplative as he watched the harbor, and Mustafa walked back down from the fort's walls.

The next day, Hajji Murad's galley arrived in the Grand Harbor. Philippe, while technically a captive and prisoner of war, entered Hajji's retinue of his own free will. Hajji Murad greeted Philippe with a smile. "I am glad to have you in my company, Knight." Hajji bowed to Philippe when they met on the ship's gangplank. Philippe bowed in reply and wordlessly followed Hajji to his quarters.

The galley remained in port in the Grand Harbor for a day to resupply before setting off again. Two other ships from the Ottoman fleet accompanied the galley as it sailed northwest through the contested Western Mediterranean in case they ran into any Spanish warships.

The sailing was smooth and the small Ottoman ships glided over the calm waters with ease. They made the journey from Malta to Marseilles in a brisk two days. Philippe remained in his cabin for most of the journey. He shied away from sea travel, and felt isolated in the company of the Turks. Hajji and his retinue were the only ones on the galley who spoke French, and much of the conversation among the retinue was in Arabic anyway.

Philippe lay on his bunk, taking the journey as an opportunity to fast to prove his devotion to the Lord. Despite this, Philippe questioned his career as a Knight every hour of the trip. He had spent many years in the Order, always working for the good of Christendom. Yet all the Knights ever met with during the past decades was defeat. Was the Lord punishing the Order? Is that why the Spanish relief never materialized? What sins had they committed?

And amid all the Order's defeat, Philippe was the only one that he knew to survive. What made him special in the eyes of the Lord? Was it his devotion that spared him? It could not be, for surely Grandmaster de Vallette was more devoted to Christ's teachings, and yet even he was not spared during the battle. What, then, set Philippe apart?

Philippe's mind struggled with these questions and more all during the voyage. When the three ships docked in Marseilles, Hajji permitted Philippe to join his retinue until he could set off somewhere on his own. Philippe stayed in Marseilles for another week, wandering aimlessly.

Hajji Murad found Philippe one day near where the Turkish fleet was docked. "Friend Philippe, I hear you are having a crisis of faith."

"Yes." Philippe said, lost in thought. The port around them bustled with merchants moving goods to and from the ships. "I simply do not know where to go next. I devoted my life to the Order, and now the Lord has seen fit to take that life from me. Where shall I go now? I'm only a disgraced soldier."

"Some things in life we have no control over; in this life, and the next. This life is to be treasured, and the fact that the Lord saw fit to spare yours at Mdina means your should treasure it that much more."

Philippe ruminated on Hajji's words. They were oddly comforting. "I believe that is the tenet of one of Christendom's recent scholars, is it not?"

Philippe's eyes opened wide. Hajji Murad was suggesting that Philippe look into the works of John Calvin. But that meant breaking with the Catholic Church. He could not do that. And yet, something about it felt right.

Philippe grew more open to the idea after the Ottoman envoy continued their mission and left Marseilles. Philippe parted with the Turkish envoy, and went up into the hills of Provence. Philippe settled in Avignon, near where he had lived before joining the Knights. There was a thriving Calvinist community in Avignon, and it did not take long for Philippe to find the local parish.

Philippe entered the door of the church. The inside bore a stark contrast to the ornate exterior of the building. The church had been converted from a Catholic church, and much of the outside walls kept the detailed sculpture of the original construction. However, the interior walls were plain and white. Philippe could see the faint shadows of where paintings had once hung. Much of the church was just as bare. The vaulted ceilings were also a pure white. The few decorations adorning the walls were several small crosses, and one large cross that gave Philippe the comfort of familiarity. A large eight-pointed cross, similar to the Maltese cross of the Knights Hospitaller he knew so well, adorned the wall to the side of the barebones oak altar. The midnight shade of the cross made it the most striking element of the entire church, and Philippe found himself staring in awe and drawn slowly toward it.

Philippe's footsteps echoed through the chasmic chamber as he walked slowly toward the altar. "Hello?" Philippe jumped at the sound of another person in the church. He looked down from the altar and saw a small elderly man with wrinkled features standing near the door to the side of the altar.

"Oh, hello." Philippe uttered. He noticed the black collar adorning the old man's neck. "Are you the priest here?"

The old man smiled. "Why yes, I am. Are you seeking guidance, my child?" Philippe nodded and the old man opened his arms toward him. He followed behind the priest as he went around the altar. He motioned for Philippe to join him in the presbytery. Philippe did so after a moment of hesitation.

"Now, friend," the priest began, "what guidance may I provide to you?"

Philippe looked up at the back of the altar, then at the old man's face. The priest radiated a gentle nature. Philippe felt himself relax in the presence of the priest. "I am, was, a Knight Hospitaller," he began, and recounted the siege of Malta to the priest. "I fear that the Lord has forsaken me, but I do not know why. I have shown Him my undying faith even in the face of the horrific loss of the siege."

The priest closed his eyes and slowly nodded his head. Philippe almost felt he could hear the man's bones creaking. He reopened his eyes and stared straight at Philippe. "You are not lost. God has been with you throughout your trials. Your undying faith is what has gained you His favor. That is the reason He has remained with you and has helped you survive these ordeals."

"But then, why did the Knights perish at Malta?"

The priest shrugged. "Perhaps the Lord wishes to teach the Church and the Pope humility, and how to properly seek His favor. The Church indulges in a glorification of itself, declaring itself the higher authority over all of Christendom in both spirit and legal matters. Each Pope considers himself the sole authority on who is worthy of sainthood, when Paul the Apostle taught us that every Christian who keeps the faith alive in their soul is worthy of sainthood."

Something struck Philippe at the mention of Paul the Apostle. He diverted the conversation to the teachings of Paul and found that both the priest and he were in agreement on the interpretation of Paul's teachings.

Philippe's face brightened with excitement as their conversation drew on, until the priest held up a hand to stop Philippe from continuing. "Now, I may not be as eloquent or as spry as Jean Cauvin, but you seem ready to join his faith."

Philippe stepped forward, eagerly. "Yes, of course."

"You do realize this will require renouncing your allegiance to the Pope and the Catholic Church, correct?"

Philippe hesitated. A knot suddenly wrenched at his stomach as he weighed the decision. He was fully devoted to the Catholic Church, just as he was devoted to the Knights Hospitaller.

Then something clicked inside Philippe's mind. He was not devoted to the Knights, or the Church. He was devoted to God. And he had already renounced his allegiance to the Hospitaller Order. Surely he could muster the strength to join the Calvinist Church as well, if it meant being able to devote his life to the Lord once again.

Philippe nodded firmly. "I am ready."

"Wonderful," the priest raised his hands toward the altar and exclaimed. He led Philippe out of the presbytery back into the main expanse of the church.

Philippe and the priest exited the side of the church. Philippe glanced back at the baptismal font as they left, but continued to follow the priest. They walked down the gentle slope of the town, skirting the edge of the main road. Soon they reached the stream that flowed through the center of the town. The priest continued walking calmly and silently following the bank upriver.

Philippe quietly followed the priest, cautiously taking in his surroundings. Birds chirped in the trees overhead. Across the valley brown fields of wheat grew, punctuated with the color of small patches of lavender. The path along the bank hardened from dirt to gravel as they left the town. The small gurgle of a waterfall from a nearby mill marked the edge of the town.

Half a mile upstream from the mill, the priest stopped. He removed his sandals and motioned for Philippe to do the same. Philippe removed his well worn leather shoes and laid them by the bank. The priest was pensive as he stared at Philippe. "Your tunic will need to go as well." The priest lifted the tunic over Philippe's head and threw it on the ground. Philippe stared at it a moment. The bright red of the Knights' cross had faded into a softer shade of salmon.

Philippe's battered body ached with the bright light of the sun hitting his chest. Philippe was uncertain if it was just fatigue from walking or something else.

The priest led Philippe into the middle of the stream until they were both waist deep. The chilly water was refreshing against his tired legs and ankles. The priest, his robe wet and heavy, positioned one arm around Philippe's abdomen and the other on the back of his neck.

"Do you renounce your allegiance in the Catholic Church, and your allegiance to the Pope?" The priest stared firmly into Philippe's eyes.

Philippe felt as if the priest was staring straight into his soul. The boring eyes brought Philippe's true word to his lips.

"Yes. The only faith I have or need is in the Lord Almighty." His body felt strangely calm despite the chill of the passing stream.

"Do you accept Jesus Christ as your Lord and Saviour above all others?"

"I do." Philippe said firmly. He always had his entire life.

"Then let the Lord absolve you of all previous transgressions and sins you have committed, and through this act of baptism may you lead a life of faith down the path to eternal salvation!"

The priest bent Philippe's body forward. Philippe closed his eyes and took a quick breath. He kept the breath in him as his head was pushed under the water. For three seconds, Philippe was submerged in the water.

His head breached the water and he let the air out of his lungs. He opened his eyes to see the priest holding him steady, smiling softly at him.

"It is done, Philippe," the priest said. Philippe was staring wide eyed, but he was relieved. It certainly felt as if his sins had been cleansed from his body. He looked down at his bare chest, and watched as droplets of water carried his past down his skin to be washed away by the current. He could start fresh.

Philippe moved slowly toward the bank. He looked at his old tunic. The cross was now even more faded after having been in the hot sun. He instinctively bent over to put it back on, but stopped short. He thought for a moment, and stood back up.

The priest handed Philippe a clean tunic and Philippe put it on. The linen felt smooth on him, and it was pure white. Philippe walked with the priest back down the bank. His renewal was complete.

The Fourth Pandemic
by Tim Moshier

Moscow, Soviet Union
15 June 1940, 1420 [Local]

"Fascist pigs in Paris! The Nazis have taken Paris!" A newspaper hawker yelled to passerby on the street, waving around a copy of *Pravda* from that morning. The doctor from Saratov already knew, of course, but didn't particularly care. Why should he? What was a war between capitalist dogs when compared to the groundbreaking research he was doing at home? Dr. A. L. Berlin ignored the man, who was now deep in conversation with passing bystanders, and opened the door to his hotel. His medical attendants trailed behind him.

Unknown to any of the group, they had more worries than they wanted to admit. *Yersinia Pestis* was already multiplying, spreading across their bodies. The Plague. The Doctor approached his room, stepping up the stairs and less than carefully down the long hallway, and tripped. He threw up his hands to protect himself before he hit the floor, and remained stunned for a minute. His medical attendants looked on in silence while the Doctor let out a self-deprecating chuckle. He was beginning to stand back up when he saw a movie flyer lying on the floor. Well, it couldn't hurt, right? And he still had a couple hours to burn.

The news bulletin before the movie showed *Wehrmacht* troops advancing through the Low Countries and France. Decadent capitalists fighting decadent capitalists. There was also something about Soviet troops aiding Polish civilians, which was par for the course in the Soviet Union. The movie wasn't bad, but the doctor had already forgotten the main plot points by the time he left. Something about a bunch of performers on the Volga. He felt slightly unwell and was seized by a fit of coughing. The crowd edged away from him, casting sideways glances, but he didn't particularly care.

Recovering, the doctor began to make his way back to the hotel. Dusk was fast arriving, and the crowds on the streets had thinned. Those who were left hurried home, hesitant to stay out in the city for much longer. The doctor began coughing again upon his arrival at the hotel, doubling over at the door and half stumbling across the lobby. His medical attendant grabbed him. "Are you okay doctor?"

"Yeah I'm...I'm just fine." He let out a deep breath. "I just need some sleep". The doctor tramped upstairs and to his room.

Moscow, Soviet Union
17 June 1940, 0900 [Local]

The radio blared, stirring the doctor from his sleep. "The glorious Red Army has begun the liberation of the workers in the Baltic territories". The Doctor groaned, his whole body hurt, particularly when he coughed. His medical assistants were similarly bedridden, wracked by pain and coughing fits, bloody spittle flying from their lips. "Our forces have encountered no resistance. Comrade Marshall Stalin says victory will be quick".

The only quick victory Dr. Berlin cared about was a victory over the ailment that was destroying his body. The news didn't even register with him. The noise did though, and the good Doctor reached over his bed towards it, probing with extended fingertips. There must be a way to turn the racket off. Somehow. There wasn't, his fingertips crashing back down to the mattress before he reached his goal. The doctor slipped back into restless sleep.

Downstairs, a clerk leaned against the wall, eyes drooping. He was feeling rather strange, perhaps a cold? Well, that wouldn't do, the damn doorman was visiting his home village for the next week, somewhere down in the Caucasus. The clerk resolved on a good night's sleep and to try and get through at least the rest of the day. Thankfully, it wasn't long before it was time to go home.

The clerk's wife was waiting for him at the door of the drab apartment, identical to every other in the neighborhood, just as she did every night. Next to her in the doorframe was standing a shadowy figure, half hidden and half obvious. The clerk warily walked up the steps. Who was it? The police? What had he done wrong? Then he was close enough to see, and his worries were forgotten. "Vasily!"

"Hello father!"

"What are you doing here?"

"We're transferring through the city, Sergeant gave me a day's leave and—are you okay?" The clerk had begun coughing, leaning against the frame of the door. Vasily took him by the arm and led him into the apartment.

"Yeah I'm alright, it's just a cold. You were saying?"

"Just that we're leaving in the morning. I can't tell you where we're going, but I also can't tell you not to guess". The clerk smiled, and Vasily continued as his mother served dinner. "How have you guys been?"

Moscow, Soviet Union
18 June 1940, 1450 [Local]

Dr. Berlin was dying. He could feel it. The shortened breath and bloody froth settling on his lips were signs, but the doctor could also just feel himself slipping away, drifting in and out of consciousness. The medical attendants were silent, engaged in something resembling a deep sleep, though it this point it was probably a coma. The doctor's head pounded, and he had recently been experiencing hallucinations.

How had it come to this? The doctor knew how it had happened, the sprayed aerosol full of deadly virus. But no, that wasn't what mattered. He tried to remember why he'd come to Moscow. He couldn't recall any meeting, nor any friends he hadn't seen in a while. Somewhere deep inside the doctor knew he was losing it, but that didn't matter either. Every thought led to one overriding emotion. The doctor was scared. He wasn't ready to die. But to the world, that just didn't matter. It never really mattered.

His chest ached and he felt that he was going to be sick, and the doctor couldn't do anything about it. There was no medicine to take, no technique that could make him any better. It was just too late. The doctor rolled over in the bed, groaning. Some sort of white light had appeared. All the lights in the room were off, and this new source of light was blinding, bathing him in white. It bobbed around the room, over him, over his attendants, back out into the hallway. The doctor stretched his hand to it, and the light turned back to him. Dr. Berlin closed his eyes.

Botkin Hospital, Moscow, Soviet Union
19 June 1940, 2030 [Local]

Boris Shimeliovich—head of Botkin Hospital—sat at his desk, eyes half closed and ready to go home after what had been a very long day. The first call had come that morning, a hotel clerk called to report he had dead bodies in one of his rooms. Personnel had dispatched to check it out, and it wasn't long before Shimeliovich had gotten another call from the same hotel, this time from his doctors. Four men were dead of some sort of infection, and the doctors on scene were requesting extra help. Shimeliovich dispatched another team.

Once again, the call came not long after, and this one sounded more frantic. One of the responding doctors had been present in Vladivostok in the early twenties, and he'd seen this before. It took only three words from that doctor to turn the city upside down. "It's the plague." And the plague it was. Shimeliovich got nearly a dozen other calls from across the city that day, every single one of them reporting at least one new victim. That morning, Shimeliovich had expected a calm, non-noteworthy day. Then again, Boris had never really gotten what he expected. The phone rang yet again, bringing Shimeliovich back to the situation at hand. "Yes, what is it now?"

"We've found another case. Apartment block near the center of the city. Small problem. The NKVD are already here." The man on the other hand seemed out of breath, as if he'd been running from something, or perhaps from someone.

Boris swore. "Alright, give me a minute." Shimeliovich put down the phone and ushered his secretary into the room, a pretty blond girl with deep blue eyes. "Natia, I need you to get me a meeting with Commissar Miterev. Make it quick." Shimeliovich halted with the phone halfway to his ear and smiled sheepishly. "And Natia? I could use a coffee, please. The day isn't over yet." Shimeliovich put the phone back to his ear. "Hello?"

A gruffer voice than before answered. "I am Captain Pyotr Sokolov of the People's Commissariat for Internal Affairs. Your men are interfering with an official investigation. I'd like them to leave. Now."

"Captain, I need you to listen very carefully. There's a chance that a very dangerous disease is present in that apartment. Your men need to take the utmost precautions, and I urge you to allow my men to check it out first."

The Captain's sigh was audible. "Yes, doctor, your men have already told me this. You misunderstand. We will not interrupt our work to partake in the fantasies of a few old men. There is no Plague here. Anyone interfering with our investigation will be considered to be complicit in any crimes we may uncover." The line went silent and Shimeliovich shrunk at his desk. It wasn't every day one got threatened by an NKVD officer.

Natia walked back in, handing him the cup of coffee. "The Commissar says he'll meet you in his dacha at your earliest convenience, sir."

"Thanks Natia."

Commissar Mitrev's Dacha, Near Moscow, Soviet Union
19 June 1940, 2140 [Local]

The People's Commissar for Health ushered Shimeliovich into his house and out of the rainy night. "Would you like something to drink, doctor? Vodka, perhaps?"

Shimeliovich smiled thinly. "No." He paused to let the Commissar pour himself a drink. "We have a rather serious situation developing in the city. Several calls have come into Botkin reporting victims of some sort of bacterial infection. I haven't examined it personally yet, but several of my doctors report the infection exhibits signs of plague."

The Commissar nearly spit out his vodka, but held it in, appearing rather red faced in the afterwards. "Plague? You're sure?"

"I wish I wasn't."

"How many cases?"

"We've counted at least a hundred so far, and calls keep coming in. Someone spread this thing far and wide. And sir, the mortality rate is high. Most of the calls have included dead bodies."

"What's our plan for this sort of thing Boris? Do we have one?"

"We're already distributing antibiotics across the city, though our stocks aren't exactly high. But George, my friend, I need a favor. I need you to get the military, and the NKVD, behind me on this. They haven't been willing to do anything so far."

Miterev only thought about it for a second. "I'll call an emergency meeting and talk to the Politburo. The others need to know."

"Good." Shimeliovich grinned. "I think I could use that drink now."

Ludza, Occupied Latvia
21 June 1940, 0320 [Local]
　　The private lie awake in the infirmary, cursing just about anything he could think to curse. He hurt. The day before, the private had reported to his medic with aches and a bloody cough, today he could barely move without being wracked by intense bouts of pain. The medic had said it was just a bad case of the flu. It sure didn't feel like the flu. Coughing, Vasily fleetingly recalled that he had visited his parents only a few days before, and noticed his father coughing most of the time he was there. Was that why he was sick?
　　A local nurse walked over to his bedside with a cold flannel. Vasily hadn't noticed the fever, but apparently she had. She was singing something under her breath, but it was in a language the private didn't understand. He faintly recognized the tune though, it sounded like one of his mother's old songs. The memory brought a smile to Vasily's face. Relaxing slightly, Vasily began to drift back into sleep. It was just the flu, right?
　　After the private had fallen asleep, the nurse walked back towards the entrance to the infirmary. Her shift would be over soon, which was nice. Still, she couldn't help wonder exactly what that Russian private had. The medics said it was the flu, but she had noticed flecks of blood on the boy's sheets. Flu didn't usually cause people to spit up blood, or at least not much of it. Still, the kid could just have a bad cough. There wasn't really anything she could do about it, so she pushed it out of her mind until her shift was over.
　　Veronika walked home through the city, which seemed far more depressing now that the Soviets had arrived. Some Latvians quietly complained about the occupation, though never where it was possible any Soviets could hear. Veronika wasn't one of those Latvians. She just tried to get on with her life just as it had been before, like the majority of the population. Like with that private's flu, it was out of her hands, and she didn't much care anyways. As her husband had taken to saying in the last few days, the Reds paid just about as well as anyone else.
　　By the time Veronika got home, her husband had already gone off to work, which meant she could go straight to sleep. She didn't wake until the afternoon, at which point she again went out to buy

something she could cook in time for her husband's return to the house. Veronika didn't mind, if she lived alone she'd be playing out much the same routine, except without any company. She waited patiently in line for food, noticing the lines seemed longer since the Soviets had invaded. Near the front of the line, Veronika started to cough.

Moscow, Soviet Union
26 June 1940, 1340 [Local]
Shimeliovich stared worriedly at the maps hanging next to each other on the wall. One portrayed the city of Moscow and was covered in red and black pins, representing infections and deaths. Most of the pins were clustered near the center of the city, but some were outside of it too. Notably, a cluster of black pins appeared at Lubyanka, spread by the Captain who had refused to listen to Shimeliovich a few days before. The poetic justice of that incident was at the back of Shimeliovich's mind, and refused to come forward. Such subversive thinking could get one executed in Stalin's Soviet Union. There was even a rumor that Beria had been infected, though no one was willing to try and confirm the validity of it.

The second map was of the Soviet Union as a whole, and scared Shimeliovich even more. Plague had spread far and fast. Leningrad, Rostov, Kiev, Smolensk, Moscow, and a dozen other cities—not to mention the various towns and villages—were experiencing outbreaks. People were starting to panic despite government warnings to stay indoors and away from public gatherings. Apparently people were beginning to try to leave the cities. Several thousand people had been infected, and nearly four hundred were dead so far. Even worse, there were indications that several Red Army units had similarly been exposed.

Prevention and treatment worked, to a point, but the state hadn't been ready for an outbreak this size, not across as much land as it had already affected. The disease appeared incredibly contagious, and attempts at quarantine had failed miserably. Shimeliovich was contacting as many infectious disease experts as he could, but so far not many doctors had expressed an expertise in the plague. Still, at least Shimeliovich had been able to set up this makeshift operation, which so far lacked a name. Commissar Miterev walked into the room and grimly walked over to the map of the Soviet Union.

He picked up yet another of the red pins and stuck it into the board. "Stalingrad reports 3 infected, but no dead. Not yet, at least."

Shimeliovich got up to talk to the Commissar. "They shut the city down, right? No public events, no major traffic, people have been ordered to stay inside?"

Miterev frowned. "If they haven't already, someone is going to be shot."

Boris, not quite knowing how to take that, ignored it. "Make sure they know to conserve antibiotics in case it gets out of control."

"We've done all of that Boris. Don't worry, we'll get it under control." The Commissar looked down at the doctor. "When was the last time you got a sensible amount of sleep Boris? I think you should go home and get some rest."

Shimeliovich rubbed his eyes. "I'll be alright sir. It might be safer here than walking home anyways." The Commissar frowned and opened his mouth to speak, but Boris cut him off.
"Maybe I'll find a quiet room later. But right now I've got work to do."

Berlin, Germany
26 June 1940, 1425 [Local]

Generalfeldmarschall Walther von Brauchitsch sat uncomfortably across from Hermann Göring. Neither of the pair had ever liked the other, and both resented that they were often forced to work together. Brauchitsch was in the middle of a sip of water when the *Führer* appeared in the doorway. The Field Marshall awkwardly stood and saluted in the traditional fashion. Göring went with the Nazi salute. "Heil Hitler!"

The *Führer* walked silently past them and sat at the opposite end of the table, gesturing for the two to sit down. The leader of the Third *Reich* leaned towards his two top generals. "*Generalfeldmarschall. Reichsmarschall.* We have been given an opportunity. The decadent communists and Jews to our East have been stricken by a disease no doubt inherent in the Slavic race. Several Eastern Poles have fled to our nation, telling tales of a coughing sickness that has struck Moscow itself."

Brauchitsch stirred. He'd expected something serious, given that the meeting had been called out of nowhere, but this? This sounded more like propaganda or disinformation than reality. Still, it didn't seem like something the *Führer* would just make up, and Brauchitsch was willing to listen.

The *Führer* continued his monologue. "This offers a unique opportunity." Brauchitsch almost smiled at that point, it sounded as if the *Führer* was selling them a business proposal. "Conflict with the Soviet Union is inevitable. All of their space and resources, wasted by a corrupt, inefficient regime. Their oil, land, agriculture, even the people can be used to serve the *Reich*. I remain convinced that only a couple well landed blows will knock that decadent country down. France, Belgium, Norway, the Netherlands, and Denmark. All have fallen before the *Reich*. The communists are next."

Hermann Göring had a worried look on his face. "Mein *Führer*, what about the British? I am confident that my planes and airmen can overwhelm their country in no less than a month. Should we not take that island before any consideration of dealing with the Reds?"

The *Führer* glared at Göring. "With the fall of the Soviet Union, Britain will be completely alone. Perhaps they'll even be willing to sign a deal." The *Führer* kept his gaze on the *Reichsmarschall*. "Any other objections?"

Göring shook his head, looking rather miffed, and Brauchitsch spoke up instead. "When is this operation expected to take place, mein *Führer*? Most of our troops are still in the West. It could take as much as half a year to fully redeploy, and invading in winter would not be efficient."

"You have three months."

The curt answer took Brauchitsch off guard. "Three months sir? That's not—"

Hitler stood. "Three months is all we have *Generalfeldmarschall*. Dismissed." The *Führer* left the room, as did Göring, leaving Brauchitsch to consider what had just happened. Three months. The man was insane.

Moscow, Soviet Union
5 July 1940, 1230 [Local]

The plague seemed to have finally reached its peak in Moscow, or so Boris Shimeliovich thought. New cases over the last couple days had been declining, although were still high, and patients were beginning to recover, due in large part to the judicious use of antibiotics. Still, while cases in Moscow were declining, reports continued to come in from far flung areas of the country reporting new disease outbreaks. What worried Shimeliovich right now was the report that had just landed on his desk.

The large scale outbreak had taken the Soviets unaware. First many medical doctors had succumbed, in large part to the disease's highly contagious properties. Now it appeared that antibiotics stocks across the country had fallen exponentially. Worse, the disease had spread to several remote villages in the Caucasus, villages far from any potential hospitals or medical personnel. It had already proven extremely difficult to isolate the disease once it had escaped from Moscow, and over the past couple days red dots had been appearing across the map of the Soviet Union.

Shimeliovich was particularly concerned about the disease's tendency to infect doctors who didn't take the proper precautions, precautions that many still didn't know to take. While rumors flooded the country, the government was still trying to maintain an element of secrecy when dealing with the disease. As a result, only high ranking doctors had received word of the outbreak and its spread and many hospitals were now reporting high rates of infection among the staff.

Piling on to the problem was the fact that many citizens had avoided medical attention and were instead remaining home and infecting their family members. Nothing is more frightening to a populace than the idea that hospitals are spreading the disease, and that is exactly what appeared to be happening here. Doctors were getting sick, as were patients who had entered the hospital for reasons other than the disease. If the doctors couldn't protect themselves, why should the civilians expect the doctors to be able to protect them?

As Shimeliovich brooded, a phone began to ring. An aide picked it up, talked for a few moments, and hung it up again. "Doctor?"

Boris started. He wasn't in the kindest of moods, though he'd always been somewhat of a cold, calculating person with little room for the niceties of social life. "What now?"

"Commissar Miterev wants to see you. He's at Number 1."

"Yeah alright." Dr. Shimeliovich grabbed his coat and searched the pockets for pencil and paper. Miterev always seemed to need someone to take notes. Finding it, Boris left the building.

Number 1, Moscow, Soviet Union
5 July 1940, 1340 [Local]

Emergency Hospital No. 1 was actually nothing more than a sprawling complex of army tents on the outskirts of the city. The

Commissar had hoped that placing it here would avoid any panic that may have been induced by the sight of patients overflowing from major city hospitals, but it didn't actually seem to have done much. The complex itself contained nearly 1000 patients and had become the go-to repository for plague victims arriving at hospitals across the city.

It wasn't hard for Shimeliovich to find the Commissar, who had set up an administration tent near the center of the hospital. Miterev beckoned to a seat in front of him when he saw Shimeliovich walk in, and the Doctor went to it. The administration tent was rather bare, furnished only with a couple desks strewn with papers and assorted chairs around them. An armed guard was posted outside, and Shimeliovich waited for the Commissar to finish scribbling something on a piece of paper before noticing him.

Miterev sighed. "Boris, I'm going to get straight to the point." His grim, mournful tone had Shimeliovich worried. "This disease is beginning to get out of control, and I'm beginning to think it may have gone too far for us. We are looking at a worst case scenario, and the Politburo knows it." Miterev sighed again. "Tomorrow, we'll be declaring nationwide martial law and deploying the army to major cities. This disease needs to be stopped, and Marshall Stalin is willing to do anything to stop it."

Shimeliovich wasn't surprised, but the decision still worried him. People were already scared, and this decision had the potential to spread panic across the country. Not to mention the weakening effect it might have on the Soviet Union's relations across the world. The doctor couldn't very well argue with a direct government order, however, especially not when it came directly from the Politburo itself. "What do you need me to do sir?"

Berlin, Germany
15 July 1940, 0230 [Local]

Brauchitsch waited worriedly in his office, eyes wide open and unable to sleep. A high stakes game was playing out across Berlin, and within the next 24 hours Brauchitsch knew he would either be dead or the next *Führer* of Germany. The *Reich* needed a strong, capable leader, and Brauchitsch intended that it get one. It had been a long few weeks in getting there.

The general was aware immediately that the orders to invade the Soviet Union were foolhardy, but there had been no one to voice his dissent to, or at least no one who had the capability to change the plans. The *Führer* appeared confident that his plan was flawless, despite the fact that it involved an attack on the communists with minimal planning and organization and, even worse, right before fall and the *rasputitsa*. Brauchitsch and the rest of the generals aware of the operation were also aware that it was doomed to utter failure. It was as if the *Führer* actually wanted the *Reich* to be destroyed.

It wasn't long before Brauchitsch heard rumors of rumblings among several of his top commanders, rumblings that could be considered treasonous and get all of them killed. Confronting one of his generals about it, Brauchitsch became convinced that they were right nevertheless. His country was on a path to destruction. The French armies may have collapsed, but the Soviets were simply not the French. It was becoming clear that even Britain would be able to stand against the *Reich's* forces, at least for now. Unless the nation's course was altered, everyone in the *Reich's* government would go down on the wrong side of history.

The question, once Brauchitsch was convinced the *Führer* had to go, was exactly how it was to be done. The answer to this came again from one of Brauchitsch's generals, who pointed out that the *Führer* had provided the means for his own downfall. In order to transfer troops to the East, some army units invariably had to go through Berlin. If a couple of these *Wehrmacht* units could be moved into the city, they could be used to overthrow the Nazi government and institute one more amenable to the army. The final plan was for *Wehrmacht* troops to secure government buildings across the city and arrest all top government officials. A select company of men would drive straight to the *Reich* Chancellery and ensure that the *Führer* was captured.

Of course, not all plans went perfectly, and this was what had Brauchitsch worried. The plan was already in motion, and the dark night seemed stifling as Brauchitsch waited anxiously for news of its success or failure. Twice gunshots had shattered the silence of the night, but it did not appear that things had developed into a full street battle. At least not yet. Two men stood guard at the entrance to Brauchitsch's office, and he was interrupted by their knock at the door.

"Sir, *Generalfeldmarschall* Keitel has arrived." Kietel, a close friend of Brauchitsch's, had been instrumental in the planning of the coup, and was directly in charge of the group that had been sent to the Chancellery. "His convoy is stopped in front of the building."

Brauchitsch eased himself out of his chair and walked out into the hallway. His guards escorted him down the stairs and into the night. Outside was a convoy three armored carswith two jeeps to the front, Kietel in the foremost of them. In the back of the second jeep was a hooded, weeping man. Brauchistsch walked to Kietel's vehicle. "Is that him?"

Kietel smiled. "Yes. We got him without a problem. I heard over the radio that Himmler was killed, and Göring is in custody. Goebbels and a few others are on the run, but we'll get them."

Brauchitsch's mouth was agape. The operation had gone off almost without a hitch. He let out a breath of air he hadn't known he was holding in, and grinned at his friend. "It's over."

Kietel, ever pragmatic, shook his head. "Not quite. We've still got to figure out what to do with him." Both had avoided using the man's name or title in open conversation. Both, up till now, had been loyal, patriotic men of the *Reich,* and it was hard enough to overthrow the government without humanizing the man they had purposely dehumanized over the last month. "Is there a plan for him?"

"Yes. Bring him to a remote holding facility and keep him there. We'll announce there was a stroke and that certain subversive elements attempted to wrest control of the government in the wake of it. No need to kill him. Yet."

After Kietel's convoy had driven off again, Brauchitsch remained deep in thought. The *Reich* was still embroiled in war, Mussolini was still screwing around in the Balkans and the British still continued to hold out on their little island. It seemed as though so little of the present had changed, but so much of the future had. The Soviets would eventually have to be dealt with, even if Brauchitsch didn't plan on dealing with them immediately, and the Americans seemed supportive of the *Reich's* enemies. The country was doubtless not going to function entirely smoothly in the aftermath of a military coup, Brauchitsch doubted the hardcore loyalists would just back down and let their beloved *Führer* be replaced, assuming they didn't buy the stroke story. Still, despite all these problems, Brauchitsch was certain he had changed the course of the nation. It was time now to steer it in a more specific direction.

London, United Kingdom
19 July 1940, 1420 [Local]

Malcolm MacDonald was an apprehensive man. He never felt comfortable meeting with the Prime Minister, a formidable character who wasn't easy to argue with, energetic even in his older years. MacDonald had reason to be worried, the suggestion he was about to lay out had possibly negative consequences for foreign affairs, and Malcolm didn't feel that Churchill would be entirely willing to sacrifice foreign capital in the interests of public health. Still, it was a conversation that had to be had.

MacDonald had learned only two weeks before that a freighter inbound to the United Kingdom had been quarantined in port after it was found that all aboard were suffering from an unknown disease. This was MacDonald's first indication that something sinister may be occurring on Europe's eastern flank. Investigation by public health officials concluded that the disease bore an uncanny resemblance to the pneumonic plague in Manchuria two decades before.

Was there actually a plague outbreak in the Soviet Union?

After several days of asking questions to that effect, MacDonald had his answer. Unequivocally yes. Rumors abounded of a mysterious disease striking Soviet cities, and Malcolm found himself increasingly surprised that he had not been informed of the situation. His aides told him this was because before the Soviet ship had arrived there was no reason to give credence to these rumors. The Minister of Health's theory was that it had simply been overlooked. Either way, it was a problem that needed to be immediately addressed, and this was the goal of his meeting with Churchill.

Malcolm decided to walk most of the way to the meeting and get some air. Perhaps by the end of the walk he'd be feeling slightly better about his decision, though he doubted it. Walking through London's streets and listening to the news hawkers advertise their papers was always the surest way to discover what was on the people's minds, and it was clear from the first five minutes of MacDonald's walk that the people were enthralled by the news coming out of Nazi Germany. There had been an attempted coup and the *Führer* was apparently down for the count, having suffered a major stroke.

The Minister of Health considered that for a few minutes, wondering if the official Nazi story was to be trusted, and decided after some reflection that it was. After all, the recent news hadn't exactly been bad for the *Reich*, why else would there be a coup attempt if not for a stroke? It sounded as if there was some disagreement as to who was to succeed the *Führer*, and strangely it appeared one of his top generals was going to do so, rather than a major Nazi party member. Of course, this was hardly MacDonald's concern, and after a few more minutes of thought his mind turned back to the Soviet plague.

Upon arriving at Churchill's bunker, where he had been since German bombing raids had begun—though the raids had tapered off in the last couple days—Malcolm was met by armed guards who, emotionless as usual, allowed him into the building. MacDonald nodded to the men, scrupulously polite as he was, and ventured down the stairs. As usual, the room where the Minister of Health found Churchill was thick with cigar smoke, particularly where the man sat reading the most recent reports and sipping some drink or another. The Prime Minister looked up. "Would you like something to drink? Tea? Scotch?"

Malcolm chuckled a bit. "No sir, I'm afraid I'm not quite in the mood."

"A shame." Churchill glanced back down to his papers, and then back up to the Minister of Health. "Can you believe these bloody Krauts? The foreign ministry says they got a suggestion through backchannels that Brauchitsch might be interested in peace! As if we're going to let them hold on to the whole continent."

MacDonald was taken aback, he hadn't heard anything of the sort. "Peace?"

"Well that's what I said isn't it?" Churchill took another sip and regarded Malcolm with slightly narrowed eyes. "Well, you must be here for something. Spit it out."

MacDonald cleared his throat. "Sir, we need to cease trade with the Soviet Union."

Churchill had been in the midst of taking another sip and began coughing on hearing Malcolm's suggestion. Red faced and incredulous, he took a moment to compose himself before responding. "You mean to tell me we should alienate the eastern half of the continent when we're already at war with the western half? Does that sound like good politics to you MacDonald? Because it certainly doesn't sound very good to me."

"Sir, the Soviet Union is experiencing a plague outbreak. If we do not cut trade with that country, we run the risk of being infected.

There are already rumors of plague cases in Turkey and Finland." MacDonald took a deep breath before going on. "And sir, if the political environment makes it unfeasible to do this, I'll have to tender my resignation. I will not stand by while we jeopardize the nation's health in the interests of helping a country which doesn't seem very interested in helping us."

The Prime Minister sighed. "Malcolm, all I can say is that I'll consider it. This is a big step you're asking me to take. We need to be absolutely sure. The best we can hope for is that the outbreak spreads to the damn Krauts too. Give me a few hours to confer with some others and I'll get back to you." Churchill glanced at his desk and pushed his chair back. "I guess these papers can wait for later."

Moscow, Soviet Union
2 August 1940, 1930 [Local]

It was not a good day in Moscow, Shimeliovich thought. Sure, it had started off normal. Well, about as normal as it could be within the context of the plague, anyways. The day had even started with some small amount of hope, Moscow was about the only city in the Soviet Union where the disease had actually started to abate. That hope had quickly evaporated, however, when Shimeliovich had received reports of bubonic plague outbreaks following the pneumonic plague across the country. Still, it was normal. Until the riots, that is.

The Soviet Union was breaking down. Reports of sporadic outbreaks across Central Asia, Europe, and the Middle East continued, but they were just that, sporadic. The western Soviet Union had been thoroughly affected. Virtually everyone in the nation knew somebody who had been infected. Mass desertions in the Red Army had become common, and resistance movements had popped up in the former Baltic States, Eastern Poland, and the Ukraine, even if the government tried to quell that sort of news. More importantly, major Soviet cities were experiencing serious food shortages and rumors of civil unrest pervaded the nation.

Sometime around noon Shimeliovich had been roused from his work by the sound of passing armored vehicles. Attempting to go outside to see what was going on, he was stopped by a couple of scared looking Red Army privates. "Sir, we need you to stay inside right now. There is a developing situation near the Kremlin. Some number of citizens have apparently decided to protest." Two thoughts took up

Shimeliovich's mind at that moment. If even one person in that protest had the plague, they would rekindle its spread across the city. And two, he didn't particularly want to be around if a street battle began in the streets of the Soviet capital.

Not much later the same two Red Army troops were ordering him and his colleagues to leave. "Sir, you really don't want to be here when the protesters arrive". They were right. Shimeliovich could hear gunshots from a few blocks away, and watched as black smoke billowed into the grey sky. Boris eventually pieced together that some of the army units had refused to fire on protesters and provoked an angry response from the NKVD. At that point an open battle had begun in the center of the city. In the moment, however, all Shimeliovich knew was that it was time to get out of there.

Now Shimeliovich found himself on the outskirts of the city, watching as more loyal army units moved in to put down the protesters. Smoke hung low in the sky over the city, and gunshots carried across the empty streets. The events had done little to boost his confidence on the state of the nation. The outbreak still seemed very far from ending, and he remarked as much to Commissar Miterev, who wasn't happy at the statement.

"Boris, you can't say things like this."

"Even if they're true?"

"Boris!" Miterev hissed under his breath. "Do you see what's happening as we speak? Do you want it to happen to you? If not, I suggest you shut up and get back to work."

Shimeliovich understood Miterev's anger, but wasn't exactly happy himself. "Fine", he hissed back, stalking off into a small concrete building that had been temporarily converted into office space for the anti-plague team.

Not quite feeling like going inside yet, Shimeliovich lit up a cigarette. He hadn't smoked much before the outbreak, but it had proven to be remarkably good at masking the smells. It had also helped to calm his nerves, something he'd desperately needed ever since Miterev's death, which had come rather unexpectedly after a routine visit to an emergency hospital. Cigarettes were somewhat of a rare commodity in the Soviet Union, though Moscow had a better supply than most.

As he smoked, Shimeliovich heard a couple of men talking around the corner, and ambled over to see what was going on. There were three Red Army officers huddled around a table and a map. One of them was clearly giving the instructions while the other two listened several minutes before snapping off salutes and walking swiftly away, presumably to perform their duties. The leader began rolling up the map, and Boris approached him. "Excuse my asking, but who are you?"

"Marshall Zhukov. I'm in command of the troops that are putting down these subversive elements, as ordered by Marshall Stalin himself." Zhukov looked suspiciously at the doctor. "More importantly, who the hell are you?"

"Dr. Boris Shimeliovich, head of the anti-plague effort." The last Boris had heard Marshall Zhukov and his troops had been out in the far east. "What were you doing here in the first place? Siberia is a long way off."

"We were ordered here to reinforce disease ravaged units. That's really all I can say to you Dr. Shimeliovich." Boris' title seemed to be stressed, the words infused with sarcasm. Before the doctor had the chance to question him about it, Zhukov had flagged down one of his vehicles and hopped up, leaving Shimeliovich with just one pressing question on his mind. If the eastern garrisons were here, who was guarding the east? And if no one was guarding the East, what happens next? His mind soon turned back to thoughts of the plague, however, the subject that had been torturing him for months. The pneumonic plague epidemic appeared to be fizzing out, but the bubonic plague had just begun. As usual in the Soviet Union, it was not a good day.

Near Vladivostok, Soviet Union
30 November 1940, 0720 [Local]

Mitsuo Fuchida listened to the drone of his engine as it carried him through the air over endless tracts of sea. There really wasn't much else to listen to, radio silence had been enforced an hour already and Fuchida's pilot wouldn't be able to communicate over the wind even if he wanted, though the man probably wouldn't have anyways. So here he sat, thinking about what had led him here and what was to come. The former was easy, of course. The Soviets were in shambles, and that was something it was best for the Japanese Empire to exploit.

The latter's explanation wasn't quite so simple. Though the immediate future seemed clear—Fuchida was confident of Japanese victory in the upcoming war—anything beyond that was murky. His friend Minoru Genda and their boss, Admiral Yamamoto, were both worried about exactly what the Americans were going to do when they heard about renewed Japanese expansion in Asia. They had been angry enough lately over the war in China and the occupation of Indochina, two things Fuchida felt his country had been totally in the right to do. Yamamoto had tried to explain something about the way the Americans thought, but it had come out as nothing but nonsense to him. The Americans had built an empire in Asia. Why couldn't the Japanese?

Beyond American interference, Fuchida wasn't particularly worried. Information from Soviet defectors suggested the country was being devastated by an outbreak of disease, and Manchurian and Japanese scientists confirmed the possibility that it was the plague. Fuchida had once heard an obviously unsubstantiated theory that the Japanese themselves had used plague, presumably on Chinese civilians. That theory had been largely dismissed out of hand, though Fuchida wasn't exactly repulsed by the idea. It seemed to have worked effectively in the Soviet Union, at least, even if it wasn't intentional.

In Fuchida's opinion even without the disease the Soviets would have been easy pickings, a nation of degenerate communists and foreign defectors. When it was confirmed that large Siberian garrisons had gone west, however, it became clear to the Japanese command that it was time to act. Even the navy wasn't completely opposed to the idea, though it still favored the southern strategy as the best course for the nation to follow. Fuchida's men were excited, while they hadn't been told directly of the plans it had hardly been difficult to infer.

Distracted from his musings by the signaling of his pilot, Fuchida looked up. "There it is". He knew no one else could hear his voice, but he said it anyway, anything to allow himself to let the sudden emotions that had come to him out. Excitement and apprehension warred within him. Fuchida flipped on the radio, ending radio silence. "Attack, attack, attack". Within only minutes, the port was aflame.

Moscow, Soviet Union
1 December 1940, 0010 [Local]

The disease had begun six months before, and during the course of that six months Shimeliovich had virtually never taken a day off. The former head of Botkin Hospital had done as much as he could, and his diligence had paid off. The plague had all but disappeared from Moscow, and pneumonic plague had abated across the nation, though sporadic cases still flared. The news would be good if it wasn't so bad, which made sense to Shimeliovich and his colleagues if no one else. It appeared that bubonic plague had once again become endemic in several parts of the country, and the epidemic of that particular strain of *Yersinia* was still at undefeatable levels.

The pneumonic plague outbreaks had left the country devastated, and this following outbreak of bubonic plague added fuel to what was already an out of control fire. Commissar Miterev had been struck down by the disease, and Stalin was purging his officers left and right. Shimeliovich had never been a religious man, but he couldn't help but to draw parallels between his nation's current situation and the Book of Revelations. The people's morale was shattered, and even the once mighty Red Army had trouble keeping order. No one seemed to know exactly how many had died or how many would die in the months to come.

The winter cold compounded difficulties, with social services barely working, and in some cities nonexistent, it was almost guaranteed even more people were going to die. Quite simply, Boris was living in the apocalypse, or so he felt. Yet there was still a job to do.   Shimeliovich opened his office door and peered into the hallway. Not quite realizing how late it was, Shimeliovich didn't expect the entire hallway to be dark and nearly tripped over something while his eyes adjusted to the lack of light.

A flyer lay in the hallway with the stylized image of a worker on it. Underneath was a biodanger sign and a caption. 'The fight against disease is the worker's fight. Report any signs of sickness in your family or neighbors.' The posters seemed rather useless to Boris. There wasn't even anybody to report to, much less something to do once the disease had been reported. Hospitals had collapsed along with society during the peak of the epidemic, and most still weren't back up to pre-epidemic operating standards. Botkin Hospital itself had lost at least half the staff to the disease.

On his way down the hallway Shimeliovich passed the old map room, where he and others had plotted the disease's progress in the early days of the epidemic. It wasn't long before that become unfeasible, however, and experts had begun labeling affected cities rather than specific cases. Even that was too much to keep up with, and eventually the map had been abandoned and tossed to the side, the map room converted to a rest area for scientists who wished to get a little bit of sleep instead of going home. Boris never used the room, preferring instead to sleep on a couch he had dragged into his office. Upon turning the corner he arrived at the back entrance to the building, from which he exited and walked to his car.

Tonight was to be the first official Politburo meeting since the start of the outbreak, and Shimeliovich was to be officially confirmed as the new People's Commissar for Health in the Soviet Union, a post he had unofficially occupied since Miterev's death. More importantly, he would be informing the assorted Soviet officials of the progress his scientists were making on plague research. While they weren't yet ready for human trials, scientists in the eastern Soviet Union, which had suffered only minor outbreaks, had created a possible vaccine for the virus. While antibiotics could cure it, if they were administered in time—in many cases they hadn't been due to shortages and rural outbreaks—a vaccine could officially eradicate the disease.

Before leaving, Shimeliovich chose to turn on the radio, where he heard what sounded like the trailing end of a news broadcast. "—forces have pushed into the Eastern Maritime Provinces and are suffering heavy losses. The Soviet Union will prevail." Boris, intrigued, turned the knob to another station. "Again, forces of the Empire of Japan have bombed Vladivostok in an unprovoked and dastardly attack on the peaceful workers of the Soviet Union." Vladivostok wasn't far from where the vaccine was being tested, Shimeliovich remembered. Damn. His country never caught a break.

Berlin, Germany
13 December, 1940, 1550 [Local]

Chancellor Brauchitsch waited patiently in his office for the arrival of *Generalfeldmarschall* Wilhelm Keitel. He read several official reports while he waited, one of which detailed the quarantine of several blocks of Konigsberg, where the plague had broken out. Apparently the city's Jewish ghetto was the primary center of the infection, and while Brauchitsch himself doubted it was anything more than a coincidence, he was perfectly content to let the citizens of the city place blame on the Jews. They were an easy scapegoat, and Brauchitsch was willing to take advantage of that.

Besides the quarantine things were relatively normal. A low level air war continued with the United Kingdom, but Brauchitsch had ordered the *Luftwaffe* to stick to purely military targets except when dropping leaflets containing suggestions for negotiations. The British for their part didn't seem willing to push the subject of negotiations, but also weren't willing to try any major military operations. It seemed as though the phony war was back everywhere except for Africa, where troops of Italy and the Third *Reich* traded blows with the British in Egypt.

In the Far East the Japanese, who Brauchitsch was hesitant to call an ally, had invaded the Soviet Union. There was very little information, but it sounded as though Japanese aircraft had bombed the port of Vladivostok in conjunction with an invasion from Manchuria and Korea. Or Manchukuo and Chōsen, as the Japanese called them. Either way the news was especially interesting given the already weakened state of the Soviets, though the information didn't seem to have much bearing on events back home in Europe.

The Chancellor was interrupted by a knock at his door. "Come in!"

It was Keitel, arriving as expected. "Chancellor," he said, and then lowered his voice. "Or should I call you mein *Führer*?"

Brauchitsch chuckled. "Anything but that. Take a seat my friend." Kietel did so, and Brauchitsch looked him up and down. "I trust you are well Wilhelm? None of that nasty plague in your system?"

It was Keitel's turn to laugh. "No sir, though that Konigsberg outbreak is interesting. I have some scientists looking into the practical implications of the disease. But I assume that's not what I was ordered here for?"

"You assume correctly. I need you to read this over. The *Führer* was right, you know, even if he wasn't smart about it. The Japanese are right too." Brauchitsch handed Keitel a rather thick manila folder marked 'Operation Moltke'. Keitel opened it and several diagrams fell out, including a blown up map of the western Soviet Union. "It's time to deal with the Soviets."

A. E. I. O. U
by Dr. Tom Anderson

August 12ᵗʰ, 1759
Kunersdorf, Margraviate of Brandenburg

Frederick II, King in Prussia, snatched his tricorne hat from his head and stared at it in fury. The black hat was stained with white streaks as his sweat had mixed with the white powder of his wig. Besides that, it was entirely intact. Not a single hole or tear from a near miss. While all around him his men, the best men of the greatest army in all of Europe, were torn apart by the murderous fire from the Russian positions. "Isn't there one bugger of a ball that can reach me, then?" he screamed in his preferred tongue of French. It mattered not that his enemies were allied with that nation, since the Diplomatic Revolution a few years before had upended the European alliance system: French was simply the tongue of civilisation and culture among the educated classes of Europe.

Not that what Frederick now yelled in despair owed much to civilisation or culture. To look at him now, none would dream that the distraught monarch was not only the finest tactical genius of his day but also a man of philosophy and learning, who had rejected his tyrannical father's crude pragmatism out of spite. Frederick William I, the Soldier King, had forced his son to watch in tears as he executed the close friend with whom Frederick had once tried to escape to England. Frederick wondered now if Hans was looking down on him from what followed after. If there was anything. He had rejected his father's blunt religiosity, as well, in favour of private doubt. Yet, he had embraced the Calvinist Predestination that his father had opposed, which meant that whatever happened today, it was destined to happen, and there was nothing he could do about it.

Somehow that did not comfort him.

Kunersdorf was turning into the biggest defeat of his career. The Austrians and their Russian allies, usually so cautious, had finally driven their armies into the Prussian heartland under the dynamic leadership of Louden and Saltykov. A victory here would undoubtedly mean a march on Berlin and the end of everything that the House of Hohenzollern had fought for decades to bring about—the shutting out of the Austrian Hapsburgs' pernicious influence and the founding of a new alternative leadership for the German nation in all its fragmentary parts. Prussia itself could cease to exist.

Though outnumbered, Frederick had fought in his usual style, marrying brilliant new artillery and cavalry tactics to an aggressive stance that never allowed the enemy to rest on their laurels. Earlier that day he had attacked the Russian flanks and scored a victory. His brother Prince Henry had advised him to leave it at that and retreat, let their defeat unsettle the Russian conscripts and weaken them for a later engagement. But Frederick had been impatient, concerned about the Russo-Austrians' position as a dagger aimed at the heart of Prussia, and he had insisted they fight on.

His refusal to be satisfied had brought them here. Here, to the cream of the Prussian army dying on the battlefield, the Russians pushing forward and ripping apart Frederick's attacks with their artillery fire. Of Frederick's army of over fifty thousand, he guessed that less than a tenth of it remained in fighting condition. Veterans to whom he would have trusted his life were fleeing in terror like untested boys. Boys... "Children!" he cried, effortlessly switching to the German that his troops would speak. "Do not leave me today! Do not leave your King, your Father..." he trailed off. His words made no impact. One regiment remained steadfast, holding the Mühlberg against the Russians, covering the retreat. But it was futile.

Despite his reputation, Frederick had not always known victory. At the Battle of Kolin, two years before—it felt more like two lifetimes—von Daun's Austrians had defeated him in what had been, up until now, his darkest moment. Colonel von Seydlitz had saved them that day with his cuirassier charge to cover the retreat. "But Seydlitz is gone, isn't he?" Frederick muttered to himself. Earlier today he had sent the miracle worker against the Russian guns to try and force a breakthrough. Seydlitz had returned barely alive, bearing what looked like a mortal wound, his men shattered and despairing. No more miracles. This could not be another Kolin, a temporary setback. This was the end of Frederick, the end of Prussia.

Somehow, time seemed to simultaneously stand still and run at twice its normal rate, as the King gazed on his day of disaster in a state of emotional numbness. That was better than succumbing to the feelings inside. He had always struggled with depression, had contemplated suicide once before when his father had forced him into a loveless arranged marriage. And now, what more did he have to live for? Would it not be better to give up his life here and now in one last heroic stand, at least become a legend to inspire the future generations of Prussia? At least his failure would have meaning in such a case, even if his people who would now live in servitude to the Austrians.

Frederick was suddenly brought back to himself as he realised what was happening. A troop of Cossacks on horseback, red caps on head and spears in hand, were approaching. The savage horsemen from the steppes clearly had only one thought in mind: to slay Frederick. Or, perhaps worse, to capture him. The King drew his sword, the sword that had remained disgustingly clean thus far today as his men had suffered and died around him. He would not give them the satisfaction. End his life as it had begun: in blood.

"Your Majesty!" A new voice, but one he recognised. Captain Prittwitz and his Hussars from the town of Ziethen. He was young, about the same age Frederick had been when his father had died and consigned this nation to his governance. Young and eager, eyes still bright despite the disasters of the day. He grabbed Frederick's horse's reins with one hand.

It was obvious what Prittwitz wanted: he wanted Frederick to go with the Hussars, go along with the other officers who had retreated, to withdraw and fight another day no matter how hopeless that might seem. Frederick's heavy heart resisted. "Prittwitz, I am lost!" he cried.

"No, Your Majesty!" Prittwitz replied firmly. Three simple words, nothing profound or original about them, yet the spirit behind them swayed Frederick's heart.

And somewhere out there, perhaps, is a world where Frederick rode away with Prittwitz's men, left the Cossacks behind, and found himself with just three thousand men left from his army of fifty... yet also found that his enemies, divided, squabbling and overly cautious, failed to follow up on their victory. A world where they left Berlin alone, gave Frederick a fighting chance to once again build back up from a defeat, and let defeats elsewhere scupper their attempts to destroy the Prussian ascendancy. A world where, in time, Frederick's family would unite Germany under their rule and achieve his dream.

But we are not concerned with that world. We are concerned with the one where a lucky—or unlucky—musket ball struck Captain Prittwitz in the temple and threw him from his horse in a trail of blood, where the jaws of despair once more closed around Frederick's heart. "So be it, then," he cried aloud, and spoke words he no longer believed, yet gave him comfort nonetheless: "*GOTT MIT UNS!*"

Frederick raised his sword in a fey salute, grabbed his reins and charged into the mass of Cossacks. The ranks closed over him, spearpoints dripping red as they plunged down again and again. And then there was silence. An end.

An end... and a beginning.

November 15th, 1759
Vienna, Archduchy of Austria

The name of the Schönbrunn Palace meant "Beautiful Spring". And, for all that the autumn leaves fell from the trees in the gardens, the name seemed apt to Maria Theresa, Archduchess of Austria and Holy Roman Empress. For this day, they would witness a new spring for Austria.

Prince Kaunitz, the Chancellor of State, allowed his usual composure to crack and gave her a wide grin as he brandished the copy of the treaty. The Treaty of Dresden, history would name it, for it had been signed in the capital of Saxony, a state now no longer in thrall to the Prussians' military designs. The signature of Prince Henry of Prussia looked rather crabbed and Maria Theresa wondered if she was imagining what looked like the mark of a teardrop falling on the ink. Given the content of the treaty, it would be understandable. "And so it ends," she said aloud. Part of her wanted to shout in triumph that Frederick was finally gone; the slippery eel had choked on a hook at last. Yet, she told herself that that was unworthy and un-Christian. She had to be better.

"It ends," Kaunitz agreed. A frown crossed his face. "Assuming Prussia even holds together enough to honour this treaty. Count Finck von Finckenstein—" (the Prussian Minister-President) "—

has a document he claims Frederick signed in secret, saying he would become Regent of Prussia in the event of Frederick's death, not Prince Henry." He shook his head. "The prince, understandably, disagrees."

"A civil war?" Maria Theresa pondered.

"We could fan the flames," Kaunitz suggested, "weaken them further."

"No," said a new voice, young but bold. Her eighteen-year-old son and heir Joseph, already a member of the Council of State, had arrived along with his sister Maria Christina. Maria Theresa kept her expression fixed: she often disagreed with her son, with his foolish radical ideas, but Maria Christina was her favourite child and she didn't want to start a fight in front of her. "Our goal should be to rule Prussia with a firm but fair hand, not to destroy it."

Maria Theresa opened her mouth, hesitated and spoke. "I am in agreement," she said. Joseph's obvious surprise was echoed in her own heart. "It is against God to prolong the suffering of these lands for our own ends. Ours should be a realm of peace and prosperity, the envy of Europe, not the battlefield of choice for other princes."

Joseph nodded in agreement, but typically put his own spin on it. "The welfare of the people is the first law," he said.

"Cicero?" Kaunitz said with a smile. "I thought you were fonder of more... contemporary wit, Your Royal Highness."

Joseph gave him a look, then reluctantly returned the smile. "If you like, I will write to M. Voltaire and inform him that one such piece of wit born from his pen may now be outdated." He gestured at a wall hanging that displayed a highly decorative, though somewhat inaccurate, map of the German lands. "In contrast to what he writes, though its holiness may be... erratic, and its Roman-ness certainly debatable, with Frederick out of the way it is my intention that it will once again be worthy of the name *Empire*." He gave them a triumphant look.

Maria Theresa resisted the urge to sigh at her son's fondness for newfangled writers with heretical views. Still, the core of his point appealed to her. "An Empire indeed," she agreed, "led by us and with no more upstarts to divide this house against itself." A good Biblical admonition, almost subconsciously paraphrased as though it could cancel out the modern negativity of Joseph's Voltaire quote. "And speaking of divided houses, I trust that Prince Henry agreed to the other requirement?"

"Reluctantly," Kaunitz said. "He knows very well what we are doing." He tugged on a bell-pull. "Send him in."

Maria Theresa sized up the young man—no, *boy*, he could not be more than fifteen years old. Her agents had written of an amiable, indolent child who could hardly be a greater contrast to his tyrannical grandfather or mercurial uncle. A child lacking much interest in statecraft in favour of a love of art and the high life. Even if Frederick had lived and won the war, Maria Theresa realised, Prussia would still have been in trouble if the throne had passed to this one. But he was young, still young enough to be... shaped, perhaps.

"Your Majesty," said Frederick William II, Elector of Brandenburg. No longer King in Prussia; that title had been extinguished as part of the treaty, and the old Ducal Prussia lands surrounded by Poland would now pass to the Hapsburgs. A birthday present for Joseph, perhaps, Maria Theresa thought with an inward smile.

Frederick William looked rather downcast, but seemed to lack any sense of righteous fury at his fate. He would go with the flow. The sort of man, Maria Theresa realised, who could be nicely steered onto the right path by an appropriate choice of spouse. Commentators often accused her of being a domineering wife to her own meek husband— that wasn't entirely fair to Francis, but there was a grain of truth to it. Perhaps Frederick William could become an asset.

Maria Theresa noticed that his gaze had wandered to Maria Christina. Young, bright, beautiful... and the only one of her daughters with the same strength of will that marked Maria Theresa herself. Maria Theresa had always feared that she loved her daughter too much to persuade her into one of the marriages of state that the imperial house demanded. But from the way Maria Christina was returning Frederick William's gaze, perhaps there would be no forcing needed.

"Welcome to Vienna, Your Serene Highness," said Maria Theresa, gently emphasising the new title and the reduction in the Hohenzollerns' fortunes that it represented. Yes; Frederick William didn't even flinch, much less pout as many would have. He did not consider his loss to be so great providing he could have the things he valued in life. Maria Theresa introduced him to Maria Christina and made excuses for herself, Joseph, and Prince Kaunitz as swiftly as she could.

As she left them behind, she heard Frederick William point out a wall hanging—not the one with a map, but a different one. It had been hanging there for as long as Maria Theresa remembered, an ornamental design surrounding five large letters: A E I O U. "I fear, my lady, I am already well acquainted with my vowels and consonants," he was saying with a smile. Maria Theresa had to hide one of her own: she remembered thinking the exact same thing as a girl before one of her godmothers had explained the secret meaning of the five letters.

Joseph spoke as they walked away, meaning Maria Theresa missed hearing her daughter's own version of the explanation. "Let others wage wars," he quoted sardonically, "you, happy Austria, shall marry."

Maria Theresa gave him a look. "Frederick III might have lived over a century ago, but he was correct. Better to form bonds of blood than to spill it."

"In that, perhaps, we are in agreement," Joseph said. He looked out a nearby window, saw the sun setting over Vienna. "We've survived the Swede, the Turk, and the Prussian," he murmured. "Who will it be next?"

"No-one that we cannot defeat in turn," Maria Theresa said firmly. She pointed at a distant part of the city, shining in the last rays of the sun. "Do you remember when I first had them set up the porcelain factory? They said that we would never compete with the Saxons." She picked up a small decorative vase that sat on the window ledge and studied it. "Yet it turns out that anything they can do, we can do better." She smiled. "So shall it be with everyone else."

May 14th, 1773
London, Kingdom of Great Britain

William Pitt glanced up from his comfortable booth at Almack's Club, setting down his glass of port wine in annoyance. At first he assumed that the interrupter of his gloomy meditations must be one of the irritatingly foppish young men who frequented the club, the so-called "macaronis" with their exaggerated, effeminate fashions. "Do you mind..." he trailed off as he realised his unwelcome visitor was no macaroni.

"No, I don't mind," said Lord George Germain, pulling up the chair opposite Pitt and sitting down. "How is your day, sir?"

Pitt made a face. "Much like any other." He waved his hand, glass and all, at his surroundings and spilt a few drips of port in the process. "Stuck in this half-rate club since I was blackballed from the real ones after that Prussian disaster, years ago. Trying to manage my estate to pay the bills." He narrowed his eyes. "And going to Parliament to try and convince the Government you serve that it is on the course to disaster. Does Lord Rochford know—"

"I'm not here on behalf of Rochford," Germain interrupted in a long-suffering manner before Pitt could start up on his tiresome obsession with one particular subject. "I'm here on behalf of Suffolk. The Northern Department, not the Southern."

Pitt nodded. "Ah. Then you wish for my advice on the situation in Poland?" Part of him wanted to grumpily tell Germain that the Earl of Suffolk should come and ask him in person. But at this point in his life, he couldn't afford pride.

"Just so," Germain agreed. "It seems that Catherine of Russia has lost patience with her puppet ruler there being insufficiently... ah... his strings are too..."

"He's acting too independently," Pitt said tiredly. "Not everything has to be a clever metaphor."

Germain scratched under his wig to hide his embarrassment. "Perhaps. In any case, she plots to invade and annex part of the country directly to Russia. To divide Poland from Lithuania and take the latter, maybe. We know she has made approaches to Vienna, but Maria Theresa has rejected her. Says it would be a criminal and un-Christian act."

"If any lady or gentlemen would let the grubby business of foreign affairs be influenced by such concerns," Pitt opined, "it would most assuredly be Maria Theresa. If the Prussians were still a power and it was two against one, perhaps even she would go along with carving up Poland...but as it is, she can stand with the Poles against the Russians." He smiled wanly. "And ensure the Sejm elects her son as their next King, naturally. So what was your question?"

"Why, whether should we stand with the Russians against the Austrians or not."

Pitt shook his head. A small white cloud of wig powder formed a brief halo about his head. "No. Quite the opposite."

Germain looked surprised. "But the Austrians are allied with the Bourbons. If they take Poland as well, the threat of a Universal Monarchy ruling the continent..."

"The Austro-French alliance is fragile and can be undermined,"

Pitt told him. "We can undermine it all the better if we become an alternative friend for Austria, as we once were before the Diplomatic Revolution in the Fifties. And it should be of no concern to England what the Austrians choose to do on the continent." He took a gulp of port. "The Russians, on the other hand, pose a significant threat in America. Their explorations of the Nootka region in particular... we should take every opportunity to beat them back and delay the day we must fight them in the colonies. We should help the Austrians to accomplish that goal."

"Ah, America," Germain said with a thin smile. "It all comes back to America with you, sir, doesn't it?"

Pitt glared at him. "Not America specifically. But the future of which nation shall have supremacy over this earth will be determined in the colonies, not in Europe. My family made its fortune in the Indian diamond trade—" he passed over the more illegal parts of Thomas 'Diamond' Pitt's work, "—while others kept doing the same old thing in England and were left behind. It'll be the same now. It doesn't matter what the Austrians do. It matters what the French and the Spanish, the Portuguese and the Russians and the Dutch do, because they are our competitors overseas." He shook his head. "Assuming of course we can even hold onto our own colonies. This Tea Act..."

"Yes, we have all heard your arguments before," Germain said in a long-suffering voice. "But some of us have a higher opinion of the loyalties of our colonial subjects. To hear your speeches, one would think that Hampshire or Kent would rise in revolt if we raised taxes slightly."

"Are you so certain they would not?" Pitt muttered.

Germain stood up. "I will take your advice on Austria to Lord Suffolk," he said. With the unspoken addendum that Pitt's views on America, on the other hand, would continue to fall on deaf ears. Pitt sighed and drained his glass.

June 20th, 1776
Philadelphia, Province of Pennsylvania (British Empire)

"All right, then," Thomas Jefferson said, crumpling up his sheet of paper and tossing it onto the floor, "how about this: 'We hold these truths to be self-evident, that all men are created equal—'no, not now!" He pushed away one of his slaves as the man offered him a tray of drinks.

Franklin frowned at that, but let it slide.

To John Adams, one of Jefferson's few weaknesses in his undoubted genius was his refusal to take up a consistent opinion on the slavery issue, often privately condemning the idea in principle yet still being part of the system himself. "Go on," Adams prompted Jefferson. Though they had many disagreements, he respected the man's intelligence and had recommended to the revolutionary Congress that Jefferson draft this declaration. He wondered if Jefferson was quite so thankful to have the task after so many harried hours of arguments over phrasing.

Jefferson wiped his brow, smearing wig powder across it, and continued: "—that they are endowed by their Creator with certain unalienable Rights, that among these are Life, Liberty and the Pursuit of Happiness..."

"I like that," intoned Roger Sherman. The quiet theologian was the fourth member of their Committee of Five—now reduced to four since Robert Livingstone had been recalled by New York. "The people need to know that they enjoy such rights not because of the whim of a monarch, but by the will of God Himself. If even the Russian peasantry can make such a realisation..."

Adams opened his mouth, exchanged a glance with Jefferson. The Russian rebellion of last year was scarcely comparable to what the Patriots hoped to unleash here in America. That had been a bloody, primal struggle prompted by the embarrassing Russian loss in the Polish War, aided by the Cossack leader Pugachev and his claim to be Peter III, the husband whom Catherine was thought to have had murdered. After the peasantry supported Pugachev enough for him to win a few victories, the aristocracy had decided to scapegoat Catherine, have her assassinated, and allow Pugachev to be a puppet restored 'Peter III' while reversing all the Europhile modernisations that Peter the Great and Catherine had imposed on the country. No, quite unlike what America should become.

Jefferson winked at Adams. "Quite so, quite so."

Adams nodded, taking the point. It was pointless to argue over such things when they already had far too many points of disagreement over things that mattered. "So," he said, "can we go back to the part about the Indian savages on the frontier, I think 'merciless' is a better word than 'barbarian'..."

June 26th, 1793
Fleurus, Duchy of the Reunited Netherlands

    "We're so close," muttered Elector Frederick William II, watching the battlefield through his spyglass. "Break! Break, damn you!"

    "I'm sure that damn infernal machine makes the difference," said Francis, Margrave of Bergen-op-Zoom and heir to Duke Charles Theodore of the Reunited Netherlands. It was thanks to Frederick William that Francis' father had such a title. Oh, certainly it had been Emperor Joseph's idea to do a deal with Charles Theodore and let him inherit the Austrian Netherlands instead of Bavaria, which could then be annexed directly into the core Hapsburg lands. Frederick William had a feeling that his uncle would have gone to war to prevent that if there had still been a Prussia with him at its head. But the nephew, helped by the guidance of his wife Maria Christina, had lived up to the uncle in a different way. Frederick William had successfully managed to command an army that ten years ago had overthrown the Patriot movement that had seized control of the Dutch Republic from the Stadtholder. Now the former Republic had been neatly merged into Charles Theodore's Duchy. And an end to an independent Netherlands having control over the Scheldt river meant an end to the constant attempts to shut down Austria's own East India trade projects. The old Dutch East and West India Companies, along with all their wealth and colonies, had fallen into Austrian hands.

    Frederick William shook himself out of his reverie and nodded at Francis' pointing finger. An observation balloon floated over the battlefield, doubtless feeding information to the French commanders with signal flags. It made Frederick William's blood boil when he thought about it. The Revolutionaries might bleat on about how they were the coming tide, but all their wonderful innovations they boasted about, the superior artillery, the balloons, the new tactics, these were all born of the old regime they had overthrown. Frederick William was quite certain that no new idea had ever entered into any of the thick heads of the murderous peasant rebels who led this revolt. It was no surprise that a man like Robespierre—a bourgeois lawyer and undoubtedly bright despite his bitterness and thirst for blood—had risen to the top over such scum. He was now engaged in killing quite as many of his own supporters as those of the old regime, so the spies said. But Frederick William would not be satisfied until that man was fed into his own guillotine along with his other compatriots.

It was a crime against God to have slain King Louis XVI. But it was a far more serious crime to have killed Queen Marie-Antoinette as well. For Marie-Antoinette had been born Maria Antonia and had grown up in the Schönbrunn with Frederick William as her occasional playmate. She had been his wife's little sister. And now Frederick William was quite as determined as Joseph and Maria Christina that the French Revolutionaries pay for her death a thousandfold.

This battle seemed to be turning out that way. The Austrians and their allies—the Reunited Dutch under Francis, the Anglo-Hanoverians under the Duke of York and the Brandenburgers under Frederick William himself—had pushed back both the French right and left wings. Only the center remained, but it was stubborn. There was a good commander there: he must be some turncoat aristocrat only claiming to be a brainless pig farmer, Frederick William decided. "We have to break them now," he insisted. "I'm going to lead a charge myself."

"Sir!" Francis said in shock.

But Frederick William would not be dissuaded. For most of his life he had been told admiring stories of his uncle, even by those who had fought on the opposite side, and despite his wife steering him towards more productive ends, he had always felt a resentment and a sense that he could never escape the man's shadow. Well, now he would. Frederick had died leading a hopeless last stand; Frederick William would lead a heroic charge, and live.

And it worked, to some extent. The French did indeed break at last, and Frederick William rejoiced, his red-stained sword gleaming in the dying sunlight as the Anglo-Hanoverians and Reunited Dutch began mopping up the enemy as they turned to a rout. But Frederick William's own forces were now battered and wounded. Vulnerable. That damnable balloon must have spotted this and signalled, for a company of fresh French cavalrymen now galloped towards them, ready to at least make a Parthian shot. They must have been held in reserve, for the proletarian French forces lacked much in the way of trained horsemen. Before the Revolution, horses had been an expensive luxury.

Frederick William raised his blade and stood at arms. If this was the end, so be it. His son, also named Frederick William, would continue his line in turn. And he would have struck a blow to avenge his sister-in-law and bring down a vile and bloodthirsty system.

Yet just before the charging horsemen could reach him, something intervened. The red-white-blue tricolour banner held by one cavalryman suddenly turned all red. Their red Phrygian caps suddenly matched the spray surrounding them. Horses screamed and toppled, men fell from their saddles. A volley of grapeshot from a concealed gun had struck the troops. They turned and fled—most of them. Four soldiers recovered from their falls and converged on Frederick William, raising their pistols. They were painfully thin from the food shortages afflicting France, with prominent moustaches and death in their eyes. Frederick William raised his sword uselessly.

A man in a white Austrian artillery uniform appeared from a nearby copse and raised a weapon. He fired once, dropping one soldier. Then Frederick William's mouth dropped open in shock as the man sighted on a second soldier and fired again, and again. One soldier managed to return fire before he was downed and Frederick William saw the musket ball crease the back of the man's wrist. A lucky wound, superficial—he could easily have lost the use of the hand. The artilleryman promptly stuck his bleeding hand into his coat in lieu of a bandage.

Frederick William found his voice. "You saved my life, soldier!" he cried.

"You won this battle, Your Serene Highness," replied the man in a strange, unplaceable accent. Vaguely Italian? He gestured around the battlefield.

Frederick William took in groups of French troops pocketed by Austrian bayonets, surrendering then and there. This was a great defeat for the Revolutionaries. Perhaps, God willing, the beginning of the end. "I did, didn't I?" he said in wonder. "But you saved me nonetheless. Did you have that gun in place from the start?"

The artilleryman shook his head, gesturing with his free hand to where the gun's muzzle now poked from the cover provided by the copse. Two of his men were now pulling it out, one of them holding the reins of what looked like a racehorse. "A galloper gun, sir, like the British use in India. They can fly around the battlefield faster than you'd believe." He hefted the strange musket he'd been using, which had an unusually bulbous stock. "Always a good idea to be able to do things the enemy thinks are impossible. Like this Repetierwindbüchse for instance."

"Ah yes," Frederick William said. "I've heard of the repeating air rifle, but I thought only the elite Grenzer troops from the border used it. And since we've pushed the Turks back beyond the Military Frontier, I wonder if we'll even have Grenzers in the future..."

"Another war for another day, sir," said the artilleryman, "but you might want to think about training regular troops to use them. And maybe get some inventors to work on a version that works with powder instead of compressed air. Fewer moving parts."

Frederick William smiled. "You're full of ideas, aren't you? Are you Italian?" He still couldn't quite place that accent.

The artilleryman's expression turned sour. "I'm Corsican, sir. My father fought to try and expel the French from the island and when he couldn't, he sent me off to get the best military career he thought I could. It was this or the Royal Navy, and, well," he smiled, "my hero was always your uncle, sir, and I thought that any power that could beat him deserved my allegiance..."

"I see," Frederick William said. A little put out at his uncle once again playing a role in this, but never mind. "I'll see you well rewarded for this, Captain..."

"Bonaparte, sir." He gestured at the galloper gun, now freed from the copse. "Remember me by my whiff of grapeshot."

Frederick William smiled. "I think Grand Duke Ferdinand is looking for a new governor of Elba..."

July 16th, 1848
Vienna, Archduchy of Austria

"I say spit on this doggerel and send in the troops!" cried Frederick William IV, Elector of Brandenburg. "Why should you accept a crown from the gutter?"

Joseph IV, Archduke of Austria and Holy Roman Emperor, smiled. "Do not be so swift to dismiss the will of the people," he said. "My grandfather would have something to say about that."

"Your grandfather..." Frederick William hesitated, aware that he was stepping dangerously close to the boundaries of good behaviour. His opinions of Joseph II's reforms were well known. Free education for the masses, institutions for the blind and deaf, the dissolution of the monasteries and nationalisation of the priesthood into an arm of the state? Marriage transformed from a religious to a civil institution, the abolition of serfdom and the introduction of religious toleration? It mattered not that Frederick William's own grandfather had been a Protestant: he had been raised into the Catholic faith and was confident in its supremacy, no matter what 'his' people in Brandenburg might say.

"My grandfather saw the coming dawn," Joseph said. "He knew what would come to pass, whether we led the way or tried to fight it—which would be futile, as the British have proved." He shook his head.

"I still think there might be a counter-revolution," Frederick William insisted. "What they did to Queen Charlotte and Prince Leopold was horrifying... I only thank God that their son escaped here."

"Let him grieve his parents before you start proclaiming him Leopold II and planning some kind of heroic return at the head of an army," Joseph said sharply. "And return to my point. King Louis knew what he had to do after my grandfather put him back on his throne, and notice how France is doing quite well in the current unpleasantness. Their peasantry is already satisfied with their lot thanks to his reforms. But if we try to stifle them, they will only turn to democracy, and we know what that means."

"Democracy." Frederick William made the word a curse. "At least the Americans have shown their true colours now. No more rhetoric about freedom while practicing slavery."

"I fear they'll still go on talking about freedom with no sense of irony," said Joseph. "Perhaps if New England had stayed in their union instead of breaking away after that tariff war with Britain... but there's no profit in speculation. The last free states in America have accepted slavery now, and similarly horrible things will happen over here if we let Democrats gain the support of the people. We have to lead the way instead." He opened the leaves of his writing desk and showed Frederick William a much-spotted draft. "I already have a response to the Frankfurt Parliament."

Frederick William's eyes flew back and forth over the page. "What is this nonsense? The division of the Hapsburg realms into four, each with its own elected *Reichstag*... a Holy German Empire, including the Netherlands... a Holy Italian Empire, a Holy Balkan Empire, a Holy Slavic Empire?" He blinked in disbelief.

"I thought 'Polish' was too restrictive for the last one since Radetzky conquered Little Russia and Crimea," Joseph explained.

"That's not the point!" Frederick William exclaimed. "You

can't just invent new realms out of whole cloth..."

"I think you'll find that I can," Joseph said. "If that's what it takes to ensure good governance. The people's foolish nationalism should be directed to constructive ends, not suppressed like jamming the valve down on a boiling steam engine." He smiled at that. "I've been talking to poor Leopold too much with his steam engine mania."

Frederick William threw down the document. "Do what you want, but I will not support this." He turned to storm out.

"A pity," Joseph said aloud. "I thought Brandenburg and that estate in Flanders too minor for your talents. Of course these reforms will render your titles somewhat obsolete, and when I make my brother Holy Italian Emperor, he would benefit from a steadfast advisor as ruler of Naples and Sicily..."

"Ruler, you say?" Frederick William asked, his eyes suddenly keen. Not every man would see those lands as desirable, but Joseph knew all too well that Frederick William had been visiting the region for years to see the Bonaparte family, who continued to rule the island of Elba. That friendship had survived generations, and Frederick William loved the land as well as the people. "With what title?"

Joseph smiled and lifted up the paper again. "I'm making this up as I go along," he said dryly. "What title would you *like?*"

August 14th, 1931
Jozefstadt, Imperial Colony of Kongo

Oskar Schindler wiped blood from the corner of his mouth, his swollen tongue feeling the gap where a tooth had been knocked out. He made an indistinct sound. It didn't really matter: by now Leopold knew that what it amounted to was "I'll never talk!"

The true ruler of Imperial Kongo—regardless of what official documents might say—lounged on a chair opposite the one that Schindler was tied to, while his bullyboys Skorzeny and Schickelgruber beat him. "Must this go on much longer?" he asked boredly. A few people might still consider him to be Leopold III, King of Great Britain—a nation that had not had a monarch for almost a hundred years, since they overthrew and executed Leopold's great-grandmother. To Schindler, he was simply a monster and a criminal.

"Not much longer," Schindler said indistinctly. "When do the papers come out?"

Leopold frowned at him, then muttered something at

Schickelgruber. The moustachioed henchman didn't look like much of a threat compared to the muscular Skorzeny, but Schindler had already learned that there was a brutal sadist behind that moustachioed face. Only a few minutes passed before Schickelgruber returned brandishing a newspaper. If you could call it that; these papers were effectively just telegraph messages cobbled together, with limited text and no pictures. It was enough to make it clear just how late Leopold was to stop Schindler.

Leopold threw down the paper. "This was your great story?" he sneered. "So you've proven that I ordered the burnings of those villages that refused to pay their taxes. So what? Do you really think European public opinion will care about what happens to a few black Africans?" He didn't use those exact words, but Schindler mentally refined them.

"They may care more than you'd think," Schindler said. "The papers are full of horror stories coming out of Argentina and Chile since the USA took them over." The last parts of the Americas to fall to the vile ideology of Democracy, a word now synonymous with the whip hand of the slave overseer. "Enough, perhaps, for people to realise that blacks may actually be their fellow human beings."

"How quaint," Leopold sneered. "You forget, my young heroic crusading journalist, that a story can be bumped off the front page by a bigger one." He triumphantly flipped the paper over. "The so-called Premier of Britain just declared war on King Louis XXII. War between Britain and France has begun!"

Schindler closed his eyes. That had been predicted for a while, all that sniping between the rival powers in India, even as the Hapsburg powers swallowed up Africa and East Asia. Two bald men fighting over a comb, as one commentator had put it. But it had clearly escalated towards a real battle that might stretch across the earth.

And Leopold would go free. Maybe a war-weary Britain would even overthrow its republican government and install him as King again, dismissing stories of his horrific crimes as the tales of one obscure journalist with an axe to grind.

He could not let that happen. And so he pressed his feet together, feeling for the catch that Elser had installed. The man was a carpenter, not a cobbler, and would have preferred to have something the size of a briefcase to work with, but that had been impossible. Those shoes with their rather thick soles, concealing...

He found the catch, and everything turned to whiteness and

pain. Briefly.

November 15th, 1979
Sea of Tranquillity, the Moon

Arnold Schwarzenegger gave one last nod to his fellow astronauts as he took the most important step in human history. The choice of what words to speak had echoed in his head for months, despite everything else, the training and stress and heart-stopping moments as the rocket *Otto von Guericke* finally lifted off. Three days later, they were finally here at the moon. They had beaten the Americans, whose first rocket attempt, *George Washington*, had blown up and delayed their programme. Their second rocket, named after the man they considered to be the USA's second greatest president, was still on the launch pad. Schwarzenegger looked up at the Earth in the sky and imagined the great rocket *John C. Calhoun*, sitting there impotently at the American rocket launch site in their State of Venezuela surrounded by slave gangs pulling fuel tanks.

He allowed himself a brief grin at the victory, but realised that such a sentiment was inappropriate. This was not a time to divide humanity, but to unite it. "So man takes his first step onto the moon," he said in the Latin that had long been the lingua franca promoted in the diverse Hapsburg realms, and with the decline of France had become the global language. Only in the American sphere, both of the American continents plus Australia and Britain—both now reduced to American states—could English and Spanish compete. The global Cold War between the Hapsburgs and Democrats was as much a war of language as of ideology.

Schwarzenegger continued: "With this step, we finally loose ourselves from the shackles of the earth—" a good subtle jab there, "—and reach out to the heavens in all their glorious wonder, the creation of God. We stand united, nations and languages and creeds," he nodded to his compatriots, a Czech named Cernan and a Hungarian named Lugosi, "and face the new path that stands before us. All of human history up to now has been only Chapter One: now we turn the page and begin the rest of the book."

He fell silent for a moment, allowing that grin to split his face again as he kicked up the grey lunar dust in wonder, felt the weak gravity beneath his feet barely hold him down. He looked up at the Earth once again, turning in all its majesty. "And..."

"And if you'll permit me one moment of national self-indulgence...when I was a child, I once saw a reproduction of a tapestry that hangs in the Schönbrunn Palace in Vienna. It bears the letters A E I O U, and I first I thought it was only about listing the vowels. But my teacher, a great man and admirer of Professor Einstein—I wish he could have lived to see his rocket finally fly—my teacher explained to me that the letters stood for a motto. A motto coined by Emperor Frederick III many centuries ago. He said that it stood for *Austriae est imperare orbi universo* – 'Austria shall rule all the world'.'"

Schwarzenegger laughed and stamped his foot, bringing up more moon dust that streaked his spacesuit. Almost like eighteenth-century wig powder. "I see now he was lacking ambition!"

The Archers
by DJ Tyrer

I. Able Archer

"I suppose we should be glad we're not slogging all this kit on a hot summer's day," said Private Archer as they advanced through the West German countryside. Instead, they were slogging it about on a damp November's day.

Sammy Archer was a private in the Royal Suffolk Regiment and was on manoeuvres as part of the Able Archer 83 exercise. If the proverbial balloon ever went up, they'd be doing this for real in the face of the Red Army.

"Give peace a chance, eh?" grinned his mate, Mickey.

"Give the bloody Reds a damn-good thrashing, more like!" laughed Bob.

"Damn straight!" Sammy agreed. They all, just a little wished they could do it for real. The Soviet Union would never rest until it ruled the world. Everyone knew that conflict would come one day, and they'd all like to do their bit.

"Right, here we are, boys," Lance Corporal Black called. "Take up position."

They were to dig in and set up their GPMG. If this were for real, they'd be part of the front line blocking force, tasked with holding up the Soviet advance long enough for the NATO forces behind them to react.

"I heard a rumour," Bob said, "that we might be going in for real, that this is just a cover for a surprise attack on the Soviets."

"Be good if it was," said Mickey. "I mean, we beat Hitler all those years ago, then just let the Russians march in and take everything. About time we sorted them out!"

"Seems unlikely, though," said Sammy, getting the gun set up.

"Yeah," agreed Mickey. "Mrs T and Ronnie might talk tough, but nobody dares cross the line. Everyone's scared of being nuked."

"Well, if they were going to do it, now would be a good time, with the Soviets busy in Afghanistan," Bob offered.

"Nah," said Sammy, "nobody wants to see nukes detonating all over the show."

As he said that, there was a sudden flash, a wave of heat, somewhere to their left, followed by a tugging suck of air.

"What the hell!" somebody exclaimed.

Turning to look, they saw a distinctive cloud rising skyward. There was another flash and a stronger wave of heat from somewhere behind them. The wind that followed nearly pulled them over.

"Dammit..." muttered Sammy, "they've gone and done it; they've really gone and done it..."

"Ready, lads!" Lance Corporal Black was yelling."This is for real!"

They looked forwards, scanning the horizon for any signs of the Soviet advance. Then, there was another flash and they knew nothing more.

II. Alone

Cathy Archer was alone. Her father had been killed by a drunk driver when she was a little girl; her mother had died during the horrendous Winter of Discontent, from cancer. Her husband was in the army, across the Channel, on an exercise. Had been. For all she knew, he was dead.

A hand slipped to her belly and she sucked in a sob. She'd nobody to rely upon.

She was proud of him, serving Queen and Country, she really was, but she could've done with Sammy right now. But, he would've told her: that was the way it was; his family had always been soldiers. He'd told her their name derived from an ancestor who was an archer at Agincourt and she didn't doubt him.

The flat, the upstairs of an Edwardian house, was cold and dark. Raindrops trickled down the windows. Cathy went to the kitchen and checked the cupboards, but they remained stubbornly bare. Ever since the power went out, nothing had worked. Not all the cars had died, but there were no new deliveries of fuel. Whilst her radio continued to work thanks to its batteries, there was nothing but static. There was no news; no food; nothing but rumours.

There was a knock and she cautiously crept downstairs to the front door. After she'd realised there would be no more food deliveries, Cathy had ceased going out. Tempers were fraying and there were rumours of riots. She was terrified. A confusing, angry world had transformed into nightmare.

Looking through the spy-hole, she saw it was her downstairs neighbour, Mrs Leaming. She opened the door.

"Come in."

Her neighbour shuffled in. She had to be seventy.

"For you," she said, shoving a half-packet of digestives at her. "Cost a pretty penny, but I don't need them all. I thought it could keep you – Oh, now, don't cry..."

Mrs Leaming reached out to pat her shoulder. Cathy took the biscuits. "Thank you."

"Let's get you upstairs," the old woman told her, gently guiding her. "They say the Americans and Russians have destroyed each other, that there's no-one left."

When she'd last seen her neighbour, Mrs Leaming had claimed London and most of America had gone up in mushroom clouds and that the Russians had swept through Europe and were poised to invade Britain. What was true and what was false were unknowns. Perhaps the worst was over. Perhaps the worst was still to come.

"Is there no news at all?" Cathy asked.

Mrs Leaming shook her head. "Just rumours, dear. You want to know your husband's alright, don't you?" Cathy nodded as the old woman's gaze grew distant. "Oh, he was a bonnie chap in uniform."

Cathy began to cry.

"Oh, I'm sorry." The old lady hugged her tight. "Keep your faith, dear."

Cathy wished she could.

Just then, she became aware of a sound, an unfamiliar sound. Other than the constant patter of the rain on the glass, the area had been quiet since the power failed, too quiet, with none of the familiar sounds of traffic and daily life.

"Do you hear that?" she whispered through her tears.

"Eh?"

"Do you hear that?" Cathy asked again. The sound was louder, a sort of wheezing and a chikkity-clack, chikkity-clack, rhythmic.

"Hear what?"

"Outside." She stood, pulling away from Mrs Leaming, and ran to the window. The sound was close now. At the rear of the house ran a railway line and looking down it she saw a train. But, neither the sound nor sight of it was like any train she'd seen run past before – those had been diesel and this was a steam train.

Mrs Leaming swore softly. She'd never heard her elderly neighbour swear before.

The locomotive was decorated with bunting – red, white and blue – strangely defiant against the rain, and a Union Flag flew from the roof of the cab.

As it passed the house, a whistle sounded, seeming to announce hope.

Behind the locomotive were a series of covered wagons supplemented by a pair of carriages through the windows of which they could see men in uniform.

"Soldiers," breathed Cathy. To her, the word meant salvation. She'd no illusions that Sammy was on the train, but she trusted the military to set things right.

"If that's food in there," Mrs Leaming said as the train disappeared up the track, "we're saved."

"I believe we are," Cathy smiled, hugging her, "I believe were are."

They each ate a digestive in celebration.

III. ALARM

The wail of a hand-cranked siren that had seen service during the Blitz was an imperative squawk of alarm. With fallout not proving much a problem, Britain having avoided a groundburst, the sound almost certainly presaged violence: raiders or rioters.

On her way for an antenatal check-up, Cathy Archer realised she was nearer to the medical center than the shelter. Waddling as fast as she could, she headed there instead. It wasn't secure like the shelter was, but it was in what had been a newsagent's, so had a rear exit. Cathy had a fear of the shelter being breached and being trapped there.

From somewhere, Cathy could hear angry shouts, the sound of breaking glass and gunshots. It sounded like a riot. Despite the ostensive restoration of order, anger seemed to explode into violence with greater frequency than it had during the dark days of confusion before the army had restored order. Cathy had a suspicion that then most people had been in a sort of daze. Now that the army had restored a semblance of normality, people had something to complain about and the luxury to protest. Besides the bandits who preferred theft to work, there were plenty unwilling to knuckle under to the new order: the socialists were stirring trouble, of course, and there were plenty more who were disgruntled, unhappy with rationing or being put to work rebuilding society.

"Take cover!" she heard a voice shout. It was a muffled cry. Looking round, she saw a soldier in camouflage waving at her to get off the street; he wore a gasmask and carried a rifle. Behind him was a policeman, his blue uniform replaced by green fatigues, who also wore a gasmask and carried an old Lee Enfield rifle with bayonet fixed: the new face of policing.

Cathy went as fast as she could, knowing tear gas was likely to be used. Reaching the medical center, she slipped inside.

"Come in." A young woman in a neatly-pressed police uniform ushered her inside and bolted the door behind her; there was no time to pull the shutters down. Cathy gratefully realised the woman had guessed she was nearby, that it was time for her appointment.

The WPC, with a basic training in first aid, had been seconded to the center as a sort of nurse. It was her that Cathy had been seeing; she'd no idea what had happened to the midwife. She wished she could remember the girl's name.

"We should go into the back," the WPC said, hustling her through a door into a storeroom lined with basic medical supplies. "Don't worry, Mrs Archer, I'll look after you."

Between looting and the increase in illness and injuries, hospitals, doctor's surgeries and pharmacies were either unavailable or restricted to emergencies. Such temporary medical centers as this were run by WPCs and girls from the WRAF and WRVS while the Transitional Government, as the eight military districts were called, worked to rebuild the country.

The sounds of rioting grew nearer and gunshots rang out. Cathy clutched the woman's arm in fear. Seconds later, they heard the shattering of glass from the front of the shop.

"Into the yard," the WPC said, helping Cathy outside.

The rioters might be intent on looting medical supplies – a valuable commodity – or be targeting a symbol of the military authority or just venting their rage at random. Whatever their motivation, it was best to let them get on and leave them to the troops to deal with: which meant shooting them on sight.

Cathy and the WPC took shelter in a small outbuilding stacked high with cardboard boxes, with a bicycle shoved in beside them. Cathy wrinkled her nose in displeasure; the place smelt very damp. She felt a twinge in her belly and hoped it was just the baby moving position. Now really wasn't the time to go into labour.

"Stay behind me," the WPC said. "I'll protect you."

Her voice had a cheery, sing-song quality to it that was too brittle to conceal the incipient panic beneath it. Unarmed, there wasn't much she could do if a rioter came at them intent on violence. That there was also determination in her voice told Cathy she'd do her duty. Cathy found herself thinking abstractedly that it was just that sense of duty that would see Britain rise from the ashes of the electromagnetic pulse that had wiped the technological slate clean.

They stood tensely in the shadowy interior of the shed. A spider scuttled across the floor. The only sound was their breathing, which they fought to control. They heard the sound of the rear door of the shop open and someone enter the yard. A moment later the door of the shed was yanked open.

A man was silhouetted in the doorway. He had a knife in his hand. He stepped into the shed.

"Stay back!" the WPC said, her voice rising. She glanced back over her shoulder to make sure she was interposed between him and Cathy.

He ignored her, stepped forward. His face was a mask of rage.

"Please..." the policewoman whispered as he drew back his hand.

Cathy screamed as the blade stabbed into the woman. Without even thinking, Cathy reached for the closest thing to a weapon she could see: the bicycle pump.

The policewoman had slumped against the pile of cardboard boxes, blood pouring from her side.

As the man raised his knife for another strike, Cathy swung the pump as a club. It caught his shoulder and he staggered, the blow deferred as he turned to face her.

Time seemed to halt as Cathy stared into eyes filled with hatred and she knew she was going to die. She heard the WPC mumble something, but wasn't listening. She was wondering if her husband was waiting for her in Heaven or if Sammy would return home to find her and their unborn child dead. She felt cheated.

Then, thunder clapped and the man's forehead seemed to blossom open in a flower of blood.

Time suddenly sped up again. Cathy vomited and the man crashed, dead, into the cardboard boxes. A soldier stood in the doorway, his rifle levelled at the man's body.

The soldier shouted over his shoulder for assistance.

Cathy felt a surge of relief. Once more, she was thankful to the soldiers for her salvation.

IV. ACHIEVEMENT

"Things have really settled down since the bombs," opined the Major General who was in charge of day-to-day civilian government in the military district. "It is a real achievement. We are well on our way to restoring regular government and daily life."

Cathy Archer sat to the left of his desk, taking notes. Thanks to Mrs Leaming providing babysitting services for her, Cathy had been able to return to work. Praised for her intervention in saving the life of the WPC, no matter how pathetic she thought her actions, it seemed she was very much in the authority's good books and her application to do secretarial work had seen her fast tacked to assist the Major General. Despite some trepidation when she took the position, Cathy felt proud to be assisting the army that had done so much for her.

But, despite her pride, Cathy's conscience had begun to niggle at her, that something wasn't quite right. Only, she'd no idea what. It was no single point, but some trend or connection of dots that evaded her conscious mind. Unable to put her finger on just what was bothering her, she said nothing, not wishing to upset the affable officer with vague paranoid thoughts.

Instead, Cathy made a decision. Quite often, she was one of the last to leave the office that had been established in the old town hall, filing away the day's paperwork or typing up her shorthand notes. It was no problem for her to remain behind until the Major General and his staff had left. There were two WRAF girls on the reception over night and a handful of guards, but none of them would bother her.

Once she was certain she was alone, Cathy went into the room where the filing cabinets and file boxes were stored. Methodically, she began to go through the files, taking out those that caught at her mind, even if the reason wasn't apparent. Then, once she'd gathered up several high piles of such files, she began to read through them in detail, trying to tease out just what it was that didn't sit right with her, making notes.

Slowly, it dawned on her. Despite what the Major General had said, the Transitional Government had no intention of restoring 'regular' government or daily life. They would restore a semblance of it, but not what had existed before the electromagnetic pulse, that much was clear.

Cathy resolved to confront the Major General with her suspicions.

She was in the office first thing, barely having slept at all, having stayed in the office all night. She expected Mrs Leaming would not be best pleased when finally she saw her. Of course, that rather depended upon how the Major General reacted when she spoke to him.

"Ah, Mrs Archer, getting an early start, eh?" the officer said as he entered his office and laid a bundle of files on his desk.

"Sir, I have something I have to ask you," Cathy said.

"Sounds ominous," he said with a chuckle.

"It is, I suppose." She took a deep breath. "I've been looking through some of the files, because, well, things have been bothering me. Little things that add up..."

"Oh, dear," the Major General said, sitting down. "This does sound serious, please go on."

"You said, yesterday, that you'd be returning things to how they were before the bombs, but you aren't."

He didn't react.

She went on. "I've been looking at the files on the rebuilding, at the handover power, at the new laws: each innocuous enough on its own, but together...

"You have no intention of restoring things to how they were. You're lying to us. You aren't rebuilding the factories we need; you aren't replacing stuff that doesn't work anymore; you aren't putting the old Parliament back as it was; you're stripping away rights."

He gave a soft chuckle and steepled his fingers as he looked at her with a smile. "Very observant, Mrs Archer. That's exactly why you're my secretary: you're good at your job. Yes, you are quite right: we've no intention of flicking a switch and just putting things back to how they were."

Cathy looked at the Major General in confusion. She'd expected denials or threats, not an amused admission.

The officer continued. "Now, of course, we didn't want to just come out and say things would never be as they were. Partly, because we want the new system to come about naturally over time rather than through wholesale change, and partly because we want to focus on the positive aspects, not expect people to accept a raft of changes in one go that they will, naturally, mistrust."

She couldn't help but nod at that. It sounded reasonable. He smiled at her reaction.

"I think you would agree there was much about Britain before the bombs we're well rid of: trade union strikes, punks, feckless youths, corrupt politicians... I could go on. It is also a fact, however much we might like to imagine otherwise, that there is much about our old way of life that we just cannot restore. America is gone and Japan is a mess. Our own manufacturing base had died from a thousand cuts. Modern conveniences are beyond our reach; we have to look for simpler alternatives.

"Our oil imports won't resume for some time, and restoring access to North Sea oil and gas won't be easy. But, we have coal, which can supply most of our needs. Why try to build costly new diesel locomotives that may never run when we can add to our fleet of steam trains? Why build factories to make tape players that run on batteries we don't have when a wind-up gramophone can play records without them?"

"It does sound reasonable," she admitted, dreams of a grand conspiracy vanishing away like dew before the rising sun.

"We have a God-given opportunity," the officer concluded, "to rebuild the country as we would have it and we must seize it with both hands. Suez, Communist subversion, becoming a glorified aircraft carrier for America... all these things sapped the British will and ground us down. Now, we have the opportunity to make Britain great again; a country we can be proud of – and you have the opportunity to play your part in doing that..."

Cathy considered that. Were they making the right decisions? It was a seductive presentation. She wondered what her husband would think of the Transitional Government's vision. Her Sammy had always said that what the country needed was a dictatorship to sort things out; that Thatcher hadn't quite gone far enough. He'd want to see Britain strong again. She thought he'd approve of what they wanted to do, although maybe not all of them: he was quite keen on his pop music.

"Can we count on your support?" the Major General asked.

Slowly, she nodded her agreement and he smiled again. They were building a new world and she would play her part in the building of it. She just hoped it would be worth it.

V. Afterwards

Sammy Archer stepped down from the train, steam and smoke lazily escaping from the locomotive. He'd been away a long time.

Cathy Archer stood on the platform, waiting for him, waved when she saw him.

Hefting his kitbag onto his shoulder, he walked towards her.

She ran towards him, hugged him and kissed him.

"Hello, Mum," he cried, returning her hugs and kisses.

"Oh, I've missed you, love." She stood back and gazed at him, admiringly. "You look just like your dad."

Raised on tales of his father and his ancestors, and of the steam trains that had saved them after the country died, Sammy Archer, Junior, had become a Royal Engineer. He'd seen service all over the globe, wherever Britain's interests lay in the world that had risen, phoenix-like, from the ashes of the one that died in nuclear flame and electromagnetic pulse. A world as different to the one his father knew as that had been to the one his great-grandfather had inhabited.

"I've got some news, Mum," he said, as they walked along the platform towards the station exit.

"Oh, what's that love?"

"I've met a girl. Her name's Lizzy. We're planning on getting married."

She paused and hugged him again. "Oh, that's wonderful, dear!"

Cathy imagined a day, so many years before that it belonged to a different world, her Sammy telling his mother he'd proposed to her. She wished he'd lived to see this day, but, she hoped, somewhere he was looking down and smiling. His son was like him in so many ways.

She tried to imagine a world in which the fragile peace between East and West had held, rather than war burning bright for one brief, final moment. She tried to imagine what things would've been like with oil and electricity in place of coal and steam: a world that had embraced the future rather than retreating to the past. She tried to imagine her life, with her husband, in that world. Only, she couldn't. The might-have-beens had long since been drowned beneath the necessities of reality, of rebuilding.

The world had been reborn from that crucible of flame, perhaps better, certainly different. All the hopes and fears that had existed before had been erased by the pain of loss and replaced by a new set adapted to the new world. What-might-have-been no longer mattered to her. All that mattered was what-would-be. The Archers would continue for another generation, she was certain; many more, she hoped, carrying on the family's proud tradition for many years to come.

Ave, Caesarion
by Deborah L. Davitt

Not to know what happened before you were born is to be a child
forever. For what is the time of a man, except it be interwoven with that
memory of ancient things of a superior age?

—Marcus Tullius Cicero

Iunius 30, 15 *Ascensio Caesare*

On this warm summer evening, fifteen years after Julius Caesar
had been crowned in the Forum of Rome, the Empire held its breath.
Rumor—fleeter of foot than Mercury—swept through the city, from
patrician homes to plebeian ones, whispering that Gaius Julius Caesar
had suffered some manner of fit. It had long been murmured that he
was subject to the falling-sickness, perhaps contracted in tropical
climes, or meted out as punishment by the gods for having dared to
ascend so far. More troubling, however, were Rumor's sly additions to
her tale: that the seventy-year-old emperor could not rise, and that his
foreign-born wife, Cleopatra, would not leave his side, whispering
spells and incantations to keep him alive.

The freeborn muttered in the marketplaces; the Empress might
be a curse on Rome. Their beloved Emperor had divorced his third
wife, Calpurnia, after his coronation, and had extended to Cleopatra
and the Hellene-Egyptian House of Ptolemy *Roman citizenship* for
"services to the Empire." Italians who had only recently been granted
citizenship spat at those words; her *services*, in their opinion, were
those of a harlot, and the rights that their grandfathers had died for in
the Social War had been granted to her for what lay between her thighs.

Few in Rome understood that the bread distributed by the government—the *Annona*—came at such a low cost to the state solely because Egypt's fertile fields provided their plenty at the whim of their queen.

In the last light of sunset, five cohorts of legionnaires marched along the *Via Flaminia* towards the gates of Rome, accompanying two young men on horseback. The dirt and dust on their uniforms suggested a long journey, conducted rapidly. The senior centurion and all the men on foot were hardened soldiers in their thirties, members of the Legio X *Equestris*—the first legion levied by Julius Caesar. The *Equestris* formed the backbone of Caesar's Praetorian Guard, the personal protectors accorded to many a general over the centuries. Hence the distinctive white crests on the helmets of their officers.

Of the pair on horseback, the elder, who wore the long white crest of a tribune of the Tenth Legion, didn't look to have escaped his adolescent years; the younger, who wore no uniform, but rather just a tunic and cloak suitable for riding, looked barely old enough to have received his *toga virilis*. "Malleolus! Fall the men out," the older of the pair called to the centurion, reining in. "Let them eat and bathe and see their families. But be at my father's villa outside of Rome first thing in the morning."

The centurion thumped his breastplate in acknowledgement, and the weary legionnaires gave a desultory cheer. But the centurion let the rest of his men file past, and then caught the young officer's reins before he could thump a heel into his horse's flanks. "I'll be going with you, *dominus*?" Malleolus asked. It wasn't quite a question.

The corners of the young man's mouth kinked upwards slightly. "This is Rome."

"Yes, my lord." Solemn acknowledgement. "And fifteen years ago, seven men tried to murder your father. On the sacred soil of Rome."

The young man put a hand on his shoulder, imperceptible through the armor. "I'm harder to kill than my father, Malleolus. Though I thank you for your care." In the last rays of sunset, his eyes gleamed an unnatural shade under the shadows cast by his helm—the color of spilled blood. For Ptolemy XV Julius Caesarion Philopator Philomator—generally called Caesarion—was god-born.

His mother, Cleopatra, who had made her son co-ruler of Egypt with herself when he was no more than three, claimed that the blood of

Isis and Osiris ran in her veins. His father had once minted coins that reminded the people of Rome that his house claimed descent from Venus. And none could deny that Mars had favored Caesar on the battlefield as well. Yet neither of his parents had shown the signs of divine favor as clearly as Caesarion did.

Malleolus released the reins, saying mildly, "I would sleep better tonight, my lord, if you'd allow me to follow you to the villa's gates."

A quick smile. "You're going to insist?"

"I would never so presume. But I do ask, *dominus*."

"For the sake of your good rest, then, yes." A nod, and then the young patrician clucked at his horse, preparing to enter the city. But now his brother, young Alexander, caught the reins. "Caesarion," Alexander said, his voice tight, "You're not carrying a sword. You *can* enter the city legally. But . . . if you enter now, you're giving up your right to a triumph."

"I don't care," Caesarion replied impatiently. "Father had a choice once, between being accorded a triumph for his victories, and standing for election as consul. He chose the consulship. You pick the thing that's more important. And seeing him before he dies . . . that's more important." He grimaced. "And ensuring that we're here to deal with issues of succession, too. Gods. I hate thinking like this."

Alexander shook his head sharply. Five years younger than his brother, he still seemed to have more political acumen. "A triumph will ensure the love of the plebeians. And you *must* have the mob behind you before dealing with the Senate."

Caesarion's expression tautened. "It's strange, Alexander. I see your face, but I hear our mother's voice when you speak." An impatient shake of his head. "Every man who stood with me in Germania deserves that triumph. They all deserve that recognition, because without the men who *followed* me, the seventh Legion would have been cut off, surrounded, and destroyed in that damned forest." His face settled into stubborn lines. "But holding a triumph instead of making my way to Father's deathbed?" He regarded Alexander steadily. "Bad taste. It would look as if I valued his position more than his life." He stared at the Porta Flaminia, and then turned his head and spat into the dust at the side of the road. "To Dis with the damned triumph. Let's go home, brother."

Centurion Ramirus Modius Malleolus trotted silently alongside the pair as they entered the city. They looked far too young to bear the weight of the Empire on their shoulders. *But Caesarion will have to carry it.* And in spite of the young man's high rank and youth, he *liked* Caesarion. Uncannily, almost everyone did. The love of his father's legions was mostly assured, but Malleolus had seen freedmen and slaves who served the legionnaires in their camps—men who hated anyone with a patrician name—smile when Caesarion addressed them.

He sighed, and kept his eyes on the people crowding the streets. No one had yet given them more than a glance, but someone had to keep these two youngsters alive.

"Why so quiet, Malleolus?" Alexander asked as they pushed through a marketplace. The stripling had been sent on his brother's campaign mostly to learn how military camps worked.

"I don't mind fighting wars, *dominus,*" Ramirus replied tersely. "Not looking forward to another civil one, though."

Caesarion's head turned towards him. Malleolus prepared for a reprimand—he'd overstepped with that reply. But Caesarion surprised him. "Rome's always at war," he replied. "Constantly pushing out the borders. Bringing the light of our laws to the unwashed barbarians on our periphery."

The words would have been innocuous to the ears of any Roman citizen. The tone, however, distinguished them. Pure irony, inviting Ramirus in. Suggesting a hint of *likeness* between the centurion and the god-born son of the Imperator.

And for an instant, Ramirus saw it. Ramirus' Gallic mother had been taken as a slave somewhere in Hispania, explaining the centurion's blond hair and height. She'd jumped into the Tiber to save the life of one of the noble children in her care, resulting in both her manumission and the noble name that she and her freeborn son bore. *And this young patrician's mother is as much a* barbarian *to Rome as mine. While she didn't enter Rome as a slave, but as a queen . . . in this, if nothing else, he and I are alike.*

"The problem," Caesarion said now quietly, "is the same in Rome's empire as it was in Alexander's."

His younger brother's head swung towards him. Over the jingle of armor and tack, he exclaimed, "Alexander the Great conquered the known world!" The young man's tone held bewilderment. "His body is kept in a temple in Alexandria, and he's worshipped as a god, for all that he was as human as I am." A hint of pride in the young man's voice, for his namesake; *he wasn't even a god-born like you, brother. And look what he accomplished.*

"Oh, he conquered it. And our own forefather Ptolemy found himself the ruler of a kingdom for his loyalty to his lord." The irony hadn't left Caesarion's voice. "The problem, brother, isn't conquering the world. It's *holding* it. Keeping the provinces from rebelling. Keeping the government from becoming more corrupt. Keeping the lines of communications open. All the administrative details at which conquerors usually fail." He frowned. "So yes, Malleolus. As you say . . . civil war might well arise once more."

Stunned at his inclusion in this conversation, the centurion remained silent. But at the villa any misapprehensions the centurion might have had of being a kindred spirit dissipated as the young men disappeared into the elegant edifice, leaving him unattended.

Caesarion looked back to give the centurion a grateful, if dismissive wave, and then ducked through the door to dart upstairs to his father's chambers, where he knocked. "Enter," his mother's voice called, and Caesarion obeyed, Alexander at his heels.

Inside, the smells of effluvia and illness struck him, even covered by the odor of costly incense, and his nostrils twitched. He'd smelled this before in the triage tents, as bowels evacuated and wounds turned septic. *He* is *dying,* Caesarion thought, but controlled his face, stepping forward to take his mother's hands in greeting as she rose from Caesar's bedside.

Forty years old, Cleopatra had been celebrated for decades as the greatest beauty the world had seen since Helen of Troy. Some of that praise was pablum; her nose could most kindly be described as *beaky,* and a large mole interrupted the smooth arc of one of her eyebrows. Lines had graven themselves on her face in the past year, and the first traces of white flecked her dark hair. However, her eyes still captured the attention of anyone who met her: large, dark, and wrapped in kohl, they sparkled with a ferocious intellect. "I'm relieved that you made good time over the Alps," Cleopatra murmured with careful restraint, though her eyes were luminous with tears. "He's been drifting in and out of consciousness for two days."

"A seizure?" Caesarion asked, taking a seat at his father's bedside.

"Not one of the usual ones. He can't raise his right arm." Cleopatra exhaled, obviously tightly controlling her face and voice for the benefit of the Egyptian servants hovering outside the door. "He told me that once you arrived, he'd trouble me to assist him with cutting his wrists."

Caesarion's head snapped up. "I'll do it," he told his mother, immediately. "You shouldn't have to—"

"Peace. A son's hands should not be stained with a father's blood." Her lips quirked, then quivered. "No matter how many times that has occurred in my family's history."

Julius Caesar opened his eyes and extended his left hand shakily for Caesarion's. Alexander crowded close as Caesar croaked, "Bring Lepidus." His voice was nearly inaudible. "Witness."

His Master of the Horse, Marcus Aemilius Lepidus, a patrician in his own right, was quickly fetched. In his fifties and completely loyal, he stood beside his emperor's bed, face composed and without tears, as Caesar spoke again, with difficulty. "My will . . . lodged with the Vestals. Coin set aside for Alexander and my daughters. Caesarion, you are my principal heir. You know this." He closed his eyes. "Listen to Lepidus. Lean on him. Too old for a regent . . . never too old . . . for good counsel." His fingers tightened on Caesarion's. "Marry one of Crassus' granddaughters, if you can. You'll need their wealth. Keep the Legions *paid*, and they'll never betray you. Be wary of Octavius and Antony. They are . . . jealous. Hungry. Use them . . . against each other." His words slurred, and he opened his eyes once more, looking now at Cleopatra. "And if you happen to find love . . . consider yourself fortunate. But never let it dissuade you from duty."

Caesarion nodded, his throat tight. *I'm not ready, Father. You can't leave us.* But to give such weak and mewling words voice would not have comforted the dying man.

A pause, and then an almost incoherent mumble: "The sword . . . lost it at the river. Touched . . . by Mars. Find it . . . ." And moments after those final, inexplicable words, which sounded like the unraveling of mind that had lost all lucidity, Gaius Julius Caesar died without troubling anyone for the favor of a knife, after all.

Cleopatra put her head on the bed beside him and wept silently. Uncomfortable, unable to show his grief for a man that he'd followed loyally for close to thirty years, Lepidus turned towards Caesarion. "Shall I make the announcement and begin the traditional nine days of rituals?"

Caesarion stared blankly at the man for a moment. And the mill that is Rome grinds on, its great wheels churning. One man dies, and is ground to dust, and the next must take his place. "Yes. We'll need a procession with all the family images. Mummers from the theater to carry them." He didn't know what to make of the words about the sword, and since no one around him commented on them, either, he put it aside.

Lepidus cleared his throat. "You won't address the Senate until you've finished his funeral oration?" A delicate question, that. If Caesarion did address the Senate before the funeral was over, and asked them to vote on passing his father's position as Emperor to him, it could be taken greatly amiss. On the other hand, if he didn't, there would be a power vacuum in Rome for nine days.

Nine days were an eternity in which many plots and plans could unfold.

* * *

Quintilis 7, 15 AC

At a comfortable villa in the Palatine Hill district, Gaius Octavius Thurinus, generally called Octavian, lounged in the *triclinium*, his body relaxed, but his mind alert. His first guest had arrived— Marcus Antonius—the wine had been poured, and the servants dismissed. He regarded the older man, his eyes narrow as he studied the graying dark curls and the bags under Antony's eyes. "It's good to have you here," he told Antony. "You've completed your year's mourning for my sister, and are ready to rejoin the world of the living once more?" *Not that you ever truly left it.* But the polite fiction left room for Antony to behave as if they both believed he was a better man than he was.

Antony's lips curled as he sipped from his cup. "Yes, I'm ready. And yet, in the moment I leave off my mourning, I have cause to put it back on once more, for Caesar has passed." A pause, as both men regarded one another like duelists; measuring, assessing. "Caesar was, after all, the one who sponsored my marriage to your beautiful sister." Another polite fiction. Antony had merely tolerated his wife for decades, often seeking out more . . . stimulating company in Rome's teeming brothels, or among slaves he purchased for precisely that purpose.

Octavian smiled faintly, suppressing his loathing. Antony could be *useful*, if properly motivated. "Yes. My uncle brought you into the family."

"My mother was already his cousin—" Snapped with all the furious pride of a plebeian who had *one* noble relation.

"Of course," Octavian soothed. "I meant to say that he *embraced* you as kin when you married my sister." He paused, smiling into his cup. "As I still do, brother," he added. "Regardless of my sister's untimely passage, you will always be kin to me." He paused again. Affiliations and affirmations dispensed with, it was time to draw nearer to the heart of the matter. "I've heard that Lepidus was named as guardian for Caesar's younger children," he murmured, watching a muscle twitch in Antony's cheek.

"Lepidus," Antony replied scornfully. "He's spent the last fifteen years licking Caesar's arse. Of *course* he's been named their guardian."

A brooding silence followed, which Octavian could have filled with words. Could have said, *Fifteen years spent as Master of the Horse made him Caesar's right hand, not an arse-licker.* Instead, he took another sip of his wine and murmured, "You weren't named at all?"

Another twitch of a jaw muscle. "No. Seems he forgot all my loyal service."

"A pity. Though not all patricians have such faulty memories." Octavian smiled again as Antony's head jerked up. "However, I'm not sure that Lepidus is the correct man to oversee the upbringing of Caesar's children. Nor to advise young Caesarion. He's . . . cautious."

"He's been coasting for decades on a reputation for knowing when to fight and when to negotiate since that business in Hispania," Antony replied dismissively—glossing over, Octavian noted, Lepidus' notable military successes against Pompey during the civil wars. "He's an old woman these days. And this is a time that calls for boldness."

No unexpected sentiments. "It seems that perhaps young Caesarion needs more capable advisors," Octavian replied.

"Young Caesarion," Antony replied acidly, "isn't likely to listen to me. His mother has hated me since I first met her in Egypt. When she was no more than fourteen." His eyes seemed to peer through the decades between that moment and this. "So damnably beautiful, even then."

And there was another potential piece of leverage, though Octavian had no way to use it at the moment. Antony lived his life at the surface of his skin, his lusts and hungers clearly evident. "Yes," Octavian responded meditatively. "It's a shame that young Caesarion is so . . . filled with his mother's teachings. One might say that she's poisoned him against Rome."

Antony's suddenly sharp glance reminded Octavian why it never did to be incautious. "*One* might say that," he replied, baring his teeth. "I'm not, however."

Octavian raised his cup in a mild toast. "Nor have I," he returned urbanely. "However, that same hypothetical person might agree that it would be . . . better for Rome, were Caesar's heir someone, hmm. Younger. More apt to be instilled with proper Roman virtues."

To his surprise, Antony leaned forward and whispered harshly, "Are you testing my loyalties? Are there men outside this room, waiting to testify against me at a proscription?"

Proscription was a punishment that had been levied against hundreds of people in the time of Sulla. They had been stripped of their citizenship, and all the protections that it provided—for example, citizens could not be crucified. Their lands, slaves, and money were seized by the state, leaving their families paupers, while the proscribed individuals fled Roman lands, often one step ahead of an executioner. Caesar, to his credit, had used the punishment sparingly—mostly to silence those who would not acknowledge his marriage to Cleopatra and the legitimacy of his heirs by her.

Octavian shook his head, raising a soothing hand. "Never in life," he assured Antony. "Did I not say just moments ago that I consider you my brother?"

The suspicion in Antony's gaze did not fade, however. "There is the matter of Caesarion being a god-born," he muttered.

Octavian waved a hand. "That is somewhat in question. His eyes are a strange color, yes, but the mage-priests of Thebes are skilled. An illusion, some bargain with a spirit? A simple pretense. A lie to keep the boy alive past infancy."

As Antony frowned in consideration, a servant entered and announced, "Your other guest has arrived, *dominus*."

Octavian waved the newcomer in, and Antony sat up, his pouchy eyes widening in surprise. Alexander Julius Caesar entered the room, wearing a fresh white toga that swamped his slender frame. "Cousin," Alexander greeted Octavian with a polite nod, but his eyes were wide, and he seemed a little overwhelmed by his sudden introduction into adult privilege. "I was surprised to receive your invitation, as our home is in mourning, but my mother assured me that there would be no disrespect to my father's memory in dining with kin." His dark eyes took in Antony, slouching on one of the dining couches, and then returned to Octavian.

For his part, Alexander kept his mother's long-standing advice in mind. *Conceal your strength. Let everyone underestimate you, until you have their measure. When dealing with someone who is complex . . . be simple. Be water in a cup. Transparent. Speak little, hear much, and react not at all until you know who they truly are.*

So he smiled and allowed a servant to help him up onto a couch, and accepted food and drink gracefully. "This is marvelous after six months on legion rations," he admitted, and heard Antony bray with laughter.

"Six months in the legion, and you're an expert, eh? You haven't even been on short rations yet, have you, lad?" Antony bit into a dormouse from the trencher in front of him. "Doubt you've been digging many ditches or setting palisades yet, either."

Alexander shook his head, lowering his eyes. "No, not at all. I served as my brother's scribe."

Looks of intrigue on both of the older men's faces. Antony smiled and offered, "You were entrusted with official correspondence? That speaks well of you, lad!" The Tribune of the Plebs leaned in, lowering his brows conspiratorially. "Careful, though. Even *thinking* of any secrets you read is dangerous around Octavian here. He can pluck secrets from a man's mouth before a word is even spoken."

Alexander touched a ring on his hand, and it warmed. And then the spirit bound to that ring whispered in his mind, *There is no magic in play here; nothing in this room can compel you to speak.* Invisible to other eyes, a hawk made of green flame appeared, landing on his left shoulder. His mother had insisted that the mage-priests of Thebes bind protective spirits to each of her children at birth, and this was one of his.

Nothing to compel me to speak, except the weight of all this attention, Alexander thought. *A cup of unwatered wine in my hand, and two of the most powerful men in Rome having invited me to sup with them. I am supposed to be overwhelmed.* And he was—but with apprehension, not awe. His voice broke as he asked, "Are there no other guests tonight?"

"No," Octavian replied, smiling gently. "Just a quiet celebration of your having attained the toga of manhood among . . .

relatives and friends." He toasted Alexander.

"Perhaps a little business," Antony chimed in. "I have a daughter who's about your age. Might be time to consider marriage, lad. After all, you are now Caesarion's heir."

Alexander caught the look of faint vexation that crossed Octavian's face. "Caesarion's heir?" Octavian put in, raising his eyebrows. "Some would say that Alexander is the heir to the *Empire*. After all, what is Caesarion but a legitimized bastard, while Alexander here was born within the sacred bounds of matrimony?" Warm sympathy in his voice. A hint of outrage at wrongs done to a friend.

Alexander thought rapidly. It was easy to resent his older brother, some days. The gods had ladled gifts over Caesarion—from Mars, skin so tough that no weapon could cut it, and enough strength to crush a man's skull in his bare hands. From Venus, a smile so charming that few people had the will to gainsay him. From Osiris, immunity to poison. From Isis, healing. And from both of their mortal parents, gifts of shrewd intelligence and courage. They'd taken great pains to conceal Caesarion's gifts. Most of their servants were Egyptian, completely loyal to Cleopatra and unable to speak Latin, for precisely this reason.

But on the other hand . . . Caesarion hadn't been required to take Alexander into Germania; he'd *offered* to take his younger brother with him. And just this morning, he'd sent the new toga to Alexander's rooms, though Alexander's fourteenth birthday wouldn't be for months. *Our family needs all the men it can muster, with Father no longer with us*, the accompanying note had read. And warmed by his brother's trust, Alexander had worn the toga with pride, a man in the eyes of his family.

So he lowered his eyes and replied softly, "I thank you for the idea of a marriage, Tribune. I had always thought that my brother would give me one of our sisters in marriage, and send me to Egypt to rule as king there in his place." A quick glance to verify the expressions of revulsion on those Roman, patrician faces at this alien Egyptian practice. "I would have to ask my mother about any other marriage plans," he added, trying to sound tremulous and dependent on others. It wasn't difficult. He knew that he was in deep waters here, and wished, desperately, that Lepidus had sent someone with him. *But that's the wish of a child, and I'm supposed to be a man now. And they wouldn't have spoken this way in front of witnesses.* "As for the rest," he added, raising his eyes to Octavian, "I really don't know much about politics.

Or about strategy and war. I just copied my brother's letters, and wrote whatever he dictated to me."

Simple. Easily-led. As transparent as a cup of water. And he could see Octavian's eyes light up with a kind of excitement as the man leaned forward, smiling. "Oh, my dear boy! You have no idea of what has been taken from you, do you?"

Alexander let his brow crinkle. "Taken?" he repeated vaguely.

"There are those who might say that you have been cheated of your birthright," Octavian replied carefully.

Always putting words in the mouths of invisible others, Alexander noted. "My birthright?" Just reiterating the others' words. Forcing them to do more of the work. "I should be the next Imperator, and not Caesarion?" he added hesitantly, as if slowly adopting the idea as his own. *I might be going too far.*

"It's a pleasant thought, isn't it?" Antony offered, glancing over at Octavian.

Alexander shook his head rapidly. "I wouldn't know what to do," he protested. Truth, this time. "I'd need help."

Octavian's tone became soothing. "I'm sure that there would always be those on hand whom you could trust to advise you." A dismissive wave. "Of course, this is a moot discussion. There's nothing that could stop Caesarion from taking the title of Imperator in just a few days' time."

The subject dropped there, but Alexander remained nervous for the rest of the meal. And when his litter came around to carry him home over the filthy streets of Rome, he chewed on his knuckles until the moment that he escaped its confines to flee into the villa. He ran directly to his brother's room, and, finding Caesarion there at his writing table, dropped to a crouch beside him.

"That's not an expression that bodes well," Caesarion said, looking up from their father's eulogy.

"Octavian thinks that I'd make a more biddable heir than you." Alexander's voice shook. "I played the idiot, and he almost had to wipe away the drool."

Caesarion grimaced. "Mother said he'd probably make a move, such as trying to betroth you to one of his daughters—"

"Oh, so *that's* why he looked so angry when Antony suggested that—"

"Antony's in this with him?"

"He was at *dinner* with us. I couldn't tell if they were working together." Alexander caught his brother's upper arm, feeling the strength there, muscles like raw iron masked by illusions maintained by spirits. "Brother. He said that there's nothing that could stop you from taking the title of Imperator after Father's funeral rites are done."

Caesarion's red eyes bored down into his own. "In this? He is absolutely correct."

* * *

Quintilis 9, 15 AC

Novendialis, the ninth day of mourning, required sacrifices and feasting—and, since Caesar had stood as a father to the entire Empire, not just to his own family, everyone in the Empire partook of the feast. Caesarion, after Lepidus had shown him the budget, had winced and sponsored games in Rome for the *Novendialis* at the expense of the Julii family. Thus, he could hear the roar of the crowd as chariots raced in the Circus Maximus, the massed voices erupting from the structure shaking the ground as he stood in the cemetery. At his side was the entire extended Julii clan—including distant cousins like Octavian and Antony.

Lepidus held down the sacrificial sow, and Caesarion slashed a knife across its throat, letting its blood pour over the grass. "For Ceres," he said clearly. "Blood in the earth, and protection from all vengeful spirits." As the sow's struggles and squeals ceased, he went about the butchery matter-of-factly, setting aside the portion that would be cremated with his father's body with due reverence. Food for the ghost.

The rest would be served at dinner, to which all these people would be invited. Another roar from the crowds resonated up through his body, but Caesarion ignored the distraction and poured a generous libation of wine over the hungry earth, splashing the hem of a toga already stained with the sow's blood.

As everyone departed, Marcus Antonius paused to speak with him. "The mob loved your father," he said, as the ground shook once more with thunderous roars.

"They had good reason to," Caesarion replied mildly. After all, he gave them games, victory, and peace. He gave them a voice, too—for patrician though he was, he was a populist.

Antony smiled, but it didn't reach his eyes. "Just keep in mind that the mob is fickle. If they turn against you, they'll cook you and eat you in your own house."

It sounded almost like a threat. Caesarion met the gaze of the Tribune of the Plebs—a man who could whip the common folk into a frenzy with a few words, were he so inclined. "I thank you for your warning," he replied. "I think, however, that my eulogy for my father will allay much unease today."

Antony nodded. "Yes, you're the final speaker at the Rostra. Octavian's scheduled just before you. Cicero's before him."

Caesarion tried not to swallow his tongue. Cicero, a frail, elderly man these days, had been carefully carried in from his country villa, where he lived in retirement. He remained, however, the greatest orator of this age, whereas Caesarion had never spoken before the Senate or anyone but a group of legionnaires before. *I can only pale in comparison.*

Thus, two hours later, Caesarion sat in the Rostra, trying not to shake, listening as Cicero lauded his late father. "While I disagreed with him on almost every particular," the elderly republican declared, "he was a noble man, filled with high ideals and love of his country. I counted him my friend, even when we disagreed. Perhaps even more so than when we were in agreement, for out of disagreement, new ideas may grow." Leaning lightly on a stick, he gestured at the Rostra. "And out of disagreement, what an idea *has* grown. A Rome stronger than it was fifteen years ago. More united. And with less corruption in her governance. While I will ever hold to the ideals of our beloved Republic, I must admit that my friend's life was to the benefit of our home."

Polite applause as Cicero shakily made his way back to his seat. Then Octavian spoke at some length, and, in his conclusion, exclaimed, "How like a god was Caesar! No—not *like* a god. But a god, in truth, as should be recognized by the Senate. For who else but Caesar could have brought us all together, republicans and populists alike? Who else could have been a father to this entire mighty empire? While I know that grief touches every heart now, how much lighter will our spirits feel, knowing that his divine hand will govern through his successors?"

The crowd, frenzied, began to clamor for precisely this. "*Divus Iulius! Divus Iulius!*"

Caesarion stared at Octavian, trying to fathom the political motivation behind this insanity . . . . Ah. He said that my father will guide the Empire through his successors. Plural, and unnamed.

Whoever winds up in control—perhaps Octavian himself, should my brother and I mysteriously die—would partake of the divine spirit of my father. Legitimacy.

A frown on his face, Caesarion took the speaker's position. His prepared remarks had to be thrown away, for he needed to stop the runaway reaction of the crowd without causing a riot.

As such, he raised a hand for silence, and then pitched his voice to be heard. "Friends! Fellow Romans! When my father first stood before you to speak, it was at the funeral of his own aunt, Julia. He reminded you all that she descended from kings on one side, and the goddess Venus on the other." His voice rang back from the marble all around him, and the murmur of the crowd died as they thirstily drank in his words. "Yet she was not a goddess, for all her descent from the gods. Nor was my father a god. Nor am I." Yet, with that phrase, he also reminded everyone there of what he was—a god-born, if an untested one. "Rome has gods in plenty," he went on as people around him frowned. The mob did not like having its will thwarted. "My father never desired worship—only your trust. Trust me now, as you trusted him, and know that the gods speak through me, their servant. And they say that no mortal should be worshipped as they are." He turned and regarded Octavian for a moment.

"For example, it has been the custom in Egypt to worship the pharaohs. There are priests in Thebes even now who lead the faithful in prayer to my mother . . . and to me. This is a custom that I intend to abolish. For I know that I, like my father, am but a man." He caught what looked like an approving nod from Cicero, and exhaled. It couldn't be for the quality of his oration, which was flat and unbalanced, but for the sentiments it expressed. "I am not here today to speak of my father's death," he went on now, "but to celebrate his life, and express my gratitude for the services he has rendered unto Rome." Back safely into his prepared remarks, he could relax a little. And gradually, he felt the crowd accept the image of Caesar, not as a god, but as a man.

That night at the funeral feast, eating the roast flesh of the sow sacrificed at his father's grave, and drinking *conditum paradoxum*, the heavily sweetened and spiced wine served at such affairs, Caesarion tasted something bitter in his drink, and set the cup aside. Lepidus, seated to his right, and substantially tipsy himself, mistook Caesarion's cup for his own, took it in hand, and quaffed it.

Two minutes later, the venerable general doubled over on his dining couch. Saliva frothed at his mouth, as from a rabid dog's, and sweat poured down his face in rivulets. Caesarion stood beside him, hands on his shoulders, letting the power of Isis flow into Lepidus' frame. *Don't die. I need you. Rome needs you.*

The general's eyes closed, and Caesarion leaned forward, checking for breath. "He's unconscious, but alive," he announced to the shocked onlookers. "Get him to a bed, and call for a *medicus*. Also, don't let anyone leave the villa—not even a servant. I want to question them all."

Antony, who'd been seated at a different couch, picked up the cup, sniffing it. "Impossible to tell what poison was used," he said. "Concealed in the spiced wine—a clever trick." He frowned. "You drank from the same cup, lad. Do you *eat* poisons every day, like Mithridates, that it did not affect you?"

Caesarion shook his head. "It may have been painted on the rim," he answered, a well-rehearsed response. "My lips must not have touched where Lepidus' did." *Never show your full strength,* his father's voice came back to him. *Not until you need to show it. Conceal it, harbor it, and then use it, effectively and devastatingly.*

Hours later, one of the servants hired for the feast was found dead, dangling by the knotted cord of her own stola, from a tree branch in the garden. "The poison was aconite," Cleopatra informed Caesarion, her eyes dark and angry. "The trail ends with her, unless we can conjure spirits who can tell us from whose hand came the coins in her purse."

Exhausted in body and soul, for it was now past midnight, and healing others deeply drained him of his vital energies, Caesarion shook his head. "I suspect Octavian, or perhaps one of Cato's grandchildren. Poison isn't Antony's style. Father always considered him a good soldier. Honorable, after his fashion." He paused. "But without proof, I cannot accuse."

Cleopatra put a hand on his shoulder. "Tomorrow," she said softly, "you will *be* Rome. You must act decisively, and sometimes outside the laws that Romans so cherish. Be more Roman than they are, for so long as you stand on their soil. And when you go to Egypt, as you *must*, be more Egyptian than any there whom you rule." Her eyes glittered.

"Malleolus and the rest of the men are certain that a civil war is coming." The words felt like a confession, wrenched from him.

"Power struggles are endemic, my son." Her voice sounded like ashes. "I fought my war against my brother, and your father aided me. Now, it's your turn."

"Civil war has gutted this land. It's time for something else, Mother. A civil peace, perhaps." He sighed. "I just don't know how to achieve it." And in those words, a world of defeat. "Mother, how do I reach for all of old Cicero's republican ideals of truth and justice, which I know that my father prized . . . in a world in which no one else holds to those ideals?"

"Ruthlessness," she replied. "It's the language your father spoke to them. For all their pretty words about law and order and beauty and truth? Romans only understand a fist wrapped in iron."

He gave her a long, considering glance. "I need to split Antony and Octavian, somehow. Get one of them firmly on my side." His eyes burned, for all his god-born strength. "I can't tie Alexander to either of their daughters. I may need him in Egypt." A nod from her prompted him to continue. "I won't tie myself to them, either," he added. "Father was right. I need a Roman bride—" Be more Roman than the Romans themselves, he thought, "but not their kin."

"You need a blood-tie that promises one of them power and access—but choose the less dangerous of them. Antony."

Caesarion's stomach turned. "One of my sisters could marry Antony." A grimace. He'd been raised in the knowledge that if somehow, his father were deposed, and Caesarion escaped to Egypt and ruled there, that one of his younger sisters would have to become his wife. The idea didn't disturb him; duty rarely did. But it also wasn't his preference. However, giving twelve-year-old Eurydice or ten-year-old Selene to that . . . voluptuary old man sickened him.

"No! Not that." His mother's face looked stricken. "Not them. They're . . . far more sheltered than I was, at their age." Ironic words, considering she had been brought up in a king's palace.

"You just told me to be ruthless."

Her eyes gleamed, ophidian, in the low light of the lamps streaming out onto the small portico in which they stood. "In this case, my son, I will be your bond. Antony may like his women younger than I am now, but he has lusted after me for decades. The reason he was dismissed from your father's staff was his renewed attempt to *seduce* me ten years ago." She bared her teeth momentarily. "Offer me in marriage, my son. It can't be carried out till our year's mourning is complete, of course, but the offer alone will gain you his attention."

Caesarion shook his head. "I can't ask you to do that." He searched wildly for reasons not to agree. "You were married to *Caesar.* Any other marriage would be a step down—"

"You aren't asking. I'm offering." Her voice held tears, but also power. "And if I find that I cannot tolerate his advances? Once your position is secure, I have alternatives." She lifted her hand, and a snake formed of blue light blazed around her wrist momentarily. The spirit's bite left no mark on its victims, but brought a swifter and surer death than the aconite that had poisoned Caesarion's cup this evening.

Part of him shuddered at the cold certainty in his mother's voice and mien. The rest of him accepted her for who and what she was: Cleopatra, daughter of the Nile. "I'll speak to him in the morning," he replied, his voice thick. *Here is the true measure of ruthlessness. She's willing to do anything to assure that her children survive and prosper.* "Before I go before the Senate." A pause as he struggled for the words. "Thank you, Mother."

* * *

Quintilis 10, 15 AC

Caesarion met with Antony in the morning to discuss a tie of marriage between them. A queen, a former empress, offered as bait to a man who'd been born a plebeian, and now held the mob of Rome in the palm of his hands. The look of surprised delight on Antony's face couldn't entirely hide the lust in his eyes, and Caesarion rigorously repressed any thoughts of his mother in this man's arms.

At noon, he had to make the long walk through Rome, unarmed and unarmored, to the Forum. Alexander insisted on walking with him, and Cleopatra saw them off, unable to attend the investiture, for foreign kings and queens were forbidden to step on the sacred soil of Rome. "Fifteen years ago, I watched your father leave just this way," she murmured, her voice catching. "If Brutus hadn't told him of the conspiracy—if Brutus hadn't given his life to save him from the assassins . . . you and I would both be dead, my son."

Caesarion touched his mother's arm. "But we're not. And I do not intend to die today." He clapped Alexander on the shoulder, and the two set off, the sun warming the folds of their purple-trimmed togas. While he wasn't supposed to have any guards, he could see Malleolus trailing after them, his eyes on the crowds lining the streets to cheer and throw flowers at the sons of Caesar.

In sight of the Forum, the screams began. Caesarion swung around, and saw men with long knives erupting out of the crowd from both sides of the street. *Seven of them*, he realized distantly, grabbing Alexander by the arm and trying to get his younger brother behind him. And then they were on them.

People screamed and ran, or surged in on all sides, trying to catch the assailants' arms. But where Caesar had been fifty-five when he'd been attacked in this fashion, Caesarion was eighteen—and god-born.

The first knife came down on his left forearm, raised to block the strike, and he felt the impact against the bone—but it was dull, as if he'd been hit with a stick. He caught the attacker's forearm with his left hand, trapping the blade, and stepped in, punching his attacker in the throat as he stripped the blade away, taking it for his own. But the man tucked his chin, turning a lethal shot into a more glancing blow. In response, Caesarion spun, turning his back to the man. In these tight quarters, the move held an attack, as he brought the knife back, slicing deeply into his opponent's thigh, near the groin. *He'll bleed out from that.*

The turn also let him see the two men who'd been behind him as they moved in to attack. He ducked as one knife bloodlessly clipped his brow, and a second knife thudded against his shoulder.

Dizzying awareness that there were more assailants to his right; that Alexander was struggling with them, too, trying to wrestle the knives from the grasps of men who'd clearly fought in the legions, and who wore, damnably, the togas of citizens. *You are my people!* Caesarion wanted to shout. *I'm one of you! I've fought beside you! We're brothers, you and I!*

But it hadn't mattered to the conspirators fifteen years ago, and it didn't matter to these men, now. Caesarion spun, kicked one of his attackers in the groin, and managed to slash the throat of a third with the knife he'd taken from the first. A brief glimpse of Malleolus entering the fight, trying to get to Alexander, and then a sickening cry of pain from Alexander himself, as his brother went down under two more men. This pair now surged forward, trying to drive Caesarion to the ground, where they could hold him down and stab at will.

Except Caesarion couldn't be dragged down. A man landed on his shoulders, and his knees flexed slightly. He turned his face away from the blade scraping uselessly at his cheek. A second man charged into him, trying to tie up his arms. He kicked the man in front of him away, reached behind himself, and got a hold on the head of the man grappling him. Then he dropped himself forward, throwing the man over his own head and on *top* of the man he'd just kicked away. The two hit the hard pavement of the street in a tangle of limbs, and Caesarion dropped to a crouch, driving his knife home into two exposed throats.

A quick glance to verify that Malleolus, bleeding freely, stood over Alexander's crumpled form, fending off two more men to his right. With no threats behind him, Caesarion moved forward, inexorable as death, and the two men menacing Malleolus turned away from the centurion, towards him now. Which proved a mistake as Malleolus, with a knife taken from an attacker's hands, stepped in behind one of them and drove the blade into his back, threading between ribs to find lung.

The eyes of the last man appeared lost as he faced off against Caesarion. *He knows he's defeated,* Caesarion thought, and shouted, "Surrender, and tell me who else is involved—"

"Death to tyrants! Death to those who would sully Rome with foreign blood and foreign queens!" And the man attacked again, in the sure knowledge that death awaited him, no matter what his actions now were.

Caesarion let him come. Let the knife impact on his chest. Saw it bounce away, and heard the hush of the crowd as he caught the man's hand in his own, snapping the wrist with a twist. And then he drove the knife, still in the man's hand, into the assailant's belly. *That's a slow death,* he thought distantly, turning back towards Malleolus and Alexander now.

"Are you all right?" he started to ask, and then the words glued themselves to his tongue, for Malleolus had just turned Alexander over, revealing the knife buried deep in the boy's chest.

His brother opened his eyes as Caesarion gathered him up in his arms, blood spreading over the white toga he'd been so proud to wear. "Sorry," Alexander apologized, and the word burned in Caesarion's mind. "I . . . couldn't stop them . . . ."

My brother is dying, and he's apologizing *for not being able to stop assassins sent to kill me.* Numbness spread through him, and Caesarion took an experimental stride towards the Forum. The blood of his attackers had soaked his toga, and now his brother's blood, hot and wet, trickled down his arms. "Hold on," he told Alexander, his throat constricting. *I can't lose both him and Father in the same ten days.* "I can heal you. But the Senate has to see you. They have to see *us*. Or they'll never understand. So *hold on*."

He sped to a trot, and the citizens of Rome, always keen for a spectacle, trailed along behind him.

Alexander's breathing was labored as they entered the Forum, and the senators gathered there spooled forward from their seats like threads from a loom, gathering on all sides. Staring like the mob outside. *Everyone in Rome loves a show,* Caesarion reflected distantly. *The bloodier the spectacle, the better.*

He settled Alexander on the only chair here with a back—their father's throne, and how bitterly the senators had begrudged Caesar a chair different from the traditional *curule*—the knife still protruding from his thin chest. Then he pulled the blade out, tossing it away before planting his hands on his brother's body. "Heal me," Alexander begged, his voice barely audible.

"I'm trying," Caesarion whispered, crouching down to speak in his brother's ear. The power of Isis built in him, but he could feel death rising in his brother's body. *Please, my lady,* he begged silently. *Take whatever you wish of me. But do not let my brother die. Not for me.* "I should have done this in the street." *I wasted time. I wasted my brother's life so that these men, with their Roman rationalism, could see both the extent of his wounds, and my ability to heal them.* "Forgive me."

He stroked Alexander's short hair, and swallowed a spasm of grief as his brother's breathing hitched. *And then stopped. My sacrifice was not accepted. For all the powers of the god-born . . . I too, must accept when the answer of the gods is* no. *For I am but a man.* Bitter tears burned his throat, but he could not let them fall.

Voices swept through his mind then, overwhelming the chatter of the senators around him. Voices that he'd lived with all his life, but which usually spoke to him in dreams. *My gift is more than just healing,* Isis whispered in his mind. *I also bring rebirth. But at a price. Nothing from nothing, as you mortals say. A life for a life. But choose wisely.*

Her voice seemed distant compared to the thunder that was Mars in his ears. You know what you must do. My people have bled themselves dry, throwing themselves upon one another for generations. Find your strongest enemy, and defeat him decisively. The rest will hesitate to attack, and may even surrender.

It was strange, how much the voice of Mars sounded like the voice of his own father.

Staring at his brother's face, Caesarion came back to himself, realizing that Cicero and Octavian had pushed through the crowd to stand close now. Cicero shook his gray head sadly. "I wish that I had not lived to see this once, let alone a second time," he said, his voice stilling the crowd. "Our sacred Forum, profaned with blood."

Coldness filled Caesarion. No rage yet, no fury. Just emptiness. He stood, touched a ring on his finger, and whispered a *Name* under his breath. "Release the illusions you hold over me," he murmured to the attendant spirit his mother had bound to him at birth.

Are you certain? These illusions were intended to protect you—
They need to see who I am.
As you wish.

Caesarion looked down. He hadn't seen his own skin, uncovered by illusion, since the age of twelve, when the strength of Mars had first manifested itself. Thus, even for him, seeing the additional muscle that had developed over the past years came as a surprise. His frame didn't seem bulky, but definitely appeared that of an adult man in the prime of life, not that of a callow youth.

The senators around him recoiled, seeing evidence of magic used first-hand. Rome paid heed to its gods, practiced auguries, and gave daily sacrifices to house-spirits, the *lares* and *penates*. But magic, true magic, as practiced in Hellas, Egypt, and Persia, was little known here, and was viewed with suspicion.

Into the pool of silence that had gathered at Cicero's words, Caesarion now spoke, raggedly, and with only his native eloquence. "My lords, I allow you to see me now, for who and what I am. My parents both believed that my true strength should remain hidden. They feared that while I am god-born of Mars—a god of Rome!—that Romans would not permit me to live to adulthood if they truly understood what I am." He gestured to his brother's corpse, and *now* the rage began to build, almost choking him. "I see now how wise they were to practice this deception."

The men of the Senate backed up a step or two as Caesarion rested his bloody hands on his brother's limp shoulders. He could see

Malleolus hovering at the door of the chamber, unable to enter, but looking stricken. "All I have heard for the past nine days," Caesarion continued steadily, "is that with my father's death, civil war seems inevitable. And how I must be ruthless with all of you to ensure that no such thing transpires, or that if it does, that it at least will be of short duration. My lords, the gods themselves tire of your wars. I am here today to tell you that there will *be* no civil discord on my ascension to my father's offices." His hands tightened on his brother's shoulders. "In fact, I am here to assure it."

Murmurs from the crowd.

A life for a life, Isis whispered again. *Choose wisely.*

Cicero stood nearby; he was an old man, who'd given his life to the service of a republic that no longer existed. But he remained the voice of liberty, of justice, of all the old values that Caesarion himself prized. And, equally near, Octavian stood as well, his brow wrinkled with what looked like concern as he stared at Alexander's corpse. *You didn't want him dead.* Fury still burned in Caesarion. *You wanted him as your puppet. You didn't order his death, but that doesn't mean that your associates—if associates they were—couldn't have killed him by accident. No proof. Never any damned proof.*

But Octavian was the other face of Rome, the flip side of the coin from Cicero. Ruthless pragmatism. Someone who would use whatever tool he had, to accomplish the goal at hand. The two, side by side? Principles balanced against pragmatism.

And, while Caesarion *hated* to think this way, he had to do so, quickly. Octavian could be a valuable ally. He was a young man, where Cicero was old and worn. He had energy and a life still to give to the Empire, where Cicero had none. It would be the more *pragmatic* thing to do, to take the life of the old man, and use it as Isis whispered that he could. But in doing so, he'd be extinguishing the last light of the old Republic.

And this, Caesarion could not do. *Attack your strongest enemy, defeat him decisively, and conquer the rest through their fear.* He looked up after his long pause, and continued, iron ringing in his voice, "I have no evidence of who directed the attack on me that injured Lepidus last night. I have no evidence of who ordered the attack on me that cost the life of my brother. I do not *need* evidence. Justice, today, will be truly blind, for I require only that an example be made. So that you all *understand.*"

He raised one blood-stained hand from Alexander's shoulder and clasped Octavian's, almost companionably. Felt the sickening rush of energy as Octavian's life rushed through him, and into Alexander. Octavian's knees buckled, and he hit the marble floor, choking and gasping on his own blood, as Alexander coughed sharply and sat up, reaching for the wound in his chest that was no longer there. "What—what happened?" Alexander cried.

Caesarion staggered, and he had to brace himself on his father's chair to remain standing amid the cries of consternation around him. "Be silent!" he shouted over their voices, swaying where he stood, his vision skewing. "Listen, and hear me *very* well. If at any point in the future, some member of my family should be *murdered* again, the person who took that life will recompense me in exactly this way." A muscle in his cheek twitched. "You can, if you so wish, make your houses into charnel yards. And I will accommodate each and every one of you. Or you can come to understand, gentlemen, that the era in which you all squabbled for power is over. You may advise. You may consent. You may control the budget. You can impose taxes and provide services. You can and you will keep order in the city." That last, with a look at the stunned Marcus Antonius. "But you will . . . not . . . rule. That is my duty and my burden."

The senators didn't take long to find their voices, but their arguments seemed halfhearted at best. They'd seen a genuine miracle performed before their eyes . . . and none of them wished to become the next object lesson of divine power. And so, after the first hour of tedious debate, Caesarion sent Alexander home in a litter to recover, feeling guilty as he did. He hoped his brother never came to remember today as the day on which Caesarion had *let him die.*

After the Senate finally acclaimed Caesarion the God-Born as Emperor of Rome, Cicero was the last to leave. A little curl to his old, colorless lips as he moved to address Caesarion, who stepped down from his chair and offered his elder a respectful arm to help convey him to the door. "I did not realize that your father had planned for the final death of the Republic in the person of his son," Cicero murmured.

"I love the ideals of the Republic," Caesarion replied honestly. "But no one in this chamber has lived those ideals in decades. I will uphold them." He grimaced. "As best as they will *allow* me."

Cicero stopped and looked at him. "Make them see," he rasped. "Make them *see* the waste of lives, wealth, and potential in every civil war.

Turn them against outsiders if you must, but Rome herself must be reborn, and her promise extended to all within her borders."

Caesarion nodded. "That was my father's dream, too," he replied. "And I will honor it."

"*Ave*, then, Caesarion," Cicero returned. "May the Fates be kinder to you, than they usually are to conquerors."

Timeshift without an Arc
by Martin T. Ingham

Max Turner staggered across the parking garage. Every muscle in his body was aching from the Paralyzing jolt he'd received. The physical pain would quickly fade, but his pride was another matter. The shame of recurring failure persisted, but he felt fortunate to be alive.

The embarkation room seemed so empty. Half the hardware that usually lived there was missing, lost to the unwritten centuries. So many men and machines destroyed by the temporal quakes. More aptly put, they were erased from history, having never been.

It had been a day like any other, when Max reported for duty all those months ago. He'd expected to ship out on assignment, to round up some lottery rigger, or a lovelorn loser looking to change a past of unrequited love. Such minor alterations to the timeline were common enough, as the new science of time travel became affordable on the black market. The Temporal Agency was there to stop any deviation from "true reality," and preserve the integrity of the timeline. Such a noble and necessary vocation, to be the police of history.

Everything had been going well until Jack Baker arrived, all those months ago.

Max remembered his first encounter with the man with no identity. While Jack Baker claimed to be a temporal agent, there was no record of him, anywhere. As far as the Agency's database could tell, Jack Baker had never existed, making him a temporal anomaly incongruent with the true timeline. Such individuals could not be left to roam in any time, for their very presence would contaminate reality. In most cases, such anomalous individuals were erased, but this non-existent agent was a unique case.

Max had listened to Jack's initial appeal for help. The man claimed to be from the true timeline, and that someone had meddled with the past to erase him. Of course, that was impossible to believe, for if time had been altered, the Agency would've known about it. They didn't change with historical alterations, so if this Jack Baker had truly existed, they would've known about it.

The only logical explanation was that Jack was a time meddler, possibly from the future, which remained largely unexplored. A thorough interrogation could've extracted that truth, yet before they could get started, the man escaped. Chronal readings of the holding cell revealed a temporal signature, proving he'd time-shifted despite their best security measures.

Directly after Baker's departure, the first major quantum wave had hit, rewriting history in serious ways.

The Time Agency existed outside normal space-time, in a permanently phased pocket of non-linear time. This way, they remained immune from changes in the timeline, and could observe quantum deviations as they occurred. It was only because of this that they remained unaffected by the disastrous alterations Jack Baker was making throughout history.

Over a period of several days, the agents in-residence watched helplessly as the future was twisted and mutilated in innumerable ways. From high technology to primitive feudalism, the past rewrote the present, leaving an unrecognizable world in its wake. History was so distorted, nobody knew where to start with repairs. They weren't sure where the first divergence point lay, but it was crucial they find it.

For the last three months, the handful of surviving agents had worked tirelessly to locate that moment in time where their reality had been shattered, though it continued to elude them. Their best bet at discovering it was to ask the man who'd caused it—Jack Baker.

The question remained; what was Baker's true purpose, and why was he intent on dismantling reality?

The lift was empty when Max walked in. His colleagues had already gone ahead of him, ready for a shower and a hot meal. He wasn't in the mood for either. Failure weighed heavily upon him, and he would rather get back to work, hunting down the one man who might put an end to his constant quest. Stopping on the third floor, he stepped out into the long, open hallway that led to Chronal Monitoring. From there, he could see everything that was—past, present, and even limited glimpses into the future. It was becoming his second home, a replacement for the home he'd lost to time.

Stepping into the observation room, Max saw the familiar face of Tony Cross waiting for him. His former partner had been serving the Temporal Agency since its inception, and spent most of his time these days monitoring the chronal waves, watching events change with each alteration. It was a thankless job, but somebody had to do it.

"Welcome back, Max," Tony greeted, slapping him on the shoulder with massive, brown hand. "No white whale today, eh?"

"Ha ha," Max replied, finding the analogy less than humorous. "I was close this time, so damn close!"

"Yeah, well, whatever you did, it stopped any new deviations in the timeline, for now."

"No thanks to me," Max answered, still kicking himself over the failure. "Baker was just on one of his collecting trips it seems, grabbed another one from the jaws of death."

"He does like the ladies, doesn't he? What is that now, six?"

"That we know of," Max replied. "Seriously, what's he doing with all those women?"

Tony smiled and made a knowing grunt.

"Oh, come on. There's got to be more to it than that," Max said.

"Perhaps you give him too much credit," Tony said, turning to a monitor. "For all we know, he's forming that little harem of his with nothing by hedonism in mind."

"You keep thinking the obvious," Max told him. "I still say there's something we're not seeing, a pattern or a greater method to his madness."

"I can tell you one thing," Tony said, turning to one of the many monitors sitting around the room. "He's based a lot further away than we ever suspected."

"Oh?" Max said, intrigued.

"Yeah. We've long been under the impression that his base of operations is similar to our own, a structure or vessel displaced from normal space-time."

"Yes?" Max asked.

"Well, I got a partial trace on his portal, right before you confronted him. It wasn't enough for a lock, but I was able to extrapolate a partial trajectory. The trail leads backward in time."

Max had suspected the answer, even before Tony told him. "Jack Baker is hiding in the past. How far?"

"Hard to say. Millennia, at least, perhaps even further. Like I said, it was only a partial lock. The portal shut down before I could pinpoint the temporal coordinates."

"Which means Baker has an accomplice," Max said, thinking of the mechanics of time travel. "We had him dead in our sights, but someone pulled him out at the last minute."

"Leaving you to hunt another day, my young friend," Tony replied lightly.

Max didn't like his tone, and called him on it. "Why do I get the impression that you're enjoying this?"

"Hey, it's my job," Tony defended. "Besides, all I ever had out there was two ex-wives and a boatload of bills. Can't say I miss it."

"Enjoy it while it lasts," Max said, turning to one of the free computer terminals. There were a hundred to choose from, so he picked one distant enough from Tony that they could each work undisturbed.

It had been a few weeks since Max had reviewed the database, and he was feeling a spark of morbid curiosity. There was little chance he could help discover the focal point, but it would be interesting to see what the world outside really looked like these days.

The logical place to start would be the internet. The Temporal Agency's data core usually maintained a constant link, and downloaded data on a regular basis for comparison with historical documents. Unfortunately, the internet hadn't existed for weeks, deleted by changes in the timeline, so Max had to look elsewhere for information.

Clicking the "satellite telemetry," he reviewed a series of enhanced images from several surveillance orbiters. They showed him little more than landscapes, though that in itself was telling. There should have been more. He saw no smoke plumes, no skyscrapers, no major signs of human industrialism. The only scenes he could find of people were in antiquated buildings more befitting the eighteenth century, certainly not the twenty-second. Taking a look at New York City, he saw a few dozen blocks of brick and stone buildings, little more. Half of Long Island was farms.

This was not the world he'd grown up in. Here, the industrial revolution had never occurred, and the people still lived as they had in ancient times. If that were the case, what had occurred to stunt civilization's growth so drastically?

There was only one way to find out.

Shutting off his terminal and walking for the door, Max said, "Tony, call the boys down at dispatch. Tell them I'm heading out again."

"No way you got a lead so quickly," Tony replied.

"No, but it's time for another fact-finding expedition."

Leaving the monitor room, Max hurried back to the elevator. Before the doors could shut, Tony shoved his arm into the compartment and slid inside.

"Need a break?" Max asked.

"Something like that."

"Think you're up to it after two months sitting behind a desk?"

"Hey, I work out," Tony said. "Besides, this is just recon, right?"

"In theory," Max replied, remembering more than one mission that got more physical than anyone intended. You never knew what you'd find in the past these days, and there was no way to guarantee a peaceful trip unless you wanted to walk around out-of-phase the entire time, which was never fun. Being out of phase meant you couldn't interact with the environment. You couldn't move physical objects, or talk to people. What was the fun in that?

"You know, I really wish there was an easier way to uncover changes in the timeline," Max mentioned as the elevator crept downward. It wasn't the fastest of lifts.

"I'm afraid we'll have to make do for the time being, and do the leg work," Tony said, scratching at the dark stubble on his tan chin. "We're only beginning to understand the fundamentals of temporal science."

"What has it been, five years?" Max asked, alluding to the first documented temporal shift, the impetus for the formation of the Temporal Agency.

"Six. Where've you been?" Tony asked.

"Don't you mean 'when?'" Max rebutted.

The elevator deposited them in the garage, where half a dozen different vehicles waited to take them to a historic locale. Max wasted no time picking his car of choice, an archaic Jeep that could handle back roads without trouble. It was his personal vehicle, the one he'd driven to work all those months ago, when last he'd left home for this lengthy assignment. Where he was going now, he didn't expect to find pavement, so the rugged wheels were a must.

"Mind telling me where we're going?" Tony asked as they neared the Jeep.

"Whatever happened, it must have originated in Europe, based on the state of the colonies these days. So we should pick a pivotal place, say Waterloo, June 18, 1815," Max said, pulling open the driver's side door. The hinges creaked from lack of maintenance. Nobody ever used this thing except for Max, and he hadn't taken it for a spin since this whole debacle began. No time for fun in the face of duty. Well, it was time for a break.

"Going to meet Napoleon?" Tony remarked as he flopped into the passenger seat.

"If I wanted to do that, we'd be going back a lot earlier. Assuming he even exist in this timeline," Max replied.

"Yeah, I watched the telemetry from your last excursion," Tony said. "It looked downright medieval down there."

"More like Renaissance, and if that's the state of the world in 2150, imagine what things must have looked like over three hundred years earlier.'

"Forget imagining, let's go see it," Tony said with enthusiasm.

For a second, a weight lifted from Max's chest, and he could forget everything that was happening. For that brief moment, it was like old times, just he and a fellow Agent heading off for a spin through history. It was enough to give him hope, and that provided the strength he needed to keep going.

The keys were already in the Jeep, and with a quick turn of the ignition and his foot on the gas, Max revved the engine to life. He was ready to shift into first gear when a hand slapped down on his hood, drawing his attention. Looking up at the owner of the hand caused him to cut the engine.

"Agent Turner, a word, now!" the lady snapped with an expressive scowl.

"Suzanne, what can I do for you?" Max asked, feeling impertinent for a change. He jumped out of the vehicle and stepped up to the woman who sought to waylay him.

"That's Deputy Director Hayworth, Agent Turner," she replied, folding her slender arms across her chest. The heavy cloth of the blue pantsuit hid her ample bosoms, though it added distinction to her attractive face. Max caught himself staring and didn't try to hide it. She was one fine looking woman. When was the last time he'd been with a woman? Too long!

"What are you doing, Turner?" Suzanne asked, tapping her polished boot on the concrete.

"Agent Cross and I are going on a quick recon, see if we can't get a bead on the focal point."

"You might have run it by me before rushing off for a joyride," she chided. There was no fooling her.

"This isn't a joyride, Deputy Director, and if you'll recall Director Warner gave me authorization to take whatever measures I deemed necessary to restore the timeline." Max knew he was overstating his power, the power given to him by a man on his death bed. Truthfully, his autonomy would only last so long as his current boss let him keep it.

"You're trying my patience," Suzanne said, not letting up for a second. "After the results of your most recent mission, I'd expect greater caution on your part."

"Don't you get it, Suzanne? It's all the same mission. Everything I'm doing is part of that charge, to fix this God-awful mess. Why don't you just let me do my job?"

"If you were doing your job, we'd have Baker by now," Suzanne grumbled. "It's bad enough you failed, yet again, to apprehend him, but you couldn't even bring yourself to debrief! I had to hear the report from Scontras!"

"He was my Second on the mission. He was fully qualified to give the report. I had better things to do."

"Well, if this excursion of yours is so important, you won't mind taking me along, will you?"

"Excuse me?"

"You heard me, Agent. I'm coming with you. Now, where are we going?" she asked, brushing back a loose strand of black hair. A few sprigs had avoided the hair tie which kept the rest in a neat ponytail.

"The battle of Waterloo, but your presence really isn't necessary," Max said in a vain attempt to dissuade her.

"Nonsense. It's about time I got back out into the field. No time like the present, relatively speaking."

"Shouldn't you stay here? You are the senior administrator in residence."

"McCulskey's handling things. I know he'll follow procedure in my absence. To be blunt, Agent Turner, if you intend to leave the base at this juncture you will be taking me with you."

Max sighed, seeing there was no way around it. Sliding his seat forward and stepping back, he invited Suzanne into the back seat. She wasted no time getting situated as Max retook his seat behind the wheel.

"Proceed, Agent Turner," Suzanne ordered.

"Once more unto the breech, eh?" Tony asked with a wry smile.

"Oh, shut up," Max said, kicking the Jeep into gear.

The vehicle pulled out of its parking space, and headed for the open end of the garage. The large span was filled with a glowing light, the edge of the temporal barrier which kept Agency headquarters isolated. Approaching that glowing sheet of light, Max slowed to a stop. Fiddling with a keypad wired into the dashboard, he accessed the base computer and input coordinates for their time-shift. With the destination programmed, he started forward again, and drove straight through the barrier.

A wave of nausea flowed over the passengers inside the Jeep, as they passed from one time to another. In an instant, the walls of the garage vanished, replaced by a thick stand of trees that trapped them on all sides. Max had barely enough time to slam on the breaks to avoid hitting a massive oak tree.

"Did you forget to set spatial coordinates?" Suzanne asked irritably.

"I didn't forget," Max defended. "According to our historical database, this should be the center of the battlefield at mid-morning."

"History's so different, there's no way to tell where we'll end up," Tony added. "Seems like Waterloo's a bit overgrown in this version of reality."

"Obviously," Suzanne said. "Well, so much for your fact-finding expedition."

"Hey, we're not finished yet. Give me a minute to reset the coordinates," Max replied, tapping a new date into his keypad. A new ripple of light coursed through the Jeep, turning everyone's stomach again as it moved the vehicle ahead in time. The trees disappeared, replaced with a muddy field filled with hay stubble.

"Welcome to the 2015," Max announced.

"Same location?" Tony asked for clarity.

"Give or take a few feet," Max answered.

"At least we now have some sign of civilization," Suzanne mentioned, "as limited as it is."

Erring on the side of caution, Max shifted the Jeep out of phase, so as to remain invisible to any locals. Once the shift was complete, they began the drive across the hay field. The wheels rode atop the stubble, leaving behind no tracks. In a displaced state, the heavy vehicle could not physically disturb solid or liquid objects. Only the air gave way to their movement, allowing them to travel covertly.

The Jeep shook and jumped as it crossed the uneven ground. There was no racing through the field, but after a few minutes they found a wagon path. The deep ruts made it impossible for them to drive down the middle, so Max followed alongside, hoping to find a more suitable roadway up ahead. Before long, the muddy ruts took them to a large farmhouse with white clapboards. Horses were grazing in the distance, and a horse-drawn combine was being dragged into a nearby barn.

"Looks like the middle of Amish country," Tony remarked.

"It's what I expected," Max replied. "From what I saw in our own time, mankind's technological evolution has been set back several hundred years."

"We should find a library," Suzanne suggested. "The right books could explain why."

Max had the same notion, though wondered how much good it would do. They'd tried this sort of thing before, collecting history books in an attempt to identify the focal point, that moment in time where history went awry. They'd succeeded in discovering half a dozen divergence points already, but Baker was always one step ahead of them, it seemed. Before they could use their newly acquired information to repair the timeline, things would change again. Alternations would be made even further in the past, and they'd have to start from scratch to find out where and when.

This trip was merely to satisfy Max's curiosity, and his colleagues knew it. Whatever insights they gleaned in this era would be fleeting. Their only true chance for success would be to capture Jack Baker, and stop him from further damaging the past. Then, and only then, could they hope to succeed in restoring reality.

"I doubt we'll find a library anywhere around here," Tony mentioned. "Maybe we should shift to a fresh locale."

Max shook his head. "In order to teleport, we'd need to temporal shift. I'd rather not make another jump right now. We've already done two in close succession. A third could tip Baker off to our presence, or leave us with a strong dose of temporal sickness."

"Just because they're farmers doesn't mean they're illiterate," Suzanne added. "There ought to be a repository of knowledge somewhere nearby."

"Well, if we're going to find it, we'll need to contact the locals," Max said.

"I don't suppose anyone thought to bring a change of clothes," Suzanne remarked snarkily.

Of course they hadn't. How could they have known the local attire for this era? They were venturing blindly into this strange new world of the past, wholly unaware of fashion trends. They'd have to improvise.

Before venturing off to find clothing, Max parked the Jeep beside a rock outcropping, someplace out of the way, so nobody would bump into it by mistake. Even out of phase, someone could still slam into the thing, only it would be an impenetrable, invisible lump. Nobody could disturb it, but it could disturb them. Who knows what the locals might think if they uncovered such a thing! Superstitions could ignite all sorts of nasty consequences.

With the vehicle safely stowed, Max pulled three wrist-bands out of the glove box. The slender plastic straps each contained their own quantum discriminator, so they could stay in contact with the Agency mainframe and control their temporal state wherever they were. With that fundamental piece of hardware tucked under their sleeves, the three of them ventured toward the farm, remaining out-of-phase for the time being. Invisible to onlookers, they could watch and listen to a few of the laborers; figure out the local dialect and customs. Then, after gleaning all they could from abstract observation, they would hunt down some clothes to "borrow," and start some introductions. It could be a time-consuming process, but Temporal Agents were accustomed to being patient.

"You could have dropped me off at the farm," Tony complained, having to walk over a mile from the parked Jeep.

"You're getting out of shape, my friend," Max replied, knowing what three months behind a desk could do to a man. He'd played desk jockey once, but he couldn't stand the sedentary existence. He needed the action, both physical and mental, to remain sane.

There wasn't much excitement at the barn. Equipment was being secured by four men in antiquated attire reminiscent of colonial times. The knee socks and tri-cornered hats would have fit well with Napoleon's period, yet seemed a bizarre sight for the early twenty-first century.

After the farm hands put the combine in its slot, they went to work, tossing hay into a loft with pitch forks. A few words were bandied about, just enough to tell that the men spoke English of all things, though the accent was odd. It wasn't any tone Max was familiar with.

It didn't take long for the three observers to leave the workers to their task, and they headed for the inviting farmhouse. The inner door was wide open, but a secondary storm door blocked their passage. They had a choice to make. They could either wait around for someone to push the door open, or they could drop back into normal space-time and expose themselves to the world at large.

They waited for an hour, but nobody came to let them in.

"If we're just going to stand around, we might as well go home," Tony complained.

"You didn't have to come," Max said, starting to feel the minutes add up.

"There's nobody inside," Suzanne remarked, looking through a window at the empty entryway. "We should proceed."

"Hey, wait," Tony said. "We don't all have to dephase. Only one of us has to be tangible, right?"

"It would be less conspicuous," Suzanne responded. "Up for the task, Turner?"

Max didn't like the idea, but she was the boss. Grabbing at his wristband, he brought his body back into phase, and opened the outer door. It made a nasty creaking sound. He stepped inside and waited a few seconds for his invisible colleagues to follow.

Max wanted to shift back to safety, but it would be several minutes before his wrist band's energy cell recharged. For the moment, he was stuck, exposed.

"You two look around down here," Max said to his companions. "I'll see what there is upstairs."

The staircase was right in front of him; a gradual run of rough-sawn boards with a square banister. The edges on the boards had all been rounded, whether from tools or wear wasn't clear. The steps were rugged enough, though, and Max jogged up in a hurry without feeling the slightest sag.

The upstairs was a long hallway with doors on either side and a window at the far end. He moved along in a nonchalant manner, hoping to find a closet or dresser containing period clothing. He peeked into a few of the rooms, seeing beds in varying states of disarray. Clearly, it wasn't customary in this household to make your bed as soon as you got up in the morning.

A room at the end of the hall was the first Max stopped to search. It was the master bedroom, and had two large dressers filled with clothing. They were mostly men's attire, clearly cut for a stout individual. Not exactly Max's size, but he could make them work. Tony, however, would be hard-pressed to wedge himself into the things.

Completing his perusal of the right-side dresser, he spotted a spattering of coinage sitting atop it. The copper and silver pieces didn't look like much, though for a poor farmer it might have been a substantial sum. Knowing that money could be needed, Max slid the handful of coins into his pocket, covering his guilt with the cool rationale that nothing in this altered timeline really mattered—though he was hard-pressed to believe it. Stealing objects would at the very least send ripples through time, disrupting the Agency's temporal monitoring for a while. It wouldn't be as disastrous as saving or taking a life out of history, though disruption of any kind was to be avoided whenever possible.

Of course, if Max had been terribly concerned with minor disruptions in time, he wouldn't have come sight-seeing.

Turning to a closet tucked in the corner of the room, he found several dresses hanging. The black and white things made him think of the Pilgrims and the thought of Suzanne walking around in such attire made him chuckle. However silly they looked, they would do the job, so he removed one set from its hanger and tossed it over his shoulder.

Turning around, Max saw a woman standing in the doorway.

He froze as she locked eyes on him, and watched as she tensed up, clearly panicking.

"No, don't..." Max started.

Her scream drowned him out.

As the woman disappeared down the hallway, Max charged after her, wondering what he was going to do, now that he'd been exposed. He caught her at the top of the stairs and tried his best to calm her down. Her flailing limbs and thrashing head almost sent her down the stairs, but Max's arms were rugged and held her in place. She eventually stopped moving, when she realized it was a futile struggle.

"Calm down," Max said through gritted teeth. His legs were throbbing from the kicking they'd received. "Nobody's going to hurt you."

"Let me go, you Austrian pig!" the lady cursed.

"Austrian?" Max asked, relaxing his grip around her mid-section. "You have me all wrong. I'm not Austrian"

"You don't sound like any Franco-Saxon," the woman rebutted, turning her head enough to reexamine Max's face.

It was then that Max realized the source of the accent he'd been hearing from the people of this timeline. What a new development; the commingling of English and French? Yet the words were predominantly English, denoting which culture had the upper hand in the alliance.

"Have you ever seen an Austrian with clothes like mine?" Max asked, hoping to place a seed of doubt. If he could somehow calm this woman, he might have a chance of talking his way out of trouble, assuming he could spin a convincing cover story.

The woman stomped a foot on the floor. "I've not seen an Austrian before," she admitted.

"Then why do you think I'm one of them?"

"Never seen anything like you before, either," the woman replied. "That is no a Royal Army uniform you're wearing. It must be Austrian!"

Following her last word, her heel slammed down on Max's foot, and he felt it even through his heavy boots. It made him squeeze her harder around the waist, which started her screaming again.

"Damn it, woman, I'm not Austrian!"

"Then you're nothing but a petty burglar," the woman shouted. "Either way, my husband will have your head!"

Reason was not going to prevail in this situation, so Max released her, and watched her charge down the stairs into the waiting arms of a bearded man, no doubt her husband who had just come through the door. The burly beast was quick to hug his wife, then set her aside to deal with the intruder.

Max cursed under his breath and darted back down the hall. He grabbed the articles of clothing he'd dropped in order to grab the woman, and then checked his wristband. It was recharged and ready to use.

Dashing into the bedroom, Max hit the control that set him out of phase with normal space-time. By the time the angry husband was once more in view, Max was invisible and intangible, safe from harm. The husband looked around frantically, checking every nook and cranny, seeking the strange man who'd upset his wife, but there was nothing he could find. The room was empty, and the windows were locked.

The husband turned to the room across the hall, still searching for the elusive intruder. Max left him to his vain quest, and headed downstairs, where his colleagues were waiting.

"Thanks for the backup. Here," Max said, tossing the dress at Suzanne.

"Got anything for me?" Tony asked with a devilish grin on his face. He'd clearly had fun watching the show.

"You want a set, have at it," Max invited.

"The man was clearly too short and wide for your wiry build, Agent Cross," Suzanne mentioned, examining the dress.

"Not a problem for you, eh, Max?"

"Let's get back to the Jeep," Max suggested, feeling they'd best be moving on. If they hit the next farm before word spread of the "Austrian burglar," they'd be able to ask for directions to the nearest library.

"Are we forgetting something?" Tony asked, hooking a thumb over his shoulder at the closed door.

The angry husband was shouting upstairs as he checked each room for the intruder, as his wife remained near the foot of the stairs, watching for anyone who might be making a run for it. There were a couple of sturdy farm hands lurking around on the front porch, as well, but nobody was going in or out at the moment.

There was no getting around it; they'd just have to wait for someone to open the door.

* * *

The city of Calais sat as a bustling port, looking much as it had for centuries. Tall masts stood tall near the water, with block after block of stone and brick buildings to greet two newcomers to the area whose clothes and accents didn't quite fit. Few people paid them any attention on the busy streets, as there were plenty of strangers in this trading center.

Everywhere you looked, there was activity. Horse drawn carts pulled meat and produce to market, while packs of people walked to the various stores on the main streets. Some of the fashions were more modern than what the Waterloo farmers had been wearing, though nothing looked post-industrial.

It was hot and humid in the middle of summer, and Max wished these work clothes he'd pilfered breathed more. They were rugged, designed for heavy labor in colder temperatures. The sun was killing him.

Suzanne bore the heat better, and didn't seem to sweat so much, though it couldn't have been pleasant for her in the baggy get up.

Approaching a busy intersection, Max turned his attention to a boisterous boy selling newspapers. "How much, kid?" he asked.

"Two pence, sir," the lad said.

"That's highway robbery," Max replied, picking a few coins out of his pocket. He examined the unfamiliar denominations he'd snatched off the farmhouse dresser.

"I don't set the price, miser." The boy may have been saying "mister," but the French influence on his accent made it impossible to tell.

"Here," Max said, tossing a small, silver coin into the kid's palm. In return, he received four pages of newsprint.

Before Max could read the front page, Suzanne yanked it from his grasp. "That's a start," she said, snapping the page straight out of his grip, and looking at the headlines. "Austrian Atrocities in Virginia?" she read aloud.

Max moved around to get a clear view of the paper as she skimmed the news story. In the center of the page was a rough sketch of Florida, with several place-names marked along the coast, none of which lined up with his geographical knowledge.

"According to this, the Austrian Empire has landed troops on

the coast of *'Virginia,'* which seems to comprise most of Florida and
Georgia in our timeline. This is only the latest in a series of strikes
against English colonies on the North Atlantian continent." From the
elevated tone of voice, it was clear she was excited by the newfound
knowledge.

"Aye, it's bloody awful," a voice remarked over Max's
shoulder. He whipped around to see a tall man in a red and white
uniform glaring down at him. "Rotten Papists and their ungodly
attacks. And they presume to call themselves Christian."

"Have you done battle with the Austrians, *Leftenant*?" Suzanne
said, recognizing the gold markings on the officer's sleeve."

"Last year, at the battle of Barcelona, and I relish the day we
pay those bastards back for what they've done," the lieutenant
remarked.

"God willing," Max said, hoping to get out of the conversation.

The lieutenant nodded and continued on his way. Max and
Suzanne watched the man limp down the sidewalk, clearly pained with
each step, but unaided by a cane or other support. It was a curious
thing.

"A member of the home guard, maybe?" Max wondered aloud.

"Never mind him. Look at this editorial," Suzanne said,
pointing to the news story below the fold. *"Appeaser on the Throne"*
was the title, and the following was a scathing commentary on the
recently crowned King Harold III of England.

Max read the words as Suzanne spoke them aloud.

"The Crowning of King Harold III has been heralded as a great
triumph by the bureaucrats in Parliament, yet it is clear this boy-king
will be nothing less than a disaster for the British Empire. His
sympathies alone should raise more eyebrows, as his own mother was a
Papist, and it is widely assumed that this lad will be led as much from
Rome as by his advisors at home.

"It was a sad mistake for King Walter to pick the Viennese-
born Joanna as his wife, as it proved a futile attempt to stave off the
inevitable conflict with Austria. The war has come, only a few decades
late, but in the meantime our former queen sowed the seed of sedition
in her offspring.

"How many centuries have we fought to remain free from
oppression? Are we now to be handed back into the waiting hands of a
Catholic hierarchy? Even now, there is rumor of peace talks with the

Austrians, talks which threaten to not only undermine our religious freedoms, but to hand large swaths of our Atlantian Colonies over to these enemies. The wealth and homes which our cousins across the sea have cultivated for so long will become bargaining chips in some regal game. Can such a betrayal be tolerated?"

The article raged on, condemning the collusion of King Harold and the Austrians, though most of it was speculative, and the entire piece was slanted toward the writer's viewpoint.

"Well, that's a start," Max mentioned. "We're getting the lay of the land."

"It's the tip of the iceberg," Suzanne rebutted. "We're still no closer to figuring out why things are this way. Let's keep moving."

They marched through town, searching for a suitable library or bookstore, anything that could provide them with decent historical texts. This was clearly a literate society, as evidenced by the newspaper.

"There's got to be an easier way to track changes in the timeline than this," Suzanne mentioned.

"I thought you wanted to get out," Max said. "You did strong-arm your way into my Jeep, remember?"

Suzanne kept a neutral expression, even as her mind raged with anger at his insolent tone. He knew damn well she hadn't come for pleasure, but to keep him in line. This was about rank, and setting an example. If this chaotic agent would learn to keep his place and respect the chain of command, she wouldn't have to get dirty like this. She'd liked her desk even before this crisis made her a refugee in time.

There was no getting out of this without a lot of research. The Temporal Agency simply wasn't ready for this sort of crisis. Their technology was relatively new, and they were up against someone who was clearly decades ahead of them, in a relative sense. How they managed to keep up at all was amazing.

There was still hope, however. Jack Baker may have ripped history to shreds, but he was still only one man, and he would slip up eventually, or so Suzanne had to hope.

How many years would it take to beat him at his own game? The way things were looking, it could be a very long time. Suzanne hated to think of an entire lifetime wasted in a vain quest to stop a madman.

As her contemplation drew her away from reality, Max tapped

her shoulder and pointed to a large glass storefront with books sitting in plain view. "Looks like the place," he said.

Suzanne had to agree, and followed him inside, where they found a narrow, cramped room filled with bookshelves. Before they could shut the door, a dapper man dressed in something resembling spats approached from the register.

"Can I help you?" the shopkeeper asked.

"We're looking for a few good books," Max answered.

"Really? I wouldn't have taken you for a couple of bibliophiles," the man said, looking them up and down in a most discriminating manner.

"We like to keep a low profile," Max explained, jiggling the coins in his pocket. "But we are paying customers, I assure you."

"Well, in that case, welcome! How can I be of service today?"

"What do you have on history?" Suzanne asked.

"Yes, my mother and I are quite interested in the past," Max said, eager to give his boss an added jibe. She was only a few years his elder, but didn't even look it, so the absurdity of his claim was obvious.

As Suzanne gritted her teeth at Max, the shopkeeper directed them to a book rack in the back. "I have a little bit of everything here, from Prescott's *Conquest of Spain*, to Samuel Clemens' *History of the English Colonies* in three volumes. Tell me, is there anything specific you have in mind?"

"Nothing in particular," Suzanne replied. "May we browse a bit?"

"Oh, of course," the shopkeeper said, returning to the register. He kept an eye on them, but let them have space to examine the books in relative privacy.

There truly was a little bit of everything on history, and it was hard figure where to start. Max started rifling through the bottom shelf on the left side, and Suzanne checked a middle rack halfway up on the right, preferring to stay vertical. She felt it undignified to kneel, and bending over might give people lecherous ideas.

The books were arranged by author in alphabetical order, as was to be expected, but their subject matter didn't follow the same pattern as their initials, making it a time-consuming search. That, and the fact that the bindings had little descriptive notation, forcing them to open each book to the title page in order to figure out what half of them were about. Even then, it was sometimes difficult, and they had to read an entire page or two of the introduction.

The shopkeeper was understanding, at least, and didn't roust them for reading too much. He was expecting them to buy something eventually, but had the courtesy to let them search. During the prolonged perusal, a few other patrons stopped in to shop, which helped to distract him.

It was tough to pick a single book for purchase, as each one held a tidbit of altered history and could prove useful. The fascination factor alone made picking out a handful of tomes a difficult decision.

"I think we're getting close," Max mentioned as he snapped shut the cover on a little brown book. "This one talks about the Norman conquest of 1066, and it looks pretty much the same, though I'd need a few days of comparison with our own historical records to be absolutely certain."

"Well, I'd say I can do one better," Suzanne said, running his finger down the introduction page of a heavy, leather-bound volume. "This is a complete history of the Hundred Years' War, and someone is conspicuously absent."

"Who?" Max asked.

"Joan of Arc."

Suzanne checked the picture index, then quickly flipped to the back of the book. Planting her finger on a colorful lithograph, she read the description. "Crowning of King John II after his annexation of France in September 1331."

"Maybe I'm having a mental lapse, but who's John the second?"

"John of Lancaster," Suzanne mentioned. "Brother of Henry the Fifth. After Henry died, he served as regent, but he never became king in our timeline—not after the failures in France." She closed the book and tucked it under her arm. "This could be it. Without Joan of Arc to turn the tide of war, the English conquered France, and must have gone on to gobble up the rest of Western Europe afterwards."

"Are you sure? It seems a bit of a leap," Max mentioned, remaining skeptical.

"I'm a historian, remember?" Suzanne boasted. "While you were building muscle cars and training at some Police Academy, I was reading this," she said, shaking the book for emphasis. "For whatever reason, Joan of Arc never left her mark on history in this timeline, and this book might tell us why."

"It's a start," Max replied, hoping it truly was the smoking gun they'd been looking for.

Suzanne headed for the register, deciding she'd dug far enough. Locating this strong lead would satisfy her curiosity, and that comfortable desk back at the Agency was perfect for reading. Best get back to it.

Max followed close behind, carrying several books he believed to be of potential use, as well. Altogether, they held enough books to formulate a practical outline of Europe's progress during the last millennium.

Stepping up to the counter, Suzanne flopped the heavy history book down in front of the shopkeeper, who looked up at her with an amiable smile. "Aha, I see you've found what you were after," he remarked.

"For the most part," Suzanne said. "How much?"

The shopkeeper opened the cover and examined the first few pages. "The gruesome Hundred Years War, most certainly an interesting topic. Two shillings."

Suzanne didn't blink, but Max flinched at the monetary amount. That was a lot of money in this place and time, and his finances were quite limited, despite what he'd suggested to the shopkeeper. Setting his stack of books down, he dug into his pocket and retrieved the coins therein. Three silver rounds, and a fistful of coppers accounted for the full sum he'd snatched off the farmer's dresser. He set them on the counter for examination. "This is what I've got."

The shopkeeper eyed the spattering of change and said, "Are you trying to chisel me, sir? This is a sight under two shillings."

"I thought these were shillings," Max said, pointing to one of the silver rounds.

"Those are half shillings," the shopkeeper said incredulously. "What sort of people are you, that you can't even count coinage? Get out, and take your meager change with you!"

Suzanne sighed, and then punched the shopkeeper square in the nose. So much for staying above-board.

Grabbing their books quickly, Max and Suzanne reached for their wrists, preparing to shift out of phase for a quick getaway. Now that they'd found the proper documents, there was no sense wasting more time in this primitive era, when they could rendezvous with Tony and head home. Once back at the Agency, they'd have breathing room to examine the books and cross examine history. If they were very lucky, they'd find the focal point before Baker changed it again.

Hitting her wrist, Suzanne felt a tingle go up her arm. It wasn't a friendly sensation, and in a split second her eyes went dark.

Max had his eyes on Suzanne when she activated her wristband, and blinked as a flash of light coursed out from her arm. The sudden burst of energy dropped her instantly, and she fell to the floor in a crumpled heap, with the valuable book falling beside her.

With the stack of books tucked under his arm, Max hadn't been fast enough to hit his band first, and after seeing Suzanne collapse, he hesitated. Nothing like this had happened before, and he couldn't tell if it were a simple malfunction, or something far more sinister.

As the shopkeeper continued to scream and clutch his broken nose, Max looked outside to see a cloaked figure standing in front of the shop window. The hood hid most of the face, but a wicked grin was plainly visible, and a gloved hand waved an added taunt at the time agent.

"Baker!" Max shouted, as he reached for the pistol tucked under his jacket. He started to run for the door, but before he could get outside, the cloaked figure was gone, vanished without a trace.

Fearing the worst, Max tapped the side of his head, activating the subdermal implant beside his right ear. He tried to contact Tony, but received only static. Something was disrupting his equipment, which meant he was stuck here for the moment.

Tucking his pistol back out of sight, Max reached down and checked the unconscious figure of Suzanne. She was still breathing, so he hefted her onto his shoulders, preparing to carry her out of the shop. He grabbed the book on the Hundred Years' War, as well, and made for the door as quickly as possible, even as the shopkeeper shouted more protests. He doubted the shopkeeper would shoot him; if the man were armed he would have already tried something following the initial assault.

Max managed to open the door and charge outside, where the flow of active bodies helped to conceal him, but only slightly. A man carrying a woman over his shoulder was conspicuous, even in a crowd. He had to find someplace to hide, where he could bide his time until help arrived—if it came at all.

He also needed to see to Suzanne. There was no telling what sort of damage that energy burst had caused. She might not have long to live, and that could spell a whole new set of problems.

"You'll pay for this, Jack Baker," Max growled, ducking down a side-alley. "Before this is over, I'll make you cherish the day you were never born!"

A Rare Chance at the Enemy
by Mark Mellon

April 17, 1806 dawned clear and fair off the coast of France. Gulls pinwheeled in the brilliantly blue sky. The Channel was flecked by a million whitecaps. The frigate *L'Oiseau* and the gun-brigs *Lark* and *Harpy* headed shoreward, propelled by a strong south-south-east wind. In earlier years, surveillance had been fairly easy, no great matter at all to dash in close to shore to observe the French and harass and interfere with their war efforts as opportunities presented themselves. Over time, however, as numerous cannon with a range of over a mile were installed, to tack near Boulogne grew risky indeed.

Nonetheless, despite the danger, sixth raters of the Channel Squadron, the "eyes" of the fleet, must reconnoiter Boulogne and other ports several times a week. A report had to be made: how many ships' masts in the harbor; had troops stationed there increased or decreased; new shipbuilding or continued maintenance of the current fleet; and any other pertinent information.

"Ahoy above! Any doings in the harbor or the town?" Captain Linzie shouted.

"Naught that we can see, sir," came a topman's fleeting cry from his perch on the main mast a hundred pitching, yawing feet above.

On the quarterdeck, Captain Linzie scanned the shoreline through a telescope. Lookouts were posted in the masts, keen-eyed, reliable men with spyglasses, but he was determined to be vigilant himself. The last lugger to fetch supplies also delivered a confidential letter, personally dispatched by the Secretary of the Admiralty, a by no means uncertain warning to watch for a possible attack by an infernal machine or other treacherous device of the American scoundrel Fulton in an unholy alliance with the Irish renegade O'Sheridane.

A new snotty whose name Linzie had not yet learned ran up and saluted. All of 15, he piped, "*Lark* signals, sir. Wants to know if she and *Harpy* should wear away."

With their shallower draughts, the gun-brigs were well ahead of *L'Oiseau*, scudding close to the wind. They sailed nearer to the huge stone forts that dotted the cliffs along the shore.

"Say your name, young gentleman."

"Midshipman Randolph Fitzhugh, sir."

"Make it Fitz for short. Signal Shippard to hug the shore. We mice must try to lure the cat from his lair, Mr. Fitz."

"Yes, sir. Gun brigs to continue surveillance. Very good, sir." The snotty ran off. Linzie put the telescope to his eye again. Things looked no different from the last uneventful visit. Boney's flat-bottomed invasion fleet still bobbed uselessly in the harbor. Boulogne was still gray and nondescript. The Secretary's letter had described a great wooden manufactory built in the basin by a small army of Irish traitors but could provide no information concerning its purpose. The manufactory was out of sight this far from shore.

This was about the level of intelligence Linzie expected from the Admiralty so he was not particularly put out. He had no fears concerning Fulton in any event. Linzie had often dined out on the tale of the mad inventor who twice ventured forth into the Channel in his cockleshell plunging boat in hopes of sneaking up to attach an explosive charge and blow his frigate to bits. It had been simple to hoist sail the moment a lookout hailed sign and tip his cocked hat *adieu* as Fulton and his quixotic boat swiftly shrank to a tiny black dot. He expected nothing different this time either.

"Hallo the deck!" a topman shouted. "Smoke ashore, six points off the port bow."

Linzie swiveled his spyglass. Thick black clouds blossomed among the flotilla's masts and spars, bare as winter trees.

"Damn me if Boney's toy invasion fleet ain't caught afire. Is it not a pretty sight, me hearties?" he shouted to laughter from the crew.

Fitz ran onto the quarterdeck.

"Sir, *Harpy* signals an enemy vessel in the roadway."

"This is our lucky day! Prob'ly fleeing the fire. Mr. Inchington, I shall have the long guns loaded and run out."

"Yes, sir," the lieutenant replied. The bosun and his mates

gave orders.   Below deck, wooden hatches were slammed open. Barefoot sailors pushed heavy cannon on rollers over a sand-strewn deck until they protruded from the frigate's sides like black teeth.

"A rare chance at the enemy, by Jove, and on such a glorious day," said Linzie.

* * *

The populace of Boulogne was confined to their homes the night *Actium* was launched. Soldiers patrolled the streets under orders to shoot anyone who violated the curfew.

Wooden stanchions were knocked loose. The manufactory's noise that had lasted so long the citizens could not remember a good night's sleep, reached a hideous crescendo. With a jarring, pig-like squeal, *Actium* slid down a greased track out of the manufactory and into the basin. She hit with a terrific splash that rocked every boat in the basin. Her stern dipped deep into the water. For a heart-stopping moment O'Sheridane knew she would sink there on the spot, that his hopes and dreams, schemes and calculations, were entirely in vain.

The stern emerged with agonizing slowness from the black water. *Actium* lay calm.   About to crow that no physical dilemma could not be solved, O'Sheridane noticed: the keel jutted at least four feet above the waterline. At the stern the propellers protruded from the water by a good foot. He had erred badly. His estimates of the weight lost by removing the ship's guns, masts, spars, and rigging and that added by the steam engine and armor plating had been grievously low. Robert Fulton's look of long-famished spite at last gratified would usually have infuriated O'Sheridane. In a crisis, however, he had no time for petty feeling.

Already up and mounted, Napoleon restlessly prowled the basin's edge with his entourage. His hook nosed white Arab nervously paced in a tight circle; the Emperor's eagle eye searched for faltering on O'Sheridane's part. Any reluctance and O'Sheridane would be imprisoned in the Temple.

"Line the hold with kentledge until the eaves break water," O'Sheridane said.

Kentledge, blocks of pig iron, were hauled out of the manufactory and rowed over in longboats to *Actium*. Hatches were opened and the heavy, unwieldy ballast was slowly lowered and carefully positioned to keep the ship's hull balanced and in trim. When they had packed in as much as the ship could hold, O'Sheridane ruefully inspected her.

The screws were submerged, but the wood hull was still exposed in the calm, level basin. The Channel's churning swell would expose more, briefly but long enough for the King's expert gunners to hole her. Once pierced, kentledge would drag *Actium* down like a stone.

"Fulton, summon the crew. I must speak with them. That includes yourself," O'Sheridane said.

Fulton failed to salute but nonetheless rounded up Gaylan Kilmaine and the others, ten volunteers. They would fire and tend the complicated steam engine under Fulton's fussy supervision. Kilmaine and O'Sheridane would man the bridge. Aside from Kilmaine and Fulton, all were ex-Royal Navy men. They tugged forelocks and bobbed their heads when they approached O'Sheridane as befitted his status as commander. He pointed to *Actium* and said:

"Ye knew t'was but a forlorn hope when you signed articles to crew *Actium*. I have a hard new fact to tell you. She still rides high with her keel exposed. T'is my own fault, no excuses."

"I shall sail her. Kilmaine and Fulton too for she is as much their ship as mine."

Fulton was about to protest but was handily shushed by Kilmaine, dewy-eyed with pride.

"Will you sail, even as she is?" O'Sheridane asked.

"Och, sir," replied a man of Aran, rugged face as lined as his rocky islet home, "what is drowned to being flogged round the fleet?" There was gallows laughter at this reminder that each man was under a death sentence in any event for daring to defy the crown of England. In low murmured tones, the others made their eagerness plain to attack the hated oppressor, no matter the risk.

"Very well then. Kilmaine, man the longboats," O'Sheridane said.

"Yes, sir. Form ranks, men."

The men fell into orderly files and trooped into longboats tethered by a pier. Dressed in the dark blue uniform of a French naval officer, O'Sheridane leaped with cat's grace into a boat and held out a hand to steady Fulton. Aboard *Actium*, they took their duty stations. The crew lit small oil lamps. Already filthy with black dust, men shoveled soft coal into the engine's burners while Fulton madly raced about the boiler to shut off one valve and open another. Men in longboats strained at their oars to turn the ship's bow. The sky was well lit when *Actium* was fully turned. At the bridge with Kilmaine, O'Sheridane shouted through a speaking tube.

"Up to pressure?"

"No!" Fulton answered. "It is not really tested. That unreasonable tyrant never gave us a chance to try it in the water!"

"Patience, Bobbie. The engine turned over in the manufactory. Let a head of steam build. Physics will take over."

Fulton sighed, "As you say."

Fulton fiddled long and hard with various gauges and valves. The crew tied kerchiefs around their faces and shoveled coal with a will. Small tentative puffs of smoke belched from the twin smokestacks. Twin pistons trembled. One shot forward into its chamber. Its mate reciprocated. Another wrenching spasm occurred. Then another, again and again. The great boiler chuffed with increased purpose and intensity. The pistons' motion grew rhythmic and repeated. Even at the bridge, the noise was overwhelming.

"Engage the screws, Bobbie, but handsomely," O'Sheridane ordered.

O'Sheridane was painfully aware this was the first time Fulton's direct acting engine had to perform. While on stanchions, the engine had fired and the propellers turned easily enough, but never in the water, not under duress. If the engine failed, if anything failed, there would be no excuses.

The ship pushed forward effortlessly.

O'Sheridane said, "Throttle back by half!"

The *Actium* slowed to a more sedate pace, suitable for negotiating the previously cleared narrow path through the National Flotilla. Already cursing the conning ports' limited view, O'Sheridane cautiously turned the wheel by minute degrees to port and starboard, getting accustomed to the steering. *Actium* headed toward the basin's mouth. Smoke puffed from her stacks like plumes from a *philosophe*'s pipe.

"Huzza!" the Irish assembled along the shore cheered. Napoleon raised his bicorne in salute. His white Arab reared up on his hind legs. The entourage saluted also. Citizens of Boulogne eavesdropped from darkened, shuttered rooms, eaten with curiosity but afraid to stick their heads out and have them shot off. What could possibly be going on?

* * *

L'Oiseau skirted near the outer range of Boulogne's guns. The gun-brigs were dangerously past it. Already at quarters, the crews threw off lingering fatigue from long watches and keyed themselves alert in readiness for potential combat. Linzie scanned the gray notch in the green and white coastal cliffs where the Liane emptied into the Atlantic.

"Sir, *Harpy* reports something strange about the ship."
"Strange?   What   the   devil   do   you   mean,   Mr.   Fitz?"
"I do not know, sir. That is what the signal said."

"It is of no account.   Signal both gun-brigs to engage the enemy."

"Yes, sir."

Linzie put the glass back to his eye.

For a brief deluded second the mad thought occurred to him that a stray beetle, newly hatched from a dead log by the warm spring sun, had been borne by the wind and landed on his telescope lens.   He put down the glass, rubbed deeply crowfooted eyes with his hands and brought up the spyglass.

His vision did not deceive him.   There was no beetle nor was it an illusion conjured up by some mischievous mental imp.   A ship moved at speed into the Channel past the pile of rocks where Fort Rouge stood. Smoke poured from two tall black cylinders at the stern. The strange vessel gleamed in the brilliant sunlight, the iron scales of her armor wet with sea spray. Flags streamed in the stiff wind from the smokestacks: the French tricolor and a golden harp on a green field. Without masts or spars (thus that much less of a target) and powered by no visible means, the ship was a fantastic carapaced monster, a seagoing dragon of menacing steel.

Not given to fancy, Linzie said, "Damn if I know what manner of craft that is."

"I would hazard a guess, sir," said Inchington, the officer of the watch.

"What's that? Speak up, Mr. Inchington."

"The ship is most likely powered by a steam engine, sir, perhaps a new contraption devised by the American Fulton."

"Fulton! How do you know?"

"T'is no secret he has tried such tricks before or that he still lives in France. O'Sheridane the deserter may have a hand in things also. That's the flag of the Irish Legion opposite the tricolor. Had a reputation as a scientific cove before he went renegade, even wrote a monograph for the Royal Society on steam propulsion in '97. Quite well received too."

"That will suffice, Mr. Inchington. Steam powered or no, we will close with her as with any French warship and destroy her."

"Aye, sir."

The evident doubt in Inchington's brown eyes troubled Linzie. Inchington was a proven officer, the veteran of a dozen stiff actions whose conduct under fire had been cited for merit. The deep, hollow boom of cannon fire from across the water distracted him.

The gun-brigs fired culverins at the French ship. Already moving at a brisk clip, the ship increased speed with unnatural rapidity.

"'Pon my soul, sir, if she ain't doing at least 10 knots," Inchington said.

"Stuff, Mr. Inchington, utter stuff."

Heedless of the steadily intensifying cannonade from coastal artillery, the gun-brigs went straight at the enemy in the best Royal Navy tradition. *Harpy* took the lead, tightly followed by *Lark*, captained by the ambitious Lt. Shippard. The ships crossed the "T" in the best Nelson manner. They passed perpendicular to the French ship's bow so a meticulously timed and aimed full broadside of six 24-pounders could be fired by each brig as cannon came to bear upon the target.

"There's masterly sailing, Mr. Inchington."

Years of gunnery practice paid off as round shot belched at precise, short intervals from the cannons' mouths with great torrents of smoke and flame. Despite the low silhouette, each cannonball found its target and smashed into the French ship at less than fifty yards range.

The shot bounced off the overlapped iron scales with no more impact than rain on a slate roof. *L'Oiseau*'s crew stood open mouthed in amazement.

"Might as well throw their hats at the bloody evil thing," one seaman said.

"T'ain't natural," another said.

Her speed already unnerving, the French ship bolted forward, her wake a great roiling spray. She swung hard aport, headed directly for *Lark*. The crew fired off another round from the culverin. The shot bounced off like a pea from a shooter.

She crashed into *Lark* dead amidships. The brig snapped like a toy broken in two by a petulant child. The once shipshape, weatherly vessel was reduced to a tangle of rigging and shattered timbers. *Lark* sank instantly beneath the turbulent waves, her fragments swamped and dragged down by the hungry sea.

"My word. How extraordinary," Inchington said.

* * *

Actium steamed through the basin's narrow mouth into the Liane. Conditions aboard grew steadily worse. Coal fumes soon filled the poorly ventilated craft. O'Sheridane and Kilmaine tried to ignore the choking smoke but their eyes burned and their throats were raw.

O'Sheridane shouted into the voice pipe, "Bobbie! Is it to kill us you seek?"

"It is the blowers," Fulton shrieked. "They do not vent properly."

"Was it not I that said they were set too low for the Channel?" O'Sheridane muttered. "Gaylan! Open the forward hatch. Fulton, throttle back full and have a man open the rear hatch as well. See if you can not mend the blowers."

"But we shall swamp," Kilmaine objected.

"Go on or we suffocate sure!"

Smoke dwindled to intermittent puffs. The ship lost way. She bobbed in the turbulent Liane. Kilmaine scaled the skeletal iron ladder to the fore hatch and heaved it open. Another man opened the rear. A cool, fresh draft eased through the ship. Fulton adjusted the blowers, tears of frustration plowing furrows down his blackened cheeks. Kilmaine wiped the soot-smeared ports clean.

O'Sheridane took a deep breath of sea air and said, "Batten hatches. Half throttle ahead."

Fulton advanced the lever that controlled the engine's pitch. Pistons worked to a more intense rhythm. Smoke poured thick and foul from the stacks. Fulton's stopgaps had improved the situation somewhat. The smoke was noxious still, but more bearable. O'Sheridane set a course to the right of the pile fort. Her defenders waved brightly colored kerchiefs in salute from the ramparts as *Actium* sailed past.

"Two small ships head toward us," Kilmaine reported.

"So I see, lubber, *Harpy* and *Lark*. They shall fire broadsides once they close. Let us see if the armor holds."

"Faith, ye are of optimistic bent."

O'Sheridane laughed.

The gun brigs passed close by, dingy sails full and curved in the leeward wind. Sharp spikes of flame speared outward from gun ports. Shot rang with dull thuds off the iron armor, twelve regular hammer strokes. *Actium* rang like a grandfather clock's noon chimes. A few wooden ribs cracked from the stress, but the iron plates stayed in place. The crew cheered.

"Bobbie!" O'Sheridane shouted. "I shall set course to ram *Lark*. Put the throttle to full, then you and the men brace yourselves."

"We cannot set the engine to such a pitch."

"Damn ye, Fulton, obey my orders!"

Pistons reached a frantic pace. The ship literally surged under O'Sheridane's feet. She hurled herself through the sea, her clean keel slicing keenly through the choppy waves, driven on by the powerful engine. O'Sheridane could see *Lark*'s captain through the conning port, an angry, red-faced man, cocked hat worn fore and aft after the new fashion, barking orders from the stern.

"Me old shipmate Shippard! What skylarks we used to have in the after-cockpit," O'Sheridane chortled. "Fancy our meeting again."

The ram's cruel barbed tip ripped *Lark* open below the water line like a knife through a soft white underbelly. *Actium* shuddered slightly at the impact but forged ruthlessly ahead. The brig careened to starboard momentarily. She split in two, her timbers shattered. An old man was thrown high into the air and plunged into the sea, toothless mouth open wide in horror. The conning ports were showered with debris from the shattered gun-brig. O'Sheridane flinched involuntarily.

"Tchah," he said. "Look at me quaking. No better than a child."

Kilmaine grabbed the speaking tube and shouted, "Grand news, boyos. We sank one of King George's own ships this day!"

The crew gave another cheer.

"Let us stalk bigger game now. The frigate *L'Oiseau*," O'Sheridane said.

* * *

In his barracks, the Emperor watched from a room opposite his bedchamber through an enormous telescope perched on three elegantly carved mahogany legs. A wide smile lit his face when *Actium* destroyed *Lark*. The officers in the room burst into cheers.

"What a triumph for French arms, Your Majesty!" Colonel Aubisson crowed, the commander of a grenadier regiment.

"Now these English dogs will know we can beat them at sea as well as land," another exulted.

"Nothing will ever match French science, French ingenuity!" a third said, conveniently overlooking the fact that *Actium* was designed and built by an American and an Irishman.

Napoleon silenced them with a disapproving frown.

"Let us not be premature, gentlemen. It was the least among English sixth-raters. Yet to be fair, it was a British warship and O'Sheridane destroyed it as he promised. He may sink more than this minnow, perhaps a fleet of whales."

There was much laughter at the Emperor's wit. Impassive, he resumed his scrutiny.

* * *

Lark's instant, utter destruction unnerved the men. The L'Oiseaus grew anxious. The French ship's devilish speed, seeming invincibility, and fearsome aspect convinced superstitious seamen she was unnatural, a sea monster from a tall tale brought to life. Some of the more pious prayed aloud, interceding for mercy from such a beast. "It is Leviathan!" Old Duff cried, a member of a small, fundamentalist sect.

To quell panic, Linzie barked "Silence fore and aft! Each man will keep to his post and do his duty. Save your vaporing for Sunday services, Old Duff. Mr. Inchington! Sail directly for the enemy. We shall outweigh any advantage in speed with the aggression of our assault."

"Begging your pardon, sir, but the enemy has anticipated us," Inchington said.

Linzie looked leeward. *Harpy* had turned into the wind to pick up any survivors from *Lark* and was instantly in irons, unable to make headway. After destroying her sister, the French ship ignored this helpless prey. She headed toward *L'Oiseau*.

"Fire as she draws near, Mr. Inchington. We shall see how she holds up under the weight of thirty-two pound shot."

L'Oiseau had the weather-gage. That and the superior gunnery of his crew should see them through, Linzie believed, but the French ship defied expectations. Rather than come to grips, the ship headed away, heedless of contrary winds, out into the Channel.

"What are they about? She goes against God," Linzie cried.

"I fear not, sir," Inchington replied. "With an internal steam propulsion system, a ship can take any heading she pleases, regardless of wind or tide. Seeing how *Lark* broke up, she is undoubtedly armed with a ram. If I were her captain and could head where I liked, I would put the ship on just such a roundabout course to strike our vulnerable stern."

The ship did indeed head for the stern. After twenty years of command, for the first time Linzie was at a loss for what to do. Everything before had been in the realm of the possible. The French ship defied iron laws acknowledged by countless generations of seamen back to the dawn of time. It was simply beyond his ken.

"Might I make a suggestion, sir?" Inchington said.

"Yes, Mr. Inchington?"

"We might signal *Harpy* to make full sail for the squadron while the French are busy with us. Whitehall and the Admiralty will want to know about Fulton's new weapon."

In other circumstances, Linzie might have told his subordinate that he would seek counsel when he needed it. Despite his pride, however, long years at sea had taught pragmatism, to recognize sound advice when offered.

"Make it so, Mr. Inchington."

"Aye aye, sir. Shall I order the stern carronades loaded also, sir?" Inchington inquired.

"Yes, of course," Linzie replied. He was preoccupied, debating which way to tack so *L'Oiseau*'s long guns could bear upon the enemy.

In addition to her regular complement of cannon, *L'Oiseau* was equipped with four 32-pound carronades mounted on wheeled trucks on the spar deck, short, ugly weapons designed to shatter ships and their rigging at close range, two at the forecastle, two at the quarterdeck.

"Load canister," Inchington instructed the gun-captains.

The men were puzzled. Canister was typically used to mow down the enemy from the decks of a ship. Nonetheless, they followed orders. Charges of gunpowder in canvas bags were ramrodded down the barrels by loaders, followed by metal cans, each of which held a dozen small round shot. A handspike through a touch-hole near the breech broke each powder bag open. A small amount of finely ground gunpowder was then poured down the touch-hole, the last step before firing.

The French ship closed fast. Glass ports mounted at the bow, criss-crossed with metal bands, were like the orbs of some sinister insect. Linzie ordered the hands to stand ready by the running rigging for the fore-and-aft sails.

"Steady. Wait for my command," Inchington said.

The ship was less than half a knot away. Linzie shouted, "Hard to port. Smartly now!"

The double wheel spun furiously. Hands hauled the lines to shift the triangular sails' gaffs and booms. *L'Oiseau* shifted course sharply in a last second, last ditch effort to present her broadside to the enemy. The sea dragon simply changed course as well, fixed upon its prey.

"All hands brace for collision! Gun crews ready to fire," Inchington shouted.

The French were scant yards away now. Inchington thought he glimpsed a face, flashing white teeth bared in an impudent smile.

"Aim for those black pipes, where the smoke comes. Port carronade, fire!"

The stubby carronade's mouth spat smoke and flame. Canister shot riddled the smokestacks, but did not slow the oncoming monster.

The French ship steamed into *L'Oiseau* full astern at 15 knots, to the right of the rudder and well below the water line. There was an awful, ear-rending noise, closer to the death cry of some huge, dreadfully wounded animal than the sound of timbers being rent and shattered.

The impact knocked Inchington off his feet along with Linzie. Inchington struck his head when he hit the deck. He tried to command the starboard gun to fire, but the breath was knocked out of him. The masts swayed wildly overhead. The gray-green sea, the blue sky, and the holystoned spar deck merged and swirled into a nauseating whirlpool that dragged him down into unconsciousness.

* * *

"Afterwards, Bobbie," O'Sheridane shouted into the speaking tube.

"We have lost pressure," Fulton responded. "They holed the smokestacks. We can not get up enough steam."

L'Oiseau was badly damaged, perhaps mortally. The English ship took on more and more water. She tilted sternward and came down hard on *Actium*'s ram, embedded deep inside *L'Oiseau*. O'Sheridane could feel the bow tilt beneath him. Water flooded over the plate armor. Unless she pulled free, *L'Oiseau* would drag *Actium* down with her for company in the Channel's frigid deep.

* * *

Linzie got to his feet, none the worse from his fall. He ordered loblolly boys to carry a prostrate Inchington below to the surgeon, and bellowed, "Starboard carronade: fire at that glass port!"

* * *

A conning port shattered into tiny scattered jagged glass daggers. O'Sheridane instinctively threw up an arm to shield his eyes. Slivers ripped thin tracks of blood in his cheeks and arm, but left him without serious injury.

"Are ye all right, Gaylan?" he cried.

"Aye, Wolfe."

With a soldier's quick instincts, Kilmaine had thrown himself onto the deck. Canister shot and broken glass had flown over him harmlessly. O'Sheridane grabbed the voice tube and shouted, his usual genial calm quite gone, "Bobbie. Put her forward. Do you hear me, forward!"

Actium's engine paused only to resume. The ram shoved deeper into *L'Oiseau*'s gaping wound, widened it further.

"Afterwards now. Smartly," O'Sheridane commanded.

The engine stopped. There was a choking sound aft, followed by silence. Kilmaine and O'Sheridane could hear *L'Oiseau*'s gun crews reload the carronades.

"Jesus and Mary, Bobbie, do not abuse us so," Kilmaine cried.

The engine's racket started. What had but recently maddened them, thunderous rattles, bangs and roars, was comfort and balm now.

"Gaylan. Loose the lanyard."

Kilmaine pulled the cord to release the torpedo at the ram's tip. The ram pulled free from *L'Oiseau*. *Actium* backed water at a fraction of her former speed.

* * *

The French ship was pulling free. Soon, she would head for shore and be out of reach. Linzie had to destroy the newfangled French ship while he had the chance. Later, Chips, the ship's carpenter, could bowse a fothering sail to the stern so they could head to Portsmouth for repairs. But the instant task was more pressing.

"Curse your slowness," Linzie said to the gun-captain. "Hurry! She shall escape."

The gunner screamed at the men to hasten while they rammed a 32-pound solid shot down the muzzle.

"I do not understand why Inchington ordered canister. Aim for the other port and hole it."

"Aye, sir!"

"Fire!"

The spar deck was ripped apart by a huge fireball. The mizzenmast abruptly tilted over, kept upright at a crazy angle only by the rigging. L'Oiseau listed badly to port; gray smoke billowed from her cannon hatches. The powder magazine exploded.

The burning hulk quickly sank. Bits of wreckage mixed with human remains bobbed in the water.

* * *

"Stop engine, Bobbie. Gaylan, open the hatch. See if any survive."

O'Sheridane and Kilmaine climbed out onto *Actium*'s armored casemate. Caught in the Channel without propulsion, the ship heaved and fell. The men clung to a railing to avoid being hurled into the sea. They peered among the wildly scattered bits of burnt rigging, tattered sail, and pulverized timbers, but saw no imploring face, no hand frantically wave in a desperate bid for rescue.

"She went down with every man aboard fighting, give the Sassenach that," Kilmaine said.

"Aye," O'Sheridane said. "Look now, Gaylan. Two points abaft the port beam."

"Sorry, which way would that be again?"

"There, you great lubber!" O'Sheridane said.

A small white triangle on the horizon was the last sign of a swiftly retreating *Harpy*, already hull-down, tacking against the wind, headed north-north-west.

"She sails for the Channel Squadron's main station. Someone had the sense to send *Harpy* back to report us. They shall give the game away for sure."

"They were bound to find out sooner or later," Kilmaine reasoned.

"I hoped to put that day off. I like a full bag when I hunt too."

"We did well today. Enough even to impress Napoleon."

"Let's below and return to the harbor."

Actium returned to Boulogne. The gray-green Channel lay empty, no sign of the furious battle that had raged there scant minutes ago but flotsam quickly dispersed by her urgent currents.

Shaken, Shot, and Stirred
by Ryan McCall

1.

The quiet, darkness of the room was finally broken by the entrance of someone. The man had smooth, flat hair, cleanly shaven and wearing a perfectly pressed dark suit like it was his own skin.

He sat on the opposite side of the table and placed a folder down. He opened it. "Major Anthony Brooks. Tried to join the armed forces in 1939, but turned down due to youth. Do you know who I am major?" The man had a rich, baritone voice.

"Yes," replied Tony. "Ian Fleming, Director of Naval Intelligence. Why are you debriefing me?"

"Your own handler is dead and the rest of your superiors in Special Operations are being put through the ringer over this treason business. Why don't we begin with your arrival in Paris?" The older man leans forward. "The 28th of April."

He picked up the glass of water and took a long sip. He knew he would need a wet throat for all of the talking he had to do.

* * *

Paris was still the same city in spite of the new regime. France's governments had changed many times in recent history; monarchy, revolutionary republic, empire, monarchy again, the Second Republic, the Second Empire, the Third Republic, the split between Vichy and the Provisional Government, and for the last three years had been known as the People's Republic of France.

The new communist government had done much to rebuild since the end of the war, and Michael could see the Paris he had visited in his youth slowly returning in spite of the devastation it had suffered during the final, desperate battle between the Germans and the Red Army in 1945.

Tony had arrived in the city only this morning, but had already managed to complete the first step in his mission. Due to his fluent French and experience in German-occupied France, he had been selected for this particular mission.

His goal was to obtain a set of documents regarding a secret operation from the office of Andre Marty, head of the Central Planning Office. It would not be easy, but Tony had found a way in, thanks to information from an MI6 contact. He had caught the eye of Annette Buton at dinner this evening. She was Marty's secretary and would be able to get him the access he needed.

She had believed his story about being a member of the resistance in Vichy who had gone on to become a member of the State Security Directorate, France's new political commissar guard and had eaten up his tales of war time heroism and sacrifice. Much of what he had told her was in fact true; he had simply altered certain details and names to make it appear as if his background and allegiance had always been to a socialist France. Though even he had to admit, he was surprised she had believed him when he said he had been friends with the famous Resistance martyr, Jean Moulin.

He dropped the last burning end of his cigarette into the ashtray at the bar and turned around, there was Annette, standing in her fine white dress and giving him a look that said 'take me now'.

He gave her his most charming smile and walked over. "Annette my dear, I thought you were still entertaining your boss and his colleagues?"

"No, he is boring," she replied. "I'd much rather spend my time in your company, Anton," she addressed him with the Francized version of his name he was using as his cover identity. She was a gorgeous woman, no question, platinum blond shoulder length hair, fine cheekbones, and long legs. Gorgeous, but gullible, and perfect for his needs.

He leaned forward and whispered in her ear, "Well then, in that case, perhaps we should retire to somewhere with more privacy." He ran his hand along her arm and he felt her shiver in delight.

She nodded in agreement. "I have a private room upstairs, 240."

He gently touched her collarbone and brushed her neck before bringing his hand down again and taking hold of hers. He quickly and casually escorted out of the bar, past the dining hall entrance, where Marty and the other PRF bigwigs were raucously laughing, and led her up the wide, red-carpeted stairs.

When they reached the room, he patiently waited for her to unlock it and followed her inside. She was on him in an instant, hot lips crushing against his own. She pulled him towards the bed and started grabbing at his clothes and buttons before sliding her delicate hands against his skin.

An hour later Annette was fast asleep, while Tony carefully extricated himself from the warm sheets, now damp with sweat from their pleasurable exertions. As he stood on the hardwood floor, Annette stirred, but didn't awaken. Tony pulled his clothes on and made his way across the room, slowly walking in the near darkness. He did not want to trip and wake her up.

He opened her bag and put his hand inside; her keys were right on top. He clasped them tightly and a surge of triumph went through him. All he had left to do was to make his way out of the hotel unnoticed and enter the Central Planning Office in Montreuil. Fortunately, he would have help with that task.

2.

"So you obtained access on your first night?" asked Ian, he sounded skeptical.

"Yes," replied Tony. "I'm good at what I do."

"Mm-hmm," murmured Ian. "Then you met one of our French allies who helped you enter the CPO. How was that accomplished?"

"With a distraction"

"A distraction?" Ian was again skeptical.

"Alexandre Hebert. He knows how to make loud distractions."

* * *

Tony waited in the heavy darkness for his contact. After avoiding the crowd of commissars and visiting Russian officers from the Ministry of State Security at the hotel, he had walked through the back alleys until arriving at the CPO offices.

A large, iron gate surrounded the building. He could pick the locks easily enough, but he needed the many guards away from the side entrances to give him time to get in and out.

That was where Alexandre Herbert came in. Herbert was the leader of the few remaining anarchists and trade unionists who had not been purged in the last year and branded as traitors to the state for 'corrupting the revolution' and 'anti-Marxist activities'.

It was all crap of course. Herbert had been part of the Resistance and fought against the Germans and now his nation had turned against him. He had turned to Britain, one of the last few bastions against Bolshevism in Europe, for support and resources. In return he helped British agents on the ground with their covert operations.

Tony saw three shadowy figures approach his position and one of them said a phrase in English. "It has been a long spring."

"But not as long as the winter will be," replied Tony in French, as he had been instructed.

The figure who had spoken stepped closer and Tony could just make out his features. This tall, lanky figure was Alexandre Herbert. He held out his hand and Tony took it.

Herbert clasped his other hand on top and shook. "Good to meet you agent. Your French is excellent. If I hadn't known you were from MI5, I would have assumed you had been born in Savoie."

"Thank you," replied Tony. "Almost, I spent my youth with relatives in the Jura."

"What is the plan?" asked Herbert.

"I can get through the side gate easily enough and I have the keys to the building and offices. I have papers, but they won't hold up to a close inspection and with the number of guards, I could be caught before I reach my objective. I need you to create a distraction at the main entrance."

Herbert smiled. "Have no fear, agent, My men and I can provide the guards with a spectacular distraction, I think." He clicked his fingers. "Theo, Gaspard. Go prepare our items; I will join you once our ally is through the gate." The two men behind him nodded and left the area, headed for the street out front.

"Pick the lock, agent," said Herbert. "We should not dally here for long."

Tony kneeled down and pulled out his steel tools. He stabbed in the first metal piece and then with the second he gently poked and prodded until the lock gave way.

"Excellent," said Herbert. "Wait here. Be ready to move."

"How will I know when it's safe to proceed?" asked Tony.

Herbert winked. "Believe me you'll know. Wait for the noise, as soon as it starts and the guards leave their posts, you can move forward."

Tony waited and as he was starting to get nervous at the time going by, the quiet was ripped apart by a tremendous sound. Orange light reflected off the windows of the nearby building. Tony watched as the guards frantically ran from their positions towards the noise and fire. Herbert and his men had set off a bomb of significant size, based on the noise and height of the flames.

Tony had an easy time getting inside, Annette's keys giving him access. He walked through the empty hallways. He passed several doors that were closed and he could hear angry words from behind, likely in relation to the explosion, but he had no cause to be concerned. The office staff would not be checking his credentials.

All of the guards appeared to have left the building and as he ascended the stairs, Tony took a quick look outside. The bomb had destroyed a café across the street and he could see several bodies on the street, guards checking them for signs of life. He guessed it was frequented by guards and staff from this very office and Herbert would have been happy to blow it up, even without the need for his distraction.

He continued until he reached the top floor on the eighth level. Marty's office was located right at the end. He found the master key and held his breath; time to find out how much trust the Butcher of Albecete gave to his secretary.

The key went in and turned with ease. He smiled to himself, put his hand on the cold, metal of the handle and pushed the door open. Now all he had to do was find the file he was after in the time he had left.

Marty's office was immaculate and in perfect order, even the pencils on his desk were lined up like soldiers on parade. The green filing cabinet that almost reached to the ceiling was the most likely spot and he walked towards it.

He filed through as fast he could, much of the papers were useless administrative files, and then he came to one section entitled *Operations.*

The first few folders had items that were old news, the evacuation of Brittany, the withdrawal from Indochina, but then he finally came across it; the part with future operations. The first one had a date of May 12 and he pulled out the paper.

As his eyes scanned the pages, his mind whirled. This was it, it had to be! The Soviets were planning to send the Red Army into Spain along with the Spanish exiles from Franco's regime. This was incredibly valuable, he needed to get this back to London, so they could coordinate with the Spanish to stem the invasion.

He folded up the papers and tucked them under his jacket. It was time to go. He turned around and standing at the door was a man in a red uniform. The man was looking at him in shock and frozen on the spot. Tony reacted instinctively and charged the man. He bowled him over and continued running down the hallway. Outside he could hear gunfire. *Herbert must be trying to buy me more time* he thought. This were not going as smoothly as he had hoped.

He had reached the fourth floor when he heard cries of alarm from above and he sped up further, adrenaline pouring through him. A gun shot rang out when he reached the ground level and he felt red-hot pain in his left shoulder, but he kept running. Another shot rang out and this time the bullet took him in the leg. He stumbled but his momentum continued to carry him forward and slammed into the ground, his skull connecting with the wall.

"Cuff him and get him up," said a rough, voice. Two guards placed cuffs on his hands pulled him to his feet, hauling him away.

3.

"And thus you were captured," said Ian. He noted something down on his paper, the first time he had done so in their conversation. "Did you know then that you had been betrayed?"

"Not at first," replied Tony. "But it soon became clear that was the case. My interrogators had far too much information on my mission. And it was soon confirmed by the double agent who rescued me."

"That would be the man whose body was found in the plane with you?"

"Yes"

* * *

Tony blinked his eyes as the guards set him down on an uncomfortable metal chair. They pulled his hands forward and adjusted his cuffs so he was tied to the table in the middle of the room.

He licked his lips, tasting the blood, still running from lips and broken teeth. The guards had given him a rough beating, but he could tell they had held back. They were softening him up.

They guards exited and two new men stepped into the black-walled room. The first was tall and thick muscled; he had a thick black beard and piercing, dark eyes. He positioned himself at right angles to Tony, leaned back and folded his arms.

The other man was well-dressed in a blue suit and had blond hair and a thin face. He sat down and Tony noticed an exhausted look on his face.

"Agent Brooks, I am Maurice Kriegel-Valrimont, Inspector for the SSD. You were caught infiltrating the Central Planning Office with the aid of the criminals calling themselves anarchists. Herbert and your other allies are dead, agent. What happens to you depends on how willing you are to talk."

Tony wondered how the man already had his name. There was something fishy going here. He stared hard at Maurice and did not open his mouth.

"Very well," sighed Maurice. "I suppose my Russian comrade will have to take over." He stood up and stepped back from the table.

The large man in his black nodded and stepped forward. He flexed his hands and clenched his fists. He looked like he could do a lot damage with those meaty paws of his.

Tony steeled himself and waited for the first blow to land. It never did. The Russian turned suddenly and grabbed Maurice by the throat. The French man gurgled and tried to push the larger man off, but his efforts were useless. A few minutes later the Russian was lowering the body to the floor.

He came to Tony, produced a key and unlocked the cuffs.

"Get up," said the man. "We need to move quickly."

Tony was bewildered, who was this Russian and why was he helping him?

The man saw his reluctance. "Nikolai Khoklov, Ministry for Internal Affairs. I am a double agent for your government. Now, move!" he ordered.

Tony nodded and did as the man said. There not many guards in this building and Nikolai, soon had him outside and they climbed into vehicle, Nikolai driving.

"Where are we going?" asked Tony, wanting answers.

"A small airfield, north of the city. I have a plane waiting there."

"And then what? I leave? I need the documents detailing the invasion of Spain."

"Forget them," said Nikolai. "Your superiors will have to make do with everything you could memorize. You have bigger concerns than Spain."

"Such as?"

Nikolai took a sharp corner and Tony held on. If they continued like this, the man would cause them to crash before they ever reached the airfield.

"MI5 has traitors. Double agents like myself, but reporting to Moscow. They are the reason you were captured so easily." Nikolai moved one hand to his pocket and pulled out a folded piece of paper. He handed it to Tony.

"What is this?" he asked.

"The names of the MI5 traitors," answered Nikolai.

"How do I know you're telling the truth about any of this? You could still be working for Moscow."

"I could, but I am not. Give the names to Patrick Watson. He is my contact from MI5; he will ensure that action is taken. In addition, I sent him proof that those men are all traitors."

Tony did not know Patrick and he did not like the idea of going outside his line of command. "Why can't I give it to my handler?"

"Because Spencer Barrington is on the list," replied Nikolai and he took another sharp corner, this one put the car on a road leading out of the city. Tony opened the paper and examined the names. Sure enough there were six names of high level agents from MI5 written down. Tony clenched the paper tightly and out it in his jacket pocket. He could not afford to lose something as valuable as this. The lights of Paris fell away as the car sped down the country road.

4.

So you had the list of names and instead of doing as Khoklov instructed, you decided to take action yourself?" asked Ian. His voice had a skeptical tone to it.

"I had no clue whether Nikolai was telling the truth, but he died insuring I reached Britain with the list, I had no choice but to believe him," said Tony. "By the time I landed, it was too difficult to contact

Agent Watson. Spencer had already arranged to debrief me.

* * *

The car bumped violently as Nikolai drove over a deep pothole and Tony grabbed the door to support himself.

"Do you mind taking it easy?" he asked. "There's no point in fleeing from the SSD if we kill ourselves in the process."

Nikolai looked at him and shrugged, he moved his foot and the car slowed down slightly.

Another ten minutes and the lights of the airfield could be seen. Nikolai pulled the car into a small dirt road on the left, steering them in the direction of the lights. He slammed on the brakes and the car screeched to a halt in front of a white, wooden building. Tony could see that it was dilapidated, the pain peeling and wooden boards missing in places.

He exited the car and stretched his legs. A man emerged from the building; he was wearing a greasy mechanics outfit and a dirty red cap on his head.

"Nikolai? What is wrong, are you trying to crash your car?" the man asked.

"Not now Andre. I need you to get the Morane-Saulnier started. This man needs to be in the air as fast as possible," replied Nikolai.

Andre nodded, his eyes flitting between Nikolai and Tony. "Very well, it will take a few minutes to get it ready and move it into position."

All three of the men turned their heads at the sound of sirens in the distance. The SSD had managed to follow them. Nikolai ran back to the car and said, "Tony, help Andre get the plane ready."

"What are you going to do?" he asked.

"Buy you some time," replied Nikolai and he pulled out a PPSh-41 sub-machine gun from the back seat of the car.

Tony nodded and ran into the building behind Andre who had the door open and was ushering him in. He kept following the man down a corridor and out the other side to a long, grass strip. Andre ran over to a large shed and opened the large double doors at the front. Inside the shed was a silver and red monoplane.

"What are you waiting for?" he shouted at Tony. "Help me with this."

Tony responded, "Of course." He ran forward and to one side

of the plane and helped Andre to push it out on to the field. He heard the rat-a-tat-tat sound of the machine gun and knew that the SSD forces had arrived.

"Alright, that's good," said Andre. He started fiddling and checking the engine. "Do you know how to fly one of these?" he asked.

Tony grimaced. "I had some experience with Tiger Moths and Camels."

"Good. At least you're not green. This thing is similar to a Tiger Moth, so you should have no trouble with it. Go on, get in."

Tony hesitated. "What about yourself and Nikolai?"

"I knew what I signed up for and so did he," replied Andre. As if in response, Nikolai suddenly came running out of the building and on to the field.

"What are you waiting for?" he shouted at them. "More of them are coming!" He was struggling to run with the gun strap over his shoulder, weighing him down.

Tony climbed into the cockpit of the plane and started up the engine. Shots rang out and Andre went down, splashes of red appearing on his chest. Nikolai climbed up on the back section of the plane and yelled at Tony, "Take off now!"

He pulled his gun up and started firing back at the new threat. Tony gave the engine more power and pushed the plane down the grass strip. He could hear more sirens behind, closer this time, the SSD vehicles must be trying to catch up with them. Further shots whizzed past and he heard several of them hit the plane with thuds on the metal.

Nikolai fired the machine gun and drowned out all the other sounds. Then he stopped and Tony heard him grunt and slump down. He suspected that his ally had been hit, but it no longer mattered. Tony was already pulling back on the controls and lifting the plane into the air.

Below gunfire and searchlights aimed towards the plane. It was too late; he was out of their reach. He checked all of the instruments. Everything looked fine, so at least none of the shots had hit anything vital. He guided the plane around in the dark sky and headed towards England.

5.

"I managed to land in a field a few kilometers outside of Bexhill and the rest you already know," said Tony.

"Indeed I do," said Ian. "You met with Agent Barrington at Crawley. You killed him and then proceeded to secretly track down each of the names on this list and eliminate them- Anthony Blunt, Donald Maclean, Guy Burgess, Kim Philby, and John Cairncross. You took rogue actions on your own initiative. You're fortunate that Agent Wilson had the evidence that Khoklov provided or you could be facing trial for murder and treason. As it is you have likely done your country an enormous service."

"Thank you, sir," replied Tony.

"Don't thank me so fast. You may have eliminated traitors in our ranks, but that doesn't mean everyone thinks what you did was right. You won't suffer any charges. It was decided that your skills need to be put to use, so we are sending you to Spain."

"Have the Soviets begun their invasion?" asked Tony. It had been his original mission to bring back the details of that operation and he wanted to know what the status of it was.

"Not yet," answered Ian. "Which is why we want you in place there, before the invasion begins. The French are contributing a significant portion to the invasion and you would be well–suited to aid the Spanish in bleeding them dry."

"So you think they can't take Spain?" asked Tony.

"Oh, they can take it. But it's a question of whether they can keep it or not. The Spanish Ulcer broke Napoleon and I have no doubt it will also break Stalin and his lapdogs. You ship out the day after tomorrow, along with several other SOE and OSS operatives."

Tony smiled. He was eager to get back into his role as a behind-the-lines spy, causing as much chaos as he could for the enemy.

The Fire Tulips
by Mike Jansen

You get the best price with a musket in hand
—old VOC proverb
(VOC – Dutch East India Company)

The proud steamer *Van der Decken* struggled its way into the outer harbor of Herakleion, accompanied by three, green copper clad Cretan frigates. Despite precautions, the deep draft steamer encountered an Ottoman float mine that damaged several of the paddles. Damage was limited, but had delayed the ship's arrival by several days.

Hans Cornelisz sighed with relief. He stood on the bow of the ship among the other passengers, mostly tourists. For them the trip was an exciting adventure, the destination their holiday resort on the main island of the kingdom of Crete. For Hans Cornelisz it was just work.

As soon as the *Van der Decken* passed the antique Venetian fortress, people pulled out their tiphaignes. The clicking of the devices formed a dissonant symphony that reminded Hans of the noise of a bootstrapping computant street. He shook his head. It was all part of the job. The steam ship was a better cover than one of the VOC's war steamers. One of those giants appearing in these waters would quickly cause open war with the Greater Ottoman Empire. This would be bad for trade.

The quay that was reserved for the steamer was nearly empty, except for a handful of dockworkers. As opposed to the other quays that were choked with passengers, dockworkers, sailors and stevedores as well as rows of donkeys loaded with diverse merchant wares from the bellies of the moored ships.

Hans noticed a squad of soldiers at the entrance to the quay, dressed in the white and red of the royal guards. They scared interested parties from the quay with angry looks and in some cases the well aimed butt of their repeating rifles. Although Hans did not condone military violence against civilians, he appreciated the relative peace and quiet on the quay. The goods he had brought along were too valuable to be handled by just any dockworker.

The passengers debarked first, most of them loaded with cabin trunks and large bags, some with young children on their arms. They gathered at the bottom of the gangway and formed a restless mob that searched for a way out. Three quay meisters approached and introduced themselves to a number of them. Soon they guided the mob through the line of soldiers toward the customs office to show their traveling papers before being allowed into Herakleion.

When the quay emptied, a single, somewhat stout man remained, an elegantly dressed gentleman. Hans estimated him to be in his early forties. His skin was Dutch white and his dark blonde hair was sun bleached. He wore the tight, white uniform with the gray jacket Hans had seen on previous assignments. This was his liaison for the VOC Admiralty. He smiled and walked down the gangway. Once down the man addressed him cordially in Dutch. "Greetings, Hans Cornelisz, I presume?"

Hans nodded and replied: "And you must be Adrian Pauwelsson the Third, correct?"

"The one and only." Pauwelsson laughed. "The governor asked me to convey his apologies. There were some issues with the king, Nikolakonios."

"I thought Crete was in compliance with the rules laid out by the VOC?" Hans asked slightly surprised.

"Nikolakonios is in compliance with anything that will hurt the Ottomans, as long as he can get away with it. The Ottoman Corridor allows trade in and out of Constantinople, but he would much rather see that trade land in Crete," Pauwelsson explained. "However, outside our protection, he also would like to gain from our own trade with his island nation."

"All local taxes are paid, are they not?" Hans asked.

"That's the state. Nikolakonios' lifestyle is rather... excessive,"

Pauwelsson said with a smile.

Hans shook his head. Same as everywhere. "How is your experience with local staff?" he asked. "My equipment requires delicate handling. Can I trust proper care will be taken during unloading and transport?"

Pauwelsson nodded. "Rest assured, each of the carriers has been selected for intense hatred and revulsion of anything Ottoman. And my overseers will make certain your crates are loaded into the carts without too much bumping."

Somewhat reassured, Hans said: "Excellent. I shall get my personal belongings from my cabin. After that we can go to my hotel. I've booked a room at Hotel *Akropolis*."

"That old dump?" Pauwelsson asked. "That really won't do. I propose you allow me to take you to the governor's palace. It has enough rooms with full amenities available."

Hans thought it through. He was never really at ease with changing plans. Especially ones for which he had extensively prepared. He also suspected Pauwelsson to have motives that were not immediately clear, yet he found himself curious about the wealth and grandeur of the governor's palace. Proximity to the fortress settled it for him. That would save several hours of travelling time through the busy, crowded streets of Herakleion. "I accept your proposal," he said with a smile.

* * *

Herakleion's streets were awash with traders from all corners of the Earth. Crete was strategically placed between Constantinople, Christo-Venetia and the entire coast of Africa with its exotic wares, just across the Mediterranean. Of course it was by no means a metropolis such as Holland-under-the-Sea or Constantinople, but seeing the crowds in the streets could give you a different impression.

Pauwelsson sweated and puffed in the heat of the carriage, obviously unused to the stuffy afternoon air that sweltered in the narrow streets.

"You rarely visit the city?" Hans asked.

Pauwelsson grunted assent. "I try to avoid the unwashed Cretan plebs as much as possible."

Hans grinned. That remark confirmed some of the earlier thoughts he had about his liaison. The movement of air through the small windows of the carriage alleviated the stifling heat, but

Pauwelsson sighed in relief when they rode onto the shadowy inner court of the governor's palace in the south east of Herakleion.

Two Cretan servants accompanied Hans and Pauwelsson to a cool porch with a view of the low hills surrounding Herakleion. Pauwelsson took one of the reed chairs and dropped into the big, fluffy pillows. One of the servants handed him a glass of ice water that Pauwelsson first moved across his forehead and cheeks.

Hans drank from the water. It had a mineral taste, but it was cold and certainly much better than the tepid, machine cleaned water of the steamer in the last few weeks.

From the southern end of the porch Hans could just see the dark gray hulk with its near vertical walls of the VOC fortress *Hollandia*. It crowned the next hill over and rose several dozen feet above the land. On each of its corners two-hundred foot long barrels pointed skywards at an angle of some forty five degrees. Hans knew that the central observation tower would have an unobstructed view of the area and would have multiple telescopes and measuring devices. Standard equipment for all the fortresses the VOC had built around the world.

Much higher than the observation tower was the Tesla coil, a slender, graceful behemoth that reached skyward for nearly a thousand feet like an accusing finger. A monfier bobbed halfway up the mast from one of the maintenance posts. Engineers kept constant watch on the prime source of power for the fortress.

"Personally I would rather look out over the sea, from a nice, shaded terrace in the harbor," a new voice said, "preferably with a good glass of wine."

Hans stepped from his corner and noticed a man in a gray jacket with the accoutrements of a governor, next to Pauwelsson's chair. He was bald on top with a small edge of hair around his head. A large brown moustache drooped from his upper lip and on his left he carried the ceremonial governor's sable, relic of the time of the first colonists who sometimes needed to defend themselves with more than just words. Hans knew the governor was required to spend sufficient time to learn its proper use.

"Governor Jacobsen, I presume?" Hans said with a smile. He gave a curt bow.

The governor inspected him stoically. "Mister Cornelisz, it's sad that we should meet in these circumstances."

Hans looked at him, trying to figure out what he meant. "How so, governor?"

The governor looked at Pauwelsson. "You did not tell him yet?"

Pauwelsson shook his head. "Not out in the streets. Here, it's safe."

The governor walked to the doors and shut them. Next he closed the windows and inspected the walls and the three book cases against the wall. "You never know," he said. "Yesterday evening we received word from Holland-under-the-Sea. One of the Lords Seventeen has been murdered. Your patron, in fact, Henrietta Van Spijck-Hoekenes."

Hans gasped but he quickly suppressed his emotion. It was bad news, but it made his mission even more important. "That is indeed sad news, governor. Who in the world knows this?"

"The Napoleonic Empire and Greater Germany are strangely subdued, despite their strong language of the past months. Christo-Venetia won't care and for Hisperica, Europe is far and strange. The Pashas seemed to know first and they consider it the final blow to the VOC, if you believe their papers. The telegram from the Ottoman ambassador that I received this morning, mentioned something along those lines." The governor snorted.

"You suspect their involvement?" Hans asked. He had his own immediate assumptions and they had just been confirmed. It meant he would work here under a magnifying glass with many people trying to look over his shoulders.

"There is speculation a Dutch street robber committed the act. The Admiralty has confirmed your suspicions, however," the governor answered. "They also repeated the need for secrecy and delicate handling of the situation."

"It doesn't change anything for my assignment, governor," Hans said with a firm sounding voice.

"Good, that's the spirit," the governor said. "I trust you'll have dinner with us tonight?"

* * *

The next morning his servant, Can Agiapos, handed him a pristine, white uniform that would have looked at home on a colonel or an admiral, but in his case there were no gold pips, only the small, copper circle that identified him a civilian.

A small, but hearty breakfast, with the strongest coffee ever, got him started.

It was still very early as he walked towards his destination, along the neatly paved road that ran from the governor's palace to *Hollandia* fortress. At the foot of the hill he saw the first Dutch soldiers behind a sand bag barrier with their repeating rifles at ready. A broad canvas canopy protected them from the sun.

His attention was drawn by a large, colorful parasol, further up on the hill. Beneath it, a woman in a red dress was setting up an easel with a blank sheet of canvas. He showed the soldiers his pass and the accompanying, bronze ring around his left ring finger.

"Can you explain to me who that woman is on the hill over there?" he asked.

The soldiers shrugged. One of them said: "She's here every day. Paints the surroundings. Higher ups don't care."

"Intriguing," Hans said. "Could I go and visit her?"

Again they shrugged.

Hans left the path and walked up the hill. The ground was parched and only a few clumps of tough grass managed to survive. The morning sun rose and first lit up the Tesla coil that sharded the sunlight in blindingly brilliant beams, with the fortress a dark, brooding void beneath it.

The woman in red just started mixing various colors on a large, wooden palette. A small chest contained her painter's tools, brushes, spatulas and other small items.

"Good morning," Hans greeted her and gave her a friendly smile.

She looked up from her work and beamed a laugh at him. Her deep black hair and dark eyes complemented her perfectly symmetrical face and Hans felt an unfamiliar flutter in his stomach.

'Good morning soldier... civilian," she said and her voice had just the right, sultry tone and the perfect, exotic accent to intrigue and mesmerize men. She made Hans feel rather ill at ease.

He smiled back. "Your Dutch 'g' sounds perfect, ma'am, my compliments."

"Why, thank you, mister..." She gave him a questioning look.

"Hans Cornelisz," Hans introduced himself. "And you are?"

"My pleasure, Mister Cornelisz." She smiled again. "My name is Alistera Gavanides. As you may have noticed, I paint."

Hans looked around. The view from the hill was magnificent; the only thing out of place was the ugly hulk of the fortress on the hill proper. With a friendly voice he said: "I also notice your view is aimed at that ugly stone building."

Alistera nodded. "So I've been told, often. However, I look further than the ugly exterior and try to imagine the unfolding of the Fire Tulips and how they bask the fortress in their resplendent glow."

Hans laughed. "You may be better off with a tiphaigne to shoot some pictures. A fire tulip's discharge lasts only seconds. With such pictures you would at least have something to paint by."

Alistera rummaged in her chest and produced a silvery, recent model tiphaigne with a large, detachable lens and a rotor dial. "All is taken care of. Alas, the number of shots the fortress has fired in its thirty year existence can be counted on the fingers of one hand. And even so, to see the fortress in its full glory, those shots need to be fired at night." She sighed. "The odds are astronomically small."

Hans spread his hands. "You never know." He coughed and checked his horologium. "If you will excuse me, ma'am, I must be on my way. Thank you for your time and explanation."

"It was my pleasure, Mister Cornelisz," Alistera said and blinked her eyes seductively.

Hans continued down the path to the fortress. He undid the top button of his jacket. *Because the temperature was rising quickly*, he told himself.

* * *

The entrance to the fortress was fully automated. It held two entrances and two exits, lock chambers really. One was for the regular bronze collar workers, the other was for soldiers, officers and irregular personnel. Hans turned the ring on his finger round a few times, then entered the smaller of the lock chambers and placed his hand in the designated hole. A clamp closed on his hand like a vise and it pulled him deeper into the chamber, pinning him between thick, glass plates. On a bronze number pad he had to type his personal pin code, before the clamp released him to the inside of the fortress.

The bronze collar workers did not have to remember complicated codes, but their wide, bronze collars formed a similar clamp as the one that had fixed his hand. In a much more claustrophobic process their heads were completely enclosed and their faces measured using volta, then compared to existing Bode-diagrams.

The sides of the fortress were nearly two thousand feet long and the immense inner court was only interrupted at the four corners, where the huge, globelike bronze casings of the Fire Tulips rose from the ground. The center of the court contained the observation tower and a deep, round pit from which the Tesla coil rose. Hans knew that below him were dozens of floors filled with exotic machinery, high frequency generators, steam turbines and several hundreds of tons of explosive munitions for the giant cannon.

From the shadows of the walls he saw regular small volta discharges from the Tesla coil to the edge of the pit. As always he felt a deep, cautious reverence for the unquantifiable forces the coil generated in its movement through the Earth's magnetic field.

On the other side of the inner court were the offices, square, functional buildings with simple latticework windows that held matte glass panes. A central gate with baroque bronze ornamental panels allowed access. It was a busy crossroads of soldiers, administrators and engineers, all coming and going.

Above the gate Hans read the legendary words in brushed steel that Viceroy Willem IV purportedly said to Napoleon after their twelfth battle in the Southern Netherlands that resulted in a stalemate: "Every step will cost you." After that last battle Napoleon recognized the sovereignty of the Republic. Flourishing trade resulted in fast economic growth in the Netherlands and the worldly power of the VOC reached unimaginable heights.

Inside he wandered the narrow corridors that held small doors. Through half closed blinds he saw claustrophobic cubicles with desks, reams of paper and an occasional mimeograph. Administrators toiled in their cubicles, filling books with arcane numbers using their old fashioned fountain pens. Hans shook his head. Volta driven ILM typographs were common in Holland-under-the-Sea, but not on Crete. Still, he had at the very least expected a few Mill typographs.

Access to the core of the building was through a set of double, mahogany doors with the word 'Staff' in gold lettering. He knocked on the door, politely, and in response an impeccable, young soldier opened it for him.

"How may I help you?" the young soldier asked.

"I am Hans Cornelisz," Hans said with a smile. "I have an appointment with Commander Pels."

The young man opened the door wider and motioned him to

enter. Next he walked ahead and brought Hans to a large, glass walled office. Inside was a well stocked book case and behind an impressive walnut desk was the Commander, dressed in full regalia, leafing through a pile of documents.

The Commander looked up when Hans was ushered inside. He was in his early fifties, with a bald head and a dark brown beard. He took off his fine copper wire reading glasses when he saw Hans.

"Hans Cornelisz, I presume?" the Commander asked and he reached out his right hand to shake hands.

"That is correct, Commander Pels. It is an honor to finally meet you," Hans said.

"The Admiralty speaks highly of you. How long will you need to set up your machines?" The Commander took a box of fine Java Gold tobacco and offered Hans a cigar.

Hans politely refused and answered: "If the preparations were carried out as planned and with the help of a few strong men, I should take about two weeks at most."

The Commander grinned. "The Ottomans will never know what hit them."

Hans nodded. "I think so too, Commander, I think so too."

"It's too bad you didn't get to meet the other engineers. Bloody float mine really messed up the time tables." The Commander pushed a button and moments later an officer entered. "Captain Adriaensz," the Commander addressed him. "I told you about Hans Cornelisz before. Will you assist him? After all, you've been working very hard the past few months to get his requirements in place. You'll have to get him up to speed on this place."

"It will be my pleasure, Commander," Captain Adriaensz said. He shook hands, and then led Hans to the deep basement of the fortress.

* * *

The walk down the stairs took several minutes until Adriaensz reached a large metal door sporting the red number "-11", beyond which was a sizeable hall only partially filled. Three soldiers leaned against the back wall, next to a pile of crates. They looked up when Hans and the Captain entered, but upon seeing their superior's uniform and rank, they immediately relaxed.

"The Huygens stabilizers are over there." Adriaensz pointed out a couple of man sized gray cubes that stood softly humming in one of the corners. "Couldn't fathom why you needed so many, but I can assure you not a single spike of Volta, high or low, will come out of this contraption."

Hans caressed one of the crates that were delivered to the fortress yesterday. "The machine I am going to set up requires perfect surroundings. A bit too much or too little, either way the calculations will be influenced."

The Captain smiled. "The Commander often hands me these delicate assignments, so I understood you require utmost precision." He looked at the three soldiers. "These gents will assist you with the heavy lifting." He identified them one by one. "Janszen, Gerritzen and Van Braekel. They will also guard the hall, day and night. I assume you'll be having lunch and dinner here?"

"Yes, please," Hans said. "Would it be possible to take a break outside of the fortress?"

"Why of course. And if you need an escort, one of my men can accompany you." With those words the Captain made a short bow, turned on his heels and marched off.

The first crate Hans opened contained his tools. Next he opened the crates that contained the racks he would need to mount all the equipment he had brought to Crete. Together with the soldiers he toiled all morning and all afternoon to complete the setup.

Over the course of the following days the doubly sealed crates were opened. They contained the devices that Hans' family business supplied. Slowly they filled up the racks with panels full of micro-relays. These were connected through black panels as thick as a thumb, with edges covered in gold contacts. At certain angles all sides showed the International Lovelace Mills logo in silver. Hans treated the computant parts like the most delicate of crystal.

Time and again he was surprised at how an underdeveloped country like England managed to grow a flourishing, innovative computant industry. The ILM factories were unmatched throughout the world in the field of miniaturization of Volta drive components or their persistent ring core memory that was considered the newest and most advanced machine available on Earth today. He considered himself lucky to be working with this state-of-the-art equipment.

At the end of the week Hans opened the final crates and took out the heavy pen reliefs, screens containing minute metal pens that formed signs and diagrams though application of volta.

One by one he followed the complex procedures to test each of the components and on Friday morning, before lunch, he placed the last of the checkmarks on his forms.

"It is done," he said to soldier Gerritzen who was nearest to him.

"Should I fetch the captain?" Gerritzen asked.

"Thank you, but not quite yet," Hans said. "I expected the work to be finished at the end of the day, so I think I deserve a good lunch, somewhere outside. Do you think you can get a picnic basket from the kitchen?"

Gerritzen grunted his assent and walked off to the kitchen to convey Hans' request. Hans in the mean time inspected the many racks and shelves that held the complex machines that were the life blood of his family. This was the first time he saw it all assembled and he was relieved to find everything fitting together seemingly perfect. Technology could do weird things sometimes.

With a sizeable picnic basket Hans left the fortress.

* * *

"Might I invite you to share lunch with me?" Hans asked Alistera Gavanides who was just painting ethereal landscapes on one of her canvases. Today she wore a revealing, green dress in old Cretan style that showed more than was common in Dutch society.

"Why Mister Cornelisz," she replied and batted her lashes at the sight of the picnic basket. "What gallantry, and such from a Dutch person, who, in general, I thought to have no class whatsoever. I guess I was mistaken." She took a blanket from her own basket and spread it on the ground beneath her parasol.

The shade left just enough room for the two of them and the picnic basket and not much later Hans and his charming guest enjoyed Cretan wine, various local cheeses, freshly baked Dutch white bread and a green salad.

"I always thought soldiers couldn't cook, but now I know better," Hans said.

"Perhaps Dutch soldiers are an exception to the rule," Alistera confirmed. "I've seen you enter the fortress a few times in the past days. You left really late each time. That is quite uncommon for civilians. Would you consider it impolite for me to ask what it is you do inside the fortress?"

"Not at all," Hans said. "I am an engineer and I work with some of the systems of the fortress." He kept a low profile on purpose.

He remembered the modern tiphaigne the woman carried with her, her near flawless Dutch and her inexplicable and stubborn habit of creating paintings of the fortress.

"Ah, you must be one of those who cannot abandon their work until it has reached perfection. Am I right?" Alistera asked with a glimmer in her dark eyes.

Hans just grinned. "It runs in the family."

"I recognize it," Alistera said. "My father was just like that."

"You inherited your fascination with ugly fortresses from him?" Hans asked innocently.

"No, but he did pass on a deep interest in technology and the ways in which it changes and shapes our lives," she explained.

"I never think much about it," Hans said. "Sounds like an interesting view."

"It is," Alistera said. "Take those Fire Tulips. We see barrels, some hundred or two hundred feet in length. However, most of the technology is far below ground, not just the barrels, but also the infrastructure needed to fire them."

Hans tried to read the expression on her face. This was much more than general knowledge. "And this influences our lives how, exactly?"

"Infrastructure requires maintenance and service. More wheels and cogs means more people to work on them. In the past few weeks I have seen many engineers come and go. Now you have arrived, with dozens of wagons filled with crates and boxes. Just after the arrival of the *Van der Decken* from Holland-under-the-Sea." She looked at him and arched a delicate brow. "What does it all mean?"

"The acumen of your artistic view is only surpassed by your information sources," Hans said in a cool voice.

Alistera noticed his change in attitude. She gave him a radiant smile and placed her hand on his knee.

Hans was startled by her intimacy and he turned pale.

Alistera quickly retracted her hand. "I apologize," she said. "I did not mean to…"

Hans shook his head. "It's alright. It's just… It's not common in my family…" He tried to find words. "We are quite reluctant to form relationships outside our family."

"I think I understand," Alistera said carefully. "Could I show you around sometime, by way of apology? Crete is historically rich."

Hans smiled. "It will be Sabbath soon. Time for relaxation."

"Shall we meet here, tomorrow? Around eight? It should be cool enough, still. Do tell me you ride horse!" Alistera said.

"I do and I shall be there," Hans replied. They ate the rest of their lunch in silence.

Afterwards Hans took the basket back to the fortress and he finished his reports.

* * *

A soft knock on his door alerted Hans that someone was trying to get his attention. He put his book down and opened the door. His servant, Can Agiapos, stood before him, smiling.

"Mister Cornelisz," he said in bad Dutch. "Is visitor. With governor."

"For me?" Hans asked.

Can nodded vigorously.

"Well, alright then." Hans pulled on his shoes, straightened his shirt, and then followed Can to the governor's quarters.

On the second floor, Can opened the double doors that gave access to the atrium, which was part of those quarters. Merry splashing sounded from the fountain downstairs. His servant guided him past a well stocked library and a large, richly decorated living room in which the governor's wife was just reading a children's story to her son and daughter.

On the cooler north side of the palace was the billiards room. Folding doors allowed access to the terrace and on both ends of the large billiard were luxurious, brown leather seats next to small, mahogany cigar tables. Crystal decanters filled with various liquids were displayed in a wall cabinet, illuminated by several electrophorus lamps. A delicate Lichtenberg was displayed in its own alcove on a Cretan column of white marble with gray veins.

From the terrace someone called Hans' name. He tapped Can's shoulder, and then stepped out onto the terrace where he found the governor in leisure clothing. Next to him was a wide shouldered Cretan with a hint of a paunch, his head covered in unruly, black curls and a narrow, black moustache. The Cretan wore a military uniform that was brimming with gold medals, pips, cords and stripes.

"Ah, Hans, allow me to introduce you to his Royal Highness, Nikolakonios," governor Jacobsen began.

Hans gave a short bow.

"So you're the genius engineer?" Nikolakonios asked in perfect Dutch.

Hans looked at him. "I don't think I know what you mean by that," he said.

Nikolakonios waved his hand. "Don't be so modest. You know about the systems inside the fortress, do you not?"

Hans looked at the governor who nodded ever so slightly.

"I am familiar with the workings of those systems, that is correct," Hans answered.

Nikolakonios nodded. "Those vitally important systems. Top secret. To protect the kingdom from attacks by the despicable Ottomans. The systems you are improving to make us even more invulnerable in this treacherous world."

Hans spread his hands. "That is my task," he said.

Nikolakonios snorted. "Then what are you doing, talking to that Ottoman spy? No less than half a dozen reports on my desk concerning your conversations with that woman."

"You mean Alistera Gavanides?" Hans asked. "I believe she is Cretan. Her Dutch is perfect."

"The VOC has visited our harbors for more than three hundred years, Mister Cornelisz. Dutch is the second language hereabouts," Nikolakonios explained. "The woman you were talking to is Cretan, no doubt, but employed by the Ottomans."

"I thought all Cretans hated the Ottomans with a vengeance?" Hans asked.

"This is true," Nikolakonios confirmed. "But everyone has a price. Her price is the life of her father who fell afoul of the Ottomans, a few years ago."

"And what is your price?" Hans asked with extreme politeness.

The governor turned white, but Nikolakonios grinned and winked at him.

"He's a smartass, Jacobsen. I hope his work is as good as his jokes." He turned back to Hans. "I hope you know what you're doing, boy. The VOC enforces the Pax Batavica, so we need sufficient evidence. But I wouldn't mind locking that woman in a deep dungeon." With a wry smile he added: "And perhaps all those she has been in contact with."

Hans remained silent until Nikolakonios snorted and took his leave from the governor. With big steps he left the billiards room. All was silent until the front door was thrown shut with some force.

The governor sat down into one of the lounge chairs in the room and held his head in his hands. "There is no political career in your future, Mister Cornelisz, I can assure you," he said.

Hans noticed the governor's tired appearance. A man with worries. He shrugged. "My family has no political ambitions. We are only interested in the latest technologies."

"Obviously,' the governor said. 'Nikolakonios has become more demanding. The Ottomans are trying to weaken his position. And I wonder how long Nikolakonios can pay his cronies more than the Ottomans."

"Does the VOC not have enough?" Hans asked.

"There are limits to our good will. Nikolakonios reached those almost two years ago. The Admiralty has curtailed his allowance," the governor explained "The situation in Crete is less stable than you might think, especially with the Ottoman's most important trade artery to Constantinople only a few hundred miles from Herakleion."

Hans thought about that for a moment. "I shall keep it in mind," he said. "To maintain the cordial relation with the current government."

"Thank you," governor Jacobsen said. He gestured that Hans should leave.

* * *

Alistera Gavanides talked to the soldiers that guarded the road leading to the fortress. Hans saw from afar she was dressed like a fashionable Amazon. Her ponytail was held in place by a cap that resembled an antique helmet from ancient Cretan times. She rode a night black Arabian.

He guided his chestnut right up to hers. "Fine horse," Hans said.

"Leonidas," she corrected.

"Why of course." Hans tapped the neck of his own horse. "Graetel. There was a Hans in the stables as well, but I did not deem that suitable."

Alistera laughed, baring sparkling white teeth. "Hans on Hans, no, definitely not good. Shall we?" She blew a kiss at the soldiers who saluted her.

Hans followed. They left the road and took a horse trail that led into the hills. The fresh morning air and the sun rising bathed the

Cretan landscape in a diverse pattern of vibrant reds.

After half an hour they stopped next to an impressive heap of stone, thousands of years old ruins that were partially hidden under olive and fig trees. In the shade of a clump of trees was a small horse meadow to which Alistera guided Leonidas. Hans allowed Graetel to follow and Alistera closed the fence behind them.

"Welcome to Knossos, Hans Cornelisz," the Cretan woman said and she waved at the ruins.

"Never heard of them. How old are they?" Hans asked.

"Thousands of years. Before Christ. Before the ancient Cretans. Before the Romans. Before the Venetians, the Ottomans and the Dutch," Alistera said with a bitter tone to her voice. She sighed and walked in the direction of an excavated row of columns. Hans followed. She stopped at the remains of a relief and studied the merry, colored lines depicting dancing satyrs. "So powerful back in their time. Now all but forgotten." She sighed again and pointed both hands at the piles of stone debris. "All that remains."

Hans nodded. "Makes you think, doesn't it?"

She looked at him. "Why do you do the things you do, Hans Cornelisz? Whatever that may be."

Hans blinked and thought carefully before he answered. "My family has served the VOC for generations. We are inventors, tinker, creators of new technologies, makers of complicated machinery. Always have been. Once we were called gypsy, but we can trace our heritage to the Bukharian tribe of Canaan. Holland-under-the-Sea sheltered us after the pogroms against my people in Poland, Walachia and Moravia. In return we swore allegiance."

"I am certain your family was similarly repressed as mine on mainland Greece," she stated. "The Ottomans were beastly in those days."

"It is my impression they still are," Hans said.

Alistera nodded and bared her teeth, her thoughts clear on her face. "That is true, but it's more refined now, insidious and much more dangerous than before."

"It seems to me you know them well?" Hans asked innocently.

"You could say that," Alistera said. "But not all Ottomans are animals, most are regular people, like you and me."

Hans smiled affably. *Here it comes,* he thought.

"For instance, I know a few who are very interested in the

activities of the VOC in these regions," she continued. "Nice people who pay good money to gain insight into these activities.

"Really?" Hans asked. "And how good would that money be?"

"Think what you could do with a million," she said while observing him closely.

"I do not really care about money, I'm afraid. The VOC pays well." Hans smiled. "Which does not mean other things do not interest me."

"So what is your interest?" Alistera asked and she stood quite close to him. "Power? The Pashas can provide a palace with a whole tribe of slaves and supervisors, to whoever helps them understand the secrets of the VOC fortresses."

Pashas, went through Hans' mind. *Nikolakonios was right about this woman, this spy.* He shook his head. "My family abhors slavery and so do I."

Alistera looked at him sideways and Hans noticed the attractive line of her face. She approached him even more. Carefully she laid her right hand on his chest and Hans had to suppress an urge to cringe. "And what of the favor of a beautiful woman?" she asked, her voice husky.

Hans took her hand. "Alistera, you are all that I could wish for in a woman, but you are not meant for me. The sovereign, Nikolakonios, warned me about you. Know that there are many eyes watching you, wherever you go."

She shook her head and Hans noticed tears in her eyes. "You don't get it, Hans Cornelisz. My father..." She pulled her hand free and ran off.

Hans just stared dumbfounded and soon heard the distinct gallop of her Arabian. The sound soon disappeared in the distance.

"That's no way to treat a lady," a dark voice behind him said.

Hans turned around and saw a bald man with a large, drooping Ottoman mustache sitting on a low wall. He was dressed in black, adorned with Uzbek gold brocade. "I was under the impression the local populace hated the Ottoman Empire something fierce, yet your dress does not reflect proper caution," he observed.

The Ottoman grinned. "Times change. The popularity of the VOC around these parts is similar to ours' these days. Pleased to meet you, by the way, Mister Cornelisz. My name is Bashar."

"You are Alistera's contact? Did she know you were here?"

Hans asked.

"She is one of my best agents and most times she manages to extract any and all information from you Dutch people. Sadly, not this time." Bashar sighed and shook his head.

"So you are also her father's kidnapper?"

Bashar grinned. "Always the drama. He is a guest of the Ottoman Empire with some temporary obstacles to traveling."

Hans looked Bashar in his eyes. "What does it take to set him free?"

Bashar's smile vanished. "Information, Mister Cornelisz. Your VOC communicates with secret messages. I have to deduce from its actions what goes on. And sometimes I have to send my people to get information from your people. So far that has worked well." Bashar bowed his head to Hans' level. "In the past month much work has been done inside the fortress. Many systems were upgraded, modernized. Does the VOC expect to have to wage war?"

"I do not know that," Hans answered. "I'm just here for maintenance work on the Fire Tulips."

"Ah, yes, the toy cannons of the VOC. Do the countries where you built your fortresses still not get that protection also means occupation and that your cannons shoot to all sides?" Bashard asked.

"I am just an engineer, but I understand your distrust," Hans said. He knew quite well that the VOC built its fortresses to serve VOC interests, not anyone else's.

"What do you know of the VOC's plans?" Bashar asked. "Why spend so much money on Crete, now, at this moment in time. Constantinople is close, is that the target?"

Hans shook his head. "I do not have that information. I only perform maintenance on the Fire Tulips."

Bashar pondered his words. "A hiatus exists in our understanding of the inner workings of the Fire Tulips."

Hans was unmoved. "Is that information required to release him?"

Bashar was silent and just looked at him, then said: "You negotiate?"

Hans shrugged. "I am Dutch, after all."

A wide grin appeared on Bashar's face. "An engineer-trader, that's rare. You wish to negotiate? For the release of Alistera's father?"

"Why not? You want information that I possess. What do you

offer in return for what?" Hans asked.

"Tell me all relevant facts of the Fire Tulips and I shall arrange his release," Bashar said.

"Ottoman word of honor?" Hans asked.

"You believe us honorable?" Bashar pinched his eyes closed. "Very well, you have my word."

"Great," Hans said. "It's a deal. I will hand Alistera the information and have her deliver it to you." He gave the Ottoman a short bow, got on his horse and returned to the governor's palace.

* * *

The palace was in an uproar when Hans returned his horse to its stable. Cretan soldiers patrolled the outer gardens and court yards. They seemed nervous and fidgeted with their repeating guns at the ready.

Near the entrance he was made to hold and questions or orders were yelled at him in Cretan.

"Does anyone here speak Dutch?" Hans asked. He was getting anxious with so many guns aimed at his head.

Momentarily Can Agiapos exited the palace, preceded by a Cretan soldier. Hans was surprised to see him in a uniform with obvious officer's pips on the sleeves.

"Can, do you know what is going on?" Hans asked him.

"Hans Cornelisz," Can said. "Big problem. Come." He motioned Hans to follow him and the soldiers who surrounded him opened their ranks with some reluctance.

They moved into the large reception hall of the palace. A group of cleaners was at work, unsuccessfully so, to scrub a red stain from the white marble. A little further, lying on a litter was a shape covered by a white sheet.

Hans gasped and pulled Can's sleeve. "Is that the governor?" he asked.

Can bowed his head.

"I can't believe it," Hans said. "Do they know who killed him?"

Can lifted his head. His eyes were bright and angry. "Ottoman!"

Hans nodded. It was as he expected. "Who is in charge now?" he asked Can. "Will you take me to him or her?"

Can guided him past the offices in the governor's palace, done in VOC colonial style with bamboo and mahogany. Hans did not think it an explicit choice, just acquired in the time the palace was built, when such interiors were modern. Can said goodbye and left. Broad leafed ceiling fans cooled the air only slightly, but Hans was happy with even the smallest of fresh breaths. The secretary's face was pale, but she announced Hans through the copper speech tube.

Pauwelsson opened the door and waved him inside. In the office Pauwelsson sat down in the governor's chair. In one of the guest chairs sat the sovereign, Nikolakonios. Hans looked from one to the other.

"Sit down," Pauwelsson said with a smile.

"What happened?" Hans asked.

"An Ottoman assassin," Pauwelsson answered. "Here in the palace, no less. Dreadful situation. I spoke to the Admiralty and they have appointed me for the interim."

"But how did this happen?" Hans sat in the proffered chair. He addressed Nikolakonios. "I though you were watching everything? How did you miss this?"

"We follow dissidents, spies and assassins as good as we can," the sovereign explained. "Insofar we have the means to do that. Pauwelsson understands this much better than former governor Jacobsen."

"Can is one of your agents?" Hans asked.

"Indeed he is," Nikolakonios said. "The Ottomans are highly intrigued by your activities, Mister Cornelisz. That fuels my own curiosity. What is it that you do, deep inside that fortress?"

Hans sighed. "Just my job, your excellence, nothing more."

"Our relationship with the VOC and the Ottoman Empire is precarious, Mister Cornelisz," Nikolakonios explained. "We are on the knife's edge between two rival nations that try to best each other at every turn. The balance we need, must be maintained to avoid destruction."

"I understand that, your excellence," Hans said. "I can assure you that my work only strengthens that balance. However, I cannot reveal any details."

"And that won't be necessary. Your superiors convinced me long ago of the necessity of this extensive upgrade, and I understand very well what double edged weapon a heavily armed VOC fortress within our borders actually is." Nikolakonios sighed.

Hans remained silent. He understood the sovereign's position.

"At least the Admiralty thought it appropriate, in light of these events, to allot the reasonable funds that I requested," Nikolakonios said. "With some help of the excellent diplomacy by Pauwelsson of course."

Pauwelsson grinned. "I always advised Jacobsen to supply the sovereign with sufficient funding. It is quite obvious he does sterling work for the VOC."

The looks Pauwelsson and Nikolakonios gave each other made it all very clear for Hans. He nodded slowly.

"And that's why it's good you're here now, Cornelisz," Pauwelsson said. "To maintain a proper balance between Crete, the VOC and the Ottoman Empire, the sovereign and I both agree that we should be able to influence the functioning of the fortress."

"How so?" Hans asked.

"Your maintenance work seems aimed at increasing the reach and accuracy of the Fire Tulips," Pauwelsson explained. "We figured," he glanced at the sovereign, then back at Hans, "it would be prudent to decrease that accuracy somewhat to less than the intended values."

"That is trade treason," Hans fumed.

The sovereign pulled out an Ottoman Eightshooter and placed the beautifully engraved barrels against Hans' forehead. "No, my dear Mister Cornelisz, it's called self preservation."

Hans swallowed and was slowly pushed back into the chair by Nikolakonios.

"Should you cooperate, the reward will be sizeable," Pauwelsson said. "Our Ottoman friends are generous. Otherwise, the assassin will, unfortunately, strike a second blow today."

"Why?" Hans asked.

"Why we would rather have you cooperate?" Pauwelsson asked. "Because two murders would attract unwanted attention. This would then result in the arrival of a full VOC delegation with accompanying military personnel to turn this place upside down."

"Obviously," Hans said. He thought fast. "I may know something…"

"Good," Nikolakonios said. "I'm not keen on changing into a clean uniform again." He checked his horologium and grinned. "And just enough time to go out and inspect my new yacht and perhaps sail it around the island of Dia a couple of times the coming week."

Pauwelsson laughed. "Any room for me? Or will you keep the Ottoman houris all to yourself?"

Nikolakonios leered. "You're quite welcome, Pauwelsson."

Hans had to explain his plan and was then allowed to leave. Every step of the way back to his rooms he felt observed.

* * *

The next days Hans worked from early in the morning till late at night. He installed high frequency Marconis on the observation towers and tested their reach by sending signals to far away war steamers, often more than a thousand miles removed from Crete.

From his high post he saw Alistera Gavanides' brightly colored parasol. She seemed occupied with her next painting. Hans smiled whenever he thought of her and he felt an uncommon happiness. This was new to him. In his profession it was rare to encounter women and certainly never exciting ones like Alistera.

To make absolutely sure, he took the wrist thick folder from captain Adriaensz in which all installations, additions, interfaces and connection were noted and very precisely checked off each and every component for fitting, tests and results. Only a few pieces troubled him and he took his time to traverse the fortress and inspect the suspect components himself.

When he was convinced everything was as perfect as it could be, he decided the time had come to activate the whole of the system. Down in the cellars of the fortress he sat behind the main control panel. The cabinet beneath it contained the ring readers. Large electrophorus lights illuminated the room with their typical yellow glow. Janszen, Gerritzen and Van Braekel sat next to the many racks of equipments at their makeshift table of empty crates. They played a game of cards that looked to Hans like Amsterdam Jack Hunt.

Hans took the final part that he had not installed yet, a small, bronze box, lined with black velvet. Inside was a neat row of nine, matte finish bronze rings. He opened the door of the ring reader and revealed a panel with numbers from one through nine. He pressed the number one and a ring shaped opening appeared.

With some adjustments to the closest electrophorus lamp, the now almost white light was bright enough to allow him to read the miniscule signs on the edge of the rings, through a magnifying glass. Only the correct sequence would activate the systems according to the complicated patterns that Hans and his family had designed in their laboratories in Holland-under-the-Sea.

In his mind Hans deciphered the signs, using the cryptographic keys he had memorized in the past months. Within half an hour the rings were aligned according to the proper sequence and he closed the ring reader. He leaned back in his chair, took his own, bronze identification ring from his finger and held it up in the light.

One ring to bind them, Hans thought and he smiled. Without his ring and the code in his brain the entire system was worthless. He placed the ring in the recess in the main control panel and closed the main switch. A soft clicking started from the direction of the large ILM installation, indicating that tens of thousands of micro relays were beginning to implement the carefully programmed controls that Hans had so diligently installed in the past weeks. *Like a dissonant symphony,* he thought.

The pen reliefs blinked and on the main relief thousands of small pens formed a raised image of the ILM logo. Next appeared a dozen squares beneath the logo with a dot in the first square to indicate the place where Hans could begin entering his code.

He looked around. Janszen, Gerritzen and Van Braekel paid him no heed; he had become part of the furniture. With a few clicks he opened a special screen only for maintenance engineers. Here he entered a few commands and changed some algorithms. The first shot from the Fire Tulips he gave a margin of error of several percentage points. He adjusted a few more parameters and added small, subtle directives to the existing list of directives he had for a large part written himself while in Holland-under-the-Sea. He then closed the screen and the ILM logo and the entry squares appeared again.

As soon as he entered his code, the Admiralty took over. Hans only needed to verify the proper functioning of the system and, after letting it run autonomous for a few days, he could start his journey homeward.

One by one he entered the proper numbers and characters and finally the center button that read 'execute.' The silence lasted only seconds before the clicking of micro relays reached crescendo in a monotonous noise like the ticking of countless grains of sand against a sail car on a stormy day on a Dutch beach.

The large pen relief showed system messages. The smaller side reliefs showed incoming messages from far off war steamers, listening posts, mobile observers and the Admiralty itself and the answers the system sent back to acknowledge.

Hans knew that now everything would be tested and calibrated. It would all seem well, but the first shot would have a strong deviation. He checked his horologium and calculated. The plan that formed in his head a few days ago, became ever more clear and the lines he had started were converging to their final solution.

* * *

Alistera Gavanides seemed uncomfortable when Hans stood next to her and observed her painting a threatening, dark sky behind the fortress. The day was bright with a clear blue sky.

"They say a painter puts his or her mood in the painting," Hans said.

"Yes? Do they also say when that mood lightens up?" Alistera said in a bitter voice. "This morning there was a test firing of the Fire Tulips and I missed it."

"Alas," said Hans.

Alistera bowed her head. "I'm sorry if I caused you any problems," she said.

Hans touched her shoulder. "No harm done, Alistera."

"Good," she said. "I yelled at Bashar and kicked his shins when I found out he followed us."

Hans grinned. "I feel sorry for him already."

Alistera turned moody again. "Again, I'm sorry. I have my reasons, but no need to worry you with my problems, Hans Cornelisz."

"I think I understand. Can I ask you something?" Hans asked.

She looked up at him, waiting.

"Do you know the restaurant 'Sea Dike'?" he asked.

Alistera pulled up her nose. "That megalomaniac attempt to recreate part of Amsterdam in Herakleion harbor? Who doesn't?"

"I have obtained a reservation through interim governor Pauwelsson, for tonight. He was in a good mood, something about a long weekend on a yacht. There is a roof terrace that is only available on special occasions," Hans explained.

"That I did not know," Alistera said. "What about it?"

"The view is extraordinary," Hans said and smiled. "I would be honored if you would accompany me for dinner tonight."

Alistera sighed and looked at him. Then she smiled, causing electric shivers to run through his stomach. "All right, Hans Cornelisz."

"Excellent, that pleases me," Hans said. "Pick you up at the foot of the hill? I'll ask for a coach to take us there."

"What time?" Alistera asked.

"Around seven. Reservation at eight," Hans said.

"I shall be there," Alistera said.

"And bring your tiphaigne along," Hans said. He smiled benevolently. "And your sketch block and some pencils."

"I don't do portraits, Mister Cornelisz," Alistera said.

"Humor me, my dear," Hans said. "After all, it is my last night on Crete."

"All right," Alistera said and she smiled her most brilliant smile, once more.

* * *

On the East side of Herakleion Harbor five Amsterdam Canal warehouses rose up. They were at least five times higher than the surrounding low structures of the Cretan houses, and stores, and were complete replicas of the stately buildings on the Fifth Emperor's Canal near the Van Pels Park in Amsterdam.

The governor's coach delivered Hans and Alistera near the restaurant around half past seven. A pompous red carpet ran all the way from the square in front of the buildings to the entrance of the 'Sea Dike.' Hans had dressed for the occasion in his Sunday dress suit while Alistera wore the green gown that had impressed him a few days ago and he had trouble keeping his eyes off her.

Hans accompanied her inside and talked to the host who immediately took them into the back and along narrow, steep staircases to the upper floors. All specific details of the Amsterdam Canal buildings had obviously been copied.

The stone floor of the terrace was made of identical stone as used in Fortress *Hollandia* and a low, cast iron fence surrounded it. Hans thought it suitable for his last night on the island.

A single table and two chairs were on the West side of the terrace such that they would see the evening sun sink into the sea.

Two Cretan servants in traditional outfit helped them into their chairs and poured their first wine.

Hans looked out at Herakleion. Far away he noticed the threatening shape of the fortress and the gun barrels that rose above the surroundings as well as the lonely Tesla coil pillar. He raised his glass. "To Fire Tulips," he said.

Alistera raised hers' "Fire Tulips," she repeated. "Sure, why not?"

The servants brought several appetizers accompanied by traditional Cretan dishes. Alistera told about her youth on Crete and Hans listened with interest. Occasionally he glanced at his horologium.

Alistera noticed. "Is this terrace rented by the minute, Hans?" she asked.

Hans grinned. "Not at all, we have all the time we want."

"Hmm, I wouldn't be surprised," Alistera said. "You Dutch will always be frugal."

Now Hans really laughed. "Wherever I go, I hear people repeat that myth." Demonstratively he looked at the horizon where the sun touched the sea, next at his horologium.

"Then why do you keep staring at that clock?" Alistera asked.

"I will show you," Hans answered. "Did you bring your tiphaigne?"

"Like you asked," Alistera said.

"Switch it on," Hans said. "And take out your sketch block."

Alistera complied. "Are you going to explain to me why?"

Hans moved his chair until he was next to her. Together they watched in southerly direction, over Herakleion, straight at the grotesque fortress. Again he checked his horologium. "Any moment now," he said.

He barely uttered the words when one of the cannons of the fortress belched a huge steam cloud. Hans tapped Alistera's elbow and mimicked pressing the button of the tiphaigne.
Alistera was half in shock, but she began taking pictures.

The steam cloud expanded and during the expansion the accumulated, excessive volta of the Tesla coil discharged through the vapor, a furious bundle of glowing red sparks that traversed the edges of the cloud like blood red veins.

A sound like thunder rolled over Herakleion.

"Did you get that?" Hans asked Alistera who was very busy snapping dozens of pictures.

She looked at him. "I think so, yes. How did you know?"

"Take your sketch block," Hans said.

Alistera complied.

Two other Fire Tulips discharged and again the typical white clouds with red fiery veins that the cannons derived their name from, occurred.

"The new Fire Tulips are controlled directly by the Admiralty." He tapped Alistera's sketch block and made writing movements with his hand. "In this modernized version everything is automated, from loading to aiming and firing. Before, one grenade per cannon per half hour could be fired. This system however can maintain a firing rate of one five thousand pounder every three minutes, per cannon."

Alistera looked up. "That's fast."

Hans nodded. "It gets better. The distance has been increased to over one hundred and fifty miles. The accuracy over that distance is roughly thirty feet."

While explaining, the cannons threw grenades a hundred miles or more into the air, every minute, accompanied by the thunderous noise of the Tesla coil discharge.

"Why are you telling me this?" Alistera asked.

"I have many reasons," Hans said. "First, you can use this information to remind Bashar of his promise to me."

"Promise?" Alistera asked.

"Information in exchange for the release of your father," Hans said.

She opened her eyes wide. "You would do this for me?" she asked. She shook her head in disbelief. "No one has ever done anything like that for me."

"Before you thank me, there are more reasons. On behalf of the Admiralty please convey the following message: 'The Ottoman cruisers in Cretan waters have been destroyed. We now cover the Ottoman Corridor that is the main trade artery for Constantinople. We request formally that you abide by the Pax Batavica.'." Hans handed her the official, sealed document from the Admiralty.

"Why give this to me?" Alistera asked.

"You are in contact with Bashar and likely with other Ottoman agents," Hans said. "You can get this into the hands of the right people, fast. Right?"

"Yes, I can do that," Alistera confirmed.

"Consider this, the VOC does not wish to go to war. Whoever starts a war, be assured the VOC will finish the war," Hans continued. "The Fire Tulips are instrumental in this. Right next to the main trade artery of the Ottoman Empire. And in the coming months most other fortresses in VOC occupied territory will be equipped with these systems."

"I always knew Holland-under-the-Sea was dangerous, no matter how derogatory the Ottomans spoke of you," Alistera said.

One of the Fire Tulips fired a grenade that swooshed by not a hundred feet above their heads and quickly disappeared over the horizon. Seconds later a ball of fire appeared and a minute later a deeper thunder rolled over Herakleion.

"What was that?" Alistera asked. "Did something go wrong?"

"No, the system does as instructed. It was aimed at a certain yacht near the coast of Dia."

"Did you do that?" Alistera asked.

Hans nodded.

"Was anyone on board?"

"Yes, a trade traitor with his accomplices," Hans answered.

"Then you have shown them mercy." She looked at him intently. "I know the punishment for trade traitors. No need to feel guilty."

Hans sighed. He moved his chair back and made to get up, but Alistera stopped him.

"Why leave?" she asked.

"My work here is done, Alistera. And hopefully I did some good today," Hans explained. "For you as well," he added.

"Please sit back down, Mister Cornelisz," Alistera said. "Like I said, no one has ever done something like this for me. Such a person I would like to get to know a little better. If said person is agreeable with that, of course." She batted her eyes at Hans.

With good wine and good food, Hans and Alistera talked until, at the end of the evening, they sat next to each other, holding hands, enjoying the lovely bouquet of Fire Tulips that unfolded far above them.

Voyage
by Murray Braun

"When all else is lost, the future still remains."
—C.N. Bovee in "Eyewitness to Jewish History,"
Rabbi Benjamin Blech (Wiley, 2004)

August 2, 1492.

Aboard the expedition's lead caravel were *Almirante,* the admiral Cristobal, with his Hebrew translator, Luis de Torres. Born as Jews, both were *conversos* who practiced Judaism secretly after converting to Christianity. Torres conveniently knew Arabic as well, believed to be the tongue spoken not only by Chinese but Japanese and Indians. Alas, it was a notion later dispelled as a mistranslation in Marco Polo's "Travels."

The day before the three rather humbly-built craft were launched from their anchorage on the Iberian coast, Cristobal and Torres watched as a swath of a half-million Jews descended on foot onto the glittering shores of an ominously-darkened Mediterranean Sea. Even the ocean smelled foul that day. Banished Jews, *converso* or not, crowded docks in search of a meager number of unseaworthy boats, hastily arranged for the voyage into uncertain waters, and sailing for doubtful harbors.

Frowning, Cristobal said, "See well, Torres, our Golden Age ends with another diaspora."

Torres said, "Almirante, where will they all find passage?"

"Few options are left them. Could you trek through mountain passes as small children or as the elderly?"

Torres shook his head, but gleaming hazel eyes reflected unwavering optimism.

Cristobal would depart on the third day of August rather than the second day since it boded ill to do so on the anniversary of the destruction of Jerusalem's Temple. Superstitious, Almirante feared the expedition would be foreshadowed if they embarked that same day.

Cristobal said, "A tragedy is on display before us."

Despite the sad scene, Torres wasn't thinking of these poor souls but of the lost Israelite tribes who sailed the oceans due west. It was as if Cristobal read Torres' mind and said, "Imagine, sailing west like the ancients we hope to encounter."

Torres said, "Surely, one can't voyage there by keeping land in view."

Cristobal said, "Do not fear—the stars will navigate our swift course to Asia."

Torres knew Cristobal promised the Spanish royals speedy establishment of an Indies trade. But how much faster, Torres thought, with assistance of the Hebrews, *los de tierra firme*, already in place.

Cristobal no longer listened as he watched the course of the lead ship out of the harbor. The sea, opaque the day before was now the color of sapphire. Breezes wafted the briny-scent that was no longer foul. A foamy ocean bid them forward. But Cristobal wasn't uplifted by the freshness of sea-spray. He already looked weary as if his eyelids wanted to close on him.

The funds for the expedition came from Jews, Luis de Santangel and Isaac Abravanel, in the financial employ of both Portuguese and Spanish courts. Santangel and Abravanel arranged the meeting with the royal duo hastily because of Cristobal's determination to seek the funds elsewhere. The Queen Isabella and King Ferdinand, resplendent in their bejeweled costumes in bright satins and delicate lace, awaited the esteemed financiers, themselves dressed in finery though more modest. In the grandiloquent royal Castilian residence, lush Persian rugs stretched from the entry to their gilded throne.

After introductions, Santangel the first to speak said, "We've come to dissuade you from further procrastination and to avail yourselves of our aid." Santangel thought, *Have I put that correctly? I didn't want to offend them.*

Queen Isabella shook her red curls about, and staring with her deep-blue eyes at Santangel said, "Cristobal's ideas are those of a madman. One knows these voyages can only be made in sight of land. Why, the courtiers jibe, 'Almirante sails to the moon'."

Abravanel chuckling, took out the letter addressed to the Portuguese king from respected cosmographer, Paolo dal Pozzo Toscanelli. He read out loud: "Navigation by way of the stars is a feasible means of sailing west into the oceans."

Isabella said, "And why has the Portuguese monarch chosen to ignore this?"

Santangel trying to suppress hiccups after laughing along with Abravanel said, "Their coffers are depleted more than Spain's, though they aren't burdened with fighting the Muslims in Granada. This is why we've proposed to fund Cristobal ourselves."

The Jews and *conversos* sought to avoid their own exile by backing both Spain's crusades and Cristobal's proposal.

Queen Isabella, appearing more and more interested, said, "I'd offer to pawn my jewels instead."

Santangel sighing replied, "Would that it were sufficient."

Abravanel calmly added, "Meet with him again, your majesties. He'll not fail to convince you to give the voyage your blessing."

* * *

Shipwrecked on the coast of Portugal, Cristobal had the good fortune to join his brother, Bartholomew, employed in the city of Lisbon as a cartographer. He would come to meet Abravanel for the first time there as well, before the financier took flight from Portugal to Spain.

Standing in his brother's tidy workroom in the early afternoon sun, Abravanel said to Cristobal, "Your brother tells me of your good and bad news. You seem to have recovered from your sea trial."

Cristobal said, "And the good?"

Abravanel said trying to suppress the hiccups, "Bartholomew speaks of your proposal to sail to Asia as the Portuguese, Vasco Da Gama, proposes to do."

Cristobal interrupting him said, "DaGama plans to sail to the Cape of Good Hope to reach the Indian Sea and Calcutta. A quite different philosophy from mine. But anyway, can you procure the funds for the expedition?"

Abravanel said, "That's why I'm here to meet you. Born Jews and *los de tierra firme*, we can't ignore our bond."

Cristobal shook Abravanel's hand and patted both the men on the shoulder. He said smiling for the first time to Abravanel, "Your reputation is known to all in Spain and Portugal. And I might add, your spirit is unimpeachable."

* * *

At his first audience in the royal court soon after the financiers' visit, some noticed that Queen Isabella was taken by Cristobal's reddish-hair and blue eyes, the features not unlike her own. Disregarding the jibes at him of "sailing to the moon" from the courtiers, at the age of twenty-one Cristobal already captained ships as a corsair or a privateer, protecting merchant convoys or reinforcing war fleets.

Queen Isabella and King Ferdinand, catching wind of Cristobal's search for funds from their enemy, France, realized that Spain had no one else but Cristobal to enlist to bring them the Indies' riches, known to all from the fables written by the priest, Prester John.

Isabella said, "Your letters have preceded you, Almirante."

Cristobal said, "I wanted to assure you the mission, should you command me, not only promises the Indies' riches, but conversion of the native population."

Isabella nodded and said, "As expected from a pious man such as you."

At that moment, Torquemada, the Grand Inquisitor, entered the hall uninvited. He said imperiously, "This a foul bent in your majesties' favor." Coming to stand with a thud beside Cristobal, the Grand Inquisitor's usually sallow complexion was flushed with outrage. He held a golden cross on a short-chain tightly to his chest. Obvious to all that he ignored Cristobal next to him, Torquemada said to Isabella, "Aha, now the Queen consults with *los marranos*. Do you not adhere to our Inquisition, your majesty?"

Dumbfounded, Isabella finally said, "My conference with Cristobal doesn't at all concern you. This is a matter of state."

Torquemada glared at a usually sober Cristobal, who steeling himself then broke into a wide grin, further enraging the beet-red Inquisitor. The priest cocked his arm back throwing the cross and striking Isabella in the forehead. Shockingly, no one seized the irate cleric. Torquemada didn't relent. With a wave of the hand at the Almirante, he said to Isabella—as she sat trying to rub away the pink welt on her forehead—"And, when will you, my Queen, issue the edict to expel *these* Jews from our midst?"

Ferdinand said nothing. Cynically, the King knew that his royal coffers would be replenished when the Jews' possessions were confiscated by his exchequers after their expulsion six-months hence.

Torquemada himself planted rumors across the land, such as *conversos'* use of black magic and crucifixion of a male child in the village of La Guardia. Ironically, it was said that the Grand Inquisitor had been a *converso* himself. Such unexpected retaliatory behavior wasn't unheard of among *conversos.*

* * *

Both navigator and cartographer, Cristobal felt destined to sail west without the coast as a guide. And if their return to Jerusalem in pilgrimage—a preoccupation of Cristobal and other Jews—wasn't in the offing, then the Temple would be built in Asia. While there, even if temporarily, the Almirante's feigned Catholicism would be cast-off as well as the fear of retribution from anti-Semites no matter how long one resided in Gentile lands.

Six-years' wait for a commission clearly demonstrated to Cristobal the *conversos'* disadvantages. Once a Jew, always a Jew? The common refrain of anti-Semitism. After conversion to Christianity, *conversos* were accused of "Judaizing" by informers. Despite the absurd and preposterous canards spread about them, such as their contamination by other evil-Jews, blood rituals and worshipping the devil, the *conversos* didn't relent in their hidden faith. They knew at some point the Jews would suffer. Alas, hundreds of Jews and *conversos,* during two Inquisitions, were burned at the stake. They were burned instead of decapitated because executions that caused blood to be spilled were forbidden in the Catholic faith.

Abravanel, like other Jews on Cristobal's expedition who had not converted under duress, also sought to sail to freedom. Fortuitously, they found refuge in Naples, the only Italian republic that would have his and the three other boats. Since the plague had broken out aboard, all were quarantined upon their arrival.

* * *

Leonardinho, or Dinho for short, was a *converso* from Portugal. The *conversos* were distrusted by the Portuguese even more than in the kingdom of Spain. The Church felt cheated by Jews who disregarded the faith it placed in or demanded from them.

Such distrust led to the exile of Jews from France in the twelfth and fourteenth centuries, and the thirteenth century in England. The trespass leading to their banishment? Practice of the faith by keeping the *sabbath*. In the so-called German-states, Jews were massacred instead as retaliation for the Black Death. *Why would anyone convert to an inimical religion, but to stay alive?* thought Dinho.

Like Cristobal, for whom home was where one could often get killed, Dinho decided to be a seaman, and learned to navigate by the stars. Thus, he avoided the ill-fate of fellow-Portuguese *conversos* who chose to stay put.

Dinho believed Cristobal's map would lead them to South America, not to Asia. Was the Almirante attempting to disprove Ptolemy's theory of 100 A.D. that Asia was much farther from Europe than believed? Perhaps, and it may have been Toscanelli's competing belief that Asia was indeed closer that had influenced him.

The sailors steered badly and fell off-course. Reprimanded by Almirante, and not only the once, the men's stares and sneers aimed at him multiplied. It got even worse when the third boat went missing.

Dinho remembered the words of Almirante when they pulled up anchor and set sail. Cristobal said to an assembled crew that first day, "I warn all of you. I'll not tolerate any deviation from our path."

The men grunted and twitched with uneasiness under his glare. For that was how he always addressed them. Dinho looked over the sailors and counted among them not less than half who were *conversos*. He wondered, was Cristobal another *converso*? He didn't know, but felt it unimportant. Like him, he had fled the Inquisitors. For Dinho, it was a permanent flight. Cristobal, on the other hand, was to return.

Nearly two-months out, Cristobal spoke to the sailors, "You've steered off-course, by my calculation." An uproar ensued, with much shouting. Men bellowed curses that Cristobal only eventually succeeded in halting by shouting over the top, "Enough! Back to work!" Unbeknown to them all, it was not the crew's steering at fault, but rather the map used by Cristobal.

Martin Alonso, the captain of the second caravel, shouted, "I claim the *precio!*" Almirante, undoubtedly, would pocket the reward of gold ducats for having first sighted land upon their return to Spain.

Two long days after first spotting signs of land ahead, they discovered it wasn't land at all. Rather, it was an enormous, stagnant, low-altitude cloud that had duped them. It had meant nothing to have spotted twigs and branches, birds that were known never to venture far from land, seaweed that only grew on rocks, crabs that lived exclusively in river weed, and shore-loving whales and dolphins.

A fourth caravel, the ghost-ship *Fantoma,* indeed existed. Jewish ghosts likewise believed they would meet up with their *landsmen—los de tierra firme—*in Asia and create a new life without trepidation. The Great Plague nearly eliminated the Jews in Spain, but a hundred years later, they found a means of escape from the finality of their existence, or be ousted *in toto.* One still heard ghosts, who remembered being told themselves, recount that more superstitious Christians placed a good-sized stone in the mouths of the dead so they couldn't eat their way out of the coffins.

Eliezer, the ship's-boy, settled into the *Fantoma's* routine, sailing alongside the Almirante's trio. Given a large hourglass, he timed the crew so the sailors knew when to sleep above-deck between shifts, despite the obvious exposure and discomfort.

Eliezer also worried about his ghost-cousin, Menachem. Forced to stay behind in Spain with a case of the flu when the *Fantoma's* captain signed-on their crew, Eliezer feared Menachem might not be able to avert the Inquisition's crushing maw. Ghosts wouldn't be spared. For the ghosts, the end came when rendered incorporeal. The diabolical Inquisitors had kept their means of accomplishing this particular feat to themselves.

During the first leg of the voyage by way of the Canaries, Eliezer recalled the last time he saw Menachem. He had been in his Cordoban garret, lying prostrate on his sleep roll, the one he had hoped to bring with him on this voyage. Holding a cloth soaked in rosewater to his forehead, Menachem looked most ghostly, and grunted at every word his cousin blurted out. Quickly, Eliezer forgot his cousin already felt abandoned.

Not in hearing range of the kingdom's spies, Eliezer bantered in an ancestral and clandestine Ladino instead of Castilian, of the provisions, "There's barreled water, hard ship's biscuits, salted meats, and freshly-caught fish while in harbor, then salted. But no citrus after it spoils below-deck en route."

Sounding oracle-like, Menachem through a haze said, "All food will be infested with rodents, worms and maggots halfway out to sea. Sailors' limbs, riddled with black patches of skin and bleeding sores from scurvy."

Looking at him incredulously, Eliezer said, "Aye, you're

jealous, left out and all."

Menachem sighed and said, "Perhaps, I can blend in with Gentile ghosts."

Eliezer thought his cousin could hardly do so since his face read like a map
of Palestine. Fleeing to next-door Portugal, like many *conversos*, only guaranteed that Lisbon would follow in Castile's path by imposing their outrageous levies on Jews. And after less than a year, mass conversions would be forced upon them.

Since the Inquisitors would lay the ghost of hope avoiding death a second time, Menachem mused, "Perhaps I could transform into my former human self?" But reincarnation was unwelcome to Menachem just then. *Better to stay a ghost than be charred whole or killed in a ghastly manner*, thought Eliezer.

The Iberian peninsula was Eliezer's birthplace, his parents hangers-on to the Ottomans who invaded southern Spain. Like folk in the wake of Roman legions, his parents worked for the Ottomans. His father, an ironworker, crafted implements of military and peaceful or domestic intent. His mother, a cook, made some difficult adjustments to oriental taste.

His grandparents, forced to leave the Iberian peninsula during the bloody *pogroms* of 1391, were swept-up in the migratory wave East, mixing with diaspora Jews arriving as traders, or the indigents in Bukhara. They retained Israelite identity but like other exiles, they attempted to avoid further disrespect and persecution by disguising their Jewishness from the Sultan and Muslim populace. But because of a yellow badge, a Muslim invention that they were forced to wear, this was ultimately impossible.

Eliezer's parents found themselves in Iberia again after the Ottomans chose to employ, rather than do-away with them, as the Muslim soldiers traversed central Asia with unstoppable momentum. Eliezer last saw his parents in Castile. Already *conversos* after fleeing from the Ottomans in Granada to Spain, they absent-mindedly wore their old winter coats with yellow, circular Jewish badges sewn on to them.

Brought before the Inquisitors, his agitated mother and impassive father knew that an informer, neighbor or stranger, was responsible for an enquiry into their heresy: lighting the *Menorah* candles on Friday nights. *Thank goodness the Inquisitors were unaware of his father's dislike for pork*, thought Eliezer. Outside the tribunal doors, the Christians scornfully shouted, *"Marranos!"*—meaning "pigs" in Spanish.

All three succumbed to an *auto-da-fe*, or "act of faith," burned to death on display in the town-square. Engulfed in flames, Eliezer—only being a lad and having not even had a *bar mitzvah*, one's coming-of-age—heard his father recite *Kaddish*, the prayer for the dead, or tribute to an absent God, never mentioning the deceased. His mother's screams were deafening and heard by the other terrified and imprisoned victims awaiting their ends. Victims were carried to the stakes in cages after torture made it impossible to walk.

Eliezer wept until totally dehydrated. His parents' ghosts, rendered incorporeal soon afterwards, left him a "survivor." Thus, Eliezer and Menachem were the last Jewish ghosts in Spain. Only Eliezer was fortunate enough to escape by sailing away. No other Jews remained.

* * *

Cristobal was like many seamen of the time. Little was known of his childhood origins or the enigma he harbored. No one suspected Cristobal's Jewishness or the cunning with which he kept it clandestine.

On the third night out, Torres joined him as Cristobal watched the course of the caravel. Torres looked over a section, or *haftorah*, from the Book of Prophets copied by Cristobal in Latin for his son.

Cristobal said, "Am I in keeping with *bar mitzvah* practice?"

Not until the Fifteenth Century was the *bar mitzvah* formalized into the Jewish repertoire.

In exasperation, Torres replied, "Yes, but I must translate it into Hebrew. The *haftorah* is to be chanted in Hebrew by memory in the synagogue so God can hear—and as closely as possible to the boy's birth date."

"So, in less than a year's time."

"Is he the son of your wife or your mistress, Almirante?"

Unperturbed, Cristobal said, "Diego is my eldest, the son of a Jewish wife who died, unfortunately. A younger son was born to my mistress, also a Jewess. I cherish them all."

Ferdinand, Cristobal's younger son, was sent letters on his future voyages as more ships returned to Spain. Appended to Almirante's signature was an anagram in Hebrew, *Sh'ma Yisrael* or "Hear, Oh Israel," one of four rolled parchments inserted in a *phylactery*, a box strapped onto the forehead in morning prayer. A leather strap was wound down the arm. The anagram's significance was misconstrued by Gentiles who believed it to represent the Trinity.

Onboard the *Fantoma*, Eliezer gazed at the hourglass on a galley post to see if the six hour mark drew near. On the ship's other end, sailors began to stir from naps, or began their rests between shifts. Sailors about to sleep above deck thought of bedrolls of sturdy fabric used as pillows. Despite the fatigue, heavy sweating and a brilliant morning sun in their eyes, sailors finished work on the sails, it being windless. The heat of the day began its ascent.

Then, Eliezer listened in on the *Fantoma's* ghosts in-command. The captain said, "We shouldn't wait any longer after being at sea two months."

Seigneur admiral winced, or maybe it was a facial spasm, and said, "The ship's-boy will go and find out what seems to be wrong with the course."

Eliezer couldn't hold back his excitement and said, "I shall do your will's justice, *seigneurs*."

Under the veil of midnight, with no moon or light from the lead boat in the distance, Eliezer with a ghost's keen night-vision made his way in the dinghy, the oars transporting him quietly across calm waters.

Cristobal's other secret was soon discovered after Eliezer, now stolen aboard, confronted Dinho studying the ship's log, while the Almirante was on-deck watching the course sleeplessly, as was his habit.

Dinho found two separate columns of daily numbers Cristobal kept.

Recognizing the ghost near him, Dinho said, "Your pallor doesn't belie your provenance."

Generally, neither ghosts or their vessels were seen by others, but there were many exceptions.

Eliezer said, "The *Fantoma's* command sent me."

"And what do they say?"

"The distances recorded by Cristobal are inflated, then transmitted to the other two boats."

"Why would Cristobal do so?"

"A ruse to elevate Christian sailors' spirits, or else they would continue to worry about their return passage to Spain."

Dinho knew Cristobal was to return with only some Christian

crew and without *conversos*. Another map would be used after Cristobal was unseated. His submission was to be handled without harm, thus assuring the Almirante's return to Spain.

The famous Jewish cartographer, himself a Catalonian *converso*, named Jafuda-Cresques, had supplied Dinho with his own drawings and perhaps those of the Almirante himself, since it was said Cristobal also hailed from Catalonia. Dinho realized, as had the *Fantoma's* command, that while the position of the stars changed day-by-day, the compass needle always pointed in the same direction. Cristobal was unaware of this. Assembling the sailors to plot an insurrection, Dinho said, "Cristobal is surely more off-course than he admits."

Dinho said, "I condemn your treatment by Almirante." The crew's hiding by Cristobal fresh in their minds, this furthered their support for the Portuguese.

Dinho hastily conspired with a *converso* sailor, Rodrigo, and the ship's-boy, Eliezer, to immobilize an unwary Cristobal. After much struggling, when he stopped thrashing, they tied the Almirante with rope, ignoring his relentless curses. He called them "*Marranos*" although he himself was a *converso*. His grandfather sojourned in Spain before the family fled to Genoa. Coming from a family of weavers, like many of the Genovese Jews, wasn't very profitable. Yet another reason Cristobal went to sea.

Cristobal said, "You'll pay dearly for mutiny, Dinho."

Dinho replied, "I'm not subject to the kingdom of Spain. So it's of no import to me, Cristobal."

Grimacing at the tightness of the rope, Cristobal said, "Rodrigo, what do you say?"

"We know of your deception, Almirante."

Dinho, curious to know if the two maps had derived from the very same Jafuda Cresques asked, "Was the Catalonian the source of your map, Cristobal?"

Cristobal's eyelids shut like curtains dropped suddenly upon a stage. Asleep, no doubt from exhaustion, he disregarded his ankles being tied by Eliezer, crouched in front of him after his torso was lassoed to a chair. The ship's-boy was thus invisible to him. Binding Almirante hand-and-foot secured him within the cabin.

After transcription onto parchment in ink, the message sent on a line strung between them to the second boat, then finally relayed to the third boat, read: *Be it known Almirante is overthrown but unharmed—Dinho is placed in his stead—hereon-in, a new map will lead us to land.*

* * *

The small island of Lucayos in the San Salvador chain was first sighted by the same sailor Rodrigo, his full-name, Juan Rodrigues Bermeo. But before the captive Cristobal was granted freedom, they sailed all along the Cuban coast but never quite reached the harbor of Havana. Tracking back, they were lulled by monotonous tropical shores. After sailing through straits with the Tortuga Islands starboard, they docked at La Navidad on the north coast of Hispaniola, the harbor of Santo Domingo far to the south.

Wherever they anchored, the natives were immodest and wore no cover. They stared at the too-clothed foreign men with awe. But their native tongues weren't familiar to Torres. By the use of hand signals and remarking on the presence of wounds on the natives' bodies, the sailors learned that cannibal tribes attacked, plundered the villages, and carried away males or females, both the children and adults.

The morning sun's tropical heat made the sailors' skin sizzle. At nightfall, every conceivable sort of hungry insect at once alighted in swarms. Exquisitely pruritic small lumps burgeoned on the sailors' already scorbutic legs, since the insects flew low to the ground. Even the men's leggings were of no protection. But the natives weren't bothered in the least by the insect bites.

The modest quantity of gold used in their tribal dress and ritual was traded for the Europeans' cheap trinkets, clearly delighting the natives. Their land was arable, but few crops grown there were recognizable to the crew. All the villages smelled of foul rotting plants not unlike the smell of old, watery potatoes, leaving sailors no choice but to cover their noses with their shirtfronts.

Cristobal thought that he found Asia, but not Hebrew landsmen. He realized the last leg of the voyage as the crew kept him informed, that robust trade from the Indies was of limited or even dubious value. Forced to use his imagination and plain magic to win further pecuniary support from the King and Queen, he would resort to fabrication. That is, until the royal's own lackeys were sent to spy on him.

Stubborn as ever, Cristobal would go on to report to the King and Queen that he had found the Asian coast. He returned to La Navidad in future voyages, especially the second of four, with replacements for the settlers, as every one of them died after the first trip.

Young Eliezer couldn't have possibly imagined the daily mayhem of La Navidad. The *converso* sailors hadn't planned on working after reaching paradise. They had not resisted the temptation of the native women there. Settlers were overwhelmed by disease, including the syphilis scourge at its outset in the New World. Carousing and being soused perpetually, the drunken hordes became a threat to the ghosts' survival and their final obstacle. It was but a short year before Almirante returned to discover the obvious tragedy of his mutinous crew's demise.

Cousin Menachem found his way, in part, thanks to safe houses and ghettos in the German states. Arriving safely in the Old City of Prague, where the so-called "good" Jewish ghetto stood, flying its contrasting blue-and-white flag with the Star of David since the early Fourteenth Century, he reveled in his good fortune.

Imagine Menachem's reaction when learning of his cousin Eliezer's demise after Cristobal's second voyage. Fortunately, Menachem was "saved" by the flu from a similar fate as his cousin. Like other inhabitants of Hispaniola, Eliezer was a victim of internecine struggles among settlers. An innocent ghost caught in a human web of the time's making and the actions of unruly men.

The Forbidden Fuel
by Sergio Palumbo
(translated by Michele Dutcher)

> "In visions of the dark night
> I have dreamed of joy departed-
> But a waking dream of life and light
> Hath left me broken-hearted..."
> from *A Dream* by Edgar Allan Poe

By properly adjusting the copper ocular device that the middle-aged man wore on his right eye, Tyshawn was able to shoot a glance at the varied representatives of mankind who crowded the streets. He was walking close to the town's river bank, where over the course of an average day, a person could see an abundance of homeless people. There were old men searching for any sort of job they could get and poor individuals trying to get an occupation somewhere, while at night that place became something different, more insidious, certainly.

Overall those were great years, and the nation's economy was growing thanks to the modern technology that made almost anything possible. Many things which once could only be dreamed of a few years ago were now easily accessible. On the other hand, it was exactly those new technologies that had cast many workers from their active jobs and relegated them to the border of modern society...

It was still hours until dawn and a cough in the shadow of a tall wall, a few footsteps on a dark alley, and some gusts of wind coming from the river flowing in the distance made you feel ill at ease with that place. But the slender man knew he had to go on, there was no other choice. Tyshawn was there in search of the truth, and the truth at times led you to the most dangerous and farthest spots. As an experienced licensed detective, he knew this very well.

The man wore his long hair in a peculiar style and his dark eyes seemed to reveal a deep perceptiveness. His usual clothing tended to favor gray leather jackets worn under a wide buttoned-up topcoat, which was exactly the outfit the man had on at present. In a way, the detective thought it better outlined his slim though muscular figure along with his stature of medium height.

This was an area very far away from the most fashionable streets in Bristol: Small Street—where the great splendor of the olden times was still maintained; along with Broad Street, Nicholas Street and Great George Street. It was also very distant from the famous Clifton Bridge which was, undoubtedly, one of the must-see sights within the town. The bridge had been built in 1864 and had since drawn many tourists to see it every year, people who enjoyed strolling across its notable length from where they could have expansive views across the entirety of the city—which was extremely breathtaking.

Bordering the counties of Somerset and Gloucestershire, Bristol was one of the warmest cities in England, but was exposed to the Severn and Bristol Channel anyway. Rain fell all year round but autumn and winter were the worst seasons, most of the time. Bristol was already wealthy, and in point of commerce, superior to any town apart from the capital. The freeing in 1698 of the African trade from the control of the Royal African Company had already opened immense new fields to the local enterprising traders in the whole Bristol area. Nowadays, Bristol's ships returned loaded with miscellaneous goods for the use of its own citizens and for redistribution to the West of the British Empire.

As a matter of fact, the lands of England were as diverse as the people who occupied them. They were continuously subject to the many changes that modern innovations and the steam engine technology were bringing to the British Isles, at a faster rate than in all the other countries in the world. Bristol was no exception, as it had undergone many modifications and alterations over the course of the last centuries.

The city had once been transformed by the opening of the Floating Harbor in 1809, in order to allow visiting ships to remain afloat all of the time. Since that time, probably nothing had changed its skyline more than the Mooring Masts.

These were used for the passenger service of the Air Stations that the new meta-planes of the Over Oceans Company, or the OOC, made use of every day. After a series of name changes, takeovers and amalgamations, it had become the biggest company in the area, with a workforce of 3 000, and was by far the largest and most profitable of the businesses at present. Its very name meant power, wealth, quality technology and speedy transportation worldwide.

Those were the years of many new scientific discoveries and ongoing progress, so the town's future and its overall production always needed innovative projects and machinery. The worldwide competition certainly was difficult and relentless. Long gone was the time when the most well-known names in town were Stanton & Champion's Steam Confectionery Works and the large Edward Packer's Easton factory, which had been opened in the 1880s by a former employee of Frys, itself another famous company. All had changed after 1876, when the first huge storage hangars of what had once been called the 'Air Vehicles and Transportation Company' began appearing outside the city boundaries. Clearly a new, important industry had officially begun, with all the consequences such an innovation could bring to the whole of society.

* * *

Even though there was a strong competition from London, Portsmouth and Glasgow, Bristol was benefiting from a series of thriving activities that had quickly positioned it at the top of the list of the more wealthy and modern towns throughout the whole British Empire. Quality wood came from the Forest of Dean, glass was produced in the city—mostly in the functional form of bottles. Lead was mined in the nearby Mendip Hills. Several bankers, being part of Bristol's professional and civic elite, were acquiring substantial and diverse interests in commerce. Three huge companies built steam locomotives, even though the local locomotive building firms never achieved the production levels of Glasgow or Newcastle. The city, however, had ranked for many years as a center of international importance, building robust engines for railways in all parts of the world.

As for the port itself, shipbuilding and repair facilities had risen to an important place in the economy of the area since medieval times. Its fortunes had continued to improve during the Seventeenth and

Eighteenth Centuries. Bristol's ship owners liked to build locally because different trades had different needs, and that made it easier for them to ensure that a vessel had precisely the features required for a particular purpose. Many actually had previously built ships for themselves or had invested large sums of money in one of the yards situated on the open ground along the banks of the river, but most of all those had disappeared with the construction of the Floating Harbor, to be replaced by more substantial and modern yards. Yet Bristol was hardly the ideal site for a modern shipyard: the largest vessels that could be built had a burden of about 3 000 tons, and iron and steel could not be had as cheaply as in the northern shipbuilding towns. Certainly, as ship owners increasingly favored large vessels over small ones, iron over wood, and steam over sail, Bristol was thought to be losing ground as a shipbuilding center in the late Nineteenth Century.

Quite differently from what a famous man had written in his essay on the economic development of the town over the course of the previous years—that "the city was a location for many activities and trades but a national center for almost none"—there was actually a field in which Bristol was the center, and that was transcontinental Air Transportation. In fact, this was where the town was already at the top of all other countries, and nothing seemed to be capable of removing it from that position of great regard.

As that profitable activity continued to grow and expand its interests, many other workers, families and businessmen had soon come to Bristol. Eventually other important needs had arisen, clearly the most obvious of those just being for more housing in town and in the suburbs. Indeed by 1891, the medieval walled city was ringed by a populous working-class on the outskirts, and by the Georgian and Regency squares of the well-to-do residences planned out on the surrounding hills and plains.

Nowadays, huge meta-planes were soaring through the skies of the British Empire as if an incredible magic was driving them. Such an air vehicle couldn't be classified as a common airship, because it was very different to the few that currently still flew over the cold lands of the Empire of Sweden or within the Russian boundaries. The extraordinary air machine used static lift generated by a pocket filled with lighter-than-air gas, and was characterized by a lowered weight center due to its long wings.

Such a design allowed the plane to have absolute stability. The correct lightness and strength were obtained by a multilayer envelope structure. Additionally, the lowered position of the propulsion system made the direct control of its energy much easier and offered high maneuverability. This innovative air vehicle was able to perform low cost aerial captures silently and safely. More and more units had already been ordered by the military so far, at least according to what the newspapers said every day. The original purpose the air machine had been built for, however, was mainly air tours for wealthy people who could afford its high cost, so they could see from above the wondrous coasts of the British Isles and its surrounding scenery. Of course, loads of cargo also went across the oceans during these same journeys.

What was Tyshawn presently looking for, exactly? Well, it wasn't easy to explain. The fact was that the graying man was investigating a delicate matter that he thought best to keep only to himself now. Strange things seemed to occur in those stinking streets, especially at night, when the dim lights made everything confused and faint; he himself had witnessed some of them directly. The first one had happened one month ago, and Tyshawn had been around there only by chance. The detective was heading back home in a hurry after a meeting with an old acquaintance of his, a cunning smuggler, who had given him some useful info about a case he was following at that time. Then, suddenly and unexpectedly, he had seen a man in flames, running along the street. It was about 11:30 PM and that was a sight he had never forgotten. Not that he hadn't tried by some means or other…

Tyshawn had done his best in order to help that poor person, but the fire was too hot and the temperature around him appeared to be equally unbearable. He hadn't been able to get any nearer and had simply remained on the site watching the body that was being reduced to ashes. Shortly after, everything was over and there was nothing else he could try. As soon as Tyshawn had done his duty and reported the event to the local police, also telling the agents that he himself would be glad to investigate as an experienced detective, things had taken a strange turn.

The policeman had explained that not only did they have some teams better suited for such research—and as such didn't need his help—but some time afterwards a friend of his, who worked as an employee at the police headquarters, asked for a secret meeting with him. He expressly told Tyshawn that he'd better not investigate further, or tell anyone about what he had witnessed.

"There are some muckety–mucks involved in all this! Forget what you saw..." he had suggested to Tyshawn one evening while sitting on a bench in the park surrounding Queen Square.

"Is this the advice of a good friend, or simply what you yourself would do under such circumstances?"

"Take it as both. I'm not joking, Tyshawn, it's better not to meddle in these things. I've already seen two of my colleagues, who were asking around about similar disappearances, killed in action because of accidents while on duty. Maybe it was only bad luck, or maybe not. Anyway, I've got my family to think about, I can't leave them alone. Therefore my hands are tied."

"I don't have a family anymore..." the detective had replied, though he had thanked his fearful, slender friend for his sincere words.

So, there were some important men of power involved in all that, from what he had heard, and the most appropriate move would be to just forget about it and leave others do their job. Even way back then, Tyshawn knew he had to investigate further, by all available means. The detective was very stubborn about such situations. He had always been.

The investigations he had made, by interrogating some ill-reputed citizens living in that area and having a look around, revealed to him that a few other common people had died in such a terrible way. Moreover, many had just disappeared leaving no trace whatsoever. Why had he been asked to step aside? He wasn't going to do so, absolutely not! But the more he found out over the course of the following weeks, the less he was thrilled about what lay ahead. That seemed to be really a very dark inquiry, full of many diversionary actions, half-truths and sad revelations.

Finally, Tyshawn had reminded himself of the fact that he was the son of an inventor. Well, probably not a very famous one, but the detective thought that his dead father had had some bad luck over the course of his life, or else he could have accomplished some truly great things. It had simply been because he didn't want to follow in his father's footsteps that the man had chosen a different path. Tyshawn had wanted adventure and an interesting life full of action, so he had become what he was now: a detective who liked to investigate delicate killings or bloody assaults perpetrated by delinquents, all in the name of justice. Of course, he would make sure justice was served only after a hefty cash payment in advance made by the ones who hired his services. Perhaps they were members of a family who wanted to know more about the abrupt death of their daughter, or maybe they searched for information about the unexpected suicide of a next of kin that occurred nearby. He was willing, for a price. Differently now, to what he had done before, he was now investigating a case without any assignment. It was his love for the truth that was enough to make him go on.

In order to get better leads, Tyshawn had turned to an old invention of his father, something the old man hadn't been able to complete before his passing ten years earlier. He had gone into his father's huge wooden shed next to the river that the old inventor had used as a lab. Left behind were many scraps of metal and other pieces of damaged copper instruments. Inside that place he had found an ocular device lying on a desk covered by dust. Even though he was not an experienced engineer like his dad, he knew some of the basics of science and could repair machines or build something completely new, occasionally. By improving and adapting thoroughly that peculiar monocle, he finally turned it into a very useful device capable of detecting the temperature of a human body from afar. Well, you had to stay within two yards of the target in order to have it work perfectly, and sometimes it didn't function right, but it was good enough for him.

Once completed, Tyshawn had adjusted that ocular device so that it looked like one of those monocles that the upper-class men were used to wearing while walking along the streets, in order not to attract too much attention. Though disguised as a monocle, its function was very different. Then, the detective had started wearing it all the time while going into the part of town where he had first witnessed that terrible death.

According to the result of the research he had done so far, most of the disappearances that were reported to the local police—or, at least, this was what his friend had revealed to him—had happened within the same area. Some of them seemed to have also occurred after they had paid a visit to a particular bar nearby. The thing Tyshawn had been asking himself was that he couldn't figure out why the agents weren't investigating all that. He had to discover something more, certainly.

There were some questions that filled his mind, all of which were still unanswered. Why someone was so interested about destitute people, and beyond that why did they disappear? Who was really responsible? And what kind of connection was there between those disappearances and the man in flames—the one he himself had seen one month ago? Tyshawn didn't know why, but he was sure there was a link. There had to be! The problem was how to discover the truth.

Furthermore, how had that unlucky individual been burned-up completely, to ashes? The night the man had witnessed that death he didn't have the modified ocular device he was wearing now, but there were some interesting doubts lying ahead. You see, you needed something endowed with a lot of potential energy in order to entirely burn-up a human body so quickly...and there was only one powerful energy source that came to Tyshawn's mind when he first started investigating. But these were only suppositions and suspicions, not enough to be sure of anything so far.

It was what happened another night that made the detective think he had been right, all along. The middle-aged man was walking through that part of town, his ocular device working in order to check on the overall temperature of the homeless and the many stray passers-by usually roaming in the area, many of who were completely drunk or drug-addicted.

It didn't take him very long. Tyshawn went past a tavern's front door and found another individual affected by a strange, notable increase in his body temperature. Today he was well equipped to investigate in a better way. That person was not in flames yet, but the brilliant colors displayed on his ocular device undoubtedly testified that something was going on, *and would be getting worse very quickly!* He appeared to be unstable, faltering as he went along, almost tripping over his own shoes. How long was he going to be able to stand up? Tyshawn   could   only   guess.

There was another detail the detective immediately noticed as the unfortunate man moved along. Two other individuals wearing dark, heavy overcoats, with their faces half hidden thanks to high collars, were apparently lying in wait at a dim corner on the left. They seemed to be keeping an attentive eye on that one and at a certain point they started following him from afar, until he changed course and almost disappeared past an old building. So, not only he had found another case of study, but it was clear that there was somebody else who had the same interest. Or worse...

Tyshawn knew he had to slow down his gait if he didn't want

to attract too much attention, while the other two immediately quickened their pace, as if they didn't want to lose the man who was walking along the way ahead of them – no matter the cost.

The wind seemed to become colder, and the darkness grew as those men moved onwards to an area even darker, and the street was in worse condition than where they were before. The sound of their feet over the rough pavement turned to an unending beating that appeared to be the only thing capable of reviving such a silent location, as the detective kept tailing the two at a distance. They definitely weren't policemen investigating that man, Tyshawn was sure about it. The problem was that he was unable to say what their true identity might be, even though he thought he already knew what their true intentions really were—and that seriously worried him. But there was almost nothing in that strange case that could be called ordinary or commonplace.

That strange, undeclared chase went on for some minutes before something happened. As Tyshawn already had the poor man in his line of sight, he saw that the two individuals who had been following him were standing next to that one and were going to act, there was no longer any reason to doubt it.

The first one ran fast and got past the other's position, then turned and stopped him. The poor man tried to speak, but all that issued from his mouth were incoherent terms and he offered no resistance in the end: he was probably already drunk as he didn't even react or noticed that someone else was next to him. So, the second individual with his face hidden immediately drew near his right side and grasped a staff that he used to hit him on the head forcefully, knocking him into unconsciousness. Then both of them approached the body of the man who was down and started carrying it to a whitish steam-powered pump-car nearby, apparently similar to one of those ice cream commercial vehicles you could at times spot in a park when there was a fair in town.

Tyshawn was able to come to a halt on time, before one of the two could have a direct look at him, so he remained past a corner, out of sight, and kept watching what was going on. It didn't seem like an act of theft or a simple attack of a weak passer-by. It was something different. On the other hand, if it was a sort of baffling first intervention in order to stop the man from bursting into flame, well, the detective just thought to himself that he didn't want to have a try at all.

The tallest one, with a slightly portly build, kept grabbing the back of the unlucky person in order to put the body aboard that wheeled motor vehicle, and it was at that time, as he removed part of the collar to take a breath that Tyshawn had, by chance, a glimpse at his face. At first the detective almost didn't believe it, as he was sure he well knew that man, but further looks made him sure about it. That nose, a wide mouth and such a pale complexion: he was a common delinquent named James, who lived in the area and who Tyshawn had already encountered in the line of his work. He had been very surprised to find out, one year ago, that he had left his life of daily thievery to begin a new life as a worker at the Ground Maneuvering Facilities of Over Oceans Company. Such a piece of gossip always spread quickly in the sinister surroundings. How had he been able to get hired? At first the detective had thought it was because of some acquaintance of James who could have helped him, but now the man had another opinion, indeed. So, that was it! Now he was sure that something seriously suspicious was going on, and his many doubts had become a certainty. The strange, subtle gleam that lurked in that delinquent's eyes looked like joy, or satisfaction. And that undoubtedly meant bad news for someone else.

While the two individuals got into their whitish pump-vehicle, Tyshawn considered that everything about his investigation now seemed to lead to the Over Oceans Company and its meta-planes. It was a strange coincidence that the OOC was the successor company to that which Tyshawn's own late father had often tried—unsuccessfully—to sell some of his inventions. This had understandably left his father dejected with what was to become the OOC. *Some names seemed to turn-up over and over again*, the detective thought. He had to follow them to their destination and discover where those two men were taking that unfortunate man, so he could find the heart of the matter. His only problem was what he might uncover at the end of that path. On the other hand, he told himself that pondering too much would only make things more complicated, so it was better simply to go on and see what turn of events the night would bring.

* * *

The detective had been following the ground pump-vehicle until it eventually got to its destination. It hadn't been too difficult, given its slow speed - *but, what car powered by an internal combustion engine was ever able to proceed much faster than a good human pace in 1891 in the whole world, after all?* Tyshawn tried to move with caution, as he didn't want to be spotted from behind the vehicle by one of the two wretches. A foolish carelessness like that would have ruined everything.

Several buildings in Tyshawn's field of vision stood out to him. There was a huge, yellowish hangar alongside the flashy features that site was best known for: a few tall Mooring Masts suitable for the cargo loading service of the meta-planes of the Over Oceans Company.

There were men servicing a secluded area protected by a tall wire netting, and the few other hangars around the one of interest to Tyshawn proved to be the main storehouses and recovery sites the meta-planes used whenever they weren't flying. His desire to go past the boundary was impractical, at least by means of the limited resources he had now. He needed to get the proper documents, along with the right uniform, in order to pose as a worker of that company before trying to enter into that facility.

Unfortunately, the detective had no other way to follow the pump-car after it had gone past the metallic gate, so he wasn't able to discover what would happen to that poor man the other two had taken. Should he call a policeman? Well, that was a naive thought. Could Tyshawn suppose they just wanted to get rid of him? There was no certainty, and at least they hadn't let him burn so far; he didn't even know that man's identity. So, his best plan was to be better prepared next time he tried to get into that place.

Just by luck, a clear detail would soon help him after he got the necessary papers. It was a definite clue to be followed for the next step of his investigation, as nothing was probably more well-known in town, and throughout the whole country, than the huge meta-plane presently soaring in the sky and towering over that place.

The vehicle was called *Brycgstow* and everyone knew that it had been named after what the town of Bristol was called in Old English: a name meaning "the place at the bridge". The original site had been founded somewhere around 1 000 A.D.. Even then, it was already an influential trading center that had its own mint, even producing pennies bearing the town's name.

The path seemed to bring everything to this vehicle. In a way, the man doubted that such a huge air vehicle was in that area simply by chance, so there had to be a connection.

The detective would be able to find it again very easily, as it wasn't a thing you could keep hidden for too long. It was the most modern and the largest meta-plane the Over Oceans Company presently had, and it was pleased to proudly show-off such a beautiful flagship.

And then that part of "A Dream", that famous poem by Poe, his preferred author, came to his mind *"Ah! what is not a dream by day, To him whose eyes are cast, On things around him with a ray, Turned back upon the past?"*

Actually, another well known quote by the same poet would perfectly represent the current situation, that is *"Science has not yet taught us if madness is or is not the sublimity of the intelligence."* This was just something the man was going to discover soon.

* * *

The incredible array of colors across the sky at sunset, lit-up the surface of the river, and seemed to be the last greeting of the daylight before the night came. Since Tyshawn had started his job as a detective, the night had never been a time of rest, and this case had really forced him to sleep less and less in order to complete his search. But now everything was coming to an end. The man only hoped that it wouldn't be *his* end.

Given the location the detective was going to try to enter late that evening, he had made all the preparations he thought to be necessary. Beyond that, he had also taken extra precautions.

While Tyshawn was going along the streets of that part of town, with those extraordinary wide structures in the sky towering above the buildings, he looked around and noticed the crowded alleys. The passers-by were wrapped in their expensive, leather embroidered mantles—that were the fashion of the moment—and the seemingly-outdated horse-drawn carts. At least, they appeared to be out of place and anachronistic today, when compared to the new pump-cars and the ocean-going steam-powered vessels. Nevertheless, Tyshawn doubted such old—though simple—means of transportation would ever truly be replaced in the machine age, given the current needs of the poorer, common people.

Above Tyshawn was a portion of sky where many meta-planes usually crowded around, as the main Air Station in town for passengers lay just below them. The only vehicle that was presently casting its shadow over that part of the city was the OOC's famous *Brycgstow*. It was extremely recognizable and conspicuous. Its characteristic features had been seen by everyone in town.

Brycgstow had a wide copper structure attached to the upper part that accommodated up to 32 passengers, night or day. Furthermore, the workers had equipped it with some refined furnishings and expensive tableware, along with gold-trimmed tea-sets to satisfy the needs of the important individuals on board. Suffice it to say that the meta-planes functioned perfectly and their business was growing by leaps and bounds.

The men who had designed such valuable air vehicles had to be persons of rare brilliance. Tyshawn had always wondered how such machines really flew, and how those designers were able to make a fortune so quickly. But the power source that made the meta-planes move was a closely-guarded secret, known only to a select few at the Over Oceans Company.

The detective was reminded of an old saying: *at times to find the truth, instead of looking at the sky or at a place in full light, you need to search the darkest recesses and the smallest alleys.* Well, everything that Tyshawn had discovered so far meant that both the statements were correct, as the evidence had brought him from the ground to that huge meta-plane soaring in the air above his head.

It had taken him a lot of time to get to this point. But now that Tyshawn was finally here, after so many days and so much difficult investigation, he was somewhat afraid of what lay ahead. He knew very well there was no way to turn back, but many worries still filled his mind.

The detective was able to enter the main station from the rear, thanks to the false documents he had obtained in order to pose as a maintenance worker. He headed for a building on his left side: inside he would change his clothes and then would try to go aboard through the passenger's entrance using a perfect forgery of a ticket, as sold at the OOC's main downtown office.

Taking courage, the detective—now disguised as a man of the middle-class wearing a stylish, dark-gray frock coat and an embroidered pair of trousers with a top-quality drape—quickly proceeded to the boarding area. A heavy hat rested above his brow in order to better conceal his features. *You never know*, he told himself.

While walking across the hardwood floor, Tyshawn noticed that a good-looking blue-eyed woman of about thirty—dressed in a slender greenish evening gown with wide whitish sleeves, her long golden hair secured in a low bun at the back—gave him a prolonged look and openly smiled. Perhaps that meant that he really looked handsome in that rich outfit? Maybe he should put on such clothing more frequently? *If only I could afford it*, the man thought.

There were a few other wealthy passengers around who were ready to board and were presently looking at the wondrous shape of the meta-plane connected at the Mooring Masts, admiring the circular windows that completely encircled the lower structure. Everyone appeared satisfied and enraptured by the prospect of such a luxurious trip. This wasn't a slice of life that commoners could currently experience. Tyshawn had never been on one of these air vehicles before, nor had he imagined he would ever have gone up there because of a case.

There were some refreshments on the main deck as soon as they got aboard, and Tyshawn drank one glass of Italian wine in order to fit in with the other passengers. Then he moved away from the small group and went to the rear of meta-plane where he could find the schematic drawings he was looking for. Once he reached the last copper bulkhead, the detective went down the stairs in order to reach the lower level that seemed to be forbidden to everyone.

Breaking that door open and going past it wasn't a difficult task. Once Tyshawn was inside the wide room full of many copper machines, bottles, jugs and other strange instruments, he finally saw before his eyes the closed tank in which water or other fluids were heated. As far as he knew, that had to be the real power generator of the meta-plane itself. The source of heat for such a machine could be the combustion of any one of several fuels. Its suitability for high-reliability use in critical applications was crucial. The detective was not so knowledgeable about such modern steam-engines, but he was sure that in this lower deck forbidden to passengers, he would find the answer to all of his remaining questions.

Actually, Tyshawn's suspicions were already based on some details he had discovered over the course of his previous research, but he lacked the final, decisive evidence. As he moved across the room, his suspicions were further confirmed when he found two huge bathtubs full of ice and water. As he went nearer, he noticed that there was a human body inserted in each of the tubs, and he began figuring out what their function really was. Such tubs seemed to be similar to those new devices that were used nowadays in modern houses to provide cold storage throughout the year for vegetables and other foods.

Those naked bodies didn't seem to be corpses, even though they proved to be unconscious—the detective wasn't able to wake them up even though he tried to shake them. They breathed, or at least they seemed to be breathing to Tyshawn, but they were unable to move or open their eyes. They had undoubtedly ingested some unknown agent that had rendered them completely helpless.

As Tyshawn grabbed one of the arms of the first inert body and put it outside of the bathtub, the modified ocular device he wore immediately showed him an important, decisive fact: the temperature of the skin started increasing as soon as it was outside of that icy water!

So, that was it! What a terrifying, incredible, and tragic development! As it happened, it was exactly as Tyshawn had quietly supposed to himself, but didn't dare believe.

The source of heat for the combustion needed to make such a meta-plane fly—which had always been a matter of controversy, due to its secret nature—wasn't just a common fuel, such as wood, coal or oil. Now everything was finally clear. That was the real energy that such air vehicles needed in order to move across the sky at a faster speed than any other known airships worldwide. It was simply *men*, some unlucky individuals who were forced to become fuel as their body's heat fatally spiraled until they burned-up completely. Humans provided the combustion that made it possible for these engines to function better than anything else! Some other questions still remained, however. How did the owners of this company keep those unconscious men inside such containers? How long could they stay in there and how many people had they already killed so far?

This place appeared to be the final, deadly destination for a lot of destitute and homeless people who had strangely disappeared over the course of the last few months.

But, as Tyshawn was inside that huge room and was surmising many other ghastly possibilities, a voice came from behind him, and a tall young woman appeared. The detective knew her face: it was the woman who seemed to have given him an interested look when he was still at the boarding area. And she was armed now.

"Don't move, please. The firearm I am pointing at you fires deadly, rapid energy bursts. I never miss a single shot." Her first words startled him, and Tyshawn understood at that point that he had foolishly let himself be caught by surprise, despite all of his great care. That woman had to be very light on her feet, as he hadn't heard a single noise until it was too late to take cover. She, too, wore an ocular device. It obviously was no ordinary monocle. The peculiar, darkly-tinted device was ringed by glistening gems. "Obviously you couldn't survive a single hit. I can assure you I can, and will, shoot to kill. And now, allow me to introduce myself: I'm Addison, a covert security agent for the Over Oceans Company. My job description says, 'special duties.' I think this qualifies, don't you?"

"I can't say that I'm pleased to meet you, madam. But at least I think you are going to be able to answer some of my questions."

"It depends on which kinds of questions you plan to ask me," the slender woman stated.

"The logical place to start is to ask how you get the body temperature of your victims to increase so quickly?"

Addison simply sneered and pointed to one of the several bottles and jugs among the clutter on the desk. "Do you know this liquid? I suppose you don't, of course. But are you familiar with this brand of whisky?" With that, she pointed to another labeled bottle with some golden-yellow alcohol in it.

Tyshawn nodded.

"We have the right people in the right places—mostly bars, obviously—and they pour a bit of this liquid, mixed in a glass along with the alcohol that customers order. Then the process begins. Nobody searches for these helpless, nameless people, nor does anyone worry about such homeless individuals who only hoped to one day find a real job with a real wage. People like them disappear every day, leaving town when their luck runs out, and so the story goes. In a way, we help them fulfill a useful purpose at the end of their unimportant lives."

The surprised detective told himself that their network had to be much wider than he first thought. "So, by simply adding such a substance to the liquors they drink, you make them burn..."

"Yes, they burn much better than coal, which is what turns their bodies into such a profitable and valuable power source."

"And then you send your men to bring these people to your..."

"—To the places where their bodies, once properly treated, become the highly energized fuel we need. But they have to act immediately, as the men who have ingested the substance start to burn very quickly. It's a matter of half an hour, more or less."

"That's the secret of the powerful engines your incredible air vehicles use. But, why didn't you try to use dead animal bodies, instead, or something else that wouldn't be mass murder?"

"I suppose, if you want to prepare some very good main courses, you first need quality meat, *the human sort...* To be honest with you, I'm not a woman of science, just a security agent. I know that the OOC tried using some animals and other matter before, but it seems that human bodies produce a better energy, perfect for its purposes."

"I see. But may I know why you burned some people before having them in position in the engine room? Why kill them so horribly without actually using their bodies?"

"Accidents happen, clearly. It is unfortunate, but it seems that our preparations work in different ways on some peculiar individuals, so they start being completely burned by the flames before our men can get to them and take their bodies to our hangars. It really is a terrible waste of corpses."

"And you keep it hidden from everyone else."

"And the owners of OOC really do want to keep it a secret, as I'm sure you can understand. Now, you're going to drink that substance, too. You'll soon become useful fuel for our company. Aren't you glad you will contribute to the growth of our business? To the economic growth that is so good for our great empire?"

"You mean, that?" Tyshawn objected, recoiling from the bottle.

"Exactly, just one drink..."

"You can't believe that I would do that, after everything I know!" Tyshawn exclaimed.

"Oh, yes, I do!" Addison's cold, blue eyes became wild, and a cruel sneer appeared on her face.

"What if I don't?"

"Look at my firearm, you have no choice."

Tyshawn swallowed and remained pensive for a while.

"Go on, have a drink, now!" she ordered, indicating the bottle with her weapon.

"Don't you think I could keep the secret, too? You didn't even try to offer me a bribe on behalf of your company for my silence. You seem to know that I'm someone that you probably can't buy."

"Well, my dear, do you see this monocle I have on? It's not just a trendy, gem-encrusted thing that I wear for the love of expensive fashion. It's an ocular device that allows me to discover at once if the person I have before me is telling the truth or is trying to deceive me. It's very useful, you know. It also works very well in combat situations in order to predict the probable moves of other assailants. Maybe we will sell it to the military in the future, but for now, only the security agents like me are provided with this technology from the Over Oceans Company"

Damn, the man thought, *this too!* It was indeed a very brilliant invention, but that monocle complicated everything, as, unfortunately, it appeared that he didn't have much room to maneuver. "Amazing!" the middle-aged detective exclaimed at once. "How does it work?"

"It operates by checking the vital temperature of the bodies of people, so I see if what they are telling me is false, or if they can be trusted from time to time," Addison explained in a plain and almost bored tone.

"How unfortunate that such advanced technology as this, and your criminal fuel, is so deadly to the citizenry."

"How bad only for the ones that we choose among the people to become fuel then, you mean?" the woman sneered.

"What you do here is obviously evil. I mean, using corpses to make the steam-engines of your meta-planes function is not exactly what I could call a good business. Making people ingest some deadly substances in order to increase their body temperatures, then killing them and benefiting from the energy coming out of their corpses, unbeknownst to everyone, is an atrocious crime.

"You know that you will have to stop it, sooner or later!" The dejected detective thought that it was incredible that such a thing was happening in the same town where Plimsoll, the so-called "sailor's friend," was currently trying his best to make the seas safer, continuously fighting for a compulsory load limit on ships, as he was terrified by the overloaded cargoes he had seen. That man was doing all of that to save lives, while the owners of the Over Oceans Company burned the bodies of the people they had decided to murder, in order to make their air vehicles fly day-by-day. And then another famous Poe quote come to his mind, that was, *"The scariest monsters are the ones that lurk within our souls."* Tyshwan shuddered.

"Just try to explain that to our shareholders. I don't believe they would agree with you!"

"I suppose they wouldn't, but the local authorities and the police will stop your vicious activities one day. There must be some men of power and some politicians around that you haven't bought and corrupted yet!"

Addison didn't respond immediately, taking a moment to sneer at his words.

"Our business is too profitable. With such huge amounts of cash, you can almost do anything you want, convince everyone..."

Tyshawn glared at her, then said, "I'm the only one you don't want to buy."

"For your kind, there are other solutions," she said, raising her firearm to point at Tyshawn's head.

He was tempted to try attacking his opponent using his experience with martial arts, but another look at that weapon convinced Tyshawn it was futile. Furthermore, the ocular device Addison wore would give away any attempt at a sudden attack or a feint before he could make it. No, the best thing to do was just play for time, or at least try to.

As the slender woman was looking at him, waiting for the detective to do what he had been ordered to, a metallic clang sounded from across the far side of the room. It sounded to Tyshawn as if another small door had been opened. Sure enough, a newcomer appeared, striding into the room.

She was a tall, young woman with long, chestnut hair. She wore a light-yellow, cross-strapped apron. It was highly polished, giving it the appearance of a uniform. The security agent turned her head briefly towards the unexpected newcomer.

"A maidservant?" Addison exclaimed, surprised. "What are you doing here? You should already be off-duty, now."

"Actually, I'm here to save my man," the other woman revealed, in a confident tone and with a broad smile.

Addison fumed. "So, you had an accomplice, detective! Very clever, but we can handle her too. Double fuel for our engines, after all..."

"I don't think so!" the younger woman exclaimed. There was a fast, sudden outburst of energy from a small, metallic device she held in her left hand. Everything was over, quickly. *Just one more useful invention by my beloved father,* the detective thought.

"I'm here to save you, my dear," said the woman dressed in the refined maidservant's uniform. "And I love you, Tyshawn, you know it!"

The man smiled and kissed her. "What would I do without you?"

"You simply couldn't go on..."

The detective smiled at her again. "Thank you very much, my dear. I can always count on you."

"Everything has gone as planned. Well, more or less. After all, you were right when you asked me to infiltrate as a maidservant aboard this air vehicle."

"And don't forget that it's thanks to you that I was able to get the false papers and the ticket I needed so that I could enter the boarding area. You're always so kind, my dear," said Tyshawn, returning the compliments, his voice heavy with bubbling relief.

"Don't mention it." The woman grabbed a rope and the two started tying-up the security agent.

"You're a person who is full of resources, Aileen," Tyshawn acknowledged out loud.

It took a few minutes before Addison woke up, as the stunning charge had been very strong. "You two. Just name your price and the owners of OOC will pay it. Our business is too valuable to be stopped by the likes of you. They can give you as much money as you want, and you can get whatever or whomever you want..."

"You're wrong, madam. My man is unique. Where do you think I could find anyone else like him?" Aileen mocked her.

"The time for negotiating is over," said the detective, abruptly cutting it short. "And here is all the evidence we need for to charge you with the serious offence of attempted murder of a policemen. Now we have to try to free those poor men from the terrible condition they are under, and I think you, madam, will help us, willingly or unwillingly, in the end."

"What if there is no way to reverse the process?" the security agent challenged them both, with eyes full of hatred.

"Then you are going to share their destiny, my dear." Aileen smiled at her.

* * *

When all was over, Aileen and the detective spent a pleasing night at the man's house, very close to the outskirts of town.

The couple had made love passionately for a long time—more vigorously than ever—and the detective didn't know if it was because of the favorable solution to that difficult case, or simply because they had just survived a lethal situation.

Tyshawn and Aileen both knew that, in the end, even if they had been capable of stopping such a cruel illegal activity, the same company owners could change their business. They would simply use that same process of producing energy—by burning innocent people alive—in another place, possibly even abroad. There did not seem to be much they could do to prevent it. As for now, their actions had saved many citizens of Bristol. There would be no public recognition of their brave actions, but they didn't do it for thanks. It was simply the right thing to, and within their power, so they had acted.

The furnishings in Tyshawn's bedroom were refined but traditional, according to the Victorian style of the late 1800s. Several combinations of veneer had been used to create elaborate patterns along the walls. A massive cupboard next to two wooden chairs with round, turned legs complemented the cosy room. There was also a stylish side table, with an ample drawer nearby and two open shelves for easy storage, full of strange devices and copper mechanisms that Tyshawn had once taken away from his late father's shed.

Being close to the window, Tyshawn turned for a while to the bed and looked at his beloved as she lay relaxed, her hair disheveled, with long chestnut curls that dropped down her bare shoulders. He smiled at her. He told himself he was very lucky, as he had such a faithful partner that loved him, and always proved to be very useful under many different circumstances.

While staring at her fair skin tone and admiring her face—a small chin and nose, soft cheeks and her wonderful lips—he simply exclaimed, "I couldn't live without you!"

"I love you, too," Aileen nodded, with a smirk, in return. Then the young woman told herself that she knew very well why she liked sleeping with him so much: the peculiar, automatic add-on he had built himself and used whenever they had sex was so incredible, so enjoyable. Tyshawn was a good detective and a brilliant inventor, too. He had the same gift that his late father had had during his time. So, wherever could she find anyone like him throughout the whole of the British Empire? Who else could be so lovely and functional—*sexually speaking*?

Aileen was well aware that there was probably no other place on earth where she could find someone like him. And the long night ahead of them held such promise that they undoubtedly wanted to make the most out of it.

Megali Hellas
by Ryan McCall

1927

Ambassador Gordon King looked at the memo in his hands with concern in his blue eyes. He had been stationed in Athens for more than three years now, and he had known this day would eventually come, ever since his appointment to the British Embassy.

After only a decade as king, Alexander I of Greece was stepping down from the throne, and tomorrow Prime Minister Eleftherios Venizelos would make a public announcement, proclaiming the Second Hellenic Republic.

"Why do you look so worried, Gordon?" asked Colonel Harold Alexander. Harold was the military attaché to the embassy and had commanded the 1st Battalion Irish Guards fighting alongside the Greeks in the Greco-Turkish War. He knew the politics and powers of the region far better than Gordon did. "Venizelos knows his people, they've had enough of monarchs, they all voted to transition to a republic."

"I know, but the conservatives won't agree back in London. The Kingdom of Greece is who they helped to back and support, not the Republic. Some of them will view this as the Greeks using us to advance their own agenda."

British and French support to Greece in the post-Great Years had been crucial to their victory over Turkey and the realization of the Megali Idea that Venizelos had proposed at the Paris Peace Conference. Greece had expanded immensely, including much of the former Byzantine Empire's territory in Anatolia-Smyrna, Eastern Thrace and the much prized Constantinople, and the Dodecanese Islands. Not to mention Cyprus—a gift of territory from the British and the Crimea, which had been seized by two Greek divisions while the Russians were busy with their civil war.

In the aftermath of the war with Turkey, Greece had sent in more soldiers, and the Red Army had decided against pressing the issue, having greater internal strife to cope with. So, Crimea had been recognized as Greek territory, but relations with Moscow had been cool ever since.

Not since the days of Alexander the Great had Greece seen such a rapid expansion, and as a close ally to Britain and France it gave both nations a great deal of influence in the region.

"They'll worry and wring their hands, but they won't do anything," Harold said. "The French won't give a damn—they have no love of royalists, and Venizelos has been slowly winning them over to this idea for years. The politicians in London have seen the benefits that an expanded and stable Greece has given us. I'm more concerned about the Italians and the Bulgarians. Mussolini has been making veiled threats about Greek influence in Albania again, and the Bulgarians have never been happy with losing Western Thrace. They may see this as an opportunity to take action."

Gordon nodded, Harold was right. The other powers had ambitions of their own. Italy, in particular, was of concern—Mussolini was eager to avenge the Italian Navy's humiliation at the Corfu Incident of four years ago.

"The king stepping down won't change anything," Gordon replied. "He had very little real power, anyway."

"I know," Harold said, "but the perception will be there, regardless. General Papoulas has requested a meeting with me for tomorrow evening. I expect he'll want to know the preparedness of our own forces in the event that the Italians do make any aggressive moves. What should I tell him?"

Gordon knew the answer to that, without needing a reply from London. "Tell him that the United Kingdom will protect its allies. If he asks about our plans and troop placements, you have authority to give him all of the details. We do have military plans in place in the event of a war with Italy, don't we?"

"Of course," Harold answered. "I look forward to reassuring him of our commitment to security of the region."

1930

Harold watched carefully through his binoculars at the sight of the approaching Italian Army. "So, Mussolini finally decided to make his move," he said.

"So it would seem," said General Anastasios Papoulas. The older Greek officer was watching alongside Harold; they were on a small hill overlooking the Drino valley in southern Albania.

Harold watched the Greek's lined face for concern or fear, but saw nothing but cold-blooded calculation. Anastasios was seventy years old; his magnificent moustache was white with age, but he still had his command instincts.

"General Demestichas," Anastasios said, calling his second in command.

The younger officer approached and said, "Yes, sir?"

"Send in your forces to meet them. Follow the plan as discussed." He looked over at Harold. "The British troops will remain on the east side of the river. If the Italians try to cross, they'll be waiting to ambush them."

Demestichas saluted and saddled his horse. The officers in the Greek Army still used horses on a regular basis; they had not seen the futility of cavalry that Harold had witnessed in the Great War.

"I appreciate you and your men aiding us in this fight, Colonel," Anastasios said.

"Of course," Harold replied.

"I know that in London there was indecision about whether to commit your forces to our cause or not."

That was an understatement. The ice-cold relations between Italy and Greece had only become worse with Greek interference in Albania. Italy saw it as a direct attack on their interests in the Balkans, and Mussolini had declared war. The catalyzing incident had occurred two days ago.

Albanian soldiers had been chasing some Orthodox rebels who had retreated across the Greek border, and the Albanians had demanded that the Greek border guards hand them over. When the Greeks refused, a fight broke out, with casualties on both sides. King Zog of Albania had used the backing of Italians to inflame the incident and now it had come to war.

The politicians in London were not eager to become involved, but if Britain didn't lend support to Greece, it could lead to another series of

Balkan Wars.

"Do you think the Serbians will make any moves?" asked Anastasios.

"Not against our forces, they'll want to position themselves to seize provinces in northern Albania. I expect they'll wait to see how the first few battles go."

"I agree but some of my advisors think I should have sent reinforcements to the north. The Serbs may hunger for Albanian land, but they also want Macedonia."

"It's never an easy decision to split your forces," Harold said. "But for now we have to meet the main threat of the Italians. I suspect their navy will be making its way around the Peloponnesian coast. Mussolini has been preparing this invasion for some time."

Anastasios nodded. "You may be right."

There was a wild shouting from behind them and they both turned. Anastasios' aide was running up the hill, waving a piece of paper in his hand.

"General!" he yelled. "An urgent message from Athens."

The aide passed on the note to Anastasios. He pulled the sheet out of the sealed envelope and read it to himself. Harold saw his eyes widen in reaction to the contents.

The general thanked his aide and turned to Harold.

"They want me back in the capital. The Bulgarians have attacked Edirne and their army is headed through Eastern Thrace towards Corlu."

Damn, Harold thought. *Mussolini actually managed to convince the Bulgarians to ally with him.* The war had become a lot more complicated.

"God speed to you, General," Harold said. "I'll do what I can from here. You, on the other hand, have the entire strategic situation to deal with."

Harold knew that Anastasios did not enjoy leading from the capital. They were similar in that regard. As an officer, it was difficult to step back from the field and command from a distance. There was always the fear of losing control. No matter the orders you gave, you couldn't be there in person to counter anything unexpected.

1932

Angelico Carta, the Italian high commander of forces in

Albania, signed his pen on the document, making his surrender official. He handed both the pen and paper to Anastasios, who picked it up.

"Thank you," Anastasios said. "You made the right decision."

Harold weaved his way through the other military officers in the room and clapped the old general on the shoulder. "Good to see you again, General," he said.

Anastasios smiled and shook hands with him. Harold could feel the lack of strength in his shake; the general was clinging to life. He had not seen the man since Drino, and the general looked like he had aged ten years in that time. His face was thinner and the lines on his face had increased significantly.

"Colonel Alexander," Angelico said, "I am surprised to see you in Tirana. I thought all of the British forces had already withdrawn." There was a hard edge the Italian's voice, he wasn't happy with the British, not after the Royal Navy had decimated Italian shipping and taken control of the Mediterranean.

"They have, but my nation wanted to have a representative at this surrender, just to make sure everything went according to plan." The now deposed Mussolini had eroded whatever goodwill Italy had once had, with his broken promises and betrayals during the war. The British had wanted to make sure the Italian army actually surrendered as they had promised.

Angelico didn't say anything in response, his silence speaking of his shame. Harold didn't blame the man; it wasn't his fault he had been saddled with a warmongering fool for a leader.

"Don't look so bleak General Carta," Harold said. "Now we start the task of helping you rebuild your nation into a worthy member of the League of Nations."

"That will not be easy," replied Angelico. "The communists control Rome and most of the towns in the north. The stories I've been hearing since then..." he shuddered. "They are rounding up anyone with the slightest connection to the Fascist Party and shooting them in the streets. God knows what will happen if the Soviets get involved."

"If they do, they will come to regret it," answered Anastasios. "The people of Greece do not hold grudges, and we have no wish to see Italy fall to the communists. If Stalin thinks he can slide his influence into Europe, he'd better think again. We control the Crimea and my forces stationed there are a dagger that can be thrust into the Soviet belly if need be."

"You see, General, even your former enemies are willing to help you. Surely now you must lift your spirits."

Harold was warmed to see a wan smile appear on the man's worn face, and while he had some concerns, he was as certain as Anastasios that Italy would not become engulfed in a communist revolution.

The Battle of Tim Hortons

(or How I Dropped the F-Bomb on the CBC and Got Away With It... but Still Got Arrested For Looting)

by Bruno Lombardi & Ben Prewitt

To begin with, I want to point out that what you think you saw on the T.V. was really taken out of context. See, that whole thing at Soest wasn't my fault, and I didn't do anything wrong. And I suppose I could tell you all some big long stories like how me and my boys blew the goddamn turret off a T-72. No shit. Point blank range through the back of a gas station. The damnedest thing you've never seen.

But you know what? I'm tired of telling those stories. And besides, you'll probably hear 'em anyway. After all, it's World War III. There's enough Soviet infantry and T-72 tanks to go around.

That wasn't what really messed me up. It was that Tim Horton's. The one in Soest, Germany. And Carol Off. And the CBC in general. There was a war on, you know? How was I supposed to know there was a camera on me? How was I supposed to give a shit?

So anyway…without further ado, this is the story of the Battle of Tim Hortons, or: How I Dropped the F-Bomb on the CBC and Got Away With It but Still Got Arrested For Looting.

So there I was. 4th Canadian Mechanized Brigade Group, and it's 1987. And all we know is that we're not going home anytime soon, because the Reds over the border were getting frisky. We couldn't go home, but that didn't piss me off since I was still like four months from my clock out. I didn't even get to go out of Soest unless it was up to our staging area on the southern end of BAOR.

Let me tell you: that's a boring fucking drive, even when you're in an APC. You can drive through all the fields you want, you can make rooster tails in the streams, no matter what: it's still a dull drive. Especially after that one time Dougy got drunk and slammed into an Oktoberfest stand. Did I ever tell you about Dougy and the Oktoberfest?

See, Dougy loved his Labatt's, but he could only get it in six packs 'cause that's how they shipped it over to the base. Then we heard they shipped, like, a *million* cases over to the local *bruehaus* and Dougy decided he wanted to grab a box. But he was supposed to be on manoeuvres that day, so he decided to take his track (Did I tell you he was a track commander?) over to the Oktoberfest in Iserlohn.

And everything's fine and he's driving his M113 through all these West German towns and they're not noticing, 'cause he's Canadian and this is where you see Canadians in West Germany, and he grabs two cases and heads off for the border to get to the practice field.

Then he gets this radio call from Gary all about how they're doing equipment checks in the vehicles to make sure everyone's got their shit, and Dougy realizes he can't sneak the beer by the officers, but he doesn't want to dump it, so him and two other guys drink two cases in forty minutes and end up ploughing through a damn Oktoberfest stand in Weserlhene.

Then they got to the damn operations area and the Captain opened it up, and the goddamn thing was covered in vomit! Can you believe it?

So anyway...the Russians were getting frisky.

I mean...they were *really* getting frisky.

So everyone's going all, 'It's fucking World War 3!' and the brass at HQ are going, 'Activate all units —and their mothers too!' and the Americans are saying to the Soviets, 'You fuck with us, we fuck you in the ass!' And the Soviets are, 'That's the way your mama likes it, I hear!' and a whole bunch of other shit. Everyone with any brains at all is trying to get the fuck *out* of Dodge. Of course, every reporter in the universe is pulling every string they got to get *into* Dodge.

Like I said – people *with* brains were getting the fuck out.

Of course, me and Dougy and Lombardi and the rest of 4th Brigade were stationed in the southern portion of CENTAG in the British Army's slice of the Rhine. HQ still had no fucking clue what exactly to do with our batch of M113s, so we were on manoeuvres and pretending to be useful until they figured that out. Dougy had a REM tape that had come out literally the same week that the Rooskies were starting to get frisky and there was this one song that pretty much summed up everyone's feelings about the whole mess—'It's the end of the world as we know it, and I feel fine'—and Dougy, well, he was like our morale dude, or at least whatever passes for one in the Brigade, he was trying to keep everyone's spirits up by playing that song over and over again as some kind of twisted joke. Fuck...I think he must have played it 50 or 60 times a day. Some of the guys wanted to empty a clip into the tape and maybe leave a few rounds for Dougy; me—I actually found it kind of a cool song, to be honest.

Anyways...where was I? Oh, yeah! So, like, we were on manoeuvres and Dougy's singing 'I feel fine!' and doing his air guitar bit and Adam is, like, joining in with *his* air guitar bit, but Lombardi is, like, 'I'm going to fucking kill you man! Kill you!' and screaming something in Italian about Dougy's mother, while Poirier is just kicking back and scoping out the scenery.

And that's when the radio squawks and we get the news.

The Soviets had stopped being just frisky and decided to get fucking badass instead. The Russians had managed to break through the cavalry screen and were coming in, tank-heavy.

Yeah—I'm not ashamed to say it; some of us needed to change our underwear when we heard that.

I mean, at the time, we were almost sure that this was it...the Big One. The one that starts the ball rolling and all the nukes start flying. But we're soldiers, and orders are orders, and we had a job to do.

If only we knew what the fuck that job was...

So Mike's on the comm and trying to get HQ and Adam is going, 'What the fuck? What the fuck? What the fuck?' over and over and over, and everyone is getting all jumpy and even Dougy realizes that now would be a bad time to be playing that REM song.

And that's when we get our orders.

Our group were basically the entire armoured component of the entire Canadian force, but we're nowhere near the line where the Russians punched through. We're way in the rear...a good 20-30 clicks away. Maybe more.

So when the Russians crossed the line, we get the call to move out and reinforce the Brits and hold the line until more reinforcements can be flown in.

Yeah—we're going right into the line of fire, so to speak. Yah, us!

* * *

So…it's like 10 or 15 minutes later and we're burning rubber through German roads and fields and checking and re-checking our weapons and we're, like, so *totally* sure that we're all gonna be dead by nightfall but, we're, like, the Royal Canadian fucking Dragoons, man…we've been in every freaking major battle in every freaking war that Canada has been in during the last hundred freaking years and we freaking kicked ass in every freaking single one of them. "It's always a good day to be a Dragoon!" as the recruitment line goes.

And that's when the radio squawks again and we get some more bad news. One chunk of the Russian breakthrough was doing better than the rest and they're, like, coming up on Soest double-time. Problem was, the evac of that place hadn't been finished yet and there still was a whole shit-load of civvies stuck in the town, as well as a few odds and ends of military staff from the Brits and American forces there.

Well—the Captain hears all this and after a few minutes he just goes, 'Fuck,' and then he turns to us.

I didn't envy the Captain right then. I mean—can you imagine how he must have felt right then? Here you are, in charge of a company of Leopards and two companies of Bisons and M113s, the Russians have just started fucking WWIII, there's allies somewhere out there who are getting killed *right at that fucking moment*, you've got orders to get your ass to the front lines and hold the line at all costs—and then you get this news that, 'Oh, by the way, there's, like, a couple hundred civvies stuck in a town that's about to be overrun by pissed-off Russians—and the town is where your HQ is located and there's a good chance that some of those civvies are friends of yours.' Can you imagine what that must feel like? Shit…

So Captain nods his head and turns to Dougy. "OK—B company—get those civvies out of there! The Leopards and Bisons are going to go block the Soviets. Double-time, everyone! We move in two minutes!"

So—two very confusing minutes later, the Leopards and Bisons get detached and us poor schmoes in the M113s from B Company find ourselves on the road to Soest.

* * *

You ever see a M113? Yeah, yeah—I know that to a civvie, everything with armour and guns is called a tank just like every ship with a big gun is called a battleship. But do you people know the difference? A M113 may be a sweet piece of machinery, but at the end of the day, it's just a big ol' fancy-ass armored car with a big-ass machine gun attached to it. Our job in a war is to come into a combat zone whooping and hollering with guns blazing, drop off a shitload of soldiers and equipment, and then haul ass out of there with guns blazing again. So yeah—our company of M113s was the perfectly logical choice to send into a noncombat situation for a quick evac, 'cause we sure as hell ain't gonna do squat against a bunch of T-72s.

Of course, with the way everyone was piling-in on the Russian breakthrough and with the distances involved and how far the Russians were from Soest compared to how close we were, there was no freaking chance that we'd meet any Russian tanks, right? Right?

Yeah—*right*...

So, it's, like, about half an hour later, and the German countryside is flying by us, and we're actually making some pretty good time, and we figure that with a bit of luck we can be in Soest in about an hour or so, when we crest this hill.

And right there, sitting all by its lonesome, is a fucking Soviet tank.

Yeah, yeah, I know—there's no freaking way it could have beaten us there, the Russians were officially still a good 20 clicks away, the main force was being blocked and attacked by everything we could throw at them...I *know* all that, okay? Maybe intel was wrong—yeah, *there's* a shock!—or this guy was part of some recon unit that slipped through. Maybe he used the freeway. Maybe the asshole teleported in—how the fuck should I know how he got there, okay?

And then we see that this guy spotted us, cause the gun starts swivelling towards us.

Ever see what a round from a T-72 can do to a M113?

Me neither.

But none of us were in any mood to find out, so we're screaming and putting our tracks into reverse. Adam pipes up with, 'Holy Jesus! There's some fucking Russians over there!' Observant dude, that Adam...he's, like, a fucking Sherlock Holmes, man. I think he was a shoo-in for officer material...

Where was I? Oh yeah—okay, so we fire a few rounds from our machine guns at the tank, for all the good that will do, and we're in full reverse, and Lombardi is shouting, 'Shit, I think a T-72 can move faster than us!' Which is, like, *way* to go with the whole boosting morale thing, man! We get back behind the ridge just in time to see a round go flying over our heads and take out a couple of trees.

So, we're, like, burning rubber in the opposite direction that we're supposed to be going and Adam is going, 'What the fuck! What the fuck!' again, and Dougy is trying to keep our company together, and Mike's on the horn trying to send-off a message and, all in all, we're, like, having a really bad day, you know?

So we're cutting across some fields, trying to stay under cover, and Ivan pops up right on top of the ridge and lets loose another round.

Wham! This round lands, takes out the top of a few trees and comes down less than twenty feet away from the command track! I swear to God, man—for this one long horrible moment, before the smoke and dust cleared, I thought for sure it got taken out. But then I see it shoot out from the other side of the explosion covered in flames and rock and shredded plants, moving like a fucking bat out of hell! I mean—*wow*! It was really fucking cool, and if I wasn't so scared out of my mind, I think I would have applauded.

But since I *was* scared out of my mind, and trying to do ten different things at once, while praying to God that I don't get killed, all I did was pee in my pants a bit.

Uh…can you edit out that last part? Thanks…

Okay—so, officially, the only weapons our M113s carried were the standard machine gun and chain gun kit. I say *officially* as back when the Russians were just starting getting frisky, somebody somewhere in the chain of command who had actual brains and intuition and motivation—a very rare combination I can assure you— decided that maybe we needed to upgrade our APVs. The Americans back in 'Nam used to slap the M40 onto their M113s with very few difficulties, and since we were right next door to the American base, we, uh, kinda 'liberated' a few of them from their surplus depot.

Unfortunately we only had time to upgrade the one M113—the one that I was in—when we were sent out on manoeuvres.

Ever see a M40? It's basically a rifle as long as a jeep. 106 mm. Single shot. It's a direct-firing gun only. Fucking pain in the ass to aim and fire, let me tell. On the other hand—it can take out a tank with a bit of luck.

Nice, huh?

Well—like I said; it could take out a tank during the Vietnam War. Against a T-72 *now*, with all that fancy-ass reactive armour shit they've got? Fuck—99 out of 100 times, all a round from the M40 will do is just piss them off. Still—better than nothing, right?

Oh—and did I mention we were only carrying three rounds for it? And that, out of the whole crew, I was the only one with any experience firing the thing? And that my experience consisted of just ten minutes?

So yeah…

Anyways…where was I? Oh yeah…so we're running from Ivan, and the fucking T-72 is, like, beginning to get its act together, and it's obvious that he realizes that he's got three easy kills here, so Ivan's probably thinking about how he's going to get a nice 'Hero of the Motherland' medal out of this, and get free vodka and pussy for the next few months when he goes home, so he puts on a burst of speed and comes after us, and even though he can't get a good lock on us, he fires another round or two at us just on general principle.

Meanwhile, we're ducking and weaving and zipping through trees at full speed, and everyone is screaming and yelling, and shit is exploding all around us, and I'm sticking my head out so I can fire this fucking M40. It's right about that moment that we zoom out of the trees and end up on this stretch of land that's nothing but fields of soybeans or some shit like that. Fields of plants that are, like, *maybe* two feet high at the most, that goes on and on for miles and miles. We've got, like, no cover *at all*.

So Lombardi goes, 'Fuck!'

Dougy goes, 'Fuck me!'

Adam goes, 'Fuck, fuck!'

Mike is, like, 'Fuckety, fuck, fuck!'

And I'm screaming, 'Motherfucker!'

The three M113's in front of us plough through the fields of fucking soybeans at full throttle and we're bringing up the rear when I notice that there's this gas station just to the right of us.

So, I'm screaming, 'Get behind the station!' while simultaneously holding onto the M40, and trying to keep an eye out for Ivan, while Lombardi pops his head up, and slams a round into the gun.

Literally five seconds after we get behind the gas station, the fucking tank comes roaring out of the woods.

I did something I haven't done since I was, like, ten years old, or something.

I prayed to God. I think it may have been...no, scratch that. Not 'may have been'. Was. Definitely was.

It was the fastest prayer I had ever done in my life. It was, like, maybe two or three seconds long. 'Please God—don't make me fuck up. Amen.' And right after I said 'Amen', well, that's when I fired the M40...

Don't ask me how. Don't ask why. Don't ask me no questions, cause I ain't got no answers—but somebody, somewhere was smiling down upon us that day, 'cause you know what?

Direct hit on the turret ring.

The fucking turret is still in one piece, but it's shaking and wobbling like a bowlful of Jell-o, and Ivan is trying to get the turret turned to us, but the damn thing is *jammed*.

Yeah—that's right; me and my boys took out a goddamn turret from a T-72.

So, I'm, like, 'Whoa?'

And Lombardi is, like, 'Whoa.'

And Adam is, like, 'Whoa!'

And Dougy is all, 'Whoa, whoa, whoa, *whoa*!'

Ivan comes to a stop and I swear you could actually hear him say, 'What the fuck?' in Russian. And that's when he clues in that, heh, he ain't got his main weapon no more, and now there's a pissed-off Canuck with a fucking anti-tank gun aimed at him.

But a T-72 is still a fucking scary thing even without its main gun, and I didn't want this fucker driving off and bringing in all his friends.

So Lombardi loads another round into the M40 and I fire off another shot.

Wham! I manage to blow a boggie wheel off the track drive!

So, I'm, like, 'Whoa!'

And Lombardi is, like, 'Whoa?'

And Adam is, like, 'Whoa.'

And Dougy is all, 'Woo-hoo!'

We decide that we're not going to stick around to see if Ivan had any friends around so I scream that we should haul-ass out of there, like, *right now*. So we grind the pedal to the metal and zoom off, away from Ivan, and sure enough, we're ploughing through the fields of fucking soybeans a minute later. I look back at Ivan. Ivan's having a really bad day. Even from where we were, I could hear Ivan grinding a few gears trying to get the tank moving. I think he managed to go all of twenty or thirty feet by the time our track crested a hill about two or three clicks from the battle, and that's the last I ever saw of him.

A few minutes later, we join up with the three other M113s, and that's when we get the bad news. Remember when the command track nearly got hit and drove through a wall of fire and debris? Guess what happened to the radio antennae? Yup—what was left of it was lying in pieces in a forest about three or four clicks back.

So, the four of us M113s are now on our own, with no way to get a hold of HQ. And there's at least one Soviet tank in the area, and you can bet your ass he's definitely trying to call his buddies. And the one and only anti-tank gun we have has just one round left. And we still had a job to do—evac the civvies. That's when Lombardi taught me a really good Italian swear word.

Marone.

What did we do? Shit—do you even have to *ask* that? We had a mission to do, so we were going to do it, okay? Remember—we're the Royal Canadian Dragoons!

So we're driving down the road to Soest, and I'm trying very hard not to think about how pear-shaped this whole mission has suddenly become, and trying to focus on just how many civvies we can pull out of the place.

You see, a M113 can normally carry only about a dozen or so people. Sure, in an emergency like now, we figure that we can cram in two, maybe even three dozen. Yeah, they'll be packed in like sardines, and air might be an issue, and God help them if somebody farts! But it could be done. Of course, with that amount of weight, our tracks will have the speed and manoeuvrability of a three-legged cow but—well— if it's a choice between that, and being over-run by the Russians, which would you choose?

Now, before we knew that there were Russian tanks in the area, that wasn't an issue. So, big deal, it takes us an hour to drive the 20 or so clicks to a safe area, right? So what?

But now—Ivan's in the area, and if we pull this evac off, we're going to be sitting ducks if Ivan pokes-up his head. Shit, we were almost sitting ducks even without being fully loaded. *With* a full load or, worse, double or triple load? Forget it, man—total sitting ducks.

I'm looking around at the others, and even though they're not saying anything, I know that they're thinking the same thing that I am.

Still—we've got a job to do, eh?

So, the sun is setting, and the sky is all these crazy shades of red and pink and purple, and we still haven't seen any mushroom clouds on the horizon, and there's been no other signs of Russian tanks, so we're thinking that things might actually be working out in our favour, when we drive into Soest about an hour after our run-in with Ivan.

So we driving through Soest and, it's, like, dead quiet, man.

I mean, really, *really* quiet.

You know that Charlton Heston movie? The one with him in LA and he's, like, the only human left in a city full of freaky white haired zombie thingies? Remember the scene of him walking through the empty streets? How fucking weird and spooky it was?

That's how it was like now.

I mean, we're driving through, making a ruckus and it's not like anybody can mistake the red maple leaf on our tracks for a red star, you know? So where the fuck is everyone?

'Hey—where the fuck is everyone?' pipes up Adam. Remember what I said about him being observant? 'How the fuck should I know?' says I. 'So, like, what we do, man?' asks Adam. I look over at Dougy and he's, like, 'Well—we go to the fucking base and see if there's anybody waiting there,' which was probably as good a plan as any.

And then Adam, who, like, is *really* into all those zombie and horror flicks, pipes up 'Hey—what if the Russians set off a neutron bomb that killed everyone, and this whole area is now glowing red hot with radiation?' Which is, like, thanks a whole fucking lot for *that* fucking image, man.

Fortunately, when we check the counters, we're totally clean, and so is the whole area. You should have heard what Lombardi wanted to do to Adam for freaking us out like that. I really had no idea how Lombardi was going to do that with his gun, and I'm pretty sure it's physically impossible, anyway, but still, we needed a good minute or two to calm him down.

So we get to our former HQ and guess what?

It's cleared out. The whole base is fucking empty.

Looks like we weren't needed. The civvies managed to get out anyway. Maybe they had help from the Americans or the Brits or maybe even the Germans themselves. Don't know then. Still don't know now. Doesn't matter how, anyways.

Of course, if our radio antennae hadn't been blown off, we probably would have been told about this. But, like, whatever.

So now we have one less problem to deal with, but that's been replaced with a new problem. Namely – what now?

The new brigade HQ, wherever that is, probably in a truck or M557 on the road or whatever, is probably wondering where the fuck we are, and trying to coordinate a counter-attack against the Russians. Well, they will have orders for us. And they'll probably have an update on that Russian tank column that, for all we know, is still making its way to Soest.

So we decide we're going to the secondary fall-back position, and figure out our next step there, and haul ass out of there.

As we're hauling ass out of there, we pass by the Tim Hortons.

Dude, I mean, seriously, nothing says 'Canada' like a fucking Tim Hortons, man. Jeez—that awesome coffee was the only thing that kept me going some days.

And those donuts, and Timbits? And the muffins? The cookies? Jesus, the freaking *chilli*! God, like divine food. Food of the Gods, man! You don't *fuck* with a Canuck and his Tim Hortons, man!

And that's when Lombardi pipes up, 'Hey—we can't leave all those Timbits behind'.

Dougy stares at Lombardi for a minute, like he's nuts, and opens his mouth to say something—and then he stops and blinks his eyes for a few seconds.

'Shit—you're right,' says Dougy.

And then Adam's, like, 'We can't allow the Tim Hortons to fall into enemy hands!'

And Mike is nodding his head, going 'Uh-huh.'

So that's when we decided to break into the Tim Hortons and save all the food…

What do you mean, that's *stupid*? Dude—I told you—you do *not* mess with a Tim Hortons! Not on *our* watch!

So, we're emptying out the Tim Hortons, and carrying armloads of Timbits into the M113, double-time.

Remember that part I told you about how so many of our

problems would have been solved if we still had our radio antennae? Yeah—well, in addition to learning that the civvies were cleared out, it probably would have helped to have been told to watch out for the CBC crew that was in the area.

So, there I am, holding a double armload of chocolate Timbits. It's now past sunset, the M113 is packed with stuff, and I'm running out of the Timmy's when I see this spotlight shine on me.

There, no more than 50 or 60 feet away from me, is Carol Off herself, with a camera crew. And the light from the camera is shining right at me, like God's very own spotlight. Carol Off is speaking and I just catch the tail-end of her speech '...transmitting *live* from Soest where we can see troops looting a Tim Hortons!'

And the camera sweeps towards me, and it's nailing me on the spot, and that's when I realize just how fucking bad all this really looks. And then—in front of 25 million Canadians, and God knows how many other tens of millions in the US and Europe who were watching the feed, I say:

"Fuck!"

And then I say—

"*Fuck me*! Fuckety, fuck, fuck!"

And then—cause I don't know when to shut up—I drop all the Timbits and I finish it off with:

"Fuuuuuuu-uuuuuck!"

Fuck.

Yeah, so what else?

Well, dropping the F-bomb on the CBC. Okay, bad. But still— you figure with fucking WWIII going on, nobody is going to give a shit, right?

Just our luck that the Russian breakthrough sucked-ass, and that our counter-attack fucked up the Russians so badly that for a while *we* were the ones doing the invading, and the Russians had changed their minds about the whole thing, and that WWIII was in the final stages of being wrapped-up at about the precise moment we were taking out all the food from the Tim Hortons, huh?

Or that, because of the time zone differences, my F-Bomb was done just in time for the noon news back home? Or that the Prime Minister had literally just finished giving a speech about how the Canadian Army had distinguished itself at the Battle of the Line when that aired?

Yeah—Karma can be such a bitch sometimes…

Like I said—nobody remembers all the rest of the stuff we did. All they remember is the Tim Hortons bit.

So, there was a big long investigation, and eventually I was up on court martial charges, and it looked pretty hairy there for a while, but—eventually—the charges were dropped. Of course, my career was over at that point—all of us in Company B for that matter—but I was the Face of Company B, as all the stupid newspaper reports said. And then there was that goddamn 'looting' charge they decided to hit me with…

Like Lombardi said…

Marone.

And here I am.

You know, I really appreciate having the chance to tell you guys this story. You have no idea how long I've waited to say all this.

Hmmm?

Oh—yeah, a few years after all the dust settled, I managed to get myself re-instated. Took some doing, but I felt like I owed it to the Forces. I still say that I did nothing wrong, and that none of that was my fault, but they had ended up with some major egg on their faces because of me, and I felt like I needed to do this to make it up to them.

Of course, I ended up getting reinstated right in time for that thing up north with Denmark. Jeez…

Uh, while I'm on the subject, I just want to say that that whole messy thing with the Danish flag, the Ski-Doo and the polar bear wasn't my fault.

Really.

There's a good explanation for that…

That'll Be the Day
by Michael McAndrews Bailey

Amira Khribin had a first class ticket on the train from Geneva to Frankfurt, but first class accommodations on the Eurostar would have hardly been considered acceptable business class accommodations back home in the United Arab Republics. Khribin had seen better on trains in the Congo. But she didn't complain, and she really couldn't all things considered. Eurostar was trying its best, and given how cash-strapped it always seemed to be, Khribin supposed that it was acceptable. She had a mostly-acceptable collection of cheap European soft drinks and beers at her disposal, and the first class carriage was scarcely a third full, so she had plenty of privacy as the train descended from the Alps and into the central plains of Europe and into what had once been Germany.

Frankfurt was the largest city in the former German Democratic Republic—excluding what was left of Berlin across the Iron Curtain that surrounded the entire German Technocratic State, though nobody could really say for sure at this point. Frankfurt Central Station sat at the center of the Frankfurt Blue Zone, a heavily fortified and heavily protected district that was supposed to be safe from insurgent attacks, but every so often, someone got through. The train station was filled mostly with foreigners—many of them occupation officials like Khribin, but a few misguided tourists here and there. Police (most of them from the East African Federation or South Africa) in sky blue berets were everywhere, vigilant eyes always alert as they kept one hand near their shock batons.

Khribin was a lean woman with long, black hair folded into a tight bun on the back of her head. She wore a scarlet Nehru jacket, with faint floral and paisley patterns, and dark trousers. The mandarin collar was starched and her trousers were neatly pressed. She had a sky-blue UN armband on her left arm and an ID card pinned to her left breast. Both had been unnecessary on the train, but people gave her a wide berth as they saw her approaching. A UN official in the Frankfurt Blue Zone wasn't someone who was to be taken lightly by anyone.

There was a war memorial outside Frankfurt Central Station. It was an old memorial, more than a century old at this point. It was a memorial to the Third World War and also a memorial to Communism—Frankfurt had been firmly in the middle of pro-American West Germany, but after the Third World War, it—and the rest of Germany—fell to the Soviet Union and Communism. The memorial was some abstract, avant-garde collection of jagged shapes that Khribin couldn't make heads-or-tails of. She recognized what she thought was the old German hammer and compass, but she wasn't entirely sure.

"Out of every piece of cultural history in Frankfurt, this is one of the few that survived."

Khribin looked over her shoulder at the soldier standing behind her. He was European, with pale skin, light brown hair that was cut short, and a matching mustache. He wore an olive-green dress uniform instead of a service uniform, with his peaked cap tucked under one arm. He had three embroidered stars on his collar tabs, two rows of ribbons in his left breast, and a sky-blue armlet on his right arm.

"Captain Niels Grimstvedt, Royal Scandinavian Army and UNPROFOR," the soldier said in English. "Amira Khribin, I presume?"

"You wouldn't be asking me that if you weren't certain," Khribin said. She turned back to the memorial. "Is this really all that's left?"

Grimstvedt took a few steps forward to stand next to Khribin. "It's not the only thing that's left, but there's not much left, ma'am," he said. "A lot of Frankfurt was damaged in the Second World War and the entire city was pretty much flattened during the Third."

"And the chaos after the Deluge took care of the rest," Khribin said with a sigh.

"I know it was rough on my grandparents watching the rest of the continent tear itself apart after the Deluge and the Soviet withdrawal," Grimstvedt said.

And my grandparents just watched it all, Khribin thought. Not that she could blame them.

"And to think, two hundred years ago, Germany was on the verge of ruling the world," Grimstvedt said. "Things have been kind of downhill for them since Hitler."

"It's been quite a slide for them," Khribin said. She turned away from the memorial to face Grimstvedt. "I'm assuming that you're my ride."

"This way, ma'am" Grimstvedt said, motioning towards the station's parking lot.

* * *

The trip to the UN Mission Building didn't take very long. Most cars that were on the road (and there weren't many) moved out of the way of the military lorry. The Mission Building had heavy security, and Khribin and Grimstvedt had to pass through several checkpoints before they were allowed to even get within a hundred feet of it. The soldiers (the ones on duty today were Argentine based on their unit markings and accents) all wore sleek and imposing powered armor. Khribin had long thought that the hulking powered armor made the peacekeepers seem like inhuman alien invaders and not UN peacekeepers. Sometimes she thought that Americans had it right with the Minutemen, but then she remembered the genocides on Io and Tethys and decided that maybe the Americans weren't *entirely* right.

Grimstvedt took Khribin to meet with Mehmet Dinçerler, one of the civilian administrators for UNPROFOR in Germany. Dinçerler was Turkish, a swarthy man with thick black hair and thick sideburns. His pants were a light blue plaid and were matched with a dark blue jacket and a white turtleneck—the type of bold, clashing patterns and colors that Khribin had come to expect from a Communist. His office, on the other hand, was small, neat and utilitarian without any personal affects. Dinçerler's handshake was firm as he greeted Khribin.

"Have you ever been to Frankfurt before, Amira?" Dinçerler asked in thick Russian. Khribin knew that Dinçerler also spoke German, so why was he bothering with Russian? She held in a sigh. *Some kind of Communist attempt at a pissing contest,* Khribin thought. That said, Dinçerler was clearly dating himself by using Russian instead of Brazilian Portuguese.

"Not to Frankfurt before, no," Khribin answered in Russian.

She wasn't in the mood to get into a passive-aggressive argument with Dinçerler already. "I've spent the better part of the past ten years in Germany with the UNCC's ongoing prosecution of war criminals."

"I saw you'd done some work on the Brandstetter prosecution," Dinçerler said. "This isn't quite as large as the initial batch; I think we're getting damn close to mopping up the VBA. Or what's left of it."

Khribin nodded her head. Brandstetter was sitting in a UNCC holding cell up in the Shangri-La orbital, but the splintered remnants of the VBA were still a threat across Germany and the rest of central Europe.

"But the *elected* government here in Frankfurt has very little power beyond the walls of the Blue Zone, so only time will tell if we can finally put a stop to the VBA." Dinçerler shrugged. "If I was a Hindu, I'm sure I'd believe that this is some kind of karmic justice for the entirety of European history."

That wasn't exactly an uncommon opinion in Khribin's experience.

"But at any rate, down to business I suppose," Dinçerler said. "The children are in the detention cells—"

"Detention cells?" Khribin asked. "They're *children*."

"They're also soldiers. Veterans who've killed God knows how many people," Dinçerler said—"You know what the recidivism rate for these children is."

Khribin bit her lip.

"This is for their own good. The detention cells aren't exactly Turkish prisons you see in those horrid American movies, you know. They're more like motel rooms."

"Still," Khribin said.

"Still nothing," Dinçerler said. "We have the first children lined up, if you're ready now."

"I'd like to get this done as soon as possible."

"Very well," Dinçerler said.

Grimstvedt escorted Khribin down to the basement of the Mission Building, and she was shown the room she'd be using as an interview room. Despite it being in the basement, it was brightly lit and the walls were calm and soothing. A large television screen had been mounted in one wall and it was showing soothing, pastoral landscapes. Khribin prepared, setting out her tape recorder and a notepad along with a variety of small items for the interviewees to play with during the interview.

Khribin had just finished when Grimstvedt brought in the first child. Markus Kroder was in his mid-teens and had a shaved head and what looked to be tattoos poking out from the collar of his simple jumpsuit. He kept his eyes down and away from Khribin as he sat down across from her.

"Hello, Markus," Khribin said in German. She was as pleasant and as welcoming as she could. "I'm Amira Khribin, and I'm a social worker attached to the United Nation's Criminal Court. Do you know what this means?"

"It means you're going to ask me questions," Markus said.

"Do you feel comfortable answering questions?" Khribin asked.

Markus shrugged. He was slouched over in his chair and looked uncomfortable. "Sure, I guess."

"Are they treating you well?"

Markus shrugged.

"Have you been getting three meals a day?"

Markus nodded his head.

"When was the last time you had that?"

"Never, I think," Markus said.

"What about a bed?" Khribin asked.

"I have a bed."

"Did you have one before?"

Markus thought about that for a moment. "Not since school. When I was eight."

"Is that when you were forced into the VBA?"

Markus nodded his head. "They attacked the school and they…and they…"

His voice trailed off.

"It's okay if you don't want to talk about it, Markus," Khribin said.

Markus grabbed one of the stress balls off the table and squeezed in his fist. He asked, "Can I ask you a question?"

"Go ahead."

"You're from Arabia, right?"

Khribin nodded her head. "I am."

"Where?"

"Damascus," Khribin answered. "Why?"

"Is that near Tunis?"

"No. Why?"

Markus seemed to hesitate before he finally said, "Because when I was really young, my father he...he ran away with this other woman. He ended up in Tunis, I think. I don't know. It's been a longtime since we've heard form him."

Khribin nodded her head. That wasn't unusual. Europeans often emigrated to the UAR for better paying jobs, often leaving behind families that they couldn't afford to bring with them. They'd save money to send to their families still back in Europe, but sometimes they'd just leave and cut all ties. Markus's father was likely a day laborer in Tunis—a janitor, a dishwasher, a construction worker. It was hard, menial work for the immigrants in the larger coastal cities, but at least it was a better life than the one they'd left behind. Khribin found it hard to blame the mysterious Mr. Kroder.

"Damascus and Tunis are on opposite sides of the UAR," Khribin said.

Markus nodded his head.

"Why don't you tell me a little bit about your school," Khribin said, changing the subject.

* * *

Markus Kroder had been taken from his school along with his entire class at age eight, and he became a child soldier in Alois Brandstetter's VBA. He was 15 years old now, which means he'd been fighting for seven years. Markus always seemed to close up when Khribin got close to anything about his service. But she was able to read between the lines based on what he did say and what he didn't say. She got a rough timeline of his service, where he'd been and where he'd fought, mostly in Bavaria.

Some of the other boys that Khribin spoke to during the next week were similar, but some were more withdrawn and others were more vocal—they were the dangerous ones, the ones who'd probably end up in Shangri-La in five years. The stories were all the same. They were either taken from small villages or from schools, many of them were orphans and all of them had been impressed into service before age ten. There was violence. Hazing was common, and soldiers were encouraged to assault new comrades to toughen them up.

All told, Khribin interviewed seventeen boys and four girls

who'd been picked up by Argentine peacekeepers the previous week. They were all minors, all of them underage. Despite the obvious crimes that many of them had committed, none would be charged. UNICEF would do what they could for them, but there were millions of children like them across Europe, and funds were limited—and with the Americans and Chinese threatening to completely cut non-INTO international funding again, things were looking to get even tighter.

"The Americans and Chinese would let everyone starve if it fit their precious mathematical models," Captain Grimstvedt said. Khribin had run into him at a café down the street from the hotel she was staying at. The café was run by a Turkish man and his European wife, and their hot chocolate was the richest, most decadent Khribin had had in a very long time. The two of them were sitting at a table in the back, Khribin going through her second mug of hot chocolate and Grimstvedt was nursing a cup of warm tea.

"I don't think they're that heartless," Khribin said. Someone would have to be as heartless as Alois Brandstetter to let these children suffer. Khribin didn't have much love for the United States—few Arabs did—but she didn't think that they were that evil. Sure, there were evil individuals—Io and Tethys alone was evidence of that—but she didn't think the entire government was evil.

"I think Io says otherwise," Grimstvedt said.

Khribin shrugged and took a drink from her hot chocolate.

Their waitress walked up to their table. She was young, about the same age as Markus Kroder and the others. Her hair was impossibly pale, so Khribin assumed that it was a wig or dyed. The name tag on her chest said *Myrthe* and she wore the café's waitress uniform: white blouse, black skirt, black apron and a black headband holding her hair back.

"How is everything?" Myrthe asked in perfect English.

"We're doing quite well," Grimstvedt said. "Maybe some more biscuits."

"I can do that," Myrthe said. She looked at Khribin. "Is everything fine with you, ma'am?"

Khribin nodded her head. "I'm fine, thank you."

Myrthe seemed to hesitate for a moment. "That's good," she said. "I know that things can be quite stressful for people like you, and people like me are here to help you with that."

"And we appreciate it," Grimstvedt. "Best damn biscuits I've had on the Continent."

"They are real good," Khribin said. "I didn't know that I could get fresh blueberries in Germany. Espeially ones this big."

Myrthe's face seemed to fall for a moment, but she composed herself. "We're just lucky like that."

"It makes for good biscuits," Grimstvedt said.

"They're an old family recipe of Helga's," Myrthe said. She held her tray flat against her chest and folded her arms in front of it. "A lot of people compliment us on the biscuits. Best in the Blue Zone, they say."

"Who says that?" Grimstvedt asked.

Myrthe shrugged. "They do," she said. "I'll go get your biscuits and bring them right back."

Myrthe turned and left. When she was gone, Khribin raised her mug of hot chocolate to her lips and said, "She's not from around here."

Grimstvedt arched an eyebrow. "Oh?"

"That accent. Non-rhotic, falling diphthongs, linking r's. Upper class. She comes from money. *American* money."

"Probably an ambassador's kid."

"What's an ambassador's kid doing working in a place like this?" Khribin asked.

Grimstvedt shrugged. "I don't know. To build character?"

Khribin nodded her head and set down her cup. "It's just not fair."

"What's not?"

"Her, this, everything," Khribin said. "Two miles in either direction from here, there's kids who are starving, and are sick, and are being forced to kill. And then there's Myrthe, who's probably lived a life of privilege, and her parents are making her work to build character."

"I'm an orphan, you know."

Myrthe's voice caused Khribin to jump. The waitress had appeared so quietly and so suddenly that Khribin hadn't noticed. Khribin felt her cheeks burning. "Sorry, I didn't...I didn't know."

"It's fine," Myrthe said. She put the basket of biscuits on the table. "I get that a lot actually. People think I'm an American all the time."

"So you're German?" Grimstvedt asked.

Myrthe shrugged. "I don't know. I really don't remember anything before a few months ago."

"That's probably for the best," Khribin said.

"Probably. I've only heard stories about what goes on beyond the walls of the Blue Zone. If I...if I did see things or did things out there, I'm glad I can no longer remember it."

Khribin nodded her head.

"I got lucky though. It doesn't end well for a lot of orphans in my position," Myrthe said. She shrugged. "Maybe I just have somebody looking out for me."

"If only everyone was that lucky," Grimstvedt said.

"That'll be the day," Khribin said.

Myrthe just shrugged.

* * *

The hotel wasn't a Hilton or a Waldorf, but it was probably one of the finer hotels in Frankfurt. During the day, Khribin could see most of the city from her window, including the dirty water of the Main (it was said that smoking was banned within a hundred feet of the river, lest it combust). But during the day, all she could see was the Blue Zone. She could see the floodlights on the Blue Zone's wall, but beyond that, there was only the occasional light, most of which flickered like candles and torches, not electric lights.

Khribin took a very long, hot shower to wash off the grit and grime that she'd picked up during the day. The Blue Zone was just as dirty as the rest of the city, and she just felt so dirty after spending a day outside. She wrapped herself in a soft bathrobe and sat on the end of her bed and combed out her hair. The television was on and tuned to Al-Jazeera and some terrible comedy—Khribin's sisters loved it, but she couldn't even remember what it was called. But it was something familiar and something Arabic, so it would do.

There was a knock on Khribin's door. She muted the television and stood up, walking over to the door. She looked through the peephole and saw the waitress from the café, Myrthe, standing just outside. She wore a warm-looking overcoat. Khribin frowned and opened the door. "Can I help you?" Khribin asked.

"Can I come in?" Myrthe asked. The overcoat was about knee-length, and Khribin could see that she wore black stockings and tall heels underneath it.

"What for?"

Myrthe grinned. "You know why."

No, I really don't, Khribin said. She had a bad feeling in the pit of her stomach. She stepped aside. "Come in."

Myrthe put her hands in the pocket of her coat and stepped in. Khribin closed the door behind her. Myrthe looked around the room. "Swanky," she said. She stopped and looked over her shoulder at Khribin. "But I should expect this from the UN."

Khribin crossed her arms in front of her chest. "What are you doing here?"

"You asked for me," Myrthe said.

"I did what now?"

Myrthe smiled and turned around to face Khribin. "Oh, so we're going to do that then?" She pulled her hands out of the pocket of her coat and undid the buttons. She shrugged out of the coat and it fell to the ground. She was scantily dressed underneath it: a white corset with black vertical stripes and lace, black panties, garter belt, suspenders and thigh-high stockings. Khribin was speechless. Myrthe took several step towards her and leaned forward, as if to kiss her.

Khribin's senses finally snapped back. She took a step back and held up her hands. "Stop," she said. "What are you doing?"

Myrthe froze and opened her eyes. She looked at Khribin, confused. "You...you asked for me."

"No, I didn't."

"But you did. Down at the café."

"No, I didn't."

"But you very specifically commented on the freshness and size of the blueberries," Myrthe said. She stood up straight and seemed to think about it for a moment. She bit her thumbnail as she thought. "That was just a coincidence, wasn't it?"

Khribin could only nod her head.

Myrthe groaned. "Helga's gonna kill me." She turned around and bent over to pick up her coat.

"You don't have to go back," Khribin said. "I can help you."

Myrthe began to put one arm through the coat, but stopped. She was frozen for a few moments before she looked over her shoulder at Khribin. "Why?"

"How old are you?" Khribin asked.

"I don't know," Myrthe said. She looked down at the ground. "Helga says she thinks I'm thirteen, but—"

"This is illegal under so many national and international laws. Exploitation of children, sexual slavery, prostitution...I can help you."

Myrthe didn't say anything.

"I can only help you if..."

"How?" Myrthe asked. She turned around to face Khribin. "How can you help me?"

"I work with the UN," Khribin said. "I can—"

Myrthe sighed and finished putting on her coat. "I wish I could believe you."

"Why don't you?"

"Because you're not the first person to tell me this."

Myrthe pushed past Khribin and headed towards the door. Khribin grabbed Myrthe by arm and pulled her back. "Stay," she said.

Myrthe didn't make eye contact.

"I promise you. I can help."

"Pay me," Myrthe said. She managed to pull away from Khribin. "Pay me, and I'll stay."

Khribin sighed. It didn't feel right, but if that's what would convince the girl to stay. "Fine, fine. How much?"

"What I'd charge normally for my services," Myrthe said. "45 dinar."

"45 dinar?" Khribin asked. That wasn't very much money. Probably enough to buy a week's worth of groceries for one person in Damascus, or one oil change, or one really nice haircut. But for Myrthe, that was probably a month's salary at the café. "I can do that. Just give me a moment."

Khribin walked over to her purse and went through it. "I only have a 50. Will that do?"

Myrthe took the bill. It was purple, with an old Arabic astrolabe on the front and a grove of date trees on the back. Myrthe stuffed the bill down the front of her corset, between her breasts. "I'll stay," she said.

"Good," Khribin said. "You can watch TV, or something."

Myrthe sat down on the end of the bed and turned the volume back on. Khribin watched her for a few moments before walking over to the phone. She dialed the UNPROFOR headquarters, and after a few transfers, she was speaking to one of their military police dispatchers. Khribin gave the dispatcher a quick rundown of the situation.

"We'll send someone over soon, ma'am," the dispatcher said,

when Khribin was done.

"Thank you," Khribin said, and hung up. She walked back to the bed and sat down next to Myrthe. Myrthe wasn't watching the television—her eyes were fixed on the floor in front of her and her arms were shaking. "What's wrong?" Khribin asked.

"They're going to kill me," Myrthe said.

"Who is?"

"Helga and Omar."

"No they aren't," Khribin said. "I promise you, everything's fine now. It's safe."

"I don't believe you."

"I'm not asking you to," Khribin said.

Myrthe nodded her head. "I should've confirmed this before I showed up."

"How long have you been doing this?"

"For as long as I can remember," Myrthe said. "Most of my clients, they're...they're like you. UN officials. They're always kind. Most don't hurt me, and those that do, don't mean to. And they always pay extra to hurt me."

"Sexual slavery is still illegal and wrong."

"I have dreams, sometimes," Myrthe said. "Dreams that I don't have to live like this. That I can make my own decisions, that I can live my own life."

"I'll get you out of this," Khribin said.

Myrthe nodded her head but didn't say anything more. The two of them sat in silence for almost half an hour before there was a knock on the door. Khribin stood up and walked over. Standing outside the door were four Scandinavian soldiers in camouflaged fatigues and sky-blue berets.

"Amira Khribin?" the officer said.

"That's me."

"I'm Major Jonas Ertsborn. Can we come in?"

Khribin stepped back and let the soldiers in. The last one in closed the door.

Ertsborn took off his beret and turned to face Khribin. "We understand that you wish to report sexual slavery?"

Khribin nodded her head. She heard Myrthe stand up and walked over towards the door. "Yes, Myrthe. She works at—"

"The Blue Turk Café, we know," Ertsborn said.

"You what?"

Ertsborn sighed. "Ma'am, you're new to Frankfurt, aren't you?"

"Yes, but—"

"Yeah, this is awful and terrible, but the Blue Turk Café is owned by Norbert Roth. As is the other side of the business."

"Norbert Roth?" Khribin repeated to herself. "You mean the terrorist?"

"He prefers militia leader," Ertsborn said. "If we stay out of his business, he stays out of ours. Usually. It's as simple as that. Usually."

"But sexual slavery? Child slavery? You seriously can't—"

"Would you rather have the entire city burning because we cut off one of Norbert Roth's most lucrative business ventures?" Ertsborn asked.

Khribin was speechless.

Ertsborn sighed. "We'll talk to Helga at the Blue Turk, and we'll see if we can work something out with this girl."

"But—"

"Sacrifices have to be made to keep the peace," Ertsborn said. "We'll take the girl back."

Khribin grabbed Myrthe's arm. "No. I won't let you."

"Ma'am, we caught you in a hotel room, in your bathrobe, with a child prostitute," Ertsborn said. "Do you really want to push it with us, right now?"

Khribin was speechless. She looked at Myrthe then at Ertsborn and then back at Myrthe. She let go of Myrthe's arm and took a step back. "Myrthe, I'm sorry."

Myrthe shrugged. "I never really believed you."

Khribin winced. She clenched her fist and faced Ertsborn. "This isn't the last of this. I'm going to go straight to Special Representative with this. There's going to be changes."

Ertsborn chuckled. "That'll be the day," he said. He grabbed Myrthe by the arm and led her to the door. "Don't be causing any more trouble tonight, Ms. Khribin."

The four soldiers left with Myrthe, leaving Khribin alone in the hotel room. She felt her legs give out and she fell to her knees. "What are we doing here?" she asked the empty room. The only answer was a bad joke from the television.

Author Biographies

Tom Anderson

Raised on a diet of *The Silmarillion* and *Star Trek: The Next Generation*, Tom Anderson has always loved science fiction and fantasy. At the age of 20 he discovered Alternate History through Harry Turtledove's Worldwar series and was instantly hooked, the idea of what if bringing formerly dull school history lessons to life and encouraging him to learn more about where the modern world came from. He is now one of the most prolific posters on the AlternateHistory.com online forum and  has contributed many pieces of writing on the subject, in particular his magnum opus Look to the West, which explores the question "What if King George II had carried out his threat to exile his son to the American colonies?" The answer apparently involves a global steam engine revolution, Lithuania colonising Namibia and an awful lot of revolutionary heroes' houses being burned down. In his day job, Tom teaches Chemistry to undergraduates at the University of Sheffield, South Yorkshire using the most inappropriate choice of metaphors possible. He is an alumnus of Robinson College, Cambridge, which may not have big names like Isaac Newton but does have the advantage of central heating that actually works.

Michael McAndrews Bailey

Michael is a graduate of Cornell College in Mount Vernon, Iowa, having graduated with a Bachelor of Arts in English Literature and Religious Studies. He is currently a law intern with a legal aid society.

Murray Braun

Murray Braun is a retired child neurologist who now writes Alternate Historical Fiction.

Dave D'Alessio

Dave D'Alessio is an ex-animator, ex-industrial chemist and ex-TV engineer currently masquerading as a practicing social scientist.

Deborah L. Davitt

Deborah L. Davitt grew up in Reno, Nevada, but took her MA in English from Penn State, where she taught rhetoric and composition. She moved on to become a technical writer in industries including nuclear submarines, NASA, and computer manufacturing, and currently lives in Houston with  her husband and son. She's the author of the Edda-Earth books; her short fiction's been featured in *InterGalactic Medicine Show*, and her poetry's appeared in close to a dozen venues. For more information on her work, please see www.edda-earth.com.

Dan Gainor

Dan Gainor is a media critic, a veteran editor, and writer with more than two decades experience. He has been published in a wide variety of publications, including *Investor's Business Daily, The Chicago Sun-Times, The Orange County Register* and *The New York Post.* He is the Vice President of Business and Culture for the *Media Research Center* and has been an editor at several news organizations  including *Congressional Quarterly* and *The Baltimore News-American.*

Martin T. Ingham

Martin T. Ingham is the author of various Science Fiction & Fantasy works, including *West of the Warlock, The Guns of Mars,* and *The Rogue Investigations.* When he isn't writing, he likes to dabble in numismatics, horology, and antique auto restoration, among other hobbies. He currently resides in his hometown of Robbinston, Maine, with his four children—Sylvia, Wyatt, Kathryn, and Lois.

Learn more about Martin's works at his website:
http://www.martiningham.com

Mike Jansen

Mike has published flash fiction, short stories and longer work in various anthologies and magazines in the Netherlands and Belgium, including *Cerberus, Manifesto Bravado, Wonderwaan, Ator Mondis, Ganymedes, Babel-SF,* and Verschijnsel anthologies such as *Ragnarok* and *Zwarte Zielen (Black Souls).*

He has won awards for best new author and best author in the King Kong Award in 1991 and 1992 respectively as well as an honorable mention for a submission to the Australian Altair Magazine launch competition in 1998. In 2012 Mike won awards in the SaBi Thor story contest, the Literary Prize for the Baarn Cultural Festival and the prestigious Dutch Fantastels award for best short story. In September 2013 he joined the Horror Writers Association (HWA).

More recently he has published in various English language ezines and anthologies, among which several publications with JWKfiction.com, Encounters Magazine and others. A full list is on Mike's site: http://www.meznir.com You can also find him on Goodreads, Facebook and Twitter.

Sam Kepfield

Sam Kepfield is a writer who is forced to earn a living as a criminal defense attorney in Hutchinson, Kansas. He has a bachelor's degree from Kansas State University (B.A. 1986), a law degree and an M.A. in History from the University of Nebraska ('89, '94), as well as doctoral work at the University of Oklahoma.

By night he writes science fiction and a few horror stories. His work has appeared in *Science Fiction Trails*, *Electric Spec*, and *Aoife's Kiss*. His story "Not Because They Are Easy," which appeared in the *Rocket Science* anthology, was considered for Best Short Story of 2012 by the British Science Fiction Association. His first novel, "Magic Man, Gold Dust Woman, and the Dream Machine" was released by Musa Publishing in March 2013.

Bruno Lombardi

Bruno Lombardi was born in Montreal in 1968. He has had a rather distressing tendency to be a weirdness magnet for much of his adult life. If your friend's cousin's brother-in-law tells you a story and swears it's true and that it 'happened to someone he knows', it was probably Bruno.

His hobbies include attempting to dissuade the cults that form around him, managing the betting pool on the next Weird Thing, and being a slave to his two cats, Mynx and Sphinx. He currently lives in Ottawa and works as a civil servant for the Canadian government. Rumours that he secretly runs the Canadian government from his nuclear bunker with an android called 'Stephen Harper' as a front have never been substantiated and are merely rumours. Honestly.

He has also met lots of people off the internet and has yet to be murdered by any of them; his cats on the other hand have other ideas. His short stories have appeared in many Martinus Publishing anthologies, and his novel, *Snake Oil*, saw its first print release in 2014.

Ryan McCall

Ryan McCall first became interested in alternate history upon coming across a *What If?* anthology. He was instantly hooked and delved into as much of the genre as he could, both in printed books and online. He has self-published two books on Amazon, *The Nanking War* and *Not By a Mine*. He is currently expanding his writing area into fantasy, with an epic fantasy series currently in progress.

Mark Mellon

Mark Mellon is a novelist who supports his family by working as an attorney. He's led a checkered life with experience as a mover, lifeguard/swimming instructor, door-to-door salesman, carpenter's helper, Russian translator, soldier, phone solicitor, collections counselor, and teacher. Recent short fiction of his has appeared in Noir Nation, Thuglit, and Polluto. He has four published novels and over forty published short stories. A fantasy novella, Escape From Byzantium, won the 2010 Independent Publisher Silver Medal for fantasy/science fiction. A website featuring Mark's writing is at www.mellonwritesagain.com.

Tim Moshier

Tim Moshier is a joint US-UK citizen who has lived in both countries and currently resides in New Jersey. He has traveled extensively across the lower 48, and has always had a fascination for disease and history. He developed an interest in reading alternate history by discovering Pearl Harbor by Newt Gingrich and William R. Forstchen, and he aquired a desire to write it after finding alternatehistory.com.

Sergio Palumbo

Sergio is an Italian public servant who graduated from Law School working in the public real estate branch. He has published a Fantasy Role-Playing illustrated Manual, *WarBlades,* of more than 700 pages. Some of his works and short- stories have been published on *American Aphelion Webzine, WeirdYear Webzine, YesterYearFiction, AnotheRealm Magazine, Alien Skin Magazine*, and *Orion's Child Science Fiction and Fantasy Magazine*, among many others. He is also a scale modeler who likes mostly Science Fiction and Real Space models. The internet site of his Model Club "La Centuria": www.lacenturia.it

William Rade

Rade is an old German occupational surname, stemming from the word for wheel. Despite any patrilineal predisposition, William has found through bitter experience that he is a poor wheelwright. He has turned his ambitions towards creative writing instead, hoping to craft stories that deliver a smoother ride, without causing serious injury. Fantasy, and other speculative fictions, are William's preferred vehicles.

William lives in the bright state of Queensland, Australia. Queensland proudly supplies the rest of the nation with its rum and fringe politicians. At time of writing, William's stories are less popular than both.

Alex Shalenko

Alex Shalenko is an accountant by day and avid science fiction writer and musician by night. He is a native of Ukraine now making home in scenic Castle Rock, Colorado with his family, and earned Bachelor's and Master's degrees in Business Administration from the University of Colorado.

DJ Tyrer

DJ Tyrer is the person behind *Atlantean Publishing* and has been widely published in anthologies and magazines in the UK, USA and elsewhere, most recently in *State of Horror: Illinois* (Charon Coin Press), *Steampunk Cthulhu* (Chaosium), *Tales of the Dark Arts* (Hazardous Press) and *Cosmic Horror* (Dark Hall Press), as well as in *Sorcery & Sanctity: A Homage to Arthur Machen* (Hieroglyphics Press), *All Hallow's Evil* and *Undead of Winter* (both Mystery & Horror LLC) and *Fossil Lake* (Sabledrake Enterprises), and in addition, has a novella available on the Kindle, *The Yellow House* (Dynatox Ministries).

DJ Tyrer's website is at http://djtyrer.blogspot.co.uk/

The Atlantean Publishing website is at:
http://atlanteanpublishing.blogspot.co.uk/

Cyrus P. Underwood

Cyrus P. Underwood's real name is Richard Anderson. Disabled since age 9, he spends his time writing and reading. He lives in Hamilton, Ontario, Canada.

Charles Wilcox

Charles Wilcox has lived in Boulder, Colorado all his life. He has always had a passion for history and creating new worlds. He holds a Bachelor's degree in International Studies from American University.

Also Available from Martinus Publishing

**21 Time Travel stories by 20 different authors.
Explore the distant past, the far future,
and everywhere in between!**

Order your copy today:
http://www.martinus.us/books.html#temporalelement
ISBN#978-0-9887685-3-6

Also Available from Martinus Publishing

Altered America:
21 "What If" Tales about America's past!

Also Available from Martinus Publishing

Bruno Lombardi's Snake Oil
A cynical "First Contact" adventure!

"A compelling exploration of what could happen if Earth's first alien visitors turn out to be a bit more like us, after all."

http://www.martinus.us/books.html#snakeoil
ISBN#978-0-6159936-6-9

Also Available from Martinus Publishing

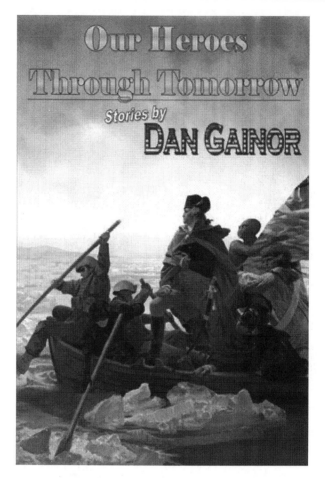

Our Heroes Through Tomorrow
-by Dan Gainor

Six scintillating stories from a modern master of
speculative fiction!

~Available exclusively for the Kindle~
http://www.martinus.us/books.html#as02

Made in the USA
Middletown, DE
25 July 2017